To Skip & Betty

Best Wishes

OLD CITY HALL

A NOVEL

BY

GERALD D. McLELLAN

authorHOUSE®

AuthorHouse™
1663 Liberty Drive, Suite 200
Bloomington, IN 47403
www.authorhouse.com
Phone: 1-800-839-8640

This book is a work of fiction. Names, characters, places and incidents are the product of the author's imagination and are used fictitiously. Any resemblance to actual events, localities or persons, living or dead, is coincidental.

First published by AuthorHouse 8/23/2007

ISBN: 978-1-4343-3092-5 (sc)
ISBN: 978-1-4343-3091-8 (hc)

Printed in the United States of America
Bloomington, Indiana

This book is printed on acid-free paper.

Books by Gerald D. McLellan

Handbook of Massachusetts Family Law*
Lawyers Weekly Publications

Handbook of Massachusetts Family Law, Second Edition*
Lawyers Weekly Publications

Equitable Distribution
John Wiley & Sons

Handbook of Massachusetts Family Law, Third Edition*
Lawyers Weekly Publications

Handbook of Massachusetts Family Law, Fourth Edition*
Lawyers Weekly Publications

Run the Cold Water - A Memoir
Unpublished

Old City Hall - A Novel
AuthorHouse Publications

*Additional Pocket Supplements

To Jean

ACKNOWLEDGEMENTS

In writing this book I was assisted by friends who read each and every chapter, who consistently encouraged me and who shared their enthusiasm with me: Judy Steul, Jack and Carol Joyce, Russ Mawdsley, John Young, Carol Sisson, Attorney Mary Jane Johnson, Professor Nancy Shuster and noted authors, Robin Cook and William Tapply.

My law partner, Ellen Zack, applied her editorial talents to the manuscript, honed by her years with the Boston Globe as a Pulitzer Prize member of the Globe's Spotlight Team.

My wife, Jean, had the patience, skill and the ability to pay attention to detail, all of which were necessary in order to remedy my mistakes.

CHAPTER ONE

I was sitting in my office in the heart of the financial district in Boston, totally engrossed in attempting to read the history inscribed on the tombstones in the old cemetery just below my window when Amy, the office receptionist, buzzed me.

"Ms. Mitchell is here," Amy whispered into the phone. I had made a special effort to get back early from lunch because I didn't want to meet my prospective client as I was coming in the front door.

She'd made an appointment to see me a week ago, and all week long I couldn't get the prospective meeting out of my mind. I'd heard rumors but all I could do was hope.

"She looks like a hooker," Amy added. "Wait'll you see her."

"Tell her I'll be out in a minute," I replied.

The person in the waiting room was Emily Mitchell, the wife of the Governor of the Commonwealth of Massachusetts, Brenden W. Mitchell and she was here to see me about a divorce. I looked around to make sure the files which I'd been working on earlier that morning were at least out of plain sight and walked down the hall to greet her.

"Good afternoon," I said to her extending my hand. "I'm Edward Eldridge."

"Oh yes, I know who you are Mr. Eldridge," she said putting the National Geographic back on the coffee table and accepting my greeting with a firm handshake. "I've been shopping around you see. A 'beauty contest' I believe you people call it and your name has come up more that once."

"Well I'm happy to meet you. Can I get you anything to drink?"

"No thank you. I've already been asked." She didn't look like a hooker as Amy said. In fact, she was dressed in Talbot's preppy finery: beige linen slacks, a white collared blouse covered by a navy blue blazer with two brass-monogrammed buttons on the front and two on each sleeve. She was trim, about forty-five years old with an apparent full figure, which was visible under at least three layers of clothes. What I think Amy meant was that she was wearing too much make-up. Her lips were covered with a dark red lipstick, which went outside the line of her lips. Her blush was too heavily applied in an almost complete circle on her high cheekbones, which, if it were red, would make one think she was part of the clown act at the circus.

"Please," I said as I gently placed my hand on the small of her back and guided her towards my office. As she passed in front of me, I noticed the reason for her heavy make-up. The blush covered a black and blue mark just under her right eye. I couldn't help noticing that the right side of her lip was swollen which I thought was the reason for the extended application of the lipstick. We settled into the two large leather chairs in front of my desk, which were separated by a small table upon which were several yellow legal pads. I seldom sat behind the desk in a first interview as I thought that sitting side by side was more intimate, less intimidating and allowed the client to relax just a bit more.

"Before we begin," she said, "I want to be reassured that whatever I tell you remains confidential. I paid your outrageous hourly rate for this consultation to your receptionist when she told me, in no uncertain terms, that this first meeting was not free. I don't think I got my coat off before I had the lecture from her."

"No need to worry, Ms. Mitchell. An attorney-client relationship was established as soon as you paid the fee." I reached for a yellow pad and prepared to take notes while she grabbed a fist full of Kleenex from the box I always kept on the front of my desk.

"I want a divorce from that son of a bitch," she said.

"He's no good, and he's fooled a lot of people in this state for a long time and I'm tired of covering up for him. No more! He's a womanizing, wife-beating son of a bitch and I don't care if this divorce brings him and his whole rotten crew down to where they belong--and that's in jail," she said between clenched teeth and sobs into her tissue. "I don't know who he's screwing but I know he's playing around. Lipstick, perfume smells that're not mine and lies, lies, lies." She looked at me with teary eyes.

"Other lawyers have told me there's nothing he can do to stop me from getting a divorce. Is that right?"

"That's right," I said, "but he can make the whole process a nasty one under some circumstances. Are you both still living together?"

She nodded. "We're living in the same household but in separate bed rooms. Danny, our only child is taking the whole situation pretty badly. He's acting up in school, his grades have dropped and he's so sullen around the house. At first, I thought it was just the advent of the terrible teens, he's fourteen, but--I don't know. He stays by himself more and more and hardly talks to either of us. Brenden tells him what to do, where he can go, what time to come home, when to go to bed, when to get up, what food he can eat. I think he'd be better off if the arguments between Brenden and me stopped and we lived in separate houses."

11

"How old is Danny?"

"He's fourteen."

"When were you married?"

"Eighteen years ago this June twenty-seventh."

"What about custody? Will the Governor let you have custody of Danny or will that be nasty?"

"He's so controlling," she sighed. "He doesn't think I have a brain in my head. He's always telling me I don't know how to handle Danny. I'm too permissive. I spoil him. I protect him too much. He's the one who decides about everything. I wouldn't be surprised if he demanded custody, not because he loves Danny so much but because of his goddamn pride."

"How does this living under the same roof work?" I said. "Who cooks dinner? Do you eat together? Who does the laundry? Who makes the beds? Who pays the bills?" I asked her.

"Oh, he goes his way and we go ours. He eats out most every night and we hardly speak when the two of us are home other than when he's giving orders to Danny and me. Otherwise, we actually glare at each other. He controls every penny and watches the money I spend on food for Danny and me. He even asks me for the grocery receipts. I have no discretionary money at all. I bring his shirts to the cleaners and wash his underwear. That's about all I do. He tells me to clean this or vacuum that but I'm trying to ignore him. I'm seeing a psychiatrist once a week and he's prescribed an anti-depressant for me but the tension around that place is too much. I can't handle much more," she sobbed.

"Has he been physical with you? Has he struck you?" I asked looking at her right cheek.

She looked down at her hands clasped on her lap, paused and said, "Yes. Just last night we had an argument and he hit me in the face with his closed fist. Danny saw the whole thing. My lip started to bleed and there was blood all over the place. Danny hollered for him to stop, I was crying and he was swearing. It was just like the tenements where he grew up in Dorchester. He's nothing but a thug."

She blew her nose in her Kleenex and, as if that act prompted her further she said, "There's something else I'm not quite sure of, Mr.Eldridge. I'm afraid even to mention it."

"Don't worry," I assured her again. "I told you this conference is strictly confidential."

"Well, I think he's recently been taking cocaine or some other drug. His nose is running, he has a glassy look in his eyes, he appears lethargic and nothing seems to bother him other than Danny and me; nothing other than when he's hitting me or hollering at Danny. He never acted as bad as this before." Another pause for a dab at her nose.

"I noticed this change ever since the election, ever since he's been out every night hanging around with Mort Haller and a bunch of his pals," she continued.

"Do you have any proof?" I asked. "He wouldn't be the first politician to depend on some kind of drug."

"No, certainly not. It's just a suspicion."

"Nothing we can do about it at this point," I advised. "But keep your eyes open."

We continued our discussion for a little longer before I got into some necessary detail. It took me the next hour and a half to explain the divorce process to her. I told her about the problem of getting him out of the house, the preparation of a financial statement, a temporary order hearing where she'd ask the court for custody, alimony and child support while the action is pending. I told her about the agonizing discovery process and what that entailed and finally told her how much it would cost.

"Two hundred thousand dollars?" she said. "Where in hell would I get that kind of money? And you want that up front? That's impossible!"

This was always the point in my conversations with prospective clients that bothered me. The fees, my fees, were outrageous and I knew they were hard to accept. Most people, in fact, didn't accept them. It was only those who wanted not only to divorce their spouse, but who wanted to annihilate the; those who had a great deal at risk whether millions of dollars or children they loved dearly who didn't question the amount of the fee. I was sympathetic to an extent but there were too many times I had to pay out large sums of money which were never paid back after the divorce was over.

"No, you don't have to pay the whole amount up front, just the retainer of twenty-five thousand dollars. The rest will come from either joint funds, funds in your own name, borrowed funds or what we can get from your husband. We bill our time here very carefully at quarter-hour intervals and send you a bill every month. All we ask is that you stay ahead of us. It may not cost that much. It may cost more, but you'll know what we're doing on your behalf every month. If you don't like our representation you can fire us at any time. But honestly, Ms. Mitchell, we don't get fired. We keep you informed as we go along because we believe that an informed client is smarter than a client who says he or she doesn't want to be bothered by the details."

"Well," she said. "You were a judge and you wrote the book. You come highly recommended and the others I've interviewed all charge as much as you for a retainer. So where do I sign."

She was right. I was a judge in the past, appointed by this Governor's predecessor, Governor Harold Lowance. After Mitchell was elected I wrote a text book for lawyers on Family Law and was a member of the adjunct faculty at a local law school. I had hoped that this new Governor would appoint me to the Appeals Court. Not only did he ignore me, not only was dealing with him like playing hand ball against a blanket, but the son of a bitch arranged for me to sit in Nantucket in December, Edgartown on Martha's Vineyard in January and Hyannis on Cape Cod in February all in an attempt to have me resign so he could appoint my successor. I stuck it out for two whole years before I accommodated him. I resigned and opened my office at Old City Hall.

I handed Emily Mitchell our standard, four page attorney-client agreement. "Here, take this home, read it over carefully and, if you still want to hire us, sign it and bring it back with your check for twenty- five thousand dollars. I'll sign it and give you a copy. We'll then have our second meeting where we'll map out our strategy and be off and running."

"OK," she said. She started to stand.

"One more thing. Wait here one minute." I went out to the secretary's station and spoke to Amy.

"Please come in and take her to the ladies room. I'll ask her to take off her make-up when she's in there and you can take some pictures of the bruises on her face with the office camera. Ask her if she has other bruises on any other parts of her body and if so, take pictures of those also."

Back in my office I said, "Ms. Mitchell, this is Amy, my secretary. She'll escort you to the ladies room. I ask that you take off your make-up so she can take a picture of your bruises. I look forward to seeing you for our second meeting in a couple of days. Just call for an appointment."

"Well, uh, I guess so." She looked at Amy apprehensively for a second. "Ok, let's go," she said.

After she left, I danced a little jig in the privacy of my office.

Revenge is best served up cold, I told myself out loud. *Sic Transit Gloria* you bastard, you're going to get yours.

It was three o'clock in the afternoon after Emily Mitchell left my office when I met with my associates. We were huddled in the conference room at Old City Hall putting together a plan of action for our new client.

"What'll we use for grounds in the complaint?" Henry Baker, senior associate, asked to no one in particular.

"Well, we could start with adultery and then list cruel and abusive treatment," I said. "The only question is whether we should name the co-respondent."

"How can we do that when we don't know her name?" Jordan Levy, my other associate, inquired.

"Not yet we don't but we can add her as a co-respondent later," I answered. "For now we say in the complaint that he committed adultery with a person to be named later. That'll start their juices flowing."

"I don't know about that," Henry said. "What good will come of stating all that in the complaint at this stage? It'll only piss them off, and what for? We can always introduce the cruelty at the time of the hearing. As for the adultery, we'd better be careful about how we handle that until we get some proof about who he's schtupping."

After listening, I changed my mind. "You know," I said. "I think you're right. Let's simply state 'Irretrievable Breakdown'. If we say anything else in the complaint now, the press will have a field day and they'll turn this case into a media circus."

"Shall I get Charley on it?" Jordan asked. Charley Randell was the private detective the firm always used. He was a big, barrel-chested, ex-marine who packed a Glock 37, 45 caliber in the middle of his back. He was the kind of guy for whom the idiom, 'an elephant in the room' was created. He could explode with the slightest provocation yet, at the same time, he had the patience to sit and wait at a stake-out forever.

"Yeah, let's get him started on the Governor. See where he goes. Get the details on the Gov's nocturnal adventures with the party whom we'll name later and see just what he's up to," I directed.

CHAPTER TWO

Mort Haller, the Governor's Chief of Staff, loved working at the State House on Beacon Street. He relished the vicarious power of his office, which he seldom failed to flaunt among his staff because of which he was not very well liked. Yet, he was an intelligent observer of the scene, a person with an obsession for detail and a person fiercely loyal to the Governor. He knew the history of Boston dating back to the early Seventeenth Century and he knew every detail of the building in which he worked.

He knew, even before the election, that the Governor's office was in Room 360 under the gold dome gilded in 1861 and painted black during the Second World War. He relished the view from the Governor's office overlooking the Boston Common, the site of a pasture owned by John Hancock before the edifice was built between 1795 and 1797.

His office was in close proximity to the Massachusetts Senate, the House, the Lieutenant Governor's Office, and the offices of the President of the Senate and the Speaker. He was also close to the scores of lesser lights connected, however loosely, to the functioning of the government of the Commonwealth. He thrived on the fact that the place was a beehive of activity with reporters from the local media watching the comings and goings of the movers and shakers from the Senate and House as they scurried from place to place. In fact, the reporters from the two major newspapers had their own little cubby holes in the building from which they sent their urgent dispatches to their editors.

Haller, a darkly complected, Levantine looking, fidgety, emaciated man with hollow cheeks, a receding hair line and piercing brown eyes was waiting in the Governor's office, pacing back and forth.

"Where the hell is he?" he stammered looking out the open door to the secretary's station, addressing Bess, the Governor's secretary. She didn't look up from her typing nor did she answer Mort's question."He's a half hour late, goddamn it," he said. "He knows he has another appointment in ten minutes. He's always late."

"He left in a hurry about an hour ago," Bess finally replied without looking up from her work. Mort knew she was among those who never liked him. He knew that from the day she first started working for Brenden Mitchell at his campaign headquarters on Cambridge Street and the tone in her voice left no doubt about her feelings for him.

"He was really upset about something some guy delivered and he stormed out without telling me where he was going," she continued, still concentrating on her computer.

"Well I'll be--" He didn't have a chance to finish what he was going to say before the Honorable Brenden W. Mitchell burst through the reception area and brushed so close to his Chief of

Staff that Mort could feel the cold coming from his boss's coat from the early April sleet.

"Close the fucking door!" he barked to Mort as he began pacing back and forth in front of his gigantic glass covered oak desk.

"She's suing me for divorce, that bitch! This will be a disaster. Mort, do you understand what this could mean to me, to us, to others who count on us? I don't believe it. The publicity could ruin us."

Mort always considered the Governor to be a rather handsome man, with a leathery, out-doors complexion, an inch over six feet tall with a full head of light blond hair turning an almost indistinguishable grey, an aquiline nose and just the beginning of a middle age bulge over his belt. His tanned face was, however, at this point, turning a beet red.

"Calm down, calm down. You're not the first politician who's ever had a domestic dispute. We'll take care of this one step at a time," Mort counseled.

"Domestic dispute? Domestic dispute? This could mean all out war, not some trivial quarrel between spouses that's reported below the fold in the City Section of the Boston Globe for chrissakes," the Governor sputtered.

"Don't worry. We'll get the best divorce lawyer in the Commonwealth or at least one with the best connections and snuff this thing out before it has a chance to spread," Mort said. "I know just the guy. I hear that lately he can be a piranha, a real man-eater when he has to be and what's more important, he's contributed to your campaign in more ways than one. This guy wants to be a judge. He'd been passed over several times by Lowance and he's not getting any younger. You've passed him over yourself so maybe now's the time to reconsider. Do you know who I'm talking about?"

"I just came back from seeing him," the Governor responded. "Paul Jed, right? Have you forgotten? I spoke to the Chief Judge years ago and have done favors for Mr. Jed when that guy Eldridge was sitting in Nantucket. Who else would I go to? He was the Chair

for the Committee of the Bar for my campaign for chissakes. I went
to him right away because I received a letter from Emily's attorney,
who just happens to be Ted Eldridge, telling me she'd retained his
firm and that I'd better get a lawyer to accept service or he'd have
a sheriff serve me with papers right here at the State House."

"And so--?"

"He told me it'll be expensive. I suppose he meant in more
ways than one. He was smarter than to ask outright whether he'd
be considered for a Superior Court appointment as a *quid pro quo,*
but he left no doubt that he expected an appointment when this
case was over," the Governor replied. "He's still miffed over the
fact that he wasn't appointed to the Superior Court several years
ago when Ted Eldridge was appointed in his place. The guy really
carries a grudge. I know he was a little pissed at me a while ago,
before I spoke to the Chief Judge about making Eldridge's winter
assignments difficult in reparation for his being passed over. It
was better at that time than putting him on the Superior Court.
You were the one to arrange the whole thing for crissakes, don't
you remember?"

"Of course I do. What else did you say?"

"And so, well-- what the hell, I led him to believe that if the
case turned out all right for me; that if the publicity was held to
a minimum and that bitch doesn't get my kid and a whopping
alimony and child support payment, he'd get what he wanted."

"We can work that out certainly but in the meantime, Governor,
we have to control the whole proceeding, maybe even the actual
outcome."

"What do you mean by that?" Mort observed that Mitchell was
nervously wringing his hands together in front of his chest.

"Look, in the past two years you've appointed three Probate
Judges to the bench in Suffolk County," Mort said. "All three were
supporters of yours and two of them wouldn't have made the cut if
it weren't for our political muscle and they know it. All we have
to do is plant the seed and any one of the three will respond, if you
catch my drift. Leave that part to me. I know what to do."

"Mort, I've got a helluva'n exposure here. If certain people are called to testify I'll be--we'll be ruined. We simply cannot let that happen. You understand? It can't happen!"

"Let me handle it. Don't worry and for God's sake don't say anything to anyone about the case other than to say, if you're asked, that it's in the hands of counsel. Let me schedule a news conference right away," Mort added. "It's better if we announce the divorce on our terms rather than have some courthouse rat call the Globe as soon as the complaint is filed. I'll also meet with Jed right away and get him straightened out about this case," Mort continued.

"Don't forget that this guy Eldridge has a reputation of being a tough litigator and he's no friend of ours," the Governor told Mort before he turned to go. "We should try and find a way to kick the shit out of him."

"Leave that to me too," Mort replied on the way out the door.

CHAPTER THREE

That same afternoon after his talk with Brenden Mitchell, Mort returned to his office just down the hall from the Governor, closed the door and called Paul Jed.

Mort knew of Jed's enhanced reputation lately. Paul Jed, who for the past two years was making his mark on the divorce bar after a big win representing one of Boston's multi-millionaires in a particularly acrimonious divorce, was enjoying his new-found fame. His one time quirky personality seemed to have morphed into a self-imposed hauteur, a feeling of confidence even arrogance.

"The Governor saw you, right?" Mort asked into the phone as soon as Jed's secretary connected him.

"Yeah, he just left. He said he wanted to hire me but didn't say anything about signing an attorney-client fee agreement or payment of any retainer."

"Look, Paul, you know there's a shit load of money in it for you if you handle this right. Also, we've been good to you in the past. It won't do your reputation any harm either to represent the Governor of the Commonwealth in his divorce action. If you do the trick for him there'll be other rewards as well."

"Do the trick! What does that mean?"

"It means keeping things clean. You know, just keep the focus on custody, alimony and child support. He'll also have to give her some money and the house as well I suppose, but keep politics out of it. Keep his personal life out of it. You understand?"

"Speaking about his personal life, what about this girl friend business? How can I keep that quiet? There's rumors around he's been screwing someone for months. He told me himself that his wife might make an issue out of this. What can I do about that?"

"We'll just have to ride that out. He won't be the first chief executive to have a girl friend."

Mort heard Jed take a deep breath, there was a pause before he replied, "Well, he'll still have to sign an attorney-client fee agreement and pay a retainer of twenty-five grand. And that's only the beginning. This'll be an enormous case. I'll need to hire experts to appraise the real estate, his stock holdings in private corporations and God knows what else he's got. He even wants me to get exclusive custody for him. Can you imagine that? Custody of their kid? How the hell can I do that? I'll have to hire a child psychiatrist who'll testify that the kid should be with him instead of his wife. Who ever heard of that, for crissakes? A full time, working Governor of the Commonwealth of Massachusctts!" Jed sputtered, almost rambling now.

"Leave the psychiatrist to me," said Haller. "Don't worry. Look, I don't want to continue this conversation on the phone now so let's meet where we can discuss this further."

"Well, OK," Jed said.

"Meet me at the Algonquin Club at six, OK?" said Mort. "See you then. Oh, one more thing. How can we put a lid on this so the media don't get wind of the details?"

"I'll go over to the courthouse as soon as my friend over there calls me and tells me that the complaint is filed. She'll hold it until I get there and I'll file an *ex parte* motion to impound all the pleadings. I'll also prepare our own complaint for divorce, back date it a couple of days so it'll look as though we started first, and have that recorded at the same time."

"All right, I'm going to schedule a press conference for tomorrow to announce that the Governor is seeking a divorce from his wife, so don't be surprised when this divorce is broadcast all over the place. I only hope the papers keep the news below the fold," Mort exclaimed.

Mort hung up the phone and let out a long sigh.

"I'm going out for a while," he told his secretary. He put on his coat, took the stairs instead of the elevator and walked out onto Beacon Street completely ignoring the magnolia trees in half-bloom up and down the street. He headed down Park Street to the "T" station and an outside public telephone. He huddled into the tiny cubicle and dialed a number he'd committed to memory long ago. He waited for almost five rings before he heard the click indicating someone had picked up.

"He's in trouble. I have to speak to you. It's urgent," Mort whispered into the phone.

"Now what?" came the reply.

"Not now. When can I see you?"

"I'll be finished at five o'clock. I can meet you then."

"No, I have to meet someone else at six. It'll have to be later," Mort said.

"You know how difficult it is for us to meet without my being seen with you. I'll meet you tonight at ten o'clock in the back-room of the restaurant. Go in through the alley entrance. I'll make sure the room is empty."

"OK," Mort replied and hung up the phone.

Rhea Andretti was forty-six years old when she was appointed to the bench two years earlier by the newly-elected Governor of the Commonwealth, Brenden W. Mitchell. Her credentials were not Ivy League. She'd graduated from UMass. Boston and New England Law School and had served two years as an Assistant District Attorney in Middlesex County before changing gears and working for Drew Langford, an old time, notorious divorce lawyer in Boston.

Rhea Andretti had known Mort Haller long before she became a judge, long before her features became more comely than sexy, before she became more attractive than beautiful. When they first met in fact, she was a tall, lanky, flat-chested teenager. Now at almost fifty, her skin was the color of a perpetual tan, her hair was dark and her brown eyes sat perfectly spaced above her Italianate nose, which although rather large, was not unattractive. She dressed conservatively making sure she never gave any notice to her ample bosom, but she couldn't hide her shapely legs, as she was five feet nine inches tall.

She lived alone in Beacon Hill on a quaint little street, an alley actually, off Mt. Vernon Street, not far from Charles Street. The entrance from the street was through an oversized door that led to another locked door at the top of rather steep stairs. That door opened into a large fire-placed dining room adjacent to a large fire-placed living room. The town house had four floors including the basement level, which consisted of a kitchen, and a small sitting room. The sitting room also featured a fireplace, used by Rhea as a cozy dining area. The kitchen could be reached without using the front door and avoiding climbing the stairs, by another locked door at the street level which opened to a passageway along the length of the outside of the house leading directly onto a small patio in the rear of the building. The patio led directly into the kitchen facilitating deliveries of groceries to the kitchen. The two top floors each consisted of fire-placed bedrooms. All-in-all, five fireplaces.

Rhea knew that Mort was well acquainted with her father, as they both became intimate players in Brenden Mitchell's campaigns over the years. Her father, Lorenzo Andretti, owned a small, intimate, Italian restaurant on Hanover Street in Boston's North End, called simply, 'Renzo's'. He'd been a mover and shaker in his neighborhood for years and still continued to ingratiate himself with the local pols, cops and the rest of his goombahs who hung out at their local "club", sitting in folding chairs on the sidewalk in their undershirts smoking anisette-flavored cheroots between card games.

His wife, Assunta, died when Rhea was fourteen years old, just at the time when little girls begin to worship their fathers, which is not to say she wasn't heartbroken when her mother died. But whatever love and mutual admiration there was between her and Renzo before, increased beyond all measure after. Renzo doted on his daughter, spoiled her without remorse, dressed her in the finest clothes, pulled strings to enroll her at Boston Latin and saw to it that she didn't go to college very far away. She was never allowed to work in her father's restaurant but Renzo made sure she had whatever money she needed for whatever purpose when she walked out the door.

For her part, she sought her father's approval for just about everything she did, whether it was getting good grades, looking her best, even cooking for him on special occasions. She never wanted to disappoint him. When she finished law school, it didn't take too much effort on Rhea's part to get the job she wanted as an Assistant D.A. She knew her father kept track of debts owed to him by many people. Of course, she also knew Mort Haller. She knew he could arrange for her appointment if he was asked to intervene by Renzo, no problem, but she was determined to get this job on her own.

When Rhea informed Mort that she wanted to be appointed assistant D.A. in Middlesex County; that she'd just been interviewed and she thought she did all right, he told her he'd 'see what he could do'. Not two weeks later she was informed she had the job. Of course, Rhea suspected her father called in a chit behind her back; she knew how the game was played.

Rhea stayed in the D.A.'s office for several years but she soon became restless. She thought she wanted to get away from criminal law and to specialize in divorce where she believed she'd get more action, more actual trial time. It wasn't long before she sought a job with a good trial lawyer by the name of Drew Langford.

In those days, she knew that Mort and Drew frequently had lunch together at Renzo's and that it would be easy for Mort to accommodate her father by getting his daughter a job with Drew. One evening, when she interrupted a conversation between Mort and her father, she made her desires known to both of them. With barely a nod from Renzo, Mort agreed to see what he could do. She knew Mort always made it his business to keep track of her comings and goings and she had no doubt that she'd get the job.

Not long after that meeting, she started working for Langford. She began sitting second-chair for him when he tried high-level divorce cases involving millions of dollars in property. Her work was stressful but exciting. Increasingly however, perhaps because Langford was so damned good, Rhea became terrified to try a case on her own. She argued motions all right, but somehow she was able to steer clear of trying full-blown cases. Besides, the clients always wanted Drew and not her.

At her father's restaurant during one of Renzo's receptions for Brenden Mitchell, and after years of listening to her father's aspirations for her to become a judge, Mort Haller found himself cornered by Rhea. He was aware that as soon as they began talking she gave an almost imperceptible nod to her father who immediately joined them at the far end of the bar. Mort listened attentively to her as she told him she wanted to be appointed a judge while Renzo looked on, nodding his assent.

Soon after the election, she applied for a vacancy on the Probate and Family Court and was interviewed by the Judicial Nominating Committee. The vetting process was supposed to be free from politics but, in reality, it was anything but. The Chairperson of the committee would assign the nominee's name to a member of the committee who would make calls to lawyers and judges seeking information about the candidate. With only a wink and a nod, the committee member appointed by the Chairperson was sure to obtain the desired result. The fact that the Governor appointed the entire Commission soon after the election made it easy for the Commission to carry out the Governor's wishes, which were communicated to the Chairperson by the Governor's Chief of Staff, in this case, Mort Haller.

Rhea's interview went well, Mort found out. No one mentioned that she hadn't tried any important cases and they certainly didn't know the depth or rather the lack of depth of her knowledge of the Rules of Evidence. Her name was submitted to the Governor along with three others for a vacancy on the Suffolk Probate and Family Court and, to no one's surprise, she was appointed. Once on the bench she was smart enough to stay out of politics.

"Look," Mort was saying to Rhea. "There are several peoples' lives involved here besides the Governor's. Paul Jed, for example, was supposed to get a Superior Court Appointment several years ago but Ted Eldridge was appointed instead. These guys hate each other. What's more, the Governor never appointed Eldridge to the Appeals Court and Eldridge bears a grudge to this day."

The two of them were sitting at "Renzo's" in a room reserved for small, intimate functions of which this meeting surely was one.

"I know, I know," Rhea said, "but there are only certain things I can do. I don't even know whether I'll be assigned the case. Who did you say is going to represent the Governor? Paul Jed?"

"I just met with him earlier this evening," said Mort. "He said he thought you'd be assigned the case. He said there was some kind of system that he was acquainted with which determines who the judge will be. I didn't know what he was talking about and, what's more, I really don't care."

"Dear God, if I am assigned, I'll have to keep it until its conclusion. We're on the single justice system in Suffolk County... I, I suppose I could recuse myself... I..."

"What do you mean, 'single justice system'?" Mort interrupted.

"Meaning that all motions throughout the life of the case will be heard by the judge initially assigned and not any other judge sitting in the motion session. But, I could only do so much... I, I have to do the right thing...I can't..." she was almost rambling now.

Her voice had trailed off. Mort noticed that she was crying. She paused and tried to collect herself. Her eyes were half closed, squeezing out the tears and her lips were tightly drawn together as she looked directly at Mort Haller. She forced herself to gain some composure before she began speaking again.

"Mort... Oh God, Mort! There are some pressures on me that you're not aware of," she exclaimed. "I don't want to be involved as a judge in the Governor's divorce case. Please, Mort. You don't understand...," she begged.

"I know this'll be a high profile case," Mort insisted. "But it may very well enhance your career in more ways than one. I happen to know that your father has high ambitions for you. Listen to me Rhea," he continued. "Your cooperation is essential. The problems we may have if this case gets out of hand will harm a lot of people, including your father. Do you understand? Besides, it won't be such a big deal. This case will settle before it goes to trial. Trust me."

"Trust you!" she said. "This isn't a question of trust. This is a situation that will put me in an impossible position. It's a clear violation of the Rules of Judicial Conduct. Besides, if I'm assigned the case I will be under a media microscope every day. I'll have no peace, no privacy." She paused. "I do have a conscience, you know."

"Rhea! Rhea, didn't you hear me? This case will settle. There will be no trial. We're not asking you to compromise yourself. At the very least you can keep a tight rein on those two lawyers in your court room. You can resolve all doubts in favor of one side or the other, if you catch my drift. Jed assured me not two hours ago that you could be an immense help to the Governor by your very presence on the bench without anything more."

"You have no idea what you're asking me to do, Mort," she said. "But …I'll do the best I can."

"That's my girl! We'll all be grateful. You'll see. Your father will be grateful too. I'm sure you know what could happen to him if you didn't do as you're told."

She stared at Haller without saying another word.

The following morning at eleven o'clock, the Governor addressed the throng of electronic and print media gathered in his third floor office, note books in hand and cameras at the ready. A tense hush permeated the entire room.

Brenden Mitchell thought he looked resplendent in a dark blue suit, pale white shirt appropriately cuffed with gold links, red tie knotted with a conservative Windsor, tight against the wide spread collars, and finished off with a small American flag pinned to his lapel.

"Good morning, ladies and gentlemen." He paused to look at each one of them.

"I've called this press conference, not because of any legislation or other issue directly affecting the good people of this Commonwealth. Rather, I have the unpleasant duty to inform you about a very personal matter, a matter that involves my family," another long, dramatic pause.

"As many of you know, I've been married for over fifteen years. My wife and I have a wonderful son, Danny, whom we both love dearly. But things change as I hope you and my friends and constituents throughout the Commonwealth understand. It happens. It happens to about fifty percent of all marriages in the United States and Presidents and Governors and Senators and Legislators are not immune. Yes, I'm talking about divorce. I'm announcing today that I'm filing for divorce." Another pause.

"I hope the good people of this Commonwealth cut my wife and me some slack. I hope the media can give us some privacy. Is that too much to hope for? I think not. Both my wife and I expect that things will go smoothly, but I can assure you things between us will go even smoother if we are not made a spectacle of, if we are treated with some degree of propriety as we go through this difficult time," Another pause, a sad look directed at each person standing before him.

"That's all I have to say. No questions please. I hope you all have a nice day. Thank you."

The Governor didn't wait for his office to clear but walked out through the crowd, excusing himself to each as he left.

Later that same day, Paul Jed filed his motion to impound the pleadings and the Governor's complaint for divorce as soon as he received the call from a clerk telling him that Emily's complaint was filed. The motion was allowed with dispatch. No trouble at all.

That night on the evening news, the Governor saw that on all three major networks, it was reported that Brenden Mitchell, the Governor of the Commonwealth of Massachusetts had filed for divorce from his wife. Attorneys Edward Eldridge and Paul Jed, the former representing Ms. Mitchell, the latter representing the Governor, were contacted but each refused public comment. Pictures of the Governor's news conference and the details of what he said were faithfully shown on each TV station, but the commentators were careful not to speculate.

The following morning the Globe and the Herald reported essentially the same story. There simply were no other details to juice up the conflict between the Governor and his wife, at least not at this stage. In both papers the proceedings were reported above the fold but not on the front page.

CHAPTER FOUR

The large, oak paneled door to the left of the cavernous courtroom and well inside the bar which separates the lawyers from the rest of mankind opened, and the uniformed court officer proceeded into the courtroom followed by the Judge. The Judge passed the court officer on her way to the bench, climbed the three steps to the dais and stood behind her high backed blue leather chair.

"Hear Ye, Hear Ye, Hear Ye! All those having anything to do with the Probate and Family Court, now sitting in Boston in and for the county of Suffolk, Justice Andretti presiding, draw near, give your attention and ye shall be heard. God save the Commonwealth of Massachusetts!" The court officer recited the ancient "cry" in stentorian tones, heard by everyone in the now hushed courtroom.

The Judge took her seat and looked at Barbara Hancock seated below the at the floor level just below the judge's bench. "Call the first case madam clerk."

I knew quite a lot about Judge Rhea Andretti. What I didn't know first hand from appearing before her I learned by other means. Lawyers talk. And they talk about judges, their peccadilloes, knowledge of the law and particularly whether they know their rules of evidence. I knew she was a stickler for formality. No first names for her. Most of the lawyers in the Suffolk County Bar Association tried to avoid her, as she was perceived to be a lightweight. She was weak on her rules of evidence, tried to avoid lengthy and complicated trials, and what was worse, had no patience with the give and take of oral arguments. Reportedly, she covered up her lack of understanding of the law, even her lack of understanding of human nature, with a formality that sheltered her from having to engage counsel in an intellectual colloquy about some arcane legal issue. She never admitted she was wrong in open court, even when it became obvious she was off the mark. When she stated a fact which she perceived to be true, she brooked no further argument. Besides all that, it was well recognized that she had her "pets" to whom she gave favorable treatment.

The motion session at the trial court level is not at all like arguing an appeal. There is usually no time limit imposed on the lawyers arguing motions at that level. Moreover, they habitually interrupt one another, raise their voices, attempt to impress their client with vitriol and hyperbole and generally try to obfuscate all the facts that do not assist their client. The fact that the underlying pleading is a complaint for divorce generally means that the plaintiff and the defendant hate one another and they have transferred their anger to their lawyers who have taken up their cudgel.

The only reason Judge Andretti had as many cases as the other four judges sitting in Suffolk was that as the complaints were initially received and filed by the clerks, they received a secret number so that each judge received one in five cases in the order of their filing. The only trouble with the system was that a few lawyers who had connections with the clerks could persuade a clerk to hold the complaint to avoid Andretti. Some, who were considered to be her "pets", persuaded the clerks to hold the complaint so that Andretti would be assigned to their case.

I was sitting inside the bar with Henry Baker, my intrepid associate, at the Suffolk County Probate and Family Court two weeks after filing our complaint for divorce. Our client was sitting outside the bar with the rest of the litigants, their friends and relatives, all waiting impatiently for the last hour and a half while other matters were argued before the Judge.

"Do you think we should be sitting with Ms.Mitchell and holding her hand?" Baker whispered to me.

"Hell no. We can catch a few minutes peace sitting here," I replied.

"I don't see Jed or his client. We're sitting here for almost two hours and those guys haven't even shown their faces," Baker continued.

"You don't think the Governor of the Commonwealth is going to sit with the proletariat do you?" I whispered back.

"Attorney Eldridge!" came a piercing voice from the bench. The Judge glared at both Baker and me.

"Is it too much to ask for a little cooperation from you while I'm hearing other arguments? If you've got something to say please go into the hall." She turned her glare to the court officer in a silent chastise. He knew immediately what to do from sad experience. "Silence please! Silence! No talking!" he bellowed.

We were in court to argue our motion for Temporary Orders which prayed for the granting of temporary custody to our client and an award of temporary alimony and child support. Usually there is a preliminary hearing before one of the Family Service Officers assigned to the Court. The hearing is held in an attempt to bring the parties to an agreement in the absence of which the FSO makes his or her recommendation to the judge prior to the hearing.

Once in a while in the past, I've been lucky enough to get someone who's intelligent as an FSO, one who could save a lot of time by having the parties agree without waiting for a court hearing. Jed must have worked his magic with one of his clerk friends I thought, because the preliminary hearing requirement was waived by the Court. After all, it would be unseemly for the Governor to subject himself to some runny-nosed court worker with a bachelor's degree in psychology.

Additionally, we also filed a motion for a Restraining Order and an Appointment for a Guardian *Ad Litem* who would investigate the issue of custody for the Court. We also filed a motion for counsel fees to be awarded us in the amount of $250,000 dollars. We had previously served on Paul Jed a Notice to Take Deposition of his client, the Governor, a Request for the Production of Documents, Interrogatories and a Notice to Admit Facts. All of these papers were served along with the motion for Temporary Orders, the Restraining Order and the Motion for Counsel Fees one week before the hearing was scheduled.

At the time of service, all of us in the firm were feeling confident. "We'll overwhelm Jed and his people with a batch of pleadings so they'll know they're in a pissing contest," I overheard my young associate, Jordan Levy state to one of the secretaries who was busy typing the forms. That was before we received the notice that the case was assigned to Judge Andretti. That was also before we received a similar batch of pleadings from Paul Jed's office, all of which were the mirror image of the ones we filed.

"Of all the gin joints in all the world…," Jordan Levy lamented when we received the court order signed by Andretti.

"That's not the exact quote," Henry replied. "But I know what you mean. We had only a twenty percent chance of getting assigned to her and we drew the short straw, I guess."

"I'm not so sure it was just the luck of the draw," I said "Jed's got a lot of sway at that courthouse. I bet he persuaded one of his toadies to manipulate the filing in order to draw Andretti. We all know he's one of her pets."

Back at the courthouse, we paced in the hall and endured the non-stop kvetching from our client as long as we could before we returned to the courtroom only to wait almost another two hours before our case was finally called.

"Mitchell vs. Mitchell," Barbara Hancock the clerk, finally announced to an almost empty courtroom. It was only ten minutes before the noon recess, which actually began at one o'clock.

Baker, Mrs. Mitchell and I took the three chairs at the table to the right of the floor microphone while the newly arrived Paul Jed and two of his associates sat at the table to the left.

"You've got ten minutes each," the Judge said. "My afternoon session is completely booked and that's the best I can do."

I stood up at the mike.

"Your Honor," I said. "I can't possibly argue my motions in ten minutes. We've been here for over three hours waiting for our turn and it's only fair that we're afforded a reasonable amount of time to present our case. We'd be glad to come back this afternoon or, in the alternative, come back tomorrow."

I paused and looked at the defendant's table.

"I don't see the defendant here. Can we assume it's inconvenient for the Governor to grace us with his presence? Perhaps it'd be better for the defendant and his counsel to postpone the hearing as well."

"Wait a minute! Wait a minute!" Paul Jed got up from his chair. "My client wasn't subpoenaed. He doesn't have to be here. This is an oral argument between counsels, not a trial where testimony is elicited. If my friend, Attorney Eldridge wanted testimony, he could have subpoenaed witnesses."

"First of all, Mr. Jed," I said, "I'm not your friend. Secondly, you didn't even show up in court today until five minutes before the case was called while we've been here all morning. It's not possible to argue my motions in ten minutes and it's not possible to argue your motions within that time either."

"Don't tell me what's ….."

"That's enough," the Judge interrupted. "I won't hear any more from either of you. I invoke Rule 78 of the Rules of Domestic

Relations Procedure and you both can submit your memoranda and exhibits in support of each of your motions in lieu of oral argument within two weeks. No need to support your motion for counsel fees Mr. Eldridge, I'll rule on that right away. That's all! This court is adjourned."

On the walk back to the office Emily Mitchell was full of questions.

"What was all that about? What's Rule 78? I don't understand. You told me there was going to be a long argument and that my husband would be there. I don't think this judge likes you. My God! What am I going to do now," she lamented.

"Take it easy. Take it easy, Mrs. Mitchell," I said. "There's no need to worry. This is just round one of a very long fight. We'll simply have to submit our argument in written form instead of arguing orally. When we get the documents that we've requested from your husband including his checking accounts, telephone records, credit card information, tax returns, copies of correspondence and diaries he's kept we'll be in good shape to take his deposition. He has to be present for that. Even Bill Clinton had to appear when he was served."

We were headed south along Congress Street, passing Faneuil Hall on the left and crossing State Street when we were interrupted as we got to the other side.

"Well, well, Judge, fancy meeting you here." It was Mary Hartigan. I almost bumped right into her engrossed as I was in my conversation with my client. She was just about to get into a limo parked on the large, grey, stone pavers next to The Old State House, not far from the spot of the Boston Massacre.

The only good thing about the new administration was the election of my good friend, Mary Hartigan as Lieutenant Governor. She ran independently from the Governor and was elected by a landslide. Mary and I were in college together in Amherst and the two of us were part of a clique consisting of five women and seven men. The seven of us guys were in the same fraternity but the girls might as well have been fraternity brothers for all the time they spent at the "House." In four years we were all inseparable. We had each other's back when one or more of us drank too much, loved too much or when some other problem occurred which tended to interfere with the harmony of the group. We studied together, cared for each other and were fiercely loyal. No one dared say an unkind word about any one of us in the presence of any of the others lest they get more than they bargained for. Over the years, we all attended each others weddings, baby showers, kid's Bar and Bat Mitzvahs and got together at football and lacrosse games back on campus as often as we could. When I'd meet Mary at different functions in the city, she was one of the few people who always still called me "Judge".

"Governor," I said. "How are you? I haven't had a chance to talk with you since the champagne became warm in the plastic cups at your swearing in," I kidded her, bending over and planting a big kiss on her cheek.

"You've seen me since then, Ted. How's the best lawyer in Boston?" she replied, looking now at Emily Mitchell for the first time.

"Emily, I didn't recognize you for a second. How are you?" Mary said to Ms. Mitchell.

"Mary. It's so good to see you again," Emily managed to say, despite her obvious distress. The two women looked at each other, not knowing quite what to say in the moment at such a serendipitous meeting.

"Ms. Mitchell, Mary and I have been friends since college," I interjected, for something to say more than anything else.

"Well, we've known each other since the campaign, Ted", Mary added, nodding to Emily Mitchell.

"Unfortunately, I haven't seen as much of you as I'd like, Emily. I guess we've all been busy," Mary said.

"It's good to see you, Governor. I've heard good things about you, not only from my husband but from several others as well," Emily replied.

"Thank you. Ted, let's get together soon", she said to me. "We have a lot of catching up to do. I have to run." She kissed me on the cheek and got into the limo, the door to which had been held open for her by a blue suit, rep tie assistant about twenty-one years old.

"Nice seeing you, Ms. Mitchell. Bye Ted." And off she went.

By the time Emily and I reached the rear entrance of Old City Hall, Emily Mitchell had calmed down and we parted after exchanging warm handshakes.

CHAPTER FIVE

After the hearing, I went directly into my office, called Jordan and asked him to come in. I wanted to ask him to bring me a cup of coffee but I didn't. In our office no one brought coffee to anyone. I wanted to avoid the secretarys' stations next to the small kitchen where the coffee pot was located because everyone would ask what happened in Court and there was no easy or quick reply.

"Have we heard from Charley?" I asked as soon as Jordan stepped in. "We sent him his retainer of five grand and he told me he'd get right on it," I continued.

"Well, uh, Charley seems to be going around in circles Ted," Jordan replied hesitantly. My associate has known me for a long time and he could sense my impatience. "He called me last night before I left the office and started talking about the Judicial

Nominating Commission, the appointment process of judges, and in particular, Mort Haller, the Governor's Chief of Staff. At first I thought he was in his cups but I'm not so sure--"

"What did he say about the Governor's mistress? Does he have a name? What has he done so far?"

"He didn't say anything about that," Jordan replied. "I think he's caught up in this rat's nest of intrigue about the selection process of judges. He--"

"I don't give a goddamn about that," I said. "I've been there. I know first hand what a sham that committee is but that's not our issue now. We have a client to service for crissakes."

"Well, the reason Charley got into it is because I told him we drew the short straw and Judge Andretti was assigned in our case. I also told him we believe that Paul Jed manipulated the process," Jordan said evenly.

"Short straw? Short straw? There was no short straw," I bellowed. "Jed got one of his toadies to wait for the right time before our complaint was filed so he'd get Andretti. So what! We'll never be able to prove that. I don't give a shit about that. I'll tell you what I care about," I continued. "I care about getting the evidence against this Governor so we can create a record at the time of trial so that even Andretti, if she has any conscience at all, will give Emily Mitchell a fair shake. And if she screws us, we'll have a record for the Appeals Court. I want to show that Brenden Mitchell is a wife beater; that he has a girlfriend upon whom he spends money lavishly while being penurious to his family. I'm sure his financial records will bear this out. I want to show that he is a control freak and that he has controlled just about every waking moment of his wife's life; that she's on the brink of a nervous breakdown if she's not there already and that his kid is a basket case."

I picked up the phone. Jordan sat in front of me stone-faced. Everybody in the office knew that I had the capacity to explode periodically and they all gave me a wide berth when I was on a rampage. The truth is that, despite my Yankee name, I am half-Italian and I have all the good points and bad points of that stereotype. My hair is not blonde, my eyes are not blue, my complexion is not fair..., and I don't get mad when someone fires a shot across my bow, I get even.

"Amy, get Charley on the phone right now," I ordered without my usual "please". While I was waiting for Charley, neither Jordan nor I said a word. Jordan knew enough to keep his mouth shut under the circumstances.

"He's on the line," Amy said to me after a few seconds.

"Charley! What have you done about finding out who the Governor's girl friend is," I said. "It's been two weeks since I gave you five grand and I've heard nothing. Jordan tells me you're off on some frolic about the politically corrupt Judicial Nominating Committee and, Charley, I don't give a shit about that. You understand? You're not writing for the Globe spotlight team, you're investigating an adulterer, a fornicator, and I want to know who the third party is before I take Brenden Mitchell's deposition.

"Ted, sweetheart, take it easy," he said. "You'll have a heart attack. I'm on it. Don't worry. I'll have a report for you shortly."

"When?" I said.

"Give me a week."

"OK. I'll look forward to it." I hung up the phone.

"He says he'll have a report in a week," I said to Jordan. "In the meantime, you and Henry prepare a draft of our memoranda in support of our position in each one of our motions that was heard today. Ask one of the secretaries to call the Court and try to get an early copy of Andretti's order so we can determine how much she's going to allow us in fees. Also, make sure we have two weeks to submit our memoranda. Call Lester Begley, you know our CPA and ask him to assign his best accountant to go over the financial documents when we get them from Jed in response to our document request."

Jordan was just the guy who happened to be in my office at the time. I would have preferred to speak with Henry directly as he was senior to Jordan by three years. Yet, I trusted both of them and I knew they worked well together.

After he left, I tried to think of all the things I had to do. I needed to make an appointment to see Emily's shrink. I needed to engage a child psychiatrist to testify that Brenden Mitchell was not qualified to be the primary care parent, notwithstanding the court appointment of a G.A.L who might turn out to be a loser. I had to prepare Emily to answer the document request that was served on her by Paul Jed as well as answering the interrogatories and, most important of all, prepare her for her deposition. I also had to begin to think of whom I should hire as a business expert to value the Governor's business ventures as well as whom I should hire as an expert to value the real estate. This was going to be a marathon case, but oh so satisfying, unless of course, Andretti doesn't give us what we asked for in our motion for fees.

On Hanover Street, Renzo was seated at one of the tables in his restaurant in his sleeveless undershirt just outside the doors leading to the kitchen. It was a quiet sun-drenched morning and the owner was reading the Globe and sipping his espresso. By contrast to the evenings when the place was filled with customers, the silence in the mornings was a welcome, peaceful interval which he thoroughly enjoyed after taking out the trash from the night before. Not this morning though.

His concentration was interrupted when his chef, Guiliano, came in around eleven o'clock to prepare the evening's menu specials.

"Buon giorno, padrone. Come sta?" Guiliano sat down at the table with Renzo.

"I'm fine. Gulie, how're you?"

"Bene, bene. But you don't look too good. Whatsamatter? Business is good. Last night was full. You were OK when I left, remember? We kidded about that customer who ordered cheese on his fritto misto di pesce."

"Rhea called me last night." Renzo put his paper down with a sigh. "She thinks someone's been following her the last couple days. She gets letters from time to time from nut cases who've appeared before her but she never had the feeling she's being followed before."

"Look boss, nobody's going to touch her," Gulie said between his teeth. "If some guy is stalking her we can find out pretty quick. You want me to fix it --just say the word."

"She could call the police but for some reason she doesn't want to get them involved. She calls me instead and asks me to do something about it. I don't know. I get the feeling she's not exactly staying home every night working on her cases but...I don't know. You saw her here with that Mort Haller last week? I don't know what all that was about but they sure didn't want to be seen by anybody."

"She's a smart girl. She's young and she must have a boyfriend. It's only natural boss, don't be so worried about her," Gulie said soothingly. "So she has an affair of the heart. So what? Lemme put someone on it-- you know, find out if someone's stalking her."

"OK, but no rough stuff. Just let me know if someone's been following her. I don't want to go any further than that, unnerstand?" Renzo instructed.

CHAPTER SIX

Paul Jed's office was at 100 Federal Street right in the heart of downtown Boston. The elevator opened directly into his office which was a nice touch, but then again, Paul never skimped on the bells and whistles. He was a fellow of the American Academy of Matrimonial Lawyers, a member of the Family Law Section of the Mass. Bar, a member of the Family Law Committee of the Boston Bar Association...and all of these designations were prominently displayed on his firm's resume.. He had four other partners each having a different specialty and the ability to draw from a pool of several associates and paralegals for assistance. It wasn't unusual to see one of the partners being trailed by two and sometimes three "bag carriers" who supposedly were brought along for assistance but, in reality, were brought along because the firm could bill their time. Five hundred dollars an hour for the least expensive of all the partners (this was Paul's recent billable rate), at least two hundred an hour for associates' time and one fifty an hour for paralegals. The cheapest team therefore was billed out at a total of eight hundred and fifty dollars an hour-- and that was when only one associate and one paralegal accompanied Paul Jed to wherever he went.

Paul Jed had the reputation of a tenacious in-fighter, a capable lawyer arguing motions before a judge in the motion sessions but woefully deficient in his knowledge of evidence at the time of trial. Everyone knew "on the street" that he'd drag a case out, milk it for all it was worth, bring motion after motion, take deposition after deposition, demand all kinds of documents and then settle the case on the court house steps on the day of trial to avoid displaying his trial deficiencies.

When he got back to his office after the hearing on the Governor's temporary order Paul had to call his client and inform him of the outcome. The news was neither good nor bad so he didn't expect any fall out... no rantings, no rages. But, neither was there any expectation of gratitude. Not yet anyway, he thought.

The trouble was he had to get the Governor to focus on his case. It had taken a whole week and several revisions of the financial statement that had to be filed with the motions that were heard today, he remembered. Even then, the Governor didn't pay attention to the fact that all of his assets had to be listed, that his income had to be exact and that his liabilities had to be specifically set forth-- under the pains of perjury!

The Governor had finally showed up at his office only three days before the hearing, Jed recalled. He and two of his associates were sitting in his conference room when they were informed that the Governor had arrived. At the time, he was delighted that the whole office would see the Governor of the Commonwealth right here at 100 Federal who'd come to see Paul Jed and no one else.

"Look," the Governor said as soon as they were all seated, "I don't have the time to pay attention to every little detail that's going to be involved in this case. I have people to do that kind of work. Call my accountant, Mark Conlin. He's a partner at Conlin and Hersey. He'll supply you with everything you need. Besides we've been busy planning the campaign for my run at the Senate and Mort has his hands full as well."

Mort Haller, as usual, was also with the Governor and added, "Don't worry Paul. Don't worry. Eldridge will have his hands full with this case. We've got our bases covered." He looked around the room.

"Uh Paul, do you think your associates could excuse us for the rest of this conference?" Mort asked after only about fifteen minutes into the meeting.

"Oh, sure. Thank you gentlemen, I'll call you back in later," Paul nodded to his two associates.

After they'd gone Paul started right in before Mort had a chance to say anything

"I don't think either of you comprehend the gravity of what we're facing," Paul said. "There's going to be experts testifying about values of assets. All the assets! There's going to be experts testifying about the Governor's income. All the income!"

He actually stood up from his chair as if energized by what he was saying.

"Testimony about parenting ability, testimony from psychiatrists, the Guardian *Ad Litem* and God only knows who else may be called. Besides, we have to submit a pile of documents they've requested, answer interrogatories, admit certain facts, and prepare for the Governor's deposition and the depositions of all the experts. We also face the possibility of a restraining order. This case is going to be a marathon and it's going to require a lot of everybody's time and it's going to cost a barrel of money." Paul stopped, almost breathless and looked nervously at his client for a response.

"I'll be goddamned if I'm going to let that bitch of a wife of mine intimidate me," the Governor thundered. "I've got some goods on her. She's not so blameless.

She and her fancy lawyer will get an ear full when the time comes. She can't hold a job. She drinks three or more glasses of Chardonnay each night and begins slurring her words after the first glass. She can't make up her mind about anything much less anything to do with parenting. She's taking medication-- some kind of tranquilizer. The combination with the booze knocks her out so she's comatose by eight o'clock at night. She can't cook, doesn't do any housework, and has a mouth on her like a longshoreman," the Governor said.

"Yes, I've hit her, but only in self-defense. She's come at me with a butcher knife and waved it right in front of my face, for crissakes. What am I supposed to do, let her cut me? She's nothing but a prima donna and hasn't contributed one asset or one dollar of income to this marriage. You know what else? I wouldn't be surprised if she was gay. She doesn't like sex. She makes me feel like some kind of deviant when, on rare occasions she relents and we've made love in positions that I read about in the Kama Sutra. For weeks, even months at a time we live like brother and sister. You won't believe this but just about the only time we've had sex is when she's had too much to drink and even then she's never the aggressor, merely submissive, like the whole act is some kind of duty. We've lived our lives of quiet desperation almost ever since the marriage began; until recently that is, when she told me she wanted a divorce."

The governor glanced around the room as he took a sip of water looking totally drained, almost pathetic, Paul thought.

After a long pause, Paul finally said, "Governor, all that may be true. We may even be able to prove most of it. But the case will be a media circus. Your career will be ruined."

"Do something about it then," Mort replied, his voice rising just like his boss. "Settle out of court. Bring pressure on them. Make things so difficult that they'll be willing to cave. We've got a senatorial campaign to worry about. We've paid you your retainer of fifty grand and we should get something for our money."

"All that's easier said than done. I'll need some help," Paul stirred uncomfortably in his chair crossing one leg over the other as he spoke.

"Paul," Mort sighed, "We'll do our thing, you do yours. Everything will turn out just fine. If we bring enough pressure on Emily she'll settle rather than airing her dirty laundry in court, or worse, having to undergo one of your scathing cross-examinations. She's already in therapy, almost completely out of control. The pressure of all the pre-trial motions, depositions and the rest of the litigation will surely become too much for her. I promised you I'll get a psychiatrist who'll testify that she's incapable of parenting the kid, not to worry, I'll do it."

Paul Jed thought back to those conversations in his office a week ago, about Mort getting a psychiatrist and all the rest and now, after the hearing this morning, Jed had a little more confidence since Judge Andretti was assigned to the case. He picked up his phone and dialed the Governor's private number. Private though it was supposed to be, it was nevertheless intercepted by Mort.

"Paul," Mort said into the phone, "What happened?"

"She entered no decision," Jed replied. "We have to submit memoranda in support of our positions. I won't know how she's ruled for a couple of weeks."

"OK. Keep us posted," and with that Mort hung up the phone.

CHAPTER SEVEN

Forty-five years old, pocked-marked, jowly, head connected to his shoulders without any neck, a middle-aged expansive chest and a protruding belly, both of which seemed to flow into one another, Jake Bauer leaned casually against the building at the corner of Mount Vernon and Charles Streets. Not twenty yards up the hill was the entrance to Cedar Lane Way where his attention was focused--at least most of the time. He'd been at his post since six-thirty that night, right after he ate his cheeseburger and Coke which he bought across the street at the 7 Eleven and wolfed down in a hurry before taking up his vigil. He started his watch at the courthouse at five o'clock that afternoon.

His surveillance was interrupted only by two trips to the convenience store for coffee and to go to the restaurant a couple of doors down the block to use the bathroom. It was now nine-forty-five. He had seen his quarry walk into the front door of her town house on the narrow street of Cedar Lane Way about seven o'clock and she hadn't left yet as far as he could tell. He was aware that she could walk down the other end of her street and exit at Pinckney Street, not Mount Vernon, but he'd be able to see her either way and he couldn't be in two places at the same time. He'd be too conspicuous if he waited right on her street but he had a vantage point nonetheless.

He watched as several people entered the street coming home from work but he observed them entering their own houses, not the one that he cared about. His boss, Charley Randell, had given him specific instructions: watch and wait, see who enters her house; if she leaves, follow her wherever she goes. Jake was armed with a small Power Shot A95 Canon and was told to snap the picture of any male who entered her house or any male she encounters for any considerable period of time after she leaves-- wherever that may be.

Jake's orders were to follow her as soon as she left the courthouse. He knew in advance that work was only a short walk from her house so she never took her car even though she had a reserved parking space waiting for her. On a few occasions he followed her as she walked from the court house to a meeting in downtown Boston. When that happened Jake was forced to wait outside the building until she left, follow her home and continue his surveillance.

Jake glanced at his watch and rolled his eyes. It was only ten o'clock. He had another two hours to go before he could go home. The passers by were all Beacon Hill types dressed in their jeans, loafers over bare feet even in this cold weather and jackets prominently displaying the ubiquitous polo player covering their turtle neck sweaters.

Then, as the strollers thinned out, Jake noticed two heavy-set men walking down the hill toward him as he slouched against the building on Mt. Vernon Street trying to be inconspicuous. As they approached him Jake became alert as they both wore black leather car coats and their heads were covered with wide brimmed hats pulled down almost over their noses. As they got closer however, Jake relaxed somewhat as they appeared to be engrossed in conversation. Yet, there was something about the way they talked as they got closer.

As they passed Jake leaning against the wall, they suddenly stopped talking. The one closest to Jake suddenly turned around, grabbed Jake by the shoulders and butted his head against Jake's brow which sent the back of Jake's head crashing off the brick building for a double hit. Jake was still dazed when his assailant grabbed him and held him up against the building while his partner got right in front of Jake's face, now beginning to drip blood .

"Who are you and what are you doing here?" Jake was asked by the face in front of him, a dark face with a large nose, thick lips and a heavy accent.

"Fuck you," Jake said between his teeth.

"Yeah? Well listen carefully wise guy. Unless you want more of the same you'd better get the hell outta here and don't come back. If we see you hangin' around this corner again you won't have any legs to stand on. Capisce?"

They let Jake slump to the sidewalk as they both calmly walked away.

Jake stayed in the same slumped position on the sidewalk against the building for several minutes not able to move. He felt the blood running down the side of his face and trickle into his open mouth but for a few minutes he was powerless to do anything about it. He was too dazed. He swallowed the thick liquid several times before he spit it out but even that motion made his head ache even more.

"Shit!" he sputtered out loud. He stayed that way not daring to move as he watched some people pass by not giving him a second look. As things began to focus a little he carefully got up on his feet, staggered and held onto the building for balance.

Ten o'clock in the middle of Beacon Hill, no cop, I've just had the shit kicked out of me and no one stops, he thought. I've got a concussion from those bastards he said to himself as he ran his fingers over the swelling on the back of his head with one hand and felt the bump on the front of his head with the other. Well, it's not the first time, he thought. His next thought was whether to walk a couple of blocks to the emergency ward at Mass General or forget about it. Well, not forget about it but--

He finally decided to report back to Charley and see what the next step should be rather than checking himself in at the hospital. He was certain his assailants were Italian and they were therefore controlled by someone Charley would know. What the hell, concussions come and go; they were part of the job, he thought.

The following morning Renzo was seated at his usual table in the restaurant after cleaning the kitchen and disposing of the considerable garbage from the night before. He was listening to Pavarotti singing Nesson Dorma from Puccini's opera, Turandot and his eyes were glassed over as Luciano hit his last several bars-- "Vincero, Vincero Vincero!"

Guiliano was careful not to slam the door as he entered the dining room. He'd heard the music from as far away as the parking lot and knew better than to startle the boss in the middle of one of his favorite arias.

"Good news, Padrone. Whoever was stalking the Judge, is no more," Gulie said after the aria was over.

"What the hell does that mean?" Renzo said turning to look at Gulie directly as he sat down at the table.

"Oh, no. Nothing bad. Just a little enforcement to insure that the problem will go away. We found some pagliaccio who was watching her. We observed him for several hours to be sure he was the guy Rhea complained about. There was nothing serious, at least not yet, so we made him an offer he couldn't refuse. I don't think she'll be bothered again," Gulie reported with a satisfactory grin as he poured himself a shot of Strega into his Espresso.

Two weeks after the hearing we submitted our memoranda together with exhibits, five separate files, which were about four inches thick as they were wheeled over to the courthouse by Jordan Levy. I was certain that Andretti would not read anywhere near all the supporting documents but rather would just go with her gut reaction without any concern for legal precedent. In that regard, she wasn't any worse than most other Probate Judges in the entire Commonwealth. I even included the pictures Amy took of Ms. Mitchell as they were supportive of our motion for a restraining order. Paul Jed had previously filed his motion to impound in order to keep the pleadings away from the public and especially the media. He had submitted his own memoranda and exhibits as well.

Two weeks later we received the Judge's order. The restraining order, which asked that the Governor stay away from his wife, was denied. The motion to impound, as we already knew, had already been granted as soon as it was filed by Jed. In addition, the Judge now imposed a gag order on all participants in the case. We were awarded only fifty thousand dollars in attorney's fees, not the two hundred and fifty we asked for. The Judge made us wait until we received all her rulings before we could find out the amount awarded despite her statement in court that she'd have it ready right away. Emily was awarded six thousand dollars a month in alimony and child support from the Governor's one hundred-fifty thousand dollar a year salary, even though the mortgage on the Brookline house was two thousand a month which Emily was ordered to pay along with other household expenses. In his memoranda, the Governor voluntarily agreed to vacate the house so Emily could live there with Danny at least some of the time. The Governor had taken up residency with his sister only three blocks away from his former residence which was the basis for the Judge to enter the killer, the absolute killer of her orders: split custody of Danny! The Governor would have him every other weekend from Friday morning to Sunday night. On the off week he'd have him Monday through Thursday. Unbelievable!

The rest of the order about health insurance, maintenance of life insurance, the prohibition of disposing of any assets during the pen-dency of the action was ordinary enough, but split custody would send Emily over the edge. The order for counsel fees sent me over the edge. The two hundred thousand difference between the fifty thousand awarded and the two hundred fifty asked for would be disastrous. My office would have to float all the costs of this litigation until the end of the trial. Emily's twenty-five thousand retainer had been used up long ago. Even when the trial was concluded, if we didn't win big, we wouldn't get paid--Emily simply wouldn't have enough assets and I didn't have almost a quarter of a million in reserve. In fact, I had nothing in reserve. I'd have to borrow the money somewhere and that was an enormous problem. We bill our time at prevailing rates and the experts I have to hire are expensive. They all want their money up front. Additionally, to make matters worse, the Judge imposed a freeze on disposing of any marital assets during the pendency of the case so nothing could be sold.

I should've known. These judges have no clue what it costs to run a downtown law office in Boston, I thought. Our rent at Old City Hall is twenty thousand a month alone. Salaries, including a partner's draw and associates pay are fifty thousand a month, not to mention pension plan contributions and health insurance -- and that's just the beginning. A trial like this will cost over two hundred-fifty thousand easy. And with the whole office working on this case alone this was a recipe for disaster.

The Judge had appointed Donald Long as the Guardian *Ad Litem,* to investigate the question of custody and ordered him to file an interim report within one month and his final report at the time of trial. Donald Long, a notorious crony of the Judge, was one of her former law clerks who had sat with her every day for over a year before he left for private practice and who, as everybody knew, met socially with the Judge regularly. I mean, I've seen them myself having dinner together at a restaurant on Boylston Street after a meeting of the bar association. They always sat together at continuing legal education programs, although I don't know what either of them could have learned from them.

Emily couldn't control her sobbing when I told her the results.

"I thought you were the best," she said between blows into her handkerchief. "How could you let this happen to me--to us? Split custody? He doesn't give a goddamn about Danny. He never did! He works all day and plays around all night. Who'll take care of my baby? Oh Jesus, what am I going to do?" She sobbed.

It took me an hour and a half to get her under control. I didn't have the heart to talk about our fees. I had all I could do to explain to her that this was just the first round; that we had a long way to go.

"Look Emily, we can probably get the Guardian Ad Litem to state in his interim report that split custody is counter-productive to Danny's best interest. If he won't, we'll hire our own child psychiatrist with credentials as long as your arm and ask the Judge to modify the order. The wheels of justice grind slowly but they grind exceedingly fine; the best interests of this kid will eventually be recognized, don't worry."

"You know something, Mr. Eldridge? I've never said this to a living soul but Brenden Mitchell isn't even the father of Danny. I tricked him when we were separated fifteen years ago," she said.

"We were living apart for about three months after a helluva'n argument where he slapped me across the face and pushed me against the wall in the kitchen. I told him to get out of the house right then and there or I'd call the cops. At that time, he was in the Massachusetts Senate and he certainly couldn't afford to be arrested for domestic violence. One night, after he'd left for about a month, I had an affair with a former boy friend of mine. It was really a nothing encounter--I just, I don't know. It was just one of those silly dalliances.

A few weeks later, I learned that I was finally pregnant after years of trying with Brenden-- but I knew it wasn't his. I knew exactly what to do. I went to the apartment he was renting and apologized even though I had nothing to apologize for. I wore his favorite perfume, black underwear and a loose- fitting blouse, and it wasn't long before we were in each other's arms. The next day he moved back in. Within a month I proudly announced that we were pregnant. With his ego he didn't dream that he wasn't the father, and besides, we were both happy to have a child on the way."

She sat back in her chair, dabbed at the corner of one eye, let out an audible sigh and looked for all the world to be completely relieved, even satisfied, at least for the moment.

I was speechless. My brain was processing this bizarre, explosive information to see where it could fit in the mosaic I was trying to build in my mind, but my thoughts were all running together. I needed some time to determine what use we could make of her revelation--and when.

I snapped back to the present after I heard her say, "Well?"

I told her we'd use that information if it was absolutely necessary; but we had to be careful of how it would affect Danny; that we'd have to weigh the pros and cons and to be sure we could prove what she just told me. To be honest I just couldn't get my mind around it just then.

"Well it seems perfectly clear to me that he won't be awarded custody of a child that's not his," she said rather forcefully, with a certainty that comes from pure conviction.

"It's not that simple," I responded.

"After fourteen or, what is it, fifteen years of Danny thinking that Brenden is his father, the courts are reluctant to conclude that someone else is the biological father despite evidence, even clinical evidence, to the contrary. There are cases--" I related, though I didn't want to burst her bubble or for that matter, even mine. There was enough bad news to digest for the two of us.

"Don't worry Emily, we'll find a place to use this to our best advantage. In the meantime, I think I'd better engage a child psychiatrist and have our accountant review the documents we'll receive from the Governor. They should prove very interesting. We also should expect a report from our investigator about his comings and goings," I said to her hoping she wouldn't notice that my voice lacked conviction towards the end...I hadn't heard from Charley in over a week.

After she left, I was alternately depressed and angry. I had such a feeling of helplessness and frustration I could hardly contain myself. The system really sucked! I knew what the right thing was this Judge should have done. A person didn't have to be a former judge to realize that-- only a person with a half of brain!

We had a weapon though. What dynamite! We could use this information Emily had just told me in several ways. We wouldn't have to go public, just use it as a bargaining chip at the right time. I couldn't wait to see the expression on his face when I dropped the bomb.

I called Henry Baker and Jordan Levy into my office and gave each of them a copy of the order.

"I can't believe it," Henry sputtered."

"What bull shit," Jordan echoed.

"Yeah well, what are we going to do about it?" I replied, looking at the two of them.

"I've got more bad news," Jordan said hesitatingly. "Charley's man, Jake, got mugged by a couple of Italians while he was on his stake- out by Andretti's street and warned to stay away. When I asked him about the Governor he mumbled that he was on it and he'd report soon."

"There's this cloud..." I said not being able to finish. Then it dawned on me.

"Will you tell me please why Charley had someone stake-out Andretti when I told him to put a man on the Governor? Get him on the goddamn phone," I demanded.

Henry picked up the phone on my desk and dialed Charley's number.

"Charley," I bellowed as soon as he got on the line, "What the hell are you doing?"

Charley, as usual was implacable.

"Ted, I had someone on the Governor since he's been living with his sister, almost two weeks now and he hasn't moved. About a week ago I got a tip that Andretti had her own nocturnal affairs and I thought I'd put Jake on a stake- out to watch her. Tell me it wouldn't be a home run if we caught her screwing around."

Henry, listening on the other phone, interrupted. "Who gives a shit if she's screwing around. She's single, for cryin' out loud."

"Yes, but it depends who she's screwing around with," Charley said.

"How long has she been under surveillance?" I asked.

"Only about a week now," Charley responded.

"Well she must have called someone, perhaps a private detective. Maybe she called her father. He's got a lot of connections in the North End. He may have sent his goons to drop Jake," I said. At that point, I was thoroughly disgusted. We weren't able to catch a break it seemed. The only good news was the fact that we could use the information about the Governor not being Danny's father--if we could prove it.

"OK. Charley, I guess we'd better stay on it for a little while, but between the two, the Governor is more important."

After I hung up, I told Henry and Jordan the story that Emily told me.

"So, he's not the father. How can we use it?" I asked both associates.

"Ted," Henry said. "Emily has just admitted to committing adultery."

"Oh come on," I replied. "That was fifteen years ago. How many times have we said that judges don't care about adultery in this Commonwealth? I've told my clients not to be intimidated when asked at a deposition whether they committed adultery. I tell them to answer 'As many times as possible'. People fall out of love with one person and in love with another, you guys know that," I said.

"Emily will get something anyway in a long term marriage unless the conduct is egregious and committing adultery doesn't fall into that category," I continued.

"Yeah, well why are we spending time and money on Charley attempting to catch the Governor in the sack with someone? Tell me that," Henry said rather smugly even for a senior associate.

"I'll tell you why," I shot back. "Because he's the Governor, that's why! And we need to win big." I didn't say anything about needing to get paid, although it was close to the top of my list.

There was such a silence in the room I thought I'd better change my tune.

"Don't forget we still have those pictures of Ms Mitchell," I said.

"I think the next step is to hire a child psychiatrist. What do you think?" I asked.

CHAPTER EIGHT

West Cedar Street runs parallel to Louisburg Square and both streets boast townhouses of the rich and famous set right in the middle of sedate, Brahmin, Beacon Hill. The mature trees between the sidewalk and the street provide an umbrella-like walkway which allows only a flicker of sunlight shooting through here and there catching small patches of grass on the brightest of days. At night, the street lamps, quaint though they are, don't shed enough light to alert any walkers to the broken bricks in the pavement or to the tree roots thrusting through their underground confinement like serpentine creatures seeking their prey.

The two strollers on West Cedar Street continued their after-dinner walk engrossed in their own conversation being careful where they stepped. Not only loose bricks and tree roots were hazardous to the unwary but dog droppings were not confined to the gutters and had to be carefully sidestepped. They paid no attention whatsoever to the silver Lexus RX 330 driving down the street.

The lone figure exited the silver car as it stopped in front of number 18 West Cedar Street. No sooner had his feet touched the pavement than he walked up the few steps to the front door, inserted a key into the lock and disappeared inside after a furtive look towards Mt. Vernon Street, the direction to which the strollers were walking. He passed the chandeliered dining room, now undergoing a substantial renovation and went straight to the back door of the kitchen, avoiding sawhorses, skill saws and various pieces of molding scattered around the rooms on the first floor. The door led from the kitchen to the fenced in back yard, which opened onto Cedar Lane Way through a hinged gate which he carefully unlatched.

As he looked to the left, he saw a figure, casually dressed in sneakers and jeans on Mt. Vernon Street walking up and down in front of Cedar Lane Way as if he was guarding the entrance, which, of course, he was doing-- in a way. The guard extended his patrol however, to a few feet from the entrance up Mt. Vernon Street so as to be hidden from view for a few seconds by the buildings on either side of the entry way. At the moment when the guard disappeared from view, the lone figure darted across Cedar Lane Way and pushed a wooden door open which was located at the side of a brick, three story town- house. He entered the passageway which ran the width of the building and exited into a private, fenced in courtyard.

She was waiting.

"I'm getting too old for this," he whispered before she led him into the kitchen.

"It's a good thing Barry and Phyllis are still in Florida while the renovations are going on, although I almost killed myself on the way through their place," he said between wheezes.

Dr. Hans Gerber leaned back in his chair and looked out the window of his office, took a deep breath and returned his gaze to Attorney Eldridge sitting before him. The doctor was in his mid-fifties with a shock of white hair, old-fashioned horn-rimmed glasses that didn't hide his piercing blue eyes and a trim, even sculptured body. He was, by all accounts Eldridge could determine, the best, the very best urologist at the Mass. General and he specialized in male infertility. It would've taken weeks for Eldridge to get an appointment with him but with a friend of Gerber interceding, an accommodation was made.

"You see, Attorney Eldridge, there are several ways to obtain DNA tests. The most common is the use of two sterile cotton swabs, where you collect samples for the test by rolling the swab firmly on the inside of each cheek of the participant about thirty times or for one minute and then repeat the process with the second swab. It's quite simple really. You allow the swabs to dry for about ten minutes and put them in separate envelopes with the person's name on the outside and bring the samples to me."

"Well that can't be the procedure in this case," Eldridge replied. "What else can we do to establish paternity or the lack of it?"

"We can do a hair analysis using a simple hair follicle as long as we have the hair root of the follicle. Hair is a protein that grows out of a follicle in the skin. The follicle produces a hair for a period of time and then the hair stops growing, falls out and a new hair grows. It's a slow process but if we can get a root of one hair follicle we can determine the DNA of the person and thus determine with a 99.9 % accuracy rate whether he is the father of the child," he answered.

Before Eldridge left, Gerber talked about male infertility; whether a sperm has a normal morphology which refers to its shape and structure. The doctor explained how a normal sperm has an oval head and a tail seven to fifteen times longer than the head. "The tail enhances the ability of the sperm to swim up to join an egg," he said. "This swimming ability is called motility. Poor motility obviously inhibits fertilization as well as poor morphology. Some win and some lose, I guess."

Gerber realized that Eldridge really didn't need to know all this stuff about infertility but Gerber thought this background information would be helpful. It was clear to the doctor that Eldridge really only wanted to know if he could get a DNA test on the Governor to show that the Governor wasn't Danny's father.

"The problem you have, Attorney Eldridge, is to see if Emily Mitchell can get a hair sample from her husband's hair brush or comb. Usually there are enough hairs on a brush every morning to conduct a thousand tests. Whether they contained a hair follicle root is another matter."

Donald Long was an associate at one of the few law firms in Boston that specialized in Family Law. The rumor on the street was that he was hired solely because he was Judge Andretti's fair-haired boy. He sat second chair every time his firm had any matter before her and the tragedy was that his presence seemed to soften her up to his client's point of view. It worked most of the time.

When he received his appointment as G.A.L in the mail, he was ecstatic. He knew instantly that with these two high profile litigants and their two high profile lawyers that this case, for certain, was going to turn into a high profile pissing contest. That meant he'd be paid for every second he spent on the investigation and, what's more, the case might very well enhance his reputation. He struggled with his conscience to make sure he'd have an open mind-- but only for a few seconds, as he realized he had a bias in favor of the Governor. What could Mrs. Mitchell do for him? Of course, he'd be forthright in his investigation but he silently prayed that the facts would come down in favor of the Governor and that he'd be rewarded with some kind of judicial appointment when all was said and done.

He knew what he had to do. He had to interview the Governor of the Commonwealth of Massachusetts alone, interview Mrs. Mitchell alone, interview Danny alone then interview each parent with the child in their home environment. He had to observe the parent-child relationship, the home surroundings, the schedule for after school activities and who was going to drop off and deliver Danny to these events. He also had to interview Danny's teachers, his neighbors, even perhaps, his friends. He had to get a release from Mrs. Mitchell to speak with her psychiatrist and get a similar release from the Governor to obtain his medical records. His credentials for all this? He was a lawyer-- and not a very good one at that. But, he'd be paid. Oh yes, he'd be paid!

Mort Haller was aware that he had to obtain a child psychiatrist on behalf of the Governor but he had second thoughts. He called Paul Jed.

"Paul, I read the Judge's order and saw that she appointed Donald Long as the G.A.L. Tell me about him."

"I think he'll be perfect for us. He's very close to the Judge and she'll more than likely accept his report and adopt his recommendations."

"Well then, why do we need to hire a child psychiatrist?" Mort exclaimed.

"Well, I'm sure Ted Eldridge will engage his own child psychiatrist because he won't have any faith in Long's report. Besides, Long won't have the designations that Eldridge's shrink will have and the Judge might have a hard time adopting Long's report over the testimony of Eldridge's heavyweight. My guess is that she'll go along with the G.A.L though."

"Paul, we can't afford to guess. It won't hurt if we hire our own shrink will it? I mean will the Judge take umbrage over the fact that we hire our own gun slinger to supplement the G.A.L.'s report?" Mort inquired.

"Naw. Just as long as we don't belittle her appointment, she'll be O.K." Paul Jed replied.

"Look Mort, another thing, the deposition of the Governor is coming up and I have to prepare him. He simply cannot ignore the possible consequences of a bad performance. Even though the pleadings are impounded, statements at the deposition can be used to impeach the credibility of the Governor at the time of trial if they are conflicting so please, get him over here this week," Paul pleaded.

After Haller hung up, his thoughts turned to the question of who he'd hire as the child psychiatrist to testify on behalf of the Governor's quest for full custody of Danny Mitchell and what a hard time he expected from the Governor when he was told he had to answer questions at a deposition in the offices of Ted Eldridge.

Almost two weeks later, after two postponements to accommodate the chief executive of the Commonwealth, Amy buzzed me.

"They're here," she whispered.

"Tell them to make themselves comfortable in the conference room and get them coffee or whatever they want," I told Amy. I had some misgivings about the deposition as I hadn't heard a word from Charley Randell about the Governor's nocturnal comings and goings. His surveillance was costing us a small fortune and I was running out of money.

"Are the carafes filled? Are the yellow pads in place? Are there pens available?" I asked her. Yes, I was nervous. It wasn't every day that I took the deposition of the Governor and it was a long time ago that I had such butterflies in my stomach.

"Tell them I'll be right in," I instructed.

I actually had no intention of going right in but rather wanted them to wait about fifteen minutes for me. After all, I was a very busy Boston lawyer. Besides, I had to calm Emily Mitchell down since she was a nervous wreck. This was going to be the first time she was seeing her husband for any substantial period of time, other than for the few moments they passed each other in exchanging Danny's visitation time.

I had instructed her to say nothing, no matter what the provocation. I told her not to engage in any puerile antics such as facial expressions of disgust or smothered derisive laughter in response to answers given by her husband. I told her she could make notes but not to interrupt my questions under any circumstances.

They were well-settled as we entered the conference room and I couldn't help but notice that Paul Jed looked at his watch just before I extended my hand in greeting.

"Ted, let me introduce you to the Governor, Branden Mitchell. Governor this is our adversary, Ted Eldridge."

"I'm not your adversary, Governor, I'm simply the opposing counsel," I replied, shaking his hand. His grip was like a lot of politician's-- not a full hand clasp but only the extension of four fingers so as not to tire himself out in a long queue.

"Mrs. Mitchell, this is Paul Jed, your husband's attorney," I said as she and I sat at the table together exactly opposite her husband and his counsel.

The court reporter sat at the head of the table poised to begin. Amy had already given her a pleading so that she could get the caption of the case and the dramatis personae.

"Governor," I began. "Are you comfortable?"

"Yes," he answered.

"If you need to take a break simply let me know. If you need to speak with your lawyer you may, but not when there is a pending question. Do you understand?" I told him.

"Look Ted, spare us the sanctimonious speech. I'll talk to my client any time I choose. So let's get on with the deposition and ask your questions," Jed said smugly.

I had to take a deep breath. Depositions are always contentious in a high stakes divorce but if you're not careful, losing one's cool could make you look like the heavy-- the bad guy at the time of trial. The reporter doesn't take down intonations, raised voices or smirks and one is always vulnerable to an accusation of "You're yelling." What is the accused supposed to do? Say, "No I'm not!"

"Yes, you are!" and so on...

I took the high road.

"Do we agree that all objections, except as to form will be reserved until the time of trial, Paul?" I asked using my best professional tone.

"Agreed," he replied. "And all motions to strike will similarly be reserved," he added.

"Governor, tell us your full name," I asked. And so it began. It went pretty well until just after the mid-morning break.

"Governor, since the day of your marriage to Emily have you had sexual intercourse with any person other than your wife?" I asked as evenly as I could.

"Wait just a minute. Wait a minute," Paul sputtered.

"Don't answer that question," he instructed his client.

"There's no need to raise your voice, Attorney Jed. I'm going to ask the question again. Since the day of your marriage have you had sexual intercourse with anyone other than your wife?"

"I want to speak to my client. Let's take a break," Jed said directing his comment to the stenographer rather than to me.

"Attorney Jed, there's a question pending. You can't speak to your client until he answers the question."

"Oh yeah, just watch me. Come with me Governor. We'll take a five minute break, Attorney Eldridge."

I'd been through this a thousand times before. I could tell the situation was getting tense as soon as we started addressing each other as "Attorney."

I could declare the deposition suspended and take Jed and the stenographer to the Probate Court, find a judge, wait for the judge to take a break from what he or she was doing and get a hearing on Jed's conduct, then resume the deposition; a two or three-hour ordeal.

Or, I could go on with the deposition, avoid the question and get as much mileage out of the Governor as I could for the rest of the day and save the testimony for the trial. At trial, his refusal to answer the question could be devastating.

When Jed and his client returned they took their seats. Jed began with a smirk on his face: "I instruct my client not to answer. He claims his Fifth Amendment Privilege against self-incrimination. As you know, Attorney Eldridge, there is still a statute in Massachusetts which makes adultery a crime."

I was content with that answer. Technically, he was right but the statute was ignored by virtually every trial lawyer across the state. Moreover, judges are allowed to draw inferences from such a response at the time of trial. The obvious inference is that the Governor committed adultery every chance he had. Jed was being stupid and grandstanding in front of his client.

As I sat across the table from the Governor, this cretin, I thought the time was right to change the smug expression on his face and, at the same time, demonstrate to Paul Jed that this was going to be a "pissing contest" to end all "pissing contests."

"Governor, are you aware that you are not the father of Danny?" I asked in a low, even voice as I leaned back in my chair waiting for the explosion.

I didn't have to wait long.

"What are you trying to pull here Eldridge?" Jed shot back ."That's ridiculous. You have no right to inflame this deposition with such reckless statements."

"Look, Attorney Jed, you just object if you don't think the question is appropriate, that's all you're allowed to do. You can't make speeches."

"I object."

"Governor, I'll ask the question again. Are you aware that you are not the father of Danny?"

"Certainly not. That's ridiculous."

"It's true, isn't it that at one point in your marriage there was a separation where you lived apart from your wife?"

"Yes, that's true."

"And at that point you'd been married for several years?"

"Yes, about three years."

"During that time you tried consistently to have children?"

"Well, yes we tried but I was very busy in those days just like I am now."

"In any event you weren't successful up to the time of your separation, that's true isn't it?"

"I guess so. I don't remember exactly."

"Danny is fourteen years old, isn't he?"

"Yes."

"And the separation was about fifteen years ago, isn't that true?"

"If you say so."

"And for all those years before, Emily never conceived did she?"

"Obviously not. What're you trying to prove here, Eldridge?"

"So Governor, Emily conceived Danny just about the time of the separation, isn't that true?"

"We reconciled after only about a month of living apart. Everything was back to normal at that point."

"During that month of separation you didn't know what Emily was doing did you?"

"I guess not. I didn't follow her around, Attorney Eldridge."

"So you don't know whether she slept with anyone who could've caused her to become pregnant at that time, do you?"

"What! I don't have to sit here and listen to this bull shit! Jed! Don't just sit there, do something!"

"Let's take a break," Jed said.

"Whew!" The steno exhaled audibly as they left the room.

I just sat there. I didn't want to go out into the office and answer questions about how the deposition was going. After a few minutes I got up and went to the window to look out, yet again, at the tombstones of King's Chapel. They invariably brought me peace as I transported myself into the lives of those great men and at once realized that all this bull shit was only temporary.

When they returned and resumed their seats, I decided to change the subject. I handed four pictures face down, to the stenographer.

"Will you mark these as Plaintiff's exhibits one, two, three and four please?"

"Let me see them first," Jed said to the steno.

"You don't tell my stenographer what to do, Attorney Jed. I'm paying her bill. You'll see the proposed exhibits when she's finished marking them."

He knew I was right. I showed him the pictures that Amy took of Emily after the steno marked them and he didn't say another word.

"Governor, I show you what has been marked as Plaintiff's exhibit number one, can you identify it?"

"Yes."

"What is it?"

"It's a picture of my wife."

"Do you see the black and blue mark on the side of her face?"

"Yes."

"You hit her with your closed fist about six weeks ago didn't you?"

"No, I don't think so."

"You also cut her lip at that time didn't you?"

"I don't remember."

"You don't remember? Do you remember Danny being there and watching the whole time you were beating up on your wife?"

"I didn't beat up on my wife, Attorney Eldridge."

"You've beaten her several times in the past haven't you?"

"No. She's come at me with a knife, threatened me in a drunken stupor and I had to protect myself on several occasions though."

"In fact, the reason you and Emily separated fifteen years ago was a beating you gave her while she was pleading for you to stop, isn't that true?"

"No. That's ridiculous."

I looked directly at him, deep into his lying eyes, before I asked the next question.

"Have you been taking any controlled substance without a prescription in the past twenty-four months?"

I could tell the Governor was getting pissed. His facial contortions and body language gave him away.

"What're you talking about, Eldridge?"

"Which one of those words don't you understand, Governor?"

"Wha--What?"

"I'll ask the question again. Have you taken any controlled substance without a prescription in the past twenty-four months?"

"Paul, I don't have to put up with this bull shit, do I?"

I looked at the stenographer to make sure she recorded every word.

"That's off the record," Jed said to the steno.

"Of course it's on the record, Attorney Jed. It's just too bad this deposition isn't video-taped, then your client's demeanor could also be recorded."

Before Jed had a chance to complain about my last comment I asked the next question.

"I show you exhibits two, three and four and ask you whether the bruises shown on Emily's body in all three exhibits were the result of you hitting or slapping her?"

"That's enough, Eldridge," Jed said. You are purposely inflaming this deposition. It's over. This deposition is over. We're leaving. C'mon Governor, let's go."

The Governor had already blanched before Jed's interruption. His lawyer must have noticed. The Governor sat almost catatonic for several seconds before the color returned to his face, and when it did, his face was beet red and his eyes were dilated. Both of his hands gripped the arms of his chair so hard his knuckles were white. After a silence that seemed to last for almost a full minute, they got up while Jed collected his papers. The Governor shot me an angry look -- they left without another word.

I looked at Emily Mitchell who appeared as though she was about to cry. I thought the reason for her distress was that she was feeling the pressure of the whole proceeding. I felt sorry for her for several reasons, not the least of which was that she was married to such a complete ass hole.

"Emily, don't worry. By the time we get to trial we'll have all the proof necessary to show that your husband is a wife beater, and adulterer and not the father of your son.

Now listen to me very carefully. I want you to look around your husband's dresser in you bedroom for any strands of his hair. Look at his comb, his hairbrush or any other place where his hair may be found. I realize he's moved to his sister's, but there must be some such evidence around the house. The expert I've spoken with needs this hair sample to establish DNA. This, in turn will help us prove he's not Danny's father.

Understand?"

She nodded her assent and started-- "But about this deposition-"

"Please don't worry about what happened today. This is just the beginning of a marathon that'll go the full twenty-six miles. There will be hills and valleys so don't jump to any conclusions."

I didn't feel like holding her hand and going through lengthy explanations so I excused myself and told her I had a lot of work to do. I bid her good-bye and went directly into my office, avoiding the staff, and, for several minutes, looked out the window.

CHAPTER NINE

"Jesus Christ," the Governor exploded to his lawyer on the way down the outside, concrete stairs of Old City Hall. The stairs opened to a large courtyard which fronted School Street where his limousine had been waiting for him all morning, parked illegally.

"What was that all about? That son of a bitch can't get away with this. Emily was frigid all right but there were times-- very few I'll grant-- but there's no doubt that I'm the father of Danny. I can't let her make those kinds of statements in public, Paul. I just can't."

"I'm amazed he asked that question," his lawyer replied. "He must have something up his sleeve. Emily couldn't have been artificially inseminated without your knowledge, she was not promiscuous according to what you've told me, I--"

"I'm telling you, there is no question that I'm the father of that child," the Governor interrupted. "I won't stand for this outrage. Someone's head will roll. I guarantee it. And what about all that bull shit about a controlled substance?"

"I think--"

"I don't give a shit about what you think," the Governor said. "I will not go to trial. I won't be humiliated with innuendo and insinuations. That bastard Eldridge will be made to pay. He doesn't know who he's fucking with. I'll show him about controlled substance. Controlled substance. I'll give him controlled substance." "Governor, I think that whole deposition was nothing but a bluff. Eldridge doesn't have any proof of any controlled substance or any proof that you're not Danny's father."

"And another thing, those pictures will not be part of any public record, you understand?" the Governor said.

"Governor, the pleadings, including those pictures, are impounded. The press won't see them."

"Oh yeah? Can you guarantee the press won't be at the trial when Eldridge introduces those goddamn pictures? Eldridge, who does he think he is. I'm going to teach that son of a bitch something he won't forget. Controlled substance! I'll give him controlled substance."

His driver opened the door to the Governor's limousine and he climbed into the back seat.

"We'd better have a meeting. Call Haller!" he instructed his lawyer before the door was slammed without another word.

"Take me to 17 Warren Street, Brookline," the Governor ordered.

When the car arrived in the driveway of the house he recently vacated, the Governor got out and told the driver to pick him up in a half- hour. He let himself in the front door and he knew instantly that Danny wasn't home, the house was silent, no one was home. He took a brown, plastic vile from his pocket and spread two lines of white powder on the glass end table next to the couch. He bent over holding one nostril and sniffed one line with the other. He reversed the nostrils and sniffed the other line.

He waited in the living room for several minutes before he felt the exuberant rush that he'd become familiar with after taking the powder for the last two years. He needed the energy boost, needed to be on his game every day if he was going to be a leader, the kind of leader he always dreamed about, the kind of leader his father expected him to be.

He heard the car in the driveway, the garage door open and then close before he saw his wife enter the house. He went into the kitchen and stood leaning against the door jamb in a casual slump.

"Hello, you bitch. What took you so long?"

"Brenden! What're you doing here!

"Did you really think you could get away with your bull shit about me not being Danny's father?" He walked casually towards her as he spoke. "So now you accuse me of taking drugs, huh? You goddamn drunk! You're nothing but a dried up old prune! You're good for nothing, not even a decent lay, you poor bitch! He swung his right arm at her and hit her on the left side of her face with his open hand. He grabbed her right shoulder with his left hand for balance and hit her again. She spun half way around and fell to the floor.

"You son of a bitch," she said. She was holding her jaw on the left side of her face as the blood from a slash on her cheek ran through her fingers.

"I'm going to see to it that you don't even come close to having custody of Danny," he sneered. "And that lawyer of yours will be sorry he ever laid eyes on you. Now you listen to me. If you open your mouth about me being here this afternoon you'll have to spend whatever money you get in this divorce on a plastic surgeon. Understand?"

"You're not Danny's father, you bastard," she said. "Fifteen years ago when we were separated, while you were probably with one of your girl friends, I spent the night with a person who had the ability to create a child. Not like you, you pathetic excuse for a man."

He tried to pick her up but she was dead weight. He bent down and slapped her across the face again.

"Just remember what I said ," he told her.

He opened the front door and left the house as he entered it just as his limousine pulled into the driveway.

Fifteen minutes after the deposition, Paul Jed was on the phone with Mort Haller.

"I'm telling you Mort, I've not been privy to many of the Governor's mood swings, but he was really upset. I don't know whether Eldridge was bluffing, but his questions certainly hit the mark."

"I can't believe he's got any proof that the Governor is not Danny's father. Emily doesn't strike me as the kind of woman who has played around. Let's not jump to any conclusions though Paul, until I have a chance to speak with the Governor. OK? What is all this bull shit about a controlled substance anyway?"

"He doesn't have any proof of any controlled substance. That whole line of questioning is just reckless witness baiting on Eldridge's part," Jed replied. "Don't worry about that. Those pictures are another matter, though. There's nothing we can do about them."

"Well, we'll see about that. This case has to settle or we'll have to get rid of Eldridge, one or the other." Mort replied.

Jed didn't like that comment. He knew Mort Haller too well. He knew what Haller was capable of and he didn't like it one bit. In fact, he was afraid not only of what Haller could do, but what he would do. 'Get rid of Eldridge' was the phrase he used. What the hell, have I gotten myself into, he thought just before he hung up the phone.

An hour and a half later the inner door to the Governor's office opened with such force it banged against the wall it was hinged on, as the Governor stormed into his office. Mort Haller followed right on his heels and quickly closed the door behind them, anticipating another outburst from his boss, something that was becoming all too frequent.

"She told me I'm not Danny's father, that bitch," the Governor said between his clenched teeth. His lips were parted, his eyes were barely open and his face was pinched from his brow to his chin, forming deep creases especially around his mouth and the sides of his eyes.

"She admitted she had an affair about fifteen years ago when we were separated for a few weeks after an argument. I don't know how she can prove it but it doesn't matter. The mere allegation will ruin me," he sputtered, pacing back and forth in front of his desk, pounding his fist into the palm of his other hand.

"When did you speak with her?"

"As soon as the deposition was over, I knew she'd be going home so I met her there. I almost slapped her across the face when she told me but at least I controlled myself to that extent. Mort, what the hell am I to do? This can't get out."

"Well, at this point the only people who know about this are Eldridge, Emily and, I suppose, the people in Eldridge's firm, not counting our own lawyer. Relax! I'll think of something. I'll make a few calls and get back to you. In the meantime, for chrissake, don't say a word to anybody about this. You've got a lot of work to do around here to keep your mind off this thing."

Only a half-hour later, Mort was on the phone. "I need to speak with you. It's an emergency," he whispered.

The following day, at seven o'clock in the morning, Mort let himself in the back door of the restaurant. Renzo, as usual, had just finished cleaning up and was enjoying his Espresso. After a brief greeting, Mort sighed audibly and sat down at the table with Renzo.

"We've got a problem, my friend," Mort began.

83

After telling Renzo about the deposition and the allegation that the Governor was not the father of his child, and how this information simply cannot go public, Renzo sat back in his chair and said calmly, "How does this affect me, Mort?"

"We need to scare the shit out of this lawyer for Emily Mitchell so he won't use this explosive stuff against the Governor, Renzo. You can help us. You know how this works," Mort replied.

"Why do you come to me?"

"Look, Renzo," Mort stated, getting somewhat agitated. "You owe us. It's as simple as that. We want him to back off this case. We want him to keep his mouth shut about the Governor not being the kid's father. We want the case settled quietly without a trial. Send him that message and if he doesn't respond, we'll just have to go to the next step." Renzo spread his hands, palms down on the table and nodded his assent. Not another word had to be said.

CHAPTER TEN

I had a lot of work to do after the deposition. Henry Baker was combing through the document production we received from the Governor, Jordan Levy was analyzing their admissions to our Notice to Admit Facts, and I was preparing to hire our business expert. The Governor had some stock options he received earlier in his career as remuneration from some of the boards of directors on which he once served and, to complicate the matter of valuation, some of the options were vested and others were not. He also owned stock in several closely held corporations which also had to be valued.

I was also preparing to hire our child psychiatrist to combat whatever the GAL was surely going to recommend to the judge. And there was more: The Governor and Emily also had some real estate holdings so I had to engage our long-standing real estate expert, Steve Lyons, to value the property.

All that was just the beginning. I had to prepare Emily for her deposition, and, more than likely, take the deposition of each one of Paul Jed's experts. Moreover, Emily had yet to report on the result of her search for her husband's hair follicles, although she called the day after the deposition and made an appointment to see me. She also had to compile her documents in response to Jed's request.

Three days after the Governor's deposition, I left the office about nine P.M., walked down the back stairs of Old City Hall and crossed the street to my parking garage. At that time of night, the garage was deserted. There was a sign at the elevator bank directing anyone needing assistance to push the buzzer for an attendant if necessary.

I got off the elevator at the sixth floor and went directly to my car which was one of only three cars parked in this cavernous space. Not a soul was around and my footsteps echoed against the cement floor as my pace quickened. When I pressed the automatic door opener to my car, I noticed a folded piece of paper on the windshield, stuck under the wiper blade. My name was typed boldly on one side so I knew it wasn't just some advertisement. I retrieved the paper, got behind the wheel of the car and locked the doors. The overhead light inside the car was still on as I unfolded the paper with some trepidation. It read:

> If you know what's good for you, you will not go to trial.
> You will say nothing about who the father is.
> You will settle this case out of court.

I started the car and, to tell the truth, I worried that there might be a bomb that would go off as soon as I turned the key. As I made my way home, I was aware of all the cars around me as I furtively looked in the window of each as it passed. At one point, I made direct eye contact with some scruffy looking guy and stared at him for so long I almost lost control of the car. I even tried to remember the license plate of a car that seemed to have stayed behind me too long.

I didn't say a word to Andrea about the note when I got home but it didn't matter. She knew something was wrong as soon as I walked in the door. She knew from experience not to pry, as I often told her it took too much out of me to repeat the dramatic events of the day because then I'd have to live them twice.

The next morning I reread the note and concluded that it must've come from some political hack working closely with the Governor. I dismissed Paul Jed from culpability as the note was such a flagrant violation of ethics that no lawyer in his right mind would be involved in such antics. But who could've been privy to such private information? The divorce papers already on file at the court were impounded, so they were not available to the public. Besides, the question of paternity was not raised in any of the pleadings so far. Certainly, it would be a waste of time to confront the Governor as neither he nor his Chief of Staff would be directly connected, at least that I could prove.

What the hell, I thought, this situation was not altogether new to me. I resolved that I would not be intimidated and that I'd continue to prepare for trial as planned.

I told Jordan and Henry what happened as soon as I arrived at my office.

"Something like this has never happened before," Harry proclaimed. "The smartest thing we can do is report this threat to the police," he continued.

"We should also report this to the Judge," Jordan added.

"Well, you know, it's not the first time I've been threatened. It's happened to me before not only as a lawyer but also as a judge. I particularly remember one time when I was sitting in Worcester a few years ago, when one nut-case called my home when Andrea and I were visiting at a friend's house next door. Josh answered the phone and the guy told this little boy that he was going to kill his father if he didn't recuse himself from a case. Josh didn't understand what 'recuse' meant but he understood the rest of the message. He became hysterical and ran next door crying, looking for us. When he found us, he threw himself into the arms of his mother and, between sobs, told us about the call. We calmed him down and before long he got over the whole thing. But I didn't. Neither did I recuse myself-- and I'm not going to let this threat change how we'll handle this case now either. Forget telling the police or the Judge. We'll continue to do our job and bring this Governor and his lawyer down."

Our meeting was interrupted by Amy telling me that Ms. Mitchell was here to see me. Jordan and Henry left as Amy ushered Emily into my office. She looked drawn and haggard as she slumped into a client's chair. I noticed she had a lot of makeup on and I knew there was trouble before she opened her mouth. I sat back expectantly, my pen poised over my yellow legal pad and waited for her to begin.

"I can't take much more of this," she said in a tremulous voice.

"Right after the deposition I immediately went home," she told me between wiping her nose and dabbing her eyes with a Kleenex. "No sooner did I arrive there, when he came barging in from the living room and demanded to know what this business was all about of his not being the father of Danny. I... I didn't know what to do," she stammered, then went on.

"So I told him the truth. I told him what happened fifteen years ago. He got so angry he grabbed me around my shoulder with one hand and pulled me close to him. He slapped me with his open hand on the side of my head then he hit me again. I don't know what happened next but he was gone when I had a chance to focus again. He must have slapped me a third time after I passed out while I was lying on the floor, as my face was puffy and swollen when I looked in the mirror. I had a cut on the side if my face from his ring and it was bleeding so hard it took me several minutes to stop the flow. I wondered whether to go the emergency room, Mr. Eldridge, but I'm afraid of him if I go public. The cut'll heal OK, I think. I was so frightened! I don't want to see any more of him.

I don't want him coming around this weekend for his visitation with Danny.

I called my mother who lives in Osterville on the Cape and asked her if Danny and I could stay with her for a while. She lives in a gated community with a guard twenty-four seven and I knew we'd be safe there. Oh God, this is awful," she continued.

"When Danny came home from school we drove down that evening and I called you the next day to make this appointment," she was sobbing now.

I came around from behind my desk and sat in the chair next to her. I put my arm around her shoulders and handed her a cup of water with the other. She took the cup and sipped some water.

"Emily, I know it's hard to believe at this point but we...you are going to be successful. First, you'll be rid of this Philistine of a husband. Second, you'll have enough money so you won't have to worry for the rest of your life. Third, you'll have sole physical custody of Danny, I promise. Fourth, all of Danny's school needs will be taken care of, as well as his health needs and your health needs. Fifth, after we take some more pictures of your face and have you sign an affidavit about the beating you took at the hands of the Governor of the Commonwealth of Massachusetts, I assure you that even Judge Andretti will give us a restraining order."

She was somewhat mollified. I told her that I'd have to speak with her psychiatrist and, after we outlined other work we had ahead of us, she left feeling more confident...at least that's what she told me. I called Jordan and Henry back into the office and asked them to give me a report on the Admissions we received and the documents that the Governor produced by the next morning. For my part, I had some experts to hire.

At our meeting the following morning, Jordan gave me a memo on each and every reply of the Governor to our Request for Admissions. As I suspected, his admissions were not helpful...at least at this point. One of the purposes of asking for them in the first place was to obtain counsel fees for our efforts in having to prove, at the time of trial, what the Governor's answers failed to disclose in our request. Fat chance with this Judge, I thought.

The documents the Governor produced were a different story. Henry made arrangements for our stellar CPA, Lester Begley, to be at the meeting and he brought with him the three large boxes the Governor had produced.

"I spent a long time analyzing this production," he said pointing to the boxes, "and I've found a few things that will interest you, Ted.

There's five years of Federal and State Income Tax returns, five years of various bank statements, stock certificates, savings account passbooks, certificates of deposit, retirement account statements, deeds to various parcels of real estate, corporate tax returns of corporations he has an interest in and a pile of other stuff including some meaningless correspondence," he stated, fingering each folder as he flipped through the nearest and largest box.

"I compared his income for each of the five years against three different sources: his Federal Income Tax returns, the deposits in his various bank accounts and the financial statements he filed with various banking institutions in the past. None of the figures add up. I figure he has over two million dollars that he's received over the past couple of years that he simply does not show on the current financial statement he filed with the court or, for that matter, any other place."

"What about campaign funds?" I asked.

"Whoa, that's a whole new can of worms," Lester replied. "He didn't produce one single document showing how much money he has access to, how much he can tap into for personal expenses from campaign contributions or anything like that. I read in the Globe though, that he's got a war chest in the millions."

"Is there any evidence of bank accounts in the Caymans or in Gibraltar? Remember the case we had concerning the guy who wired millions to his bank account in Gibraltar?"

"No, but I can put one of my guys on the trail and report back."

The meeting ended and I had to assimilate all that Lester told me. I wondered why I still hadn't heard from Charley. I wondered about many things...

We needed to know who the Governor's paramour was so we could name her in our complaint for divorce, who the experts were going to be that we had yet to hire, the names of the experts Jed was going to hire, when the G.A.L was going to submit his interim report, when we could schedule more depositions and more. I also was worried about how fragile my client seemed to be getting day by day.

There was another matter that squeezed itself into and between all the other thoughts I was having about this case. It intruded itself into my conscience no matter how much I tried to avoid it: I was going broke. The expenses of Emily's case, the expenses of the office, the fact that the entire staff was working on this case alone with no money coming in, was driving me to distraction. I had to do something about it pretty soon.

CHAPTER ELEVEN

Donald Long was frustrated. Emily Mitchell wasn't home and hadn't answered her phone in the past two days. He couldn't make any arrangements to visit the Governor because of the Governor's busy schedule. He didn't even know what school Danny Mitchell attended so he couldn't interview his teachers. How could he make any money in this investigation when he couldn't even get started, he thought. When he thought of the power he had as the G.A.L -- the power to recommend to the Judge who the custodial parent would be, a sardonic smile came to his lips. At some point these people, yes the Governor, would recognize just who he was; how he fit in the mosaic of this case and they'd knuckle under, by God. They would conform to his schedule, open their house to him and call him on the phone. Perhaps, just perhaps, he could get a judgeship out of this if he played his cards right, he thought. How bad could the Governor of the Commonwealth of Massachusetts be as the custodial parent, he asked himself. What the hell, kids adjust. Besides, the mother would have visitation privileges and I, well I would be a judge.

Once again, the visitor stepped onto the sidewalk as he climbed away from the silver car, which was squeezed, between two others. He had finally found a parking space on West Cedar Street after making the loop several times down Charles Street, up Mt Vernon, down Louisburg Square, down Pinckney and finally onto West Cedar. Even as the late spring evenings became longer, West Cedar Street was still bathed in darkness at eight P.M. as the trees, now covered with leaves from the heat of the downtown streets of Beacon Hill, had almost reached their fullness.

He entered 18 West Cedar Street yet again, walked through the first floor to the back yard, opened the gate and peered to his left, down Cedar Lane Way towards Mt. Vernon Street. He waited. In a few seconds, he saw the same figure as before, walking back and forth in front of the one-way entrance to Cedar Lane Way, but just as before, the sentry went a few feet past the entrance so his view down the street had to be blocked. At that precise moment, the lone figure crossed Cedar Lane Way, pushed open the wooden door at the side of the building and calmly walked down the covered passageway to her courtyard. He opened the door to her kitchen and she greeted him with a tender touch to his cheek before falling into his arms. They stayed locked together for a few seconds, kissed and then he held her at arms length, looked directly into her eyes, and sat down heavily at one of the chairs by the kitchen table.

"I can't do this anymore," he said while holding her hand, still looking into her eyes, as she remained standing next to him. "There's just too much going on."

He noticed she wasn't herself, on edge, distracted.

"You'll be all right," she whispered, bending down and kissing him lightly. "Is the guard dog still there?"

"Yes."

"He makes me nervous," she said.

"Call your father."

"Let's forget about it, at least for tonight," she said after a few seconds.

"This is getting way too complicated," he said to her as he looked away and slouched further down in his seat.

"Let me get you a drink. That's all you need," she said to him, as she gently pulled him to his feet and led him to the wheeled tray in the kitchen which held an ice bucket, tongs, a shaker, a bottle of Bombay Sapphire Gin, dry vermouth, Balvenie Scotch and Grey Goose Vodka.

"What'll it be? I've supplied you with all of your favorites."

"I need a martini," he said as he exhaled audibly blowing air out between his thinly parted lips.

"I'll fix it for you and you can watch and see if I do it right," she said mischievously. She picked up a hand full of ice from the bucket, disregarding the tongs, and dropped them into the shaker before licking her fingers while glancing suggestively at him. She then poured three ounces of gin over the ice and carefully let about six drops of vermouth fall into the mix. She shook the results vigorously while opening the freezer and retrieving a frosted martini glass. She fingered a large olive from a jar on the kitchen counter and dropped it into the glass, poured the strained liquid, now an emulsion of ice crystals, over it and offered the glass to him with both hands holding the stem.

"Your drink, Sire," she said bending in a half bow, making him fully aware of the exposure she created in her silk shift and the absence of underwear.

He smiled, took her hand in one of his and with the martini held carefully with the other, led her out of the kitchen and up the stairs.

Paul Jed was on the phone with Mort Haller.

"Mort, I'm not getting the cooperation from my client that I need. I realize he's a busy man but I've got a responsibility to adequately and vigorously prepare to try this case. It's not going to be a walk in the park, you know. I've yet to hire a child psychiatrist, a business expert, a real estate expert and what's more, I haven't even taken Emily's deposition. He's got to be a part of all this; he simply cannot ignore what the consequences might be if we blow this thing. These experts will all want a retainer and a signed agreement spelling out their responsibilities. I have to take the deposition of Emily's experts and..."

"Paul, Paul, calm down," Mort interrupted. "Everything in time. Look, why don't you prepare a list of the things you have to do, the things the Governor has to do, the money you need, the people you suggest we hire as experts and any recommendations you have to expedite this case. Send the list to me and I'll arrange a meeting among the three of us, you, me and the Governor so we can talk about it. OK?"

Not a week after submitting his list to the Governor and obtaining approval of the firm's usual real estate expert, Byron Hackett, Paul Jed was in the office of Dr. Sheila Monaghan who was strongly recommended by Mort Haller and who was also approved by the Governor as a possible child Psychiatrist for the defendant. Dr. Monaghan was a dowdy, heavy, even a rather dumpy, grand-motherly type woman about sixty years old, who wore her glasses on the end of her nose so she could look over them to see distance.

"You see, Doctor," Jed began, "we already have a G.A.L., Donald Long, but we believe that Ted Eldridge will hire his own child psychiatrist so we want to be prepared to combat that testimony with our own expert."

"Do you assume, Attorney Jed, that my findings will favor your client? Do you honestly believe that just because you're paying me, I'll recommend sole physical custody to the Governor?"

Jed gave a half shrug. "Uh, well no, I mean yes, I believe you will conclude that Ms. Mitchell is not the better of the two parents to have physical custody. She's a flake who is on drugs and drinking alcohol at the same time. She does not discipline that boy. She is so permissive that the child gets away with murder, and what's more, the child will tell you, in confidence, that he'd prefer to live with his father."

"Will both parents agree that I may conduct my investigation, talk to the neighbors, the boy's teachers and friends and relatives, all in the usual manner without interference from either?" the Doctor asked, in a bored, rather clinical voice; she'd been through this before.

"Certainly. You should also talk to Ms. Mitchell's psychiatrist. I understand she's on some kind of a mood elevator or some other psycho-tropic drugs. Actually, her psychiatrist is James Hurley, a psycho-pharmacologist. Do you know what a psycho-pharmacologist is? I sure don't."

"For your information, Attorney Jed, a psycho-pharmacologist is a psychiatrist who treats patient illnesses, not by traditional couch therapy sessions, but rather with cutting-edge drugs."

"That's new to me," Jed replied. "At any rate, will you take the job?"

"Yes, I'll be glad to. You'll have to make arrangements with both parents. Will you have any trouble doing that?"

"No. We'll simply sign an agreement that both child psychiatrists will have access to whatever they need to make their recommendations. You'll have to be prepared to have your deposition taken though, unless we agree to waive them in favor of exchanging your reports. The depositions in this case could easily get out of hand," Jed said while rubbing the bridge of his nose with his thumb and index finger, obviously thinking out the problem as he spoke.

"In that case, you'll have to pay a retainer of twenty-five hundred dollars and I'll make arrangements to begin as soon as that agreement is signed by both parties. You'll send me a copy?"

"Certainly, and thank you," Jed replied. "Our check will be in the mail."

"One more thing, Attorney Jed, this child is going to have three separate people meeting with him: the G.A.L. and two child psychiatrists. Don't you think it would be a good idea to have both sides agree to only one psychiatrist?"

"Well, Ill try, but getting any kind of agreement from Eldridge is difficult. I'll let you know."

CHAPTER TWELVE

One week later, Emily and I were in the waiting room of Paul Jed's firm to attend Emily's deposition.

"Don't say a word unless you are absolutely sure of your answer," I cautioned her in each of two prep sessions we had.

"For example," I had instructed, "if you're asked how much money you have in your bank account, what will you say?"

"I'd say I'd have to look and my check book is right here", she answered almost proudly.

"No! No!" I had said. "You simply say I don't know. Don't go looking things up. The more you can honestly say, 'I don't know' the better."

"If you are asked to give an estimate, you should say, 'I don't know and I'm not going to guess.'"

"If you're asked whether you prepared for this deposition, your reply should be, 'Yes, and my lawyer told me to tell the truth.' Understand? If you don't understand the question, don't be afraid to say so."

"Finally, when I instruct you not to answer, you will just sit there and wait for the next question. OK?"

The deposition went surprisingly well most of the morning. Emily Mitchell knew nothing about the family's finances so that was a dead end. She recited the events of fifteen years ago which disclosed that the Governor was not the father of Danny, but when she was asked for proof, her only reply was, "A woman knows those things, Attorney Jed."

She described the beatings she received at the hands of the Governor in detail, just as we rehearsed. She testified to the frequency of his late night comings and goings. Again, she had no proof of his trysts, but stated, "I mean honestly, Mr. Jed, I wasn't an eye witness of course, but I smelled someone else's perfume on him when he came home and saw lipstick stains on his shirt collar."

She did pretty well, all things considered, until Jed got into her medical condition.

"Are you seeing a psychiatrist at the present time, Ms. Mitchell?"

"Yes."

"What is her name?"

"She is a he, Mr. Jed and his name is Doctor James Hurley."

"Where is his office?"

"On Cambridge Street here in Boston. I don't know the number."

"What is his diagnosis?"

"Don't answer that question, Emily," I shot back.

"What's wrong with that question, Attorney Eldridge?"

"Ask your next question, Attorney Jed, I'm not answering questions here."

Jed shifted in his seat. "O.K. if that's how you want to play it."

"What medication are you taking at present?" he said to Emily, trying to ignore the glare I was shooting him from across the table.

"Tell him, if you know," I instructed after a quizzical look from my client.

"I was taking Valium for a while. Then I took Zoloft and now I'm taking Lithium."

I groaned.

"We need to take a break," I said directly to the stenographer. I placed a hand gently on Emily's shoulder and motioned her to the door.

When we were in the adjoining conference room I closed the door.

"Emily why, in the name of all that is right and holy, did you go into such detail," I admonished her.

"Did I say something wrong?" her voice unsteady, on the verge of tears.

I decided to back off.

"Well, it's just that those drugs are a progression," I said. "Valium is a minor tranquilizer. Zoloft creates a high and Lithium is given when a person's mood swings from high to low — you know, what used to be called 'manic depressive' and now is called 'bi-polar'. Without giving him Hurley's diagnosis, he can put two and two together or at least someone on his staff with half a brain can, and conclude that you are bi polar."

"Oh, God. What was I to do? I had to answer the question truthfully," she began to cry. There was not a Kleenex box in sight.

"I left my purse in the other room," she sniffed. "Can I borrow your handkerchief?"

"OK, let's forget about what just happened," I told her handing her my handkerchief from my breast pocket. "We simply have to move on. The next area he'll cover is your parenting role. Are you ready for that?"

"You bet. Don't worry about that. I'm ready," she replied getting some timbre back in her voice.

That was one area I was sure she'd do well in. Compared to her husband, she was Doctor Spock himself. To the extent I surmised she was somewhat permissive about parenting Danny, I knew she'd never admit to any deficiencies and Jed would get nowhere.

The deposition ended without our losing any more ground. In fact, her parenting role came out pretty well and, all in all, I was satisfied.

Before we parted I stopped to talk to her in the lobby of Jed's building.

"Emily, what will Doctor Hurley say about your mental state? You know there's a possibility he'll be deposed if the Court grants a waiver."

"Attorney Eldridge, I'm not crazy. I love Danny and I'm a good mother. This divorce has left me feeling insecure, even frightened-- and yes, depressed. Doctor Hurley is simply trying to find the right prescription for me. That's a hard thing to do because my mood changes so often. Sometimes I'd like to kill that son of a bitch. Other times I can't stop feeling sorry for myself and cry at the drop of a hat. I don't know..."

"All right. Don't worry about it. I'll be in touch with you regarding the experts I have to hire. Tops on the list is a child psychiatrist. Do you have any recommendations?" I asked her.

"Well, I heard from some of my friends that Sheila Monaghan does a good job. Other than that, I just don't know," she replied.

We parted on the corner of School Street and Washington Street and I made a mental note of the name of Doctor Sheila Monaghan. I've learned over the years that if I don't take the suggestions of my client, I'd better have a good reason.

Paul Jed wasn't wasting any time. Right after Emily's deposition he arranged to meet Dr. Lionel Gagne, President and CEO of Cambridge Business Investors, a think-tank and investment company composed of academics, researchers and business executives all connected to the Harvard Business School. Dr. Gagne was a Professor of Economics there, a director of several national and international companies, and the author of three books: two on methods of investing and one on the various theories of valuation of business assets.

Dr. Gagne was accompanied by two of his associates as the three of them sat in Paul Jed's waiting room not two full minutes before being greeted by their host for this meeting.

"Good morning, gentlemen," Jed said to them, extending his hand to the nearest one.

"Come in. Come in," he said as he shook the hand of each while, at the same time, deftly moving them towards his office.

"Thank you," Dr. Gagne managed to say.

"Allow me to introduce my associates, Bob Foley and Alex Graham. The three of us have read the materials you sent to us and, let me say at the outset, that we'd be happy to be engaged in this endeavor."

They all sat at the small conference table by the floor to ceiling windows and began to remove several manila folders from their briefcases.

Dr. Gagne, continued.

"The valuation of the four closely held companies in which the Governor holds a considerable amount of stock, although a minority interest in each, will not be difficult. We have used three different models in arriving at the valuation of his interest: Capitalization of Earnings, Discounted Future Earnings and Dividend Paying Capacity. Here are our calculations," the professor said, laying out four different charts.

"You can see that the method that creates the least value is the Dividend Paying Capacity method. Because not all four companies distribute earnings, we simply attribute a very conservative amount of earnings to dividends. In that way our valuation is extremely low." He paused to let all that sink in.

"What about the Real Estate Trusts?" Jed asked looking at the other folders in a pile on the corner of the table.

"That's even easier," Gagne replied.

"All we have to do is substitute your real estate expert's opinion of fair-market value of each parcel for the depreciated value on the trust's balance sheet."

After another pause for effect, Gagne continued.

"Our only problem is valuing the Governor's unvested stock options. Here we will have to use a very complicated method of valuation called the Black Scholes Method."

Forty-five minutes later, after Dr. Lionel Gagne stood at the blackboard in Jed's office explaining Black Scholes in minute detail, Attorney Paul Jed's head was spinning. What the hell, he thought. All I have to do is put this guy on the stand and let him testify. Let Eldridge spend time trying to understand what the hell he's talking about in order to prepare his cross-examination.

"I see," Jed said when he assumed the lecture was winding down.

"That's fine. I'm sure you'll do a great job at trial, Dr. Gagne. Now, tell me how much is this going to cost? Will I have to give you my first-born son?" Jed asked.

"It depends on the amount of time we have to put in. My rate is seven hundred and fifty dollars an hour. Bob and Alex bill their time at three hundred dollars an hour. Of course, I will be the only one to testify at trial. We won't know how long I'll be on the stand, will we? Neither will we know how long a deposition will take, but I assure you, Attorney Jed, we keep careful track of our time."

"Can you give me at least a ball-park estimate of the cost?" Jed asked, after a hard swallow.

"Well, this is only a 'guestimate'mind you, but I think the total will be around a hundred thousand dollars. You will have to pay twenty-five thousand as a retainer and we will bill you after that as we go along. May I remind you though, Attorney Jed, we do have quite a respectful reputation in the business world and our testimony generally carries the day."

"Uh--well, OK then," Jed replied. After he collected himself he said, "One thing that will make life easier for you, Dr. Gagne, and will also save us some money I hope, is that I'll ask my accountant,

Mark Conlin to turn over all his documents to you and to get you anything else you need."

"Yes, that certainly will help."

"All right then, let me speak to my client and I'll be back to you. I'm certain your proposition will be acceptably--your reputation precedes you."

After they left Jed was on the phone to Mort Haller.

"Mort, this will cost a small fortune," he lamented to the Chief of Staff. "A hundred thousand dollars for the business expert alone, not to mention the child psychiatrist, half the GAL fees, the real estate expert, the depositions that are left and my fees which are climbing exponentially, by the way."

"Paul, don't worry. All these expenses will be paid. We're not talking about some four-flushing client of yours. We're talking about a client who is the Governor of the Commonwealth of Massachusetts. From what you've told me about this guy, he'll save us millions."

Charles W. Randell, Private Detective, had a small office at 5 Longfellow Place in Boston. Longfellow Place was one of four towers situated in the 47 acre spread of Charles River Park, the construction of which many people blame for the destruction of the old West End Neighborhood. The office was unremarkable in that it was entirely functional with no effort made to suggest any style whatsoever. There were two chairs behind a small table in the waiting room. The adjoining room, the only one with a window, consisted of a desk, a five-drawer filing cabinet and a single chair. The walls were bare, the floor was not covered and the window had blinds that were obviously broken by the way they folded up in an uneven slant.

Jake Bauer sat slumped in the chair, his head still aching from ten days ago, while his boss sat with his feet up on the desk.

"Ted Eldridge is all over me, Jake, and we don't have a shred of evidence for him after all this time. Besides, he's complaining about our bill. Last week it was twenty-five hundred dollars and that's with his usual discount. I just don't know what to tell him."

"Tell him we're doin' our best for crissakes. I'm sick and tired of walking up and down Mt. Vernon Street waiting for some visitor to go to that broad's house. I follow her every where she goes after she leaves the court house but she only goes to her father's restaurant, some other restaurant, some meeting with the bar association or to some other kind of meeting. I've even had the shit kicked out of me while on duty. Does that figure into the bill?"

"I've had the same problem with the Governor. I tail him after he leaves the State House and believe me, that's no easy task. He's all over the place, attending one function after another before he goes home to his sister's house. When he visits with the kid, he doesn't take him anywhere. I guess he just plants him with his sister and goes about doing his own thing.

He does one thing that's strange, however. I've trailed him on two occasions so far, when he's visited somebody who lives at, or someone who meets him at 18 West Cedar Street. He stays there for two, sometimes three hours, and then drives to his sister's house. That by itself wasn't unusual I thought initially, except that, when I checked the city directory, I found out the house belongs to Dr. Barry Styles Edmonds and his wife, Phyllis.

When I checked further, I found out that Dr. and Ms Edmonds are still in Florida and their house was being completely renovated in their absence. He must be meeting someone who waits for him to arrive because certainly no one is living there during construction. There must be someone who gets there before I see him enter. I don't know. What the hell can he be doing in a house that's torn upside down. More importantly, who is he doing it with?"

"Well, at least we've got something to report to Eldridge about," Jake added.

"I could get in there during the day and install a couple of cameras and sound equipment that no one would ever notice if you want," Jake continued, sounding very confident.

"The evidence we'd obtain, if we obtained anything at all, wouldn't be able to be introduced in court," Charley said

"We'd also be breaking and entering, violating the criminal statute against recording and invading a person's right to privacy. But..."

"Yeah, besides, we're dealing with the Governor," Jake added, now becoming less certain of his proposal.

"I'd better check in with Eldridge and see what he has to say about this," Charley said rising from his nearly supine position indicating that the meeting was over.

CHAPTER THIRTEEN

"Gulie, we've got problems," Renzo was saying to his chef early one morning.

"In fact, there are two problems. Rhea tells me that she's still being stalked by some guy she sees following her when she comes home from the court house. She says the guy follows her wherever she goes. He even stays at the top of her street until late at night watching everyone who comes by."

"We can fix that, boss, no problem. We were pretty soft on the guy the last time. That was only ten days ago. Remember you said to go easy," Gulie replied sitting down at their customary table.

"Yeah, well I think the time has come to make sure we get rid of this guy once and for all. Just take care of it. Not permanently

Gulie, you understand, just enough to make him go away and leave her alone. This time for good."

"Don't worry. It'll be done. What's the other problem?"

"That lawyer didn't take our advice. The case is going ahead and I've been informed that we should send another message. This time, we have to leave no doubt that the case must be settled."

"Gulie, you understand what this is all about?" Renzo said grabbing Gulie's arm and gently squeezing it for emphasis.

"It has nothing to do with my daughter directly. This has to do with preserving our whole operation in the North End. No one has bothered us. We operate here and nobody says a word about the "clubs". You, we, control the runners, the bookies, the vig and things are going OK. I don't want anybody to interfere with us. We're also able to distribute a few drugs to people we trust. Not much, we agreed. Not enough to anger our 'friends'. I don't want those guys in 'Southie' to have their noses under the tent and get a whiff of what we've got here. If we don't do the trick with this lawyer, our protection is gone.

"Adesso Gulie, do whatever you have to do."

"Fine, anything else padrone?"

"No."

Things were coming into focus slowly but surely soon after Emily's deposition as Harry, Jordan and I began to systematically outline the issues that we expected at trial. We were in the large conference room, each with our notes, yellow pads and scattered files. We made lists of our witnesses, their witnesses and the documents we intended to introduce.

I received a proposed stipulation in the mail from Paul Jed with a covering letter asking whether I'd agree that Dr. Sheila Monaghan be appointed by the court as the child psychiatrist for both sides. After seeing her name in writing, I remembered I used her in the distant past as a GAL, but people change, sometimes drastically, in a short period of time. I wasn't taking any chances. After vetting her name with some health care professionals and receiving favorable replies and, equally as important, remembering what my client said about the fact that she heard she'd "do a good job", I signed the stipulation. I was grateful that by that act alone I was able to cut down the growing list of witnesses by at least one to save some trial time, which would also cut down on my mounting debt. I had a line of credit at the bank that was slowly running out.

Emily had recently dropped off an envelope containing hair strands, I was told. Hopefully, I thought, they contained a root or two which she could have found on one of the hair brushes her husband used. Emily had told me that when he went to his sister's house, he took his shaving kit leaving all his other toiletries in his drawer in the bathroom. I sent a messenger to deliver the envelope to Dr. Gerber but hadn't heard back from him. I also instructed Emily to bring Danny to Gerber's office so the doctor could take a swab of Danny's cheek.

"What are we going to do about a business expert?" Harry asked as we reviewed the preliminary list of witnesses, which now included Dr. Monaghan.

"We need a business expert that's a real heavy-weight," Jordan added from behind a pile of documents scattered on the table which were supplied by the Governor's legal counsel.

"Yeah, that's the guy who will charge more money than any other expert we hire. On the other hand, his testimony will be crucial in valuing the business assets of this marriage. If his testimony prevails, it could mean the difference of millions of dollars against whatever their expert testifies to," I replied.

I had no choice. I had to hire this guy, whoever we choose, however much he'd charge. Where in hell I was going to get the money, I had no idea.

"Let's review," I continued.

"We have these witnesses to put on the stand for our direct testimony," I said as I wrote their names down on the large blackboard:

1. Emily Mitchell
2. Dr. James Hurley, Emily's psycho –pharmacologist

3. Donald Long, the GAL

4. Dr. Sheila Monaghan, child psychiatrist for both sides

5. Dr. Hans Gerber, if we're lucky

6. Lester Begley, our CPA

7. Steve Lyons, our real estate expert

8. Our business expert, whoever he or she is.

9. Charley Randell, if he ever finds the person or persons the Governor is screwing

10. The screwee, so to speak.

And that's just on direct. We'll have just as many witnesses introduced by Jed when he puts his case in and I'll have to prepare my cross examination of each. What a marathon this case is going to be, I thought for the hundredth time.

"What's worse," Harry added, "is that Lester might not be able to actually trace the lost millions we want to put in the Governor's column which means we might have to hire a forensic CPA."

"You know we just may want to put the Governor on the stand in our case rather than wait for him to testify in Jed's case," Jordan added. "We can interrupt their rhythm, cross examine him on issues we choose, and present our side completely to the judge before Jed has a chance to put in his direct."

"That's a good suggestion," I replied. "We'll just have to see," I felt overwhelmed yet again thinking of all the work that had to be done. At some point I had to solve my money problems or 'overwhelmed' wouldn't be the word for it.

The meeting came to a close and they each filed out the door.

Approximately one week before Emily's deposition, Donald Long's frustration turned into downright anger. He had made several attempts to contact Danny's mother at her home at 17 Warren Street in Brookline rather than wait for her to call him. After several fruitless tries, he finally called her lawyer to find out where she was. He learned that she was at her mother's house on the Cape with Danny but that she'd be returning to Brookline after the weekend in order to prepare for her deposition. He asked her to bring Danny to his office on the Wednesday following her deposition so they could meet.

Donald Long knew that his office was not the proper setting to establish the first contact with a young boy of fourteen. It would be better to meet him in his own environment, at home. He was going to demonstrate however, that he was going to run this show and that they'd better learn at the outset, that he was damned important.

When they first came into his reception area he noticed that Ms. Mitchell looked tired and wan; that she appeared a little "spacey" and distraught. It was obvious to him she didn't want to submit to any investigation into her parenting qualifications right then so he decided that his interview with her should be postponed.

The meeting with Danny didn't last long. Danny was hesitant, appearing somewhat frightened, almost uncommunicative, answering Long's questions in monosyllables. He met with the GAL in his office while his mother waited nervously in the reception area.

"How's it going Danny?" Long began.

"Good."

"Do you understand that your mother and father are getting divorced?"

"Yes."

"Do you know that I'm going to try and see what is in your best interest?

"Yes."

"That I want to be your friend?"

"Yeah."

"How's school?"

"Good."

"What subject do you like best?"

"English."

"What do you like about English?"

"I dunno."

"How are you and your mother getting along?"

"Good."

"How about you and your father? Do you get along with him?"

"Yes."

"How are your grades in school?"

"OK."

And so it went for about fifteen minutes.

Opening the office door Donald Long escorted Danny back to the reception area where Emily Mitchell, apparently relieved to see them, got up from her chair.

"Did everything go all-right?" she asked.

"Fine, fine," Long replied. "Let's make an appointment now, Ms. Mitchell, so I can visit you and Danny at home. I'll also be going to Danny's school. Perhaps you could call the principal and alert him to my coming. What school does he attend?"

"He goes to Brookline High and there's no principal, there's a headmaster," she said rather testily.

"The teachers already know about the divorce because Danny's father made arrangements to get a duplicate copy of his grades and any reports on his health. I'll be glad to alert the headmaster to your coming," she said feigning a civility which she certainly didn't have towards this man.

"You know, Mr. Long," she continued, "Danny and I will also be investigated by Dr Sheila Monaghan," she said somewhat impatiently. "That means fitting in all these meetings with you, Dr. Monaghan, Danny's after-school activities, doctor's visits, dentist's visits and God only knows what else. I hope you'll be patient with us."

"Certainly, Ms. Mitchell. What's a good time for you to have me come to the house?" Long asked, lowering his voice.

"I can't make it this week," she replied. "In the last couple of days, while we've been at my mother's house on the Cape, Danny has missed a couple of days of school. He'll have some making up to do. I've also got a deposition I have to face. Let's make it Wednesday, in the middle of next week after Danny gets home from school about four o'clock. Would that be OK?" she said blinking her eyes.

"Let me check my calendar, Ms. Mitchell, and I'll have my secretary call you to confirm. Perhaps we can coordinate with each other a little better than we have. Good-bye and have a nice day."

"Bye, Danny!"

"Bye." Danny replied.

114

CHAPTER FOURTEEN

The Governor's sister, Helen Prescott, was thrilled that her brother was living with her. She was a sixty-year old widow who lived in the same house on Dudley Street in Brookline all her life. She and her brother were born there. Her husband, Arthur Prescott, died when she was fifty-six and she steadfastly refused all family entreaties to move to a smaller house. Mr. and Mrs. Prescott had two children born three years apart who had turned the staid, old, cavernous, paneled halls of the downstairs vestibule into their own private playground as they romped and played raucously with each other and their friends.

In those days the place was alive with noise and laughter but in the last few years, the old house was like a nursing home. In fact, Mrs. Prescott needed outside assistance to do all the household chores including all the shopping and cooking. She had a stroke just after her husband died and she was barely mobile. She used a walker to get around and had to be helped down the stairs from her bedroom on the second floor by her housekeeper Lilly, who doubled as her nurse, companion and, after three years of living together, her friend.

The house was large, almost mansion size, sitting behind a brick wall ten feet high. The only modification from the original drawings occurred when Mr. Prescott had the large iron fence at the foot of the drive-way removed five years after they moved in. He thought the scrolled, intricate iron-work was a little too pretentious.

Brenden and Helen Mitchell were siblings to the manor born. They grew up in the Dudley Street house and being only one year apart from one another, a rare situation among Yankee Protestants, they were very close. Although Brenden was older, Helen treated him like the baby of the family and 'mothered' him since the time she was old enough to walk.

Their father, Harold Daniels Mitchell, was a banker and real estate mogul who capitalized on the booming economy following the Second World War and endeared himself to the Republican Party when he made substantial contributions to the campaign of Henry Cabot Lodge, Jr. in the Fifties. Their mother, Beatrice Plummer Mitchell was the daughter of Thomas L. Plummer and his wife, Mary Lynwood Plummer. The Plummers were also Boston Brahmins who shared the Back Bay with the Mitchells and a few other Episcopalians.

It was Donald Long's intention to get into that house on Dudley Street in order to see the Governor face to face; to see how he treated Danny for sure, but really to have a chance to show off his position in front of the Chief Executive. He'd heard through the grapevine that the Governor had taken up residence there. He could hardly wait.

He didn't waste any time after his initial visit with Emily Mitchell and Danny before calling Mort Haller. He knew he couldn't get connected directly to the Governor at the State House as the two had never met. Haller informed him that yes, the Governor was living at his sister's house with Danny and that he'd make arrangements for Long to visit the house at 10 Dudley Street as soon as possible.

"What would be a good time for you, Attorney Long?" Mort asked in his most courteous voice.

Long, finally receiving some positive response was gratified.

"The sooner the better, Mr. Haller. I just met Ms Mitchell and Danny and I'd like to follow up that visit with a visit with Danny and the Governor as soon as possible."

"Certainly, Attorney Long. Let me get right back to you after I speak with the Governor and find out when Danny will be with him."

Not ten minutes later, Haller was on the phone with the GAL.

"We're in luck, Attorney Long. The Governor has Danny this very week-end. What's a good day for you?" Mort asked.

"Well, I usually don't work on Saturdays but I'll be glad to in this case," Long replied, dreaming of being fitted for his robes. "How about if I go over there at 10 o'clock? Is that too early?"

"No. That'll be fine. The Governor will see you at Dudley Street.."

That Saturday the GAL drove up the long driveway, through the port-cochere, sans the iron, filigreed gate, which led to the covered entrance of the Prescott house.. He had some hesitation about leaving his car, a Toyota Camry, parked in the circular drive right in front of the main entrance, it looked so out of place, but decided what the hell, why not?

Lilly met him at the door and immediately showed him into the family room where Danny was engrossed in his Game-Boy and the Governor was playing solitaire.

After initial greetings, during which the Governor was most gracious, Long again asked to see Danny alone. He and Danny

117

were escorted by the Governor into a den that was equipped as an office complete with computer, printer, fax machine and what looked like a scanner. Left alone and after only five minutes, it was clear to Long that the second encounter was going to be just as un-informative as the first. Consequently the meeting didn't last long. Danny stayed in the den after Long left.

"Uh, Governor," Long began when he was reunited with Brenden Mitchell in the family room, "I have to ask you some questions which I hope you won't mind answering."

"Not at all, not at all," came he reply. "Take a seat and fire away."

"Well, when Danny is here who does the cooking?" Long asked, settling into a high-backed leather chair.

"Why, Lilly does, of course. She's been cooking for my sister for over three years and she does a damned good job." Mitchell said with emphasis.

"How often are you home for meals, sir?"

"I try and make sure I'm home for dinner when Danny is with me. The three of us, my sister, Danny and I generally eat together."

"Yes, I saw the dining room on the way in just now. It's quite elegant isn't it?"

"Yes, sir," the Governor replied, proudly. "The paneling is Honduras Mahogany, you know. The chandelier, did you notice, is cut glass from Murano, Italy," Mitchell said sitting back in his chair contentedly.

"What do you and Danny do together when he's with you?"

"We watch TV together; the Red Sox, the Celtics. Danny isn't into playing any sports himself but we certainly enjoy watching them. I should point out that Danny's room is the same as mine was when I was a little boy. I'm proud of that but I don't know …Danny is, uh… into his Game-Boy quite a bit. I guess there's some hand-eye coordination involved with that, eh?" the Governor said.

"I guess it's fair to say that Lilly gets him ready for school when he's here on school nights, right?"

"Absolutely, Lilly's very devoted to Danny. She even takes him shopping for clothes. You know, Mr. Long, when Danny comes over here from his mother's house she doesn't allow him to bring a thing. I have to pay an enormous amount of child support which surely includes a clothing allowance but she simply will not pack any clothes for him. That doesn't seem right. Does it?"

"Well, no..."

"Besides, when he's here she calls him three or four times a day. Sometimes when she calls, I can tell she's been drinking. She slurs her words and calls me the most God-awful names. I have to hang up on her but she calls right back and demands to speak with Danny."

"When I bring him back home she won't even let me into the house. I have to let Danny out of the car in the driveway. My own house! She won't let me in!" Mitchell was on a roll now.

"She's so permissive with him, Attorney Long. When he comes over here, he's sullen and angry when I try and enforce some manners out of him. I'm the only one who tries to discipline the boy. All she does is give into him. She takes the easy way out all the time."

"Well, Governor--"

"Lilly and my sister are here twenty-four seven," Mitchell continued. "They take care of all of Danny's needs. He has this whole house to enjoy. We're only three streets away from Brookline High. I can help him with his homework. I can see to it that he's courteous and I will restrict his use of that goddamned Game-Boy, I assure you. Do you know she made him miss two days of school this week; that he's frequently tardy in the mornings?"

The governor finally paused. He got up and put his hand on Long's shoulder as Long also rose from his seat.

"Donald, I know you'll do the right thing. I've been hearing good things about you. Things that lead me to believe you'd make a good judge, as good a judge as you are a GAL."

"I want you to know, Governor, that I understand your situation completely. I believe you only have Danny's best interest in mind and, I assure you, so do I," Long replied.

"I'm going to visit Ms Mitchell at her house next Wednesday and schedule one or two other appointments after which I shall make my preliminary report to the Judge. Before I go though, I'd like to speak with Danny for a few more minutes if you don't mind."

"Certainly, certainly. Let's go back in the den; I'm sure he's still there."

Danny, while his father was talking to the guy named 'Long', the creepy-looking guy with the flaming red hair who seemed like such a pain in the ass when he first met him at the guy's office, was engrossed in his Advanced Game-Boy and feeling sorry for himself because he didn't have a "PSP" like the other kids.

When he had asked his father for the Play Station Portable so he could watch movies he could purchase, his father refused.

"Danny, why don't you play some kind of sport at school instead of burying your nose in that goddamn Game-Boy all the time? You're either into that thing or your ear-phones are on and you're listening to music on your iPod. Is it too late to go out for lacrosse, baseball, or track?"

Danny thought, Oh no, not again.

"I could purchase tennis and skate boarding games for a PSP and learn how to do those things," Danny pleaded hopefully. "They really help hand and eye coordination..."

"Absolutely not," his father replied.

"I see you playing hoop in front of the garage many times. Why don't you go out for the basketball team?" He remembered his father asking.

He didn't reply.

No amount of urging was successful. Danny tuned his father out. His father turned a deaf ear to him just as he did for most everything else, Danny thought.

His concentration on the Game-Boy was interrupted by recurring conversations he recalled having with his mother.

"Danny, your father and I are not getting along these days, as I'm sure you realize," she'd said to him one afternoon after school, he remembered.

"I don't believe it's in your best interest to hear us quarreling all the time. The tension around this house when your father is home, which is not very often anyway, is unbearable."

She was right about that, he thought. When he heard them shouting at one another when he was in his room, he'd put his ear phones on and turn up the volume on his iPod. When the arguments occurred downstairs, he'd run up to his room with his hands over his ears as fast as he could .On those occasions, there was always a rumbling, a kind of gurgling in his stomach which inevitably caused him to have the runs.

He remembered hearing about the arguments from his mother, her constant complaints, over and over until one day she finally came out with it.

"Danny, I've decided to get a divorce from your father, but I don't want you to worry. Everything will turn out OK. You will continue at Brookline High and we'll be together living here without any more arguments," she finally said one day.

Yeah, sure, Danny thought. No more arguments but what will happen to your drinking and the drugs I see you take? And when will I be able to see my father?

Later that night, after his mother talked about a divorce, in his room listening to "Guster" on his iPod, he brought himself to the verge of tears thinking that surely he was responsible for his mother and father breaking up. If only he was on some team, some club, like the Latin Club or the Science Club. Then his father would be satisfied, he thought.

I'm to blame, he lamented. I can't live up to Dad's expectations, I don't have any friends at school-- they all think I'm a snob because my father is the Governor. I suppose he's right when he refuses to take me anywhere or spend any time with me. Who could blame him? And my mother--I take advantage of her. She's always trying to please me and I don't give her the time of day. She tries too hard to make up to me after she has too much to drink the night before. I should have agreed to go to Nobles instead of Brookline High. Shit!

Danny also turned his thoughts to his friend, Brian Woods from school. Brian lived next to Danny's house on Warren Street. Warren was close to Tappan Street which ran right by Brookline High School. They'd become inseparable, his only friend, walking to school most every day, hanging out after school and even sharing classes together. When Danny was at his aunt's house when his father had visitation, Brian would walk to Dudley Street and the two of them would walk to school together just as they did when Danny was with his mother.

Danny recalled a conversation he'd had with Brian recently. It was the day after his mother talked to him about the divorce. They were on their way to school when Danny said, "Brian, my parents are getting a divorce."

"Bummer! My parents went through the same thing two years ago, you know. It ain't easy."

"Yeah well, that's what I want to talk to you about. What happens?"

"At first my mother and father couldn't agree on custody of me and my sister. There was this guy the court appointed to investigate which one of them was going to get us. The guy met us alone then together. He met us at our father's house then at our mother's house. He even came to the school and talked to the teachers. Finally, my father backed down. He was working full time and my mother was at home and better able to take care of us. She had the time, he didn't. The whole thing was a gigantic pain in the ass."

"What did you tell the guy who did the investigation?"

"I told him I wanted them to stay together, I didn't want the divorce. Then the guy says to me, 'which one do you want to live with?' I... I didn't know what to say to him. My sister told me after she talked to him that she wanted to live with my mother when he asked her the same question. Later, I heard from my mother's lawyer that the judge won't split up kids. Anyway, it didn't matter. My father backed down."

Danny looked up from his Game-Boy and was brought back to the present as 'red head' came back into the den with his father.

"Just give us another minute alone, Governor, please." Danny heard 'Red' say.

"Surely. I'll just be in the family room when you're finished, Donald," his father replied.

After his father left, 'Red' started right in.

"Now Danny, when we met at my office last week you weren't in the mood to give me any answers to my questions, were you?"

"Uh, I guess not."

"And you weren't very forthcoming earlier today, were you?"

"I guess not."

"Are you in a better frame of mind now? After all, we're at your father's house."

"This isn't my father's house."

"No, of course not. But your father is close by. Does that make you feel any better about answering my questions?"

"No."

"Look Danny, at some point you'll just have to be more cooperative. All of us only want what's in your best interest and you are the best person who can help determine that." 'Red' looked pissed off. I didn't care, thought Danny.

"I'm going to visit your mother and you again at Warren Street next Wednesday. I hope by then you'll realize that I want to be your friend and you can be honest with me. OK? I'll see you then, Danny. Good luck at school."

My ass, Danny thought.

The Governor waived Donald Long goodbye from the front door. As Long started his car he knew the smile on his face was hidden from the Governor's view but it didn't matter. Donald Long knew he'd made his point.

Making a list of the things I had to do, as usual, forced me once again to concentrate on what I had to do next. Shortly after receiving the proposed stipulation to appoint Sheila Monaghan from Paul Jed, I realized there were several critical areas of my case that were missing. Notably among them was the engagement of a Business Expert. I had used Ernest Bigelow in the past but I thought this matter was too much for him to handle. Across the river in Cambridge I knew there were several Harvard types who taught at the business school, even think-tank people with designations after their names using letters I had never seen before, but these people often times were too esoteric, too academic and spoke a language few Family Court Judges understood.

I interviewed several people before I settled on Dawson Associates, a CPA firm across the bridge in Charlestown, which boasted over one hundred-fifty employees. Chuck Dawson impressed me as being smart, having no pretensions, no air of superiority and yet a presence and command that was magnetic. The one qualification of his that impressed me the most was his ability to simplify the most arcane accounting concept and reduce it to a simple declarative sentence or two.

His fee was outrageous. He wanted fifteen thousand dollars as a retainer and refused to estimate what the total bill would be after I outlined the assets he'd have to value.

"All I can tell you Attorney Eldridge, is that I charge six hundred dollars an hour and the two associates I have in mind to assist me, charge three hundred. We send our bills out promptly every month so if you think we're not doing the job you expect of us, you can abandon ship at any time," he told me.

This sounded much like my own answer to the same question asked of me by countless clients.

"I have used Lester Bagley as my CPA on many of my cases in the past. He's done an analysis of the documents the Governor has supplied us with. Preliminarily, he's found about two million dollars that should be placed in the Governor's personal account but he tells me he doesn't have a forensic person on his staff to do the critical work necessary to establish the chain of events that will trace the cash. He believes there is a helluva lot more to be found and he also believes that there may be huge problems with the Governor's campaign accounts," I told him.

"I can assure you we have such a person on our staff and, if given some time, we'll be able to clearly establish where the money came from and where it went."

After the interview I talked to Emily and told her I thought I'd found the right person for the valuation and tracing issues and how much it would cost. She left the choice to my judgment resignedly, and said something like, "What the hell, we've come this far."

The trouble was she didn't have the money to lay out and neither did I. I resolved to go to the bank and see about an equity loan. I was afraid to say anything to Andrea at this point but I had to do something and quick.

I also had a problem with Charley Randell as I hadn't heard a word from him in over a week. When I called him, he asked to come to School Street and meet with me personally rather than discuss the matter over the phone. When I hung up I hoped he finally had something tangible to report. Something tangible like he knew who the Governor's girl friend was or that they followed judge Andretti to a strip joint and watched her lap-dance with one or two customers.

Instead, he told me about the Governor's clandestine visits to 18 West Cedar Street and his discovery that apparently Dr. and Ms. Edmonds were still in Florida while their house was being renovated. He thought the house was vacant and that someone was meeting the Governor there; that he wanted my permission to install cameras and listening devices to capture just what was going on and that Jake Bauer was just the guy to do it.

"Charley, I could lose my ticket, for chrissakes. It's a felony to do that. Is that the only way you can think of to get the answers we need? You, a first class private detective?" I said to him.

"Ted, it's costing you a small fortune for Jake and me to continue to keep these people under surveillance. Why don't we forget watching the Judge and concentrate on the Governor? That

way the bill will be cut in half and we won't enter the premises to
do our trick with the camera and listening devises."

"You know that suggestion sounds familiar. I think we've
wasted a lot of money so far. Yes, I guess that's our only alternative
at this point. Let's proceed that way."

"OK, but I'm leaving right after this meeting for a weekend
in Las Vegas with my long suffering wife. I won't be able to reach
Jake until I get back, OK?"

"Yeah, sure. What's two or three more days when you've
already amassed a fortune on this case? I hope you blow the whole
wad at the tables," I told him.

That afternoon as the pressure mounted, I had to do something
about my money problem. I went to the bank right across State
Street and arranged for a two hundred and fifty thousand line
of credit with my personal banker. I had a personal banker not
because I had any money invested in the bank but because I
had several firm checking accounts which sometimes had large
amounts of money in them He gave me the application to bring
home for Andrea's signature and told me they'd send the paper
work to their closing lawyer right away. The bank's lawyer had to
do a title run-down which was going to take a few days, but they
told me I'd have the money within a week.

At home that night, after dinner, I told Andrea what I had to
do.

"Do you need the entire amount right away?" she asked me.

"No," I said, "but I don't have enough right now to hire the
experts I need and I'll need the rest to keep the office running for
the next several weeks."

"Isn't there some way you can invest some of the money until
you need it?"

"Well, I never thought of that. Maybe I can talk to Clyde
Lawler, the investment guy, and see what he says."

That was the end of the discussion and I was relieved when
Andrea signed the application without another word.

The next day I had to focus on the business appraiser problem. I wasn't sure what to do--whether to hire Lester Bagley's office even though they didn't have a forensic guy as such, or hire Dawson Associates at their outrageous rates. True enough I received the OK from my client to go ahead with Dawson, but six hundred an hour--just to go digging. Of course they knew what to dig for in that morass of paper work Jed sent over. Additionally, they also would have the task of valuing the other business interests of Brenden Mitchell and they were more than well equipped for that job.

I called Chuck Dawson and told him he was hired. I asked him to contact Lester for the documents Lester had been combing through in order for Dawson to get a head start. Two million to begin with wasn't chump change. I also instructed him to begin the valuation process. He told me he'd get right on it. I had no doubt at six hundred dollars per hour.

Three days later, I called for an appointment with Clyde Lawler. "He'll see you right away, Mr. Eldridge," his secretary said after she'd asked me to hold.

"Ted, how are you?" Clyde said with his usual smile as I entered his office.

"OK, Clyde, but I've got some money problems," I replied, getting right to the reason for me being there.

"Well, the word on the street is that you're representing Emily Mitchell in her divorce, right?"

"Yeah, that's why I'm here. I just borrowed two hundred and fifty thousand dollars on a line of credit. I'll need fifty thousand in the next couple of weeks to fund the goddamn law suit and I thought I could invest the rest with you and make some money."

"Your timing couldn't be better, Ted. I have something that just came across my desk involving an investment opportunity in a building project. It's a shopping center right here in Boston. You can get in on the ground floor. The permitting process is almost over. They've received the go-ahead from every agency, every department from Washington right up to the City of Boston and they're ready to proceed. I recommend you buy in now, the owners only want a few investors to become limited partners."

"What can I expect from my two hundred thousand?"

"You should get your two hundred thousand back and another fifty as soon as all the permits are granted-- and there's only one more permit to get, they tell me."

"How long will it take to get my return?"

"Two weeks at the most. Once all the permits are granted they'll restructure the organization, get more investors and pay off the original limited partners including you, and they'll be on their way to make a few million."

"Twenty-five percent! That's fantastic, Clyde. How sure are they to get the final approval though?"

"Piece a cake. I've dealt with these people before. They're good as gold."

So what the hell, I did it. I felt relieved that at least that problem was solved. I could afford to pay the increased mortgage payment resulting from the added line of credit until Emily's case was over--as long as I won it for her. Besides, I was going to get all my two hundred and fifty thousand dollars back.

CHAPTER FIFTEEN

Jake was tired of this assignment. He'd been following the Judge every day after she left the courthouse for weeks now. Sometimes she'd go to a meeting at one of the downtown hotels where he watched her closely less she adjourn to one of the upstairs rooms after the meeting was over. Sometimes she'd go to the Mass. Bar Headquarters or the offices of Lawyer's Weekly Publications for some function or other. She'd also go shopping either for food or rarely, to Newbury Street for some items of clothing. Mostly though, she'd go right home after work, which made Jake's job a little easier.

Jake patrolled Mt. Vernon Street at the entrance to Cedar Lane Way every night until about one A.M. He was relieved every fourth day by a person whom Charley Randell had hired expressly for the purpose of giving Jake some time off. He hadn't seen Charley in the past three days and he was anxious to tell Charley that he wanted to change the schedule around to get more time off. This night, however, was Jakes fourth night and he was looking forward to spending some time away from Beacon Hill--far away.

Shortly before one o'clock, Jake noticed two men turn the corner from Charles Street and walk up Mt. Vernon on the opposite side of the street. He was instantly alerted as neither one spoke to the other but continued walking, apparently intent on their destination. He watched them carefully. Behind Jake, and unnoticed by him, a black Jeep Grand Cherokee slowly came down Mt. Vernon Street and steered into a parking space, not far from Cedar Lane Way. Four men got out. Silently they approached Jake as his back was turned while watching the other two come closer and closer.

The blow came from behind and caught Jake right on the back of his head, just below the base of his skull. His legs buckled and he would have collapsed onto the sidewalk but for the sake of being propped up by two of his assailants.

The two men whom Jake had first seen crossed the street and joined the group. Four of them crowded around the two holding Jake up as if they were taking care of their drunken friend, though they needn't have bothered as there was not a soul in sight at that time of the morning.

"Dude! This is our last warning," one of them said. "Stay outta here and don't come back."

The shortest one in the group, the one who spit out the words close to Jake's ear, swung a wooden club, which looked like a baseball bat but smaller, and connected with full force to the front of Jake's left knee cap. The blow sounded like the crack from a bat which just hit a ball for a home run. It crushed Jake's knee. Jake's cry was stifled by a gloved hand over his mouth but nothing stopped the tears of pain coming from his eyes. The pain shot up his spine and met the pain coming from the blow on his head as Jake passed out. He was left in a heap beside a brick wall of a building on Mt. Vernon Street.

The six men disappeared as fast as they had approached. Within five minutes the street was as calm as it had been before except for the groans coming from the figure propped up against the side of a building, his head bent over his chest and his left leg splayed at a thirty degree angle from his left thigh.

At 100 Federal Street, three weeks after his meeting with Dr. Lionel Gagne, Paul Jed was meeting with his four partners who were gathered around the large mahogany table in their conference room. At these partnership meetings it was required that each partner review the cases that were open and active and the status of accounts receivable more than thirty days overdue. Legal problems were also discussed, opinions obtained, arguments made pro and con, all as if the five lawyers were part of a study group preparing for an exam.

"So, Emily Mitchell is seeing Dr. James Hurley, forensic psychiatrist," he informed the group as they were discussing the case with the highest profile in the firm's history. "The Governor says she's on drugs; she has two or three glasses of wine every night and then passes out and that she simply cannot parent their kid. I want to take the shrink's deposition. I bet I'll get some juicy evidence against her. What do I have to do?"

"Well, you can't take her deposition without Mitchell's approval, that's for sure," said Jim Flahive, the med-mal lawyer.

"Won't the doctor-patient privilege prevent me from taking the deposition if she refuses to waive the privilege?" Jed asked.

"No," Flahive responded. "First of all there is no doctor-patient privilege in Massachusetts as such. There is, by statute, a psychotherapist privilege which gives the patient the right to prevent a therapist from disclosing any communication between them. If a defendant raises his or her mental condition as a defense to any allegation made by the plaintiff however, the judge may find that the communication should be disclosed in the interest of justice. That's obviously not the case here though. I vaguely remember that custody matters are treated differently however. I don't know about that. I don't have any custody proceedings."

"How do I get around that?" Jed asked the assembled partners.

"Look up the statute, Paul, for chrissakes," Donald Cooper, senior partner answered.

Unperturbed, Jed continued, "Things are heating up," he told the group.

"Donald Long, the GAL is on the war path. He's made appointments to see Emily and he's met with the Governor at the Governor's sister's house. He's talked with the child and plans to go to the kid's school. The report is that all went well so far. I'll look into how to take Hurley's deposition. Thank you," he said to the group.

Dr. Sheila Monaghan's office was on Cambridge Street in the Bullfinch Building next to Massachusetts General Hospital. She had recently received the second payment of twenty-five hundred dollars, this one from Attorney Ted Eldridge and she was pleased that both sides agreed to engage her as the child psychiatrist for Danny Mitchell.

Her first meeting with Danny was in her office which was decorated so that it was not terribly threatening to little kids, much less fourteen year olds like Danny. His mother brought him to the appointment early in the morning at the beginning of the week. She was told the earlier the better. They waited for almost a full hour however before Dr. Monaghan was finished with other patients.

When Monaghan finally appeared and after initial introductions, Dr. Monaghan escorted Danny into her office after asking Ms. Mitchell to wait for them in the reception area. After about forty-five minutes, Monaghan and Danny emerged though the office door, Danny looking no worse for wear. Emily Mitchell informed Dr. Monaghan that she knew for some time that there'd be two people investigating the issue of custody as soon as they approached one another. Ms. Mitchell made it clear to Monaghan that she nevertheless was not happy about the intrusion into her daily life now that the appointments began to escalate. Even now, Emily complained to the doctor, Attorney Long had scheduled an appointment to visit her and Danny at Warren Street later this very week. It was obvious she could hardly contain her annoyance when Dr. Monaghan requested a similar visit at her home. To make matters worse, Monaghan had to tell her that she too, was going to schedule an appointment to speak with Danny's teachers at Brookline High.

"God! What a pain this is," Emily said to Monaghan. "At least you're a qualified health care professional with a medical degree and a specialty in child psychiatry," she continued.

"Ms. Mitchell, will you give me permission to speak with Dr. Hurley?" Monaghan asked. "I really need to have his input. I assure you he'll be most helpful to me."

"I don't see why not. It seems everybody in this city will be involved in my divorce case. But honestly--let me speak to my lawyer first. I'll get back to you. OK?"

Later that week Dr. Sheila Monaghan met with Eleanor Taft, the Assistant Headmaster of Brookline High at the school.

"Yes, Doctor, I was told you'd be coming today. I'm pleased to meet you," Ms. Taft said when introduced to her visitor.

"Thank you. I don't expect to take up much of your time," Dr. Monaghan replied. "My purpose is to find out how Danny Mitchell is doing in school; whether there are any problems you could tell me about."

"I hope I can save you some time. Are you aware that Attorney Donald Long came here a couple of days ago and was asking the same questions?"

"Yes. The Court appointed him as the GAL. My role is somewhat different, though. Both the Governor and Ms. Mitchell have engaged me as the psychiatrist for Danny. In other words, I work for Danny while the GAL works for the Court. Nevertheless, we both have Danny's best interest at heart."

"Well, I can tell you the same thing I told Attorney Long. Danny is in trouble. His grades have plummeted since Christmas break. He doesn't do his homework assignments most of the time and when he does hand something in, it's late. He appears to be lethargic in class, uncommunicative. Unlike his previous behavior, he never engages in class discussions, never volunteers. He's even developed a surly attitude with his teachers."

"The only person he's been seen with is Brian Woods and, to tell the truth, Brian has been his only friend since school started in September."

"We sent him to the Guidance Office for an evaluation about a month ago. We have different programs here at Brookline High, and we wanted to make sure we delivered the right service for him. The guidance office sent him to the school psychologist who found out that his parents were going through a divorce. His reaction to the divorce was not uncommon. He blames himself, loves both parents equally even though his father is somewhat tyrannical and his mother has some personal problems of her own. Danny appears to be thoroughly confused about the future."

"He sees the psychologist twice a week but, unfortunately there is only so much she can do. Our experience is that when the divorce is over things will calm down for Danny-- if he can last that long," she said.

"You can interview his teachers but what I've just told you is the gist of what they'd tell you," she continued.

"That won't be necessary, Ms. Taft. Thank you for your help," Dr. Monaghan replied. "If it's OK with you, I'd like to be able to follow this meeting up with a telephone call in a couple of weeks to see if there are any changes."

"That'll be fine. It was nice to meet you, goodbye," Taft said as Dr. Monaghan departed.

Emily Mitchell decided to postpone the meeting she'd scheduled with Donald Long for the Wednesday following her meeting with him and Danny at his office. After her meeting at Dr. Monaghan's office, she thought she could save herself some aggravation by asking them both to come to Warren Street at the same time. When she called them to make arrangements however, she was informed that neither would agree to such a meeting. She then told Long to come at ten o'clock in the morning and Dr. Monaghan at two in the afternoon on Friday, the following week.

Promptly at ten, Donald Long pulled into the driveway at 17 Warren Street. The house stood to the right of the three car garage before which Long parked his car, got out and stood for a brief second marveling at the enormous English Tudor structure that appeared to cover half of the short, curving street from which he'd just turned. There were trees, shrubs, flowers and other plantings, which almost obliterated the house from his view.

He'd taken Storrow Drive, got lost on Beacon Street for a few moments and finally cruised to a stop at his destination.

Emily Mitchell greeted him at the front door and ushered him into the foyer where she asked if she could get him a cool drink. When he declined, she showed him into the living room but asked him to continue to the sun room at the western end of the house and make himself comfortable on the ample couch, situated in front of a gigantic fireplace.

"Let me get Danny for you, Mr. Long. I'll just be a minute," she said sweetly.

When she returned, she had a hand on Danny's back as she directed him towards Long. She and Danny sat on the couch together while the GAL sat on the lounge chair opposite.

"Hi Danny, nice to see you again," the GAL said, affably.

"'Lo," was the only reply.

"Danny, where's your Game-Boy?"

"My mother won't let me play with it unless I earn it," came the reply.

"What do you mean by that?"

"She makes me play outside with other kids before I can watch TV or use my Game-Boy. Problem is I don't have any kids to play with," Danny mumbled.

"How were your marks at the end of the last semester?"

"Not so good."

"What are you going to do for the summer?"

"Well, I'm supposed to get some tennis and sailing lessons at the Cape at my grandmother's house."

"Ms. Mitchell, can you let me speak with Danny alone for a few minutes?"

"Certainly," she replied and left them in the sun room as she closed the French doors behind her.

When she was gone, Long continued his questions.

"I spoke to the assistant headmaster at your school Danny, Eleanor Taft, and she told me you weren't doing so well. Is that right?"

"You went to my school?"

"Yes, I had to find out how you were doing."

Danny turned his face away to hide the tears.

"I'm sorry. I only have a few more questions."

"Danny, who cooks for you here?"

"My mother."

"What happens after dinner?"

"What do you mean?"

"Where does your mother go after she cleans up the kitchen?"

"Well-- she usually falls asleep on the couch and I watch TV in my room or get on the computer. Sometimes I get into my Game-Boy."

"Danny, just between us, does your mother drink a lot of wine at dinner?"

"Uh, --I don't know."

"Is she awake when you go to bed?"

"I don't need anybody to put me to bed, for cryin' out loud."

"Yes, but is she awake?"

"Leave me alone! I'm tired of all this bull shit!" Danny cried as he bolted from the room.

Within a minute, Emily came back into the sun room.

"What did you do to my son?" she yelled at Long.

"I'm sorry if I upset him, Ms. Mitchell. He seems to have a low threshold these days."

"Don't you dare blame him? He's been going through a lot with all you people prodding him, asking all kinds of questions and making him a nervous wreck.

I think it'd be better, Mr. Long if you left right now," she said as she glared at him and escorted him toward the door. She went straight to Danny's room after Long left. He was lying on his bed, his face in the pillow, sobbing.

"Danny, my sweetheart, I'm so sorry you have to go through all of this but it'll be over soon." She said as she put her arms around his shoulders. He made no response and even shifted his weight to lay on his right side, away from her.

"I'm afraid one more investigator is coming this afternoon. She's much better than this guy who just left. You have met her before and I think you'll like her. Please try and understand this is supposed to be all for your benefit."

No response.

"I'll make some lunch for you; ice cream and chocolate sauce for desert. OK? Come down in about thirty minutes. I'll have it all ready for you, my sweet."

No response.

Emily left him alone and went to the kitchen to fix Danny a grilled ham and cheese sandwich, his favorite, chocolate milk and cookies and ice cream with chocolate sauce. It took her a little over a half an hour. It took her another five minutes to look for the serving tray, assemble the iced tea, sandwich and napkin and carefully brought them upstairs to Danny's room. When she opened the door he was lying on the bed, on his back, his legs akimbo and his arms wrapped around his chest.

"Danny," she screamed as she dropped the tray and ran to his bed. She put her face next to his and heard a faint wheeze but then, in an instant, she thought he stopped breathing.

"Oh, Jesus Christ, what have you done!" she cried as she picked up the phone on the table next to Danny's bed. The bottle of Valium, the drug she was previously taking, was empty and was on the table next to a glass half full of water. She couldn't remember how many pills were in there, more than ten she thought to her horror. She dialed 911.

As soon as the phone was answered, she blurted out,

"My son has just overdosed on drugs! He's passed out! He may be dead! I can't hear him breath! Please help me! I think--"

"What address? What address? Please tell me the address!

"Seventeen Warren Street, Brookline! Please hurry!"

"What kind of drug did he take?"

"Valium! I think that's the only one! Oh God!"

"Stay on the phone! What's your name?"

"Never mind my name, just get someone here!"

"The EMT's are on the way."

When the EMT's arrived they brought Danny and Emily Mitchell to Beth Israel Hospital. In the emergency room, as soon as he was rolled in, Emily saw the nurse give Danny something she couldn't quite see. When she asked what it was, they told her it was Flumazenil –'as a precaution.' Emily was by his side when she heard the order for "gastric lavage."

"Please, what's that?" she said to the attendant. She didn't know whether she was a doctor or not, she looked so young.

"We're pumping his stomach. Are you sure he only took Valium?"

"That's the only bottle I found," she replied.

"If that's all he took, lady, he'll be OK. Don't worry."

Emily didn't get home that night until ten-thirty. When she left Danny was resting comfortably. She felt as though her nerve endings were like broken electrical wires in a rain storm.

As soon as she entered the house, with trembling hands, she poured a large glass of Chardonnay which was always available in her refrigerator. She carried the glass into the sun room and sat heavily on the couch without putting on the light.

What am I doing to myself? What am I doing with Danny? I have to get hold of myself, she thought. I can't continue like this.

I will not let those people, those investigators drag Danny down, drag me down with all their psych-babble nonsense. I can't take these drugs, can't drink. I must get hold of myself. I can't become so depressed I want to kill myself and then become so angry I want to kill somebody else. I am a capable woman. I will not let this divorce get the better of me. She remembered her comment to Monaghan a few days ago that the whole investigation of custody thing was such a 'pain'.

She stared at the Waterford goblet in her hands for just a few seconds before she got up and with all her might threw the glass of wine into the fireplace.

CHAPTER SIXTEEN

I was familiar with the Suffolk County Probate and Family Court. The Edward W. Brooke Courthouse on New Chardon Street, Boston, was completed only about four years ago, which is to say, according to old Boston standards, that it's still brand new. The corridors continue to glisten despite the heavy traffic from litigants, lawyers and witnesses. The restrooms are even devoid of graffiti.

Henry Baker and I were there together with Paul Jed, two of his associates and the very fragile Emily Mitchell. Emily had not yet recovered from the trauma of Danny's overdose the week before and she looked like a complete wreck. She had dark circles under her eyes, her cheeks were hollow, she looked like she lost ten pounds, all in her face and she began to stutter when she started a sentence. Danny had been at Beth Israel Hospital for two days after he was raced there by the ambulance and was doing OK, at least physically, she told me.

Henry and I were primed to address Jed's motion to take the deposition of Dr. James Hurley, Emily's psycho-pharmacologist. As usual, the Governor was not present. Jed had also marked for hearing a request for a status report in order to give him and his client some sense as to when the case would be ready for trial.

Anticipating a favorable report from Dr. Gerber, I filed a motion to amend the complaint for divorce by adding a Petition to Establish Paternity. Even if the report was negative, I figured the Petition would send the other side around the bend. Besides, the filing of the petition was certainly not frivolous at this point. Even if the data from Gerber was unreliable, I still had the testimony from Emily, for whatever it was worth. Certainly, the Governor didn't show what I would call a loving interest in Danny's hospitalization. Emily told me he did come and visit once at the Beth Israel and groused that the whole thing was caused by Emily's neglect, her drugs, her drinking and on and on.

I was fully aware that if the Governor was not Danny's father, the first thing he'd do is attempt to get out from under his obligation to pay child support, college expenses, health insurance premiums and uninsured medical expenses for Danny. I also knew that one year ago I lost a similar case where I represented the father in the same circumstances as the Governor's. In that case, it was the father who brought the Petition to Establish Paternity. Once found not to be the father, he reasoned, he wouldn't have to pay child support. The Supreme Judicial Court in Massachusetts held that where the parent holds himself out to be the father of the child for many years, in Danny's case fourteen years, the father is prevented from denying that he was the biological father of the child. The Court stated that it would be too detrimental to the best interest of the child to grant the Petition. The same thing would hold true if the mother brought the Petition, I reasoned. The Governor would still have to pay.

I also filed another motion for a restraining order and had the pictures of Emily we took on two occasions at the office ready to hand to the Judge. I made duplicates for Jed. Even though the pleadings were impounded to prevent public access, if those pictures were ever leaked to the press, the Governor's political life would be finished, no campaign for the Senate for him. The motion was also going to complicate the Governor's visitation privileges. If the restraining order issued, he'd have to stay away from Emily and pick Danny up in the driveway when he arrived.

After my motions were served on Jed, I anticipated some fireworks. Sure enough, on the day before the hearing I received a call from him. I signaled Amy to tell him I was on the phone and that I'd call him back. I needed some time to think about what I would say to him-- and to be sure I'd control my temper regardless of what he said to me. I really didn't want to speak with him so I called him back around noontime, hoping he wouldn't be there and that the passage of time would give him pause. I left a message to have him call me after I was told he was out to lunch. I never heard from him for the rest of the day.

When Paul Jed received the motions, he called Mort Haller. Jed told Haller that Jed's motions and those motions filed by Eldridge would be heard by Judge Andretti on the following Friday, July sixth. Haller heard the details of the petition to establish paternity as well as the allegations in the motion for a restraining order. After listening to Jed going on and on, Haller finally interrupted him, informed him that the Governor would not be present at the hearing, wished him good luck and told him to report back later.

As soon as the conversation with Jed was over, Haller walked across Boston Common to his favorite public telephone and dialed the number. He huddled between the partitions that separated the telephone on both sides and waited for a response to his call.

"Yes?"

"Renzo! What are you waiting for, for chrissakes! There is a major hearing in the Governor's case scheduled for this coming

Friday, the sixth. The case is progressing much too fast. That lawyer for the Governor's wife must settle or we're in big trouble!"

"Patienza! Patienza," was all that was said in response before Renzo hung up the phone.

At the courthouse, somehow or other our motions were scheduled for the afternoon session which began at two o'clock. This hardly ever happened in Suffolk County. Perhaps in Berkshire or Hampshire Counties where the judges were more accommodating to the members of the bar due to a reduced caseload, lawyers could expect such assignments, but not here.

The morning motion session was usually jammed with litigants and lawyers. The clerk would call out each case name and the lawyers would respond by stating how long they anticipated their argument would last. They all lied. None of them wanted to be placed at the end of the list because their case would take too long, so they lied.

Usually the afternoon session had only a few cases left over from the morning and the judge could therefore spend some time in chambers writing opinions or reading pleadings when the afternoon session was over.

This day, there were two cases ahead of ours, but because they were placed at the end of the morning list. They were long and, according to Barbara Hancock, the clerk, very contentious. Barbara also informed me that the morning session was a "zoo" and Judge Andretti was in one of her moods.

"Barbara," I whispered to her at her side bar, "How come we're in the afternoon session?"

"Are you kidding, Ted? Your case will take forever this afternoon. If it was assigned to the morning session you would have waited here all morning," she replied.

"Did Paul Jed have anything to do with the afternoon assignment?" I asked.

"All I know is that it was on the daily list marked for this session. Don't get me involved," she said to me with a sly grin.

At that point the Judge glared at me and silently told me to sit down by lifting her chin and pointing it in the direction of the chairs inside the bar. Not a good start.

Two lawyers who were obviously not prepared argued the first case called. Both of their arguments were filled with statements unsupported by facts. One didn't know what his client's own financial statement said and consequently misquoted his client's income. The Judge, reading the statement before her, picked up on the error and her patience waned rapidly.

"The least, the very least you can do counselor, is to know what you put down on your own client's financial statement," she said with one of her now famous glares.

"Well, uh...Yes, Your Honor. Can you give me a five minute recess so I can speak with my client?" the poor guy sputtered.

"Absolutely not. I have a long afternoon and time is precious," Andretti replied.

The other lawyer was no better and, by the time they finished, the Judge was wired, sitting on the edge of her high-backed blue leather chair, her face flushed, and her eyes flashing.

The second case was almost as bad. It involved the appointment of a guardian for a patient for whom the doctors prescribed psychotropic drugs. The family had to be heard, the doctor had to be heard, the lawyers had to be heard-- it went on forever while the Judge sat immobile apparently attempting to control her anxiety, I thought.

"I'll give you five more minutes," she said after both sides exchanged their view for the second time.

When they were finally finished, the Judge said,

"I'm taking a ten minute recess!" and sweeping her robe around her, left the courtroom before the court officer had a chance to say, "All rise."

It was now three-thirty and because Jed's motions were filed first, he was going to start. We had only twenty minutes to argue four motions after theJudge returned and I knew from experience, that Jed would take at least fifteen of those minutes. Gamesmanship, I thought. At least in chess the rules were always followed. I really couldn't complain though. My paternity petition was part of the game being played especially if there was no DNA proof.

When the Judge returned she had composed herself somewhat. Barbara Hancock called our case and we five lawyers approached the counsel tables, I accompanied by Emily Mitchell and Henry Baker, Paul Jed accompanied by his two associates.

"What do we have this afternoon?" the Judge asked to no one in particular.

Shit! I thought. She hasn't read the pleadings.

Jed, not one to take a back seat, immediately got up.

"Your Honor, I have a simple motion to take the deposition of Ms. Mitchell's psychiatrist and a request for a status report… nothing out of the ordinary. My brother, on the other hand, has a ridiculous request to establish paternity as an issue in this case. After fourteen years of being a devoted father, the Governor has to suffer the ignominious allegation that he is not the father of his little boy. It's preposterous! It's simply a ruse, an opportunity for Attorney Eldridge to muddy up the waters and I resent it! What's more--"

"Your Honor, I object. You simply asked to be informed of what's before you, not a one-sided diatribe from Attorney Jed. May we…"

"That's enough! That's enough. This is not the way it's going to be this afternoon," the Judge admonished.

"You are both experienced members of the bar. I will not put up with this badgering of one another. Do you hear me? Now let's proceed civilly. You filed first Attorney Jed. Proceed."

"Your Honor, I simply want the Court's permission to take the deposition of the plaintiff's psychiatrist. She--"

"I object," I said, rising and addressing the Judge, looking directly at her.

"I thought I told you, Attorney Eldridge, that we were going to proceed civilly. This is not--"

"Excuse me, Your Honor. Attorney Jed is asking to waive the psychotherapist privilege of my client. The issue is what is in the best interest of the child. The hearing, according to the statute, must be conducted in chambers."

Silence

"Get me the statute, Attorney Eldridge and I'll see for myself."

"I have it right here, Your Honor," I said as I handed the green statute book to Barbara Hancock.

After she read the page I had previously marked she said simply,

"Chambers."

"All rise," the court officer intoned as we gathered up our papers and followed him and the Judge out of the courtroom through the door to the rear of the judge's bench.

There were not enough chairs so most of us stood in front of the Judge's desk as she took her seat.

"Now, what is this all about," she said looking at Jed and me.

"I think--"

"Your honor," I began, interrupting her.

"Mr. Eldridge! You have the exasperating habit of interrupting me each time I'm about to say something. Your conduct--"

"Judge, I simply want to point out that the court reporter should be in here to transcribe the proceeding, before anything else is said," I informed her.

Silence. The Andretti glare.

"Bring her in," she instructed the court officer.

During the next several minutes while the stenographer was getting set up, the nervous tension in the room was palpable. The air was heavy with the smell of body odors as we were all standing close together. The air conditioning system in the building was not designed to cool nine persons, including the stenographer, court officer and four lawyers with their suit coats and ties on, crowded into one small room in July. The one open window had a glass partition in front of it at a forty-five degree angle from the window sill directing what little cool air there was upward toward the ceiling. No one could say a word until we received the signal from the steno and there was much shifting of weight from one foot to the other as each of us avoided looking into the eyes of the others. Meanwhile, the Judge was absorbed in reading the pleadings.

Finally, mercifully, the steno was ready and after a nod from the Judge, Jed began.

"We need to take the deposition of Ms. Mitchell's psychiatrist because we believe she is on heavy medication which prevents her from adequately parenting the child in question. Additionally, we believe she's drinking alcohol while taking this medication which makes her catatonic and therefore certainly not capable of supervising the child or even making sure he's safe. Our understanding is she's passed out on the couch right after dinner and the boy has to take care of himself. His grades at school have slipped, he is seeing the school psychologist because his conduct in class is lethargic, he arrives at school late, he doesn't hand in any homework assignments and he is morose and obstinate around his father during his visitation.

What's worse, Judge, is that recently Danny attempted suicide!" He paused to let the hush that followed become even more dramatic. Jed leveled a drilling, accusatory look at Emily. When I also glanced at her she was silently crying, her tears were streaming down the sides of her cheeks. Her handkerchief was rolled into a ball, which she was squeezing in her right hand. Her lips were quivering and her legs were unsteady. I glided over to her, put my arm around her shoulders and felt her whole body rising and falling with every breath she took.

"He was rushed to the Beth Israel Hospital after overdosing on his mother's drugs," Jed continued. "Where was his mother? This was on her watch."

Jed droned on for another ten minutes repeating the same theme until he finally ended by saying, "Therefore, I request that my motion be granted, Your Honor."

"Mr. Eldridge?"

"The truth is Judge, that Emily Mitchell is an excellent parent. She has had to combat the interference of her husband in parenting this child for years. He is nothing less than a control freak, belittling his wife and child at every turn, taking charge of every little detail surrounding the child's welfare and constantly telling his wife and child that they are both incompetent to make decisions on their own. Yes, Danny is going through a difficult time but it's his mother who is helping him, not his father."

"But you don't have to believe me, Judge. Simply wait until you receive the report from Dr. Sheila Monaghan, the child psychiatrist agreed to by both sides. She is making an independent investigation of the child's welfare and her recommendation will be pivotal in your decision. Ms. Mitchell and others like her are entitled to pour out their hearts and souls to their psychiatrist, tell the most intimate details of their marriage in order to further their treatment without fear that what they say will be disclosed to the other spouse. That's the essence of the statute."

"And there's more, Judge. We have evidence under investigation that this Governor is not even the father of Danny. We will prove..."

"What is this?" Jed bellowed. "Judge, don't fall for this smoke screen. This is nothing but a political attempt to bring down the government of this Commonwealth. These people are desperate. They'll say anything. They..."

"Enough! Enough!" the Judge interjected.

"I've heard enough from both of you. I've read the pleadings and it's not necessary to go back into the courtroom. I am going to grant both of your motions. Attorney Jed, you may take the deposition of the psychiatrist. Attorney Eldridge, you may amend your complaint to include a count to establish paternity."

"The trial of this case will not turn into a circus. I want your pre-trial memoranda and a list of witnesses within thirty days. In answer to your motion for a status report, Attorney Jed, there will be a trial September sixth."

She looked up from her papers, pushed a wisp of hair away from her right eye which enabled her to glare at counsel more effectively.

"There will be no continuances. Positively no continuances, do you understand?" Jed and I nodded in unison.

"You will both pre-mark your exhibits and submit them one week before trial. And don't forget the gag order I imposed. Any violation will subject the violator to contempt."

"I've looked at your request for a restraining order, Attorney Eldridge, and I'm not disposed to grant it."

"But Your Honor, I have these pictures I'd like to introduce to demonstrate that my client is in danger from her husband," I pleaded.

"Let me see them," she demanded.

After only a few moments she looked up and had a pained expression on her face.

"All right, Mr. Eldridge, I'll grant the restraining order. The details of visitation will be the same as my previous decree except that the pick-up and delivery of the child will be made twenty yards from Ms. Mitchell's front door. I assume the Governor will be able to see the front door from that distance for the child's safety." she paused and then looked at each of us separately.

"I hereby impose a gag order to include all attorneys associated with this case, their entire office staff, their clients, experts, and all other witnesses. I direct you, Attorney Jed, to prepare the document and to make sure it's signed by everyone involved with this case so far. I want the order on my desk by Wednesday, next week. Any additional people will have to sign as they come aboard. Do you understand? Not one word to the media or anyone else not directly involved in this litigation. If there is any violation of this order, the penalty will be contempt and a possible jail term. Do I make myself clear?"

Nothing but a shuffling of feet was the response.

"I said-- do I make myself clear?"

This time a chorus of "Yes, Judge," was the response.

"OK then. Thank you all," she said rising to dismiss the group from her presence.

CHAPTER SEVENTEEN

Emily, Harry and I stopped at Faneuil Hall for a cool drink before parting and going back to the office. Despite a throng of students and tourists strolling among the many kiosks and the frenetic shoppers seeking some delicacy or other, we were able to place our order after only a few minutes in line.

"So we have the ability to amend our complaint. Big deal. No judge would ever deny us that right," Harry said as we collected our drinks.

"Well, we received our restraining order," I hurriedly said as we quickly sat at a small table in the rotunda when it became vacant. I wanted Emily to focus on our small victory. At this point she'd paid us thousands of borrowed dollars anticipating receiving her share of the marital property when the case was over. She had long ago used up her retainer and it was important to keep her spirits up for more reasons than one.

"What about Jed taking Dr. Hurley's deposition?" Emily asked. "After all this time being treated by him I'm afraid I just don't know what he's going to say."

"Look Emily, don't worry, he's a pro. So you've taken some anti-depressant medication. So what! I sometimes think half the people in the United States are on some kind of mood elevator. It doesn't make you out to be a bad parent or a bad person. Besides, I'm going to meet with Dr. Hurley before Jed gets a chance to get his hooks in him just to see where he's coming from. Remember Dr. Monaghan is also going to see him. I will tell you this though, Emily, we have a trial date of September sixth. That's just around the corner. From now until then, I want you to parent the hell out of Danny. He's out of the hospital now. Be with him every chance you get. Show him how much you love him. Don't be afraid to talk to him about your feelings. Ask him to tell you what's on his mi--"

"You don't have to lecture me about how to care for my son, Attorney Eldridge," she interrupted.

"He's out of school for the summer and I've made arrangements for both of us to live on the Cape with my mother. He's already enrolled in tennis, golf and sailing lessons at her club. And I want you to know, I'm not coming back to Brookline other than to see Dr. Hurley for our weekly sessions for the entire summer. Speaking of Hurley, I've decided not to attend Jed's deposition of him or his deposition of the other one, Dr.Monaghan, whenever he deposes her. Let him say whatever he's going to say. To hell with it," she exclaimed.

"Emily, first there'll be no deposition of Sheila Monaghan. She'll simply submit her report to the Judge with copies to Jed and me. Second, I'm afraid to tell you this. You can't remove Danny to the Cape for the summer. Did you forget your husband has visitation privileges? If I remember correctly he has him Monday through Thursday one week, and on weekends the next."

"Oh no!" she wailed. "Don't tell me that! Please, Dear God! I forgot all about that." She got up from the chair and walked to the window holding her head with both hands, blocking her ears so she couldn't hear any more.

Emily's whole body began to shake. She held on to the window with one hand outstretched, the other holding her stomach. She began to lose her balance, but steadied herself with both hands now on the inside window ledge. Her legs still seemed unsteady as she teetered back and forth, now on one leg, then on the other.

"I've made all these plans with my mother. She's even paid the fees for me to enroll Danny in those programs," she sobbed.

Her shoulders were hunched over and she was crying inconsolably, standing there in front of the window overlooking King's Chapel Cemetery. She looked pathetic. I was tempted to go over to her and put my arms around her shoulders to try to console her but that was an invitation to disaster. I'm not her shrink, I thought. I'm not responsible for her emotions. I'm not her relative. I'm simply her lawyer. I'm responsible to deliver the very best legal representation to her that I'm able to deliver.

Who was I kidding? She was pitiable. I got up and silently moved toward her. I carefully placed my left hand on her left shoulder and stood well behind her.

"Emily, I'm sorry for this confusion. It's perfectly understandable for you to make arrangements for Danny and temporarily forget the Governor's visitation rights. You're going through a very difficult time. You probably have blocked your husband out of your mind altogether. But don't you see? That only means you'll be fine when this divorce is over. You don't want to hear it now but trust me, you are a young woman and you'll fall in love again."

"Not on your life," she exclaimed. "Never again! I'm not going through this a second time." She reached for a hand full of tissues from the ever present supply on my desk and began to calm down.

"Thank you," she said to me as she resumed her seat.

"I feel like such a fool. I'll just have to make other arrangements for Danny. I'm worried about him, though. He's been acting so strange what with the overdose and all. During this last semester at school his performance was horrible. I suppose it's understandable He'd been seeing the school psychiatrist twice a week but I didn't see much improvement in him. He's been so lethargic. I just don't know. Perhaps I should bring him to his own psychiatrist. What do you think?"

"Keep in mind that there are two psychiatrists in this case already, your Dr. Hurley and Dr. Monaghan. Long is also appointed to investigate the question of custody as the GAL."

"But there is no one to care for Danny, is there? I mean no one who can treat his problems." she said.

"That's true. It's your call," I informed her.

"We might get some grief from the other side, but you have to do whatever is in Danny's best interest. If the Governor complains I think we'll carry the day in court," I told her.

We talked some more about what remains to be done and, after we parted, on the walk back to Old City Hall, I thought about having only two short months to pull all this together. I remembered learning in law school that a trial is like a stage production. It's the lawyer who controls the players, when they enter, when they exit, what they say and when they say it. It's the lawyer who directs the unfolding of the plot and conducts the rehearsals of the actors to create an interest in the audience when the show begins. I had yet to write the stage play for this case and I had only sixty days to do it. My audience was going to be the indomitable Justice Rhea Andretti and she was certainly not a first nighter.

That evening I left the office about six-thirty. For a change, I walked out of the front of the building and down the steps to the stoned inner courtyard of Old City Hall. In nice weather, the restaurant, Maison Robert, festooned their outside seating area bordering the courtyard, with potted plants, trees and a string of lights giving their al fresco dining area a gay and elegant setting. The tables were set up with dark green umbrellas and I sometimes watched the diners at lunch or those gathered in the early evening for cocktails and dinner from my office window. It was a helluva lot more uplifting than reading inscriptions on gravestones.

154

This early evening as I stepped across the courtyard, the diners appeared to be chatting amiably, their glasses tinkling, without an apparent care in the world. The scene was reminiscent of a Van Gogh painting, 'Café Terrace at Night', that was always one of my favorites. I could hear music, a smooth jazz, coming from the three-piece ensemble playing next to the outside bar which added to the atmosphere.

For a few seconds I became lost in a reverie of delight, forgetting Emily and forgetting the ton of work that lay before me.

I was tempted to stop for a drink but I hadn't spent much time at home with Andrea and the kids lately. Kids-- there are no kids around our house anymore. Josh was seventeen and had been accepted at Boston College just this past spring. About the time Emily's case was going to trial in September, he'd be setting up his room at one of the dorms, meeting his roommate, getting settled; I was going to miss all that just as I had missed most of his lacrosse games this year, helping him with his homework and a host of other parenting duties. He was a strong kid though, handsome, self reliant and able to be by himself and like it, which to me, was always a mark of maturity.

Mandy was sixteen and was just finishing her junior year at Brookline High. I asked her if she knew Danny Mitchell but she said she really didn't know him other than that he was the son of Governor Mitchell.

"Dad, he's only a freshman," she said pointedly.

So, somewhat reluctantly, somewhat in a melancholy mood, even saddened by my episode with Emily in my office earlier, I made my way to the garage to begin my trek to Brookline.

The sun was still shining but the garage, cooling in the late afternoon, cast its shadows on the north east side of the building away from the setting sun. That's where I parked my car at seven-thirty this morning. Even at that hour the garage was half full so I had to park on the fifth floor down at the end away from the elevator. No big deal. It wasn't a long walk back and I felt lucky to be on the fifth floor instead of further up.

At this hour of the afternoon many of the downtown lawyers were still in their offices billing their little asses off. My car was parked on the inside row where cars faced other cars rather that a space where the cars faced the outside of the building. I had a vintage Mercedes 280SL which I babied for the last ten years and, who knows, it might rain and the car could get wet from the dust filled rain drops if it was parked facing out. Besides the sun, you know-- well, let's just say I liked that car.

I put my brief case in the back seat and settled into the driver's seat, smelled the leather with satisfaction, noticed the efficiency of the placement of the dials on the detailed dash, started the car and heard the quiet hum of the engine. I pushed a button to listen to music from my five speaker CD player, which had replaced the Blaupunkt radio, and began to be somewhat uplifted hearing the strains of Natalie Cole singing "The Very Thought of You".

The car in front of me, no it wasn't a car, it was a Ford F150 pick-up truck, started up just as I began to back out. Suddenly the pick- up's motor revved up and I heard its engine sounding like a 747 in the confines of the garage while the driver evidently had the truck in neutral. For a split second, the truck wasn't going anywhere until the driver shifted into drive causing the truck to lurch forward and smash into my left front fender with such force that the dashboard buckled into my chest and my head snapped back against the headrest behind me. To my horror, the truck kept coming at me pushing me into the cars parked facing the outside of the building and smashing the front of my car with its heavy duty front end so that the windshield shattered and glass shards were sprayed all over me. I felt the blood running down my face, neck and arms where the glass cut me. The front of my car caved in towards me and the last thing I remember, as I was wedged in behind the steering wheel and the once detailed dashboard, was someone saying, "Listen to me, ass hole."

I must have passed out for only few seconds as I saw four men huddled around me rather than the police or medics or the fire department. I couldn't focus very well but I saw one guy bend over me with a long thin knife with an intricate handle in his hand. I could feel his warm breath on my face and even as I was immobile and couldn't move any part of my body, I could smell the sweat, the stink, from his body and the garlic on his breath.

"Now you listen to me, Mr. Lawyer. You'd better settle the Governor's case or the next time you won't survive. Hear me? I'm going to give you something so you won't forget what I'm saying for the rest of your life."

At that moment I felt a searing pain on my left cheek and warm blood gushing down my neck. I passed out.

When I awoke I lay still, afraid to move any part of my body other than my eyes and even they hurt if I kept them open for long as the light in the room in which I was lying was blindingly bright. I was obviously in a hospital and I assumed it was the Massachusetts General. My left leg was in a cast, my shoulders were taped down to my waist, including my rib cage, so I couldn't move the upper part of my body even if I wanted to. My arms were bandaged but at least they were not strapped to my side. There was a drip of some kind embedded in my left forearm so I really couldn't move that either. My head was swathed in bandages which extended around my neck save for small openings for my eyes, ears, mouth and nose. Thankfully I was breathing on my own assisted by oxygen tubes in both nostrils.

My whole body ached; I was frightened. No one was around and I had to pee. I couldn't reach the buzzer to call the nurse so I voided my bladder right then and there and fell back to sleep partially bathed in my own warm urine.

When I awoke for the second time, I could tell it was afternoon as the sunlight suffused the whole room and my eyes didn't hurt when I opened them.

"Well, well, welcome back to the land of the living," the figure before me stated.

"You've had a tough time of it haven't you?"

My emotions at that point were mixed. I thought that the two expressions I just heard were clichés and I was going to be treated by a moron. On the other hand, I was indeed happy to be alive and thankful I was at the Mass. General Hospital.

"Where is my wife?" I managed to say through dry lips barely able to open.

"She just left. She's been here all night and all morning. She said she had to go home and be sure that the kids were all right. She said she'd be right back."

"Dr. Cunningham?" I mumbled.

"Oh yes. He was here this morning. He's your primary care physician, I guess. There have been other doctors involved in your care as well. Dr Katz, a plastic surgeon, Dr. Daniels, an orthopedic surgeon, Dr. Patelle, an anesthesiologist, Dr. LaBelle, a general surgeon and, I don't know, maybe even others. You were in the OR for quite some time."

"How do you feel?"

"Water please," I whispered.

As I drank I noticed for the first time that I had a catheter inserted into my penis. I guess they didn't want a repeat of last night's performance. After only a few moments I fell back to sleep.

When I awoke for the third time, the lights in the room were on full force but thankfully, my eyes didn't hurt once a few seconds passed. The bandages limited my vision though, as I could only see objects directly in front of me.

Andrea was sitting in a chair beside the bed reading a magazine when she noticed my eyes were open.

"Hello sweetheart. I love you," she said as she gripped my fingers and held them tight.

"I love you, too," I replied but no words came out, just lip movement.

"You're going to be all right," she told me as he squeezed my fingers even harder and bent down to kiss the bandages surrounding my face.

"They gave you a deep, gash on the side of your face which Dr. Katz said will heal. But you'll have a scar there for the rest of your life. I think it'll make you look dashing. You know, kind of a swashbuckler." She forced a laugh.

"I'll let Dr. Cunningham tell you the rest when you're ready."

I could barely make out a second person in the room but Cunningham moved from my periphery to stand along side Andrea in front of me.

"Now," I managed to say.

Cunningham looked at Andrea who gave him a shrug and a nod.

"We may as well tell him what happened. He'll think the worse otherwise," she said while looking directly at me.

"You've had a tough time Ted. The operation, I should say operations, lasted four and a half hours. You have multiple fractures of your pelvis. Four left lateral ribs were also fractured with associated pulmonary contusions. That's why it's difficult for you to breath. You also had anterior and posterior pubic rami fractures, and a fracture of the left anterior acetabular which is a cup- shaped socket in the hip bone. We inserted four screws in your pelvis and placed two bars, an external fixator, along the outside of your lower abdomen which looks like you could hang your dinner napkin on them when you go out to eat."

"You also fractured your tibia in your left leg. We inserted a titanium rod through the bone. You also sustained multiple lacerations from the shards of glass from the windshield but they should all clear up. As Andrea said however, you'll carry that scar on your left cheek forever unless Katz can work a minor miracle."

"All in all you're a pretty lucky guy. You'll have to put up with injections of a blood thinner twice a day but that's only precautionary. With therapy you should be in a walker in a few days, on crutches in a week. I've prescribed 10mg of oxycodone for pain every four to six hours."

"Kids?" was all I could manage to say.

"They're fine. They'll be here later. They send their love. I assured them you'll be all right and they're dying to see you," Andrea replied.

"When you're feeling better we have to talk about what happened to you and what you're going to do about it. The police want to talk to you also but I've been able to keep them at bay for now. You've got a lot of 'splainin' to do Lucy," but she wasn't smiling.

"E finito, padrone"

"Bene, Gulie. Will you please call Mort Haller and ask him to meet me tonight at the restaurant. Tell him the back door will be open for him at eleven-thirty."

"Certo. Subito."

At precisely eleven-thirty Mort Haller parked his car in the alley behind the restaurant and found Renzo waiting for him at his usual table, sipping a Strega. Haller could smell the anise in the small glass as soon as he sat down.

"Mr. Haller, I wanted--"

"Renzo! We've known each other for years. I've asked you many times to call me 'Mort'--"

"I prefer to keep our relationship on purely a business level. In fact it's business that I want to talk to you about."

"Before you begin, I heard from Paul Jed this afternoon. He received a call from Eldridge's office telling him that Eldridge was in the hospital with very serious injuries. We, of course, are sorry to hear that," Haller said in a low voice even though there was no one in sight. His face telegraphed a wry, conspiratorial smile.

"Yes, that took several men and was quite a risk to me. There is also the problem of money. In the past several months the "take" has gone from thirty-five thousand a week to twenty-two thousand. After we pay you twenty percent we only have about seventeen thousand to distribute to our people. That's not enough. There are too many of my people involved that make this operation to run smoothly."

"Look, Renzo! We have people who are involved also. I don't have to tell you there are three senior officers who have this precinct under their jurisdiction who have to be paid. They assign the beat cops and they have to be paid also. We're only able to add about twenty-five hundred a week to the Governor's campaign funds. We're in the throes of a run for the U.S. Senate. We'll need all the help we can get."

"Mr. Haller, that incident in the parking garage was no small affair. We don't usually get involved in such physical abuse. We run a clean book, a few drugs. It's simple. No one gets hurt. We don't do prostitution, only a little gambling—not any way near what they do in the casinos in Connecticut. You are well aware of the cocaine we get for very special people--it's a service. "

"Have you forgotten what we did for your daughter? She's on the bench now through our efforts alone."

"Yes and she's going through a tough time as a result of the pressure you're putting on her," Renzo quickly replied in a harsh tone, which was unusual for him.

"She's under a lot of stress. She calls me every day," he continued.

"Mr. Haller, I'm only recommending a cut of two and a half percent. That's only about five hundred dollars a week. If we charged you fifty thousand dollars for the recent trick, it would take one hundred weeks for you to equal the reduction. Why don't we try it for say, six months? See how it goes. See whether the "take" increases; that'd make us all happy."

"Well, uh--"

"We'll keep the price on the Governor's habit the same, no increase. How's that?"

"I'll get back to you, Renzo," Haller replied. "It sounds OK for a while anyway, but, as I've said, we have big expenses in store for us with this run at the Senate."

When Charley Randall returned from his sojourn in Las Vegas he went straight to Jake Bauer's apartment. The three day vacation with his wife turned into ten and he felt guilty especially after he heard about Jake's encounter on Mt. Vernon Street. Jake was hobbling around on crutches after his knee replacement three days earlier. He had only just returned from his first physical therapy appointment an hour before Charley arrived.

"Jake, I received a call while Eleanor and I were in Las Vegas. I'm sorry this happened. I feel responsible. We'll find out who did this and we'll make them pay, you'll see."

"Ah, this is just an occupational hazard, Charley," Jake replied as he navigated to the couch in his living room.

"No, you don't understand. Ted Eldridge told me just before I left that he wanted to call off the surveillance of the Judge and concentrate on the Governor. We didn't think another few days would matter so I didn't tell you. If I had you wouldn't be in this fix."

"They tell me my new knee is better than the old one so I'll be back in action in only a few weeks. They can't keep an old tight-end down. I've had worse injuries playing for State."

"Any idea who did this to you?"

"I've thought about it a little," Jake replied rubbing his chin thoughtfully.

"I honestly believe the Judge got a little antsy when she noticed someone was following her and watching her street. I tried to be careful, to avoid her seeing me but she's no fool. She probably spotted me and called her father. Those guys who got to me twice didn't speak the King's English, y'know. They were from the North End all right, part of Renzo's gang—that Guiliano what's his name--" He paused...

"So, now what?" Jake asked.

"So now I'm going to take over and keep the Governor under surveillance. Tommy Delaney, your temporary replacement, will spell me every other day. I'm going to pick the Governor up when he leaves the State House. I've got someone to call me on my cell phone when he leaves. The time has come when we'd better produce some results or we can kiss our business with Eldridge goodbye.

Oh, by the way, you heard, didn't you that the kid, Emily's son, overdosed on some drugs he got a hold of earlier this week? He's going to be alright though."

"That's too bad," Jake replied

"This case is turning out to be a pisser," Charley said after a long sigh.

"So far we've made a small fortune though, I suppose we can't complain," he continued.

"Take care of yourself, Jake. I'll keep you informed."

When Charley returned to his office his telephone was blinking a message.

"Charley, this is Harry Baker. Ted Eldridge is in the Mass. General. He's in pretty bad shape. We believe he was attacked by the same people who left the note warning him to settle or he could expect trouble. Well, he got trouble in spades. He'll be all right, though. He'll be out of commission for a couple of weeks at least. In the mean time, if you have anything to report, call me. I'll try and keep you up to date on Ted's condition."

Oh, and just in case you haven't heard, Emily's son overdosed on some drugs just before the hearing we had earlier this week and had to be rushed to the hospital. He'll be alright too. He's back home already.

Just another day at the office, I guess. Take care of yourself."

Those bastards, Charley thought as the message ended. First Jake and now Eldridge.

Late that evening, Charley waited outside Renzo's restaurant until the last customers, an elderly man accompanied by a young blond hanging on his arm, got into their car and drove away. The sign was already in the window signifying that the restaurant was closed as soon as they left. A few minutes later, two waiters, still dressed in their black trousers and red cummerbunds, opened the front door and disappeared into the dark of Hanover Street. Charley waited another half hour until a bent old man, a cigarette drooping from his mouth, his white shirt outside his white, soiled, work pants, opened the front door while balancing a take out carton in his left hand. He also disappeared into the shadows of the street. Charley thought he must be the dishwasher and the last to leave save Gulie and Renzo himself.

Another ten minutes and Gulie opened the door. Charley waited to be sure no one else was coming out. He withdrew his Glock from his waistband and walked carefully up behind his quarry. He was able to get so close to Gulie he could smell his acrid after shave lotion.

He grabbed Gulie across his left shoulder and covered his mouth with his left hand. With the butte of his gun in his right hand, Charley rapped Gulie on the side of his head, just hard enough to stun him but not hard enough to knock him out.

"You bastards have done enough. You've taken down my man and you went after Eldridge-- you almost killed him. Now you listen to me, you wop son of a bitch. If you or any of your people lift a finger to harm any one connected with that case, that finger and the rest of its hand will be mailed to you, special delivery. The rest of the body will be stuffed in the dumpster behind your fucking restaurant."

He let Gulie slump to the sidewalk and pointed the Glock against his left kneecap.

"Let's see, was it Jake's right or the left? I guess it doesn't matter much." He pulled the trigger and blasted Gulie's kneecap to pieces.

Amid the scream of his victim, Charley put the gun back in his pants and calmly walked away.

Three days later, the shadowed figure, resplendent in a suit, white shirt, blue tie and shiny black brogues, parked under the trees on West Cedar Street and entered number eighteen.

Charley parked his car closer to Pinckney Street but still had a full view of his target. He watched as the house, now totally in darkness, suddenly came to life as the lights went on throughout the first floor. Charley ran back to Pinckney Street and down Cedar Lane Way to look at the rear of the house to see if the lights in the back were also on. He stopped halfway down the street and flattened himself against the brick wall of town house as he saw the Governor open the wooden door at the side of Judge Rhea Andretti's house and enter.

Just as I thought, Charley said to himself. I'll be goddamned!

Once inside, they embraced and kissed even before Brenden Mitchell took his suit coat off.

"What's the matter?" the Governor asked Rhea as he held her slightly away from him but still with his arms around her.

"How can you tell so quickly?" she said to him, turning away from him towards the small bar in the kitchen to fix drinks.

"It's in the kiss, as the song goes," he replied, taking off his jacket and tie and placing them on the back of a kitchen chair.

She was surprised he knew the name of the song. He could be so out of touch with the mainstream, sometimes even with reality, as he insulated himself with only his people.

She mixed a martini for him and poured herself a glass of Chardonnay. When they were seated on the couch in the little room off the kitchen, she clicked his glass with hers.

"Cheers!" she said to him, and sipped a small portion of her wine, looking at him over the brim of her glass.

"Cheers," he replied.

"Now, will you tell me what's wrong?"

"What's wrong? You don't go to the hearings," she said to him, accusingly.

"You know, we just had a second hearing and they're getting to me. If you ever treated me the way you treat your wife-- we'd be, you'd be finished," she said.

"Those pictures--"

"I really have no excuse Rhea, but she attacks me and I lose control. She knows how to inflame me when she says I'm not Danny's father," he interrupted.

"The lawyers are so combative," she said. "I'm at my wits end. I've got a lot on the line, you know. I just found out that Ted Eldridge got beat-up in his parking garage as he was leaving work. The timing isn't lost on me, you must be aware of what's going on. Danny, as you know, overdosed on drugs. I can't take any more of this. I'm scared to death. I love you but this is too much for me to take," she repeated.

"You know if anyone found out about us --" she stopped in mid-sentence.

"Here we are," she continued. "I'm sitting as a judge on your case in the daytime while we screw each others brains out at night."

She began to cry.

Mitchell put his arm around her.

"There's a way out," he said to her in a low voice.

"I agree this was a wrong approach. We should never have involved you. It was just that Paul Jed knew how to make sure you were the judge at the beginning of the case and things just fell into place after that. Mort felt sure it'd be all right."

"I know my father is playing a role in all this," she said to him hesitantly.

"He's a big boy and can take care of himself," he replied.

"Your business with him is not my affair," she added, almost hopefully, "Is it?"

"No, you're not involved with any of that. Don't worry."

"Brenden, I'm going to recuse myself before it's too late. I can't go on. There's too much at stake," she said to him, gathering some timbre in her voice.

"I quite agree. Now, don't worry any more," he whispered as he pressed his face close to hers on the couch and slipped the strap of her shift off her shoulder.

"Let's finish our drinks later," he said into her ear."

Charley Randell was ecstatic. All that hard work, his hunch, all those hours finally paid off as he watched the Governor steal across Cedar Lane Way into the back entrance of 18 West Cedar Street. Charley skirted around Pinckney Street and looked down West Cedar as all the lights were extinguished in the Edmond's house. The Governor didn't waste any time getting into his car and Charley, at last could calmly, happily, leave his assignment, confident that there'd be no other stops that the Governor would make before he went home to his sister's house-unless he was an iron man.

The next morning, Charley called Henry Baker.

"Henry," Charley began as soon as Baker answered the phone.

"I've got him, just as I suspected. The Governor, for chrissakes, it's the Governor whose been schtupping the Judge. Can you believe it?"

"Hold on, Charley, hold on. Tell me what happened," Henry said into the phone so no one could overhear as if it was he who was making the disclosure.

Charley related the events in detail and finished his story with a flourish by saying, "How about them apples!"

"What if they're just friends and have taken steps to keep their friendship private?" Henry replied, ever the lawyer.

"In order to prove adultery you don't have to be a fly on the wall, so to speak, but you do have to prove "opportunity" and "inclination", Henry continued, processing the information he just received, trying to sort it out.

"What--are you nuts?" We've got the Governor of the Commonwealth of Massachusetts by the short hairs!"

"Look, Charley, what if the Governor develops an alibi? It was dark. You were yards away. You couldn't be sure. He says he was with someone else at a card game or something. It's not a slam dunk at this stage. Let me go to Ted with this and I'll get back to you."

"Nice work, Charley," he added.

Charley decided that he'd keep his meeting with Renzo's man to himself. No sense getting any one else involved.

"OK, bye Henry."

CHAPTER EIGHTEEN

Dr. Sheila Monaghan had met with Danny at the house on Warren Street after he returned from the hospital. Emily was not very hospitable and Danny was not very communicative. The meeting didn't last very long. The doctor knew in advance that the visit would not be very productive but she had her own agenda.

The person she really wanted to interview was Dr. James Hurley. Just what kind of parent would Emily make if she was on drugs? That was the big question.

And what about her drinking? She was anxious to get answers to these and other questions she planned to ask.

This poor kid was going through a lot she knew, taking responsibility for the break-up between his mother and father, taking drugs himself, lethargic, a vacant stare when asked the simplest question, lying about all day...

She was determined to get all the information she needed from both sides to make a recommendation to the Judge that was the right thing for Danny, a recommendation that was in his best interest and to hell with Emily and the Governor.

Dr. Monaghan also knew that Paul Jed was anxious to depose Dr. Hurley. In a telephone call, Jed told her that as soon as he had returned from the hearing authorizing him to take the doctor's deposition, he made arrangements for a date. Of course,Ted Eldridge wouldn't be there-- he was still in the hospital-- but time was running out. In fact, Jed told Monaghan, that he and Eldridge's associate had agreed to shorten the notice requirement for the deposition to accommodate her. Emily had already told Monaghan she didn't plan to be there.

There was not much Henry Baker had to do to prepare for Hurley's deposition. He visited Ted Eldridge at the hospital to get instructions from him but all Ted said was, "Let him go. He's a psycho- pharmacologist. He's got to know what he's doing. There's nothing we can do to change his diagnosis, or for that matter, his prognosis."

At the agreed upon time at Paul Jed's office, Dr. James Hurley appeared. Henry Baker watched him closely as he came into the conference room. He saw Hurley was a man about forty-five years old, thin, with close-cropped hair sprinkled with flecks of grey, a fair complexion, and piercing blue eyes set above his straight, rather small nose. He wore a silk blue blazer, enhanced by a maroon handkerchief in the left hand breast pocket, placed there in an apparent reckless fashion, but, on close observation, the points showed perfectly above the edge of the pocket. He wore a pair of light grey slacks, a white shirt and a maroon and white rep tie.

Even so, Baker prided himself on the old bromide that he could tell everything about a man by his shoes and his watch. Dr. Hurley had on a pair of black Ferragamo loafers, no socks and a Rolex watch which showed just below the cuff of his shirt. All in all, a very impressive figure, Henry thought.

When he was introduced to those around the conference table he had a quick, vulpine grin as he greeted everyone affably.

Ten minutes into the deposition, after the preliminaries were dispensed with, Henry observed that Paul Jed didn't waste any time getting into the heart of the matter.

"Dr. Hurley, is it your diagnosis that Emily Mitchell is bi-polar?"

"She has episodes of depression and times when she's ebullient."

"Does she lose control?"

"That's what the medication is for."

"Is she a good parent?"

"What does that mean?"

"When she's depressed is she able to function?"

"The medication brings her up."

"When she's, what? ebullient, is she able to function?"

"The medication brings her down."

"So when she takes the medication does she have times when she's up and/or times when she's down?"

"The medication reduces her highs and lows."

"What about her consumption of alcohol?"

"What about it?"

"Does she drink when she's taking the medication?"

"Drink what?"

"Drink wine, alcohol!"

"She used to."

"When did she stop?"

"I'm not certain."

And so it went for ninety minutes. Henry Baker didn't say a word, never accepted the opportunity to cross examine the deponent and was happy to collect his yellow pads with not much written on them when the deposition was over. He noticed, on the other hand, that Paul Jed was clearly exasperated. Baker knew the reason. Jed was never able to rattle the witness; never even able to score any hits. Dr. James Hurley was in control throughout.

It wasn't long after Jed's deposition of Hurley that Dr. Sheila Monaghan met with the Doctor. She wasn't any more successful than Jed had been but neither was she as frustrated or disappointed with the results.

She arranged with Haller to see Danny again at his father's home, or at least the home where he was staying on Dudley Street. Each time she attempted to talk with Danny, whether alone or in the presence of his father or his aunt, the boy was quiet, taciturn and uncommunicative. Something was definitely wrong.

Before she left the Governor after her meeting with Danny was being brought to a close, she spoke to him about her concern. "Governor, Danny needs help. You've got to arrange for him to see a psychiatrist, his very own doctor."

"My son doesn't need a psychiatrist, he needs to live with me and not that decrepit, alcoholic that pretends to be his mother," he said shooting her a disdainful look.

Almost as if he realized whom he was talking to and the responsibility she carried, he instantly changed his tune.

"If you really think we need to get help for Danny though Doctor, I won't stand in the way to do whatever I can to assist him. Whatever it is, I'll do," he said amiably.

"I'll speak to his mother and see if she'll agree. Do you have anyone in mind, Governor?"

"No, no. Whoever you say is all right with me," he replied.

The next day, when Dr. Monaghan called Emily to see if she'd agree to have Danny see a psychiatrist, her reaction was instant.

"Not another one, please," she said.

"There's Long, there's you, there's Hurley. How many does it take?"

"Emily, as many as we need to help your son. He's got to get his act together before school starts in September. In fact, you and his father will have to have a plan for Danny at the time of the trial. Be reasonable. You have your own psychiatrist. Danny needs his."

Toward the end of my first week in the hospital, I had made some small progress. The catheter, praise God, was removed and I could go to the bathroom on my own --with difficulty. I was up on a walker at first, and then was able to become slightly more mobile with crutches. When the bandages were all remove from my face, I could see the knife slash on my cheek. It was a bright red gash laced with black stitches which, I was assured, would dissolve eventually. The other cuts and abrasions on my face and other parts of my body were already beginning to show signs of healing and I was told that there'd be no scarring there.

My left leg was still in a cast and my chest and lower abdomen were still bandaged. My breathing improved from those first days when every breath was painful. I was even developing a positive attitude, trying to overcome my malaise and restlessness.

"You have a visitor, Mr. Eldridge," the nurse announced to me one afternoon about two-thirty.

"Hello," Emily Mitchell said tentatively as she entered the room shielding her eyes from the bright sun that was shining through the windows behind my bed.

"Hello Emily," I replied. "How are you?"

"I'm fine, the question is how are you?"

"I'm on the mend. Sit here and bring me up to date. How's Danny?"

"To tell you the truth, I'm not sure. That's one thing I want to talk to you about. Paul Jed took the deposition of James Hurley..."

"Yes, I know," I said to her.

"Henry told me all about it. Jed didn't lay a finger on Hurley, so there's nothing for you to worry about. Dr. Monaghan took his deposition also. No problem there either," I continued.

"I spoke with Dr. Monaghan about Danny. She thinks he needs his own psychiatrist and she even got George to agree," she said while knotting her handkerchief in her hands nervously.

"It can't hurt, can it?" I said to her.

"Well yes. It seems he's seeing too many people now. People who are prodding him, asking questions, making him anxious. Do I add yet another one to the mix?"

"I think you should, Emily. Don't waste any more time. The doctor will need some time to make his evaluation and we have a trial in a little more than a month."

"*We?* Are you able to represent me? Can you possibly? Shouldn't I get another lawyer?"

"Do you want to?"

"Of course not, but if you're not feeling up to it..."

"Emily, I haven't had a chance to tell anyone this, especially my wife, but I fully intend to prepare for and conduct the trial of this case. I'll hobble around the courtroom on crutches but I'll be mobile. I'll have Jordan Levy and Harry to assist me. At their hourly rate you might even get off cheaper when the case is over."

"Mr. Eldridge, I'm relieved, but at this stage, dollars and cents are important. I'm way behind your fees already. If we don't win this case I'll be in pretty bad shape. I don't know what I'll do."

"There's nothing you can do about the fees at this point. There's nothing I can do about them either," I said to her. I didn't want to tell her about my two hundred fifty thousand loan. That was my problem.

"There's going to be some rough sledding for you, Emily. Rough sledding for me too. I'm going to write out every question I'm going to ask you when I put you on the stand. After every question, I'm going to write down your answers. You will memorize the entire examination. When you're finished with that, you'll memorize the answers to the questions I think Paul Jed will ask you on his cross examination. Are you up to all that?"

"I'll do it. Don't worry about me; and thank you," she said.

All that was well and good but after she left, I still had to face Andrea and tell her I was going to continue on with this case. That was another matter entirely. And the investment? I wonder how that's going, I thought.

The day after Emily Mitchell's visit to the hospital, Henry Baker came to see me. I still had not worked up the courage to talk to Andrea about my resuming Emily's case and I was feeling guilty about that.

Henry told me about the conversation he had with Charley and at first, I was elated. As Henry and I began to analyze Charley's report, we began to take opposite sides of the issue.

"Ted, we put Charley on the stand and he testifies he saw the Governor visit the Judge at her house from about eight forty-five until after midnight. C'mon they weren't playing cribbage all that time."

"You said Charley was about fifty yards from the entrance to the houses at both Cedar Lane Way and West Cedar Street when he saw the guy go in, right?"

"So?"

"So, he could be mistaken. It was dark. The Governor develops an alibi. He was at a meeting with three of his cronies during that time. He wasn't even there, he says under oath."

"But the Governor, the defendant in a divorce case, which case is pending before the very Judge he's visiting, drops by at eight forty-five at night to say what-- Hello?"

"There's certainly an impropriety there..."

"Impropriety! Ted, that's enough to get her disbarred!"

"We have to prove it, Harry. We have to prove it was the Governor. How do we do that? At best it'll be Charley's word against the Governor's and a gang of witnesses who'll support him. Do you possibly think that as a result of my rapier cross examination that the Governor will say, 'Stop it. You win. It was I who had a sexual relationship with the very Judge that's sitting on my divorce case'?"

"Ted, there's no need for sarcasm. Of course I don't believe that. But hell..."

"I'm sorry, Henry. You're right. I shouldn't be sarcastic. It's just that it gets frustrating lying here and being out of the loop. You're going to have to carry the ball to a great extent in the next couple of weeks. Here it is August. We only have about five or six weeks to get ready for trial on the sixth of September."

"What's the status of the custody issue?" Henry asked.

"That's pretty much out of our hands. There's the GAL, Donald Long. He's been visiting Emily, the Governor, Danny and Danny's school. Dr. Monaghan has been doing the same thing, conducting her investigation. Nothing we can do to affect either of their conclusions. Then there's Dr. Gerber. His report is long overdue. Why don't you call him and shake him up a little, Henry?"

"I'm on it."

"By the way," I continued, the adrenaline taking over." Emily is going to bring Danny to his own psychiatrist. That's another witness we'll have to provide for. What he'll testify to is also out of our hands. Hopefully, we'll know what he's going to say before trial."

"Ted, what about the privilege? We'll have to get the Governor's approval for him to testify, won't we?

I don't want to go before Andretti again. I'm thinking we can subpoena Danny's shrink, put him on the stand and make Jed take the position that they don't want him to testify. They'll look like they have something to hide and I'm betting the Judge will want to hear what the doctor has to say about Danny's mental health.

That's four people testifying about custody, including Dr. Gerber. When we submit our witness list, Jed will probably hire his own doctor to counter Gerber's testimony, won't he?"

"I don't think so. He's either Danny's father or he isn't based on ninety-nine percent accuracy from the lab report. Remember, even if he's not Danny's biological father, he'll still most likely have to pay child support. We have to ask ourselves what we'll accomplish by proving that the Governor is not Danny's father. Will that sway the Judge's opinion about exclusive custody or will we look like 'bullies' and have the tactic backfire?"

"Good question," Henry replied thoughtfully.

"There's something else I've been thinking about. It will add another layer to the custody issue but if we decide not to use Gerber's testimony we could substitute someone else's," I said to Henry, knowing I'd peak his interest.

"Uh oh! Now what do you have up your sleeve besides those bandages," Henry said, with a wry smile.

"I'll bet the Governor and Paul Jed would agree to the appointment of a forensic psychiatrist, you know like the one we had in the Fitzpatrick case. The psychiatrist we mutually agree upon would see both the Governor and Emily, have his associate who is a psychologist, submit a battery of tests to each of them and the psychiatrist would then reach a conclusion about the character of each as it relates to who is more suitable to have exclusive custody of Danny. What do you think?"

"I'll bet the Governor's pride would compel him to agree," Henry replied. "He thinks his wife is a basket case, besides. He may believe that Donald Long is in his corner but he can't rely on the recommendation of Dr. Monaghan. Let's do it! What do we have to lose?"

"OK. Talk to Emily then and get her approval. After she agrees, put the proposition to Paul Jed. We'll have to find a psychiatrist who has the time to put this together in such a short period but money talks. I'm certain the Governor will take the time from his busy schedule to meet with these people if he thinks it'll benefit him."

My head fell back onto the pillow. I was exhausted. I hadn't realized I was half sitting up the whole time I was talking and planning our strategy with Henry. I think I remember seeing Henry leave but I can't be sure, my eyes were almost closed as soon as I stopped talking.

By Wednesday of the following week, Paul Jed was on the phone with Mort Haller as soon as he received phone calls from two different sources.

"Mort, I just received a call from the courthouse. Judge Andretti has recused herself from our case this morning," he was almost out of breath but he continued.

"She filed a statement with the chief judge saying she was in poor health and requested that her entire caseload be reduced temporarily until she recovers."

"Well I'll be--"

"I understand that Judge Talbot has been designated to take her place in our case. The chief divided much of her remaining caseload among the other judges."

"This is not good news for us Paul. We would have been given the benefit of any doubts with Andretti, now, who knows?"

"At least Talbot knows what he's doing," Jed continued. "He knows his rules of evidence and he understands complicated valuations."

"There's nothing we can do about it," replied Haller.

"I think..."

"Wait, there's more. The second call I received was from Henry Baker, Ted Eldridge's associate. They want us to agree to a *forensic psychiatrist*," he said with emphasis to be sure Mort understood.

"With a little over a month to go, they want to add another shrink, for crissakes," Jed sputtered.

"What will that do to us, Paul?" Haller asked in a calm, measured tone. "Will it help us or hurt us, You're the lawyer, what's your advice?"

"How the hell do I know. Those kinds of shrinks administer a bunch of tests, ask a lot of questions and come up with a composite of who the hell you are."

"How will that hurt us? Emily is one step from a complete nervous breakdown. The Governor thinks she's lost control with a combination of booze and drugs. Won't this forensic guy uncover that? Besides, the Governor is pretty cool when he's being examined. He should come out ahead on this. Let me bring this to his attention and I'll get back to you."

Later that afternoon, Haller told Jed to go ahead and agree to the appointment of the shrink.

"As a matter of fact, the Governor is quite anxious to participate, Paul. Just make sure the psychiatrist you agree to is a person with impeccable credentials. Clear?"

At this point Paul Jed needed all the help he could get. He had to prepare Dr. Lionel Gagne and listen to Gagne's two associates, Foley and Graham from Cambridge Business Investors, as they droned on with their convoluted accounting dialogue, none of which Jed really understood. He had to prepare the Governor who didn't want to listen to his admonitions against developing a belligerent attitude when he assumed the stand. But it was the Governor who had to carry the day testifying that Emily was incapable of fulfilling her role as a custodial parent. He wasn't looking forward to that. Most importantly, he had to prepare his cross examination of Emily. He was certain he could destroy her but he had to be careful with her at the same time. And that Dr. Hurley! What an inscrutable witness he turned out to be. He'd have to show that he was biased in favor of his patient, the person who was paying him his fee. And then there was his real estate expert, Byron Hackett that needed preparation. He couldn't bring himself to think of all the other people he had to cross examine and the work that that was going to entail.

Depositions were another thorn in his side. He had to arrange to take the deposition of Eldridge's experts and he certainly wasn't looking forward to getting up to speed for that confrontation no matter how important they'd be at the trial.

CHAPTER NINETEEN

I stayed in the hospital for a full week and waited until I was discharged before I opened the discussion with Andrea about resuming the case. During that week I was able to talk with Henry and Jordan mostly on the phone, but I could tell they must've received the word not to excite me or tire me with developing details because our conversations were clipped. They were smart enough not to say a word about the case when Andrea was with me.

On Thursday, following my release, Josh and Mandy weren't home. They came to the hospital with Andrea on Wednesday to take me home but left shortly after for the beach in Connecticut. Andrea and I had a nice dinner complete with candles and cloth napkins sitting in the dining room instead of the area off the kitchen where the family usually congregated at meal times. I even had a little wine against doctor's orders .We watched the six-thirty news on ABC while sitting on the couch in the living room and relaxed sipping a little of what was left of the Merlot from dinner. I wasn't looking forward to the confrontation.

"So-- let's talk." I began.

"Yes, let's talk," she interrupted.

"It's about time," she said, placing her glass carefully on the coffee table.

"And before you begin, let me tell you something," she stated emphatically.

"There are four people here, not just you, so I don't want to hear how much you want to continue with this case. You haven't talked about one other case in your office since Emily Mitchell walked in. It's like you're on a mission, you're too invested with your client; it's as if you have something to prove. Well, you don't have anything to prove to her. You have something to prove to me!" She didn't stop to allow me to say a word.

"That junior high attitude you have, that pay-back motivation you cultivate against the Governor is the cause of all this," she said sweeping her arm over the cast and bandages around my abdomen.

"Your life is in danger, for crissakes." She never swore. She was wound tighter than a drum.

"Andrea, please--listen to me. This was their best shot and I'm going to be fine. Once I'm up and about they, whoever 'they' are won't have another chance. I simply can't back out now. There's not one lawyer in the Commonwealth who'd take this case with only a month to go. The fact that there can be no continuances is already on the record. I'm determined to see this through. There are too many people depending on me…"

"We're depending on you, Ted! We, your family… your wife and two children! You could be killed by these people, don't you understand? The police haven't a clue who did this. They're not going to be any help…"

"Andrea, Andrea, nothing else is going to happen to me. Please just give me this opportunity to bring this bastard down, this cretin who wouldn't give me the time of day, this guy who beats his wife and ignores his kid, this pariah who imposes himself on the people of this state. You're right, I'm involved. I'm involved and I want to stay involved."

I took a breath and with effort, moved closer to her on the couch. It hurt too much to raise my arm so all I could do was place my still bandaged head next to hers.

"Andrea, please don't worry, I'll be fine."

She wasn't convinced, but she knew me well enough not to draw a line in the sand. She didn't say anything more. She never once brought up the money we'd just borrowed. She really never grasped the severity of our money problem, mostly because she didn't know how much it costs to run that office at Old City Hall for a month. I didn't say a word either. She patted my hand, took another sip of wine and focused on Charles Gibson and the news.

For the rest of that week, I busied myself going to the re-hab clinic every day for three hours each day. I was able to get along on crutches pretty well and tried to avoid the walker which made my progress a little slower. I kept thinking to myself about the oft repeated criticism of my personality: that I had to hit every rut in the road but it was too late in the game for any behavior modification. By the middle of the next week, all the bandages on my face were removed and the purple scar on my left cheek stood out in a purple and red line. It hurt like hell when I shaved. The stitches were still visible and it certainly didn't make me look like Errol Flynn or some other handsome swordsman from central casting. Rather, it was nothing but an ugly scar which was six centimeters long curving under my left cheek bone and pointing toward the bottom of my left ear.

The cast was still on my left leg of course, but my trousers covered that. I hobbled around on my crutches with difficulty. The bandages around the plate in my abdomen were removed and the two bars in front were all that could be seen when I lifted my shirt. The bandages around my ribs were also removed.

By the following Monday, I was ready to get back to work. Henry kept me abreast of the action which was rapidly developing while I was at home but I wanted to get back into it, to feel the dynamics, to get back into the swing of things.

It was a major task to get me into the car. Andrea, not terribly happy to begin with, fussed and fumed over my medications, my bandages, the ointment for the scar, the clothes I was wearing and a whole host of other things she thought of.

"How are you going to go to the bathroom? How will you climb the stairs? Will you be able to take a nap?" On and on--all the way into the city.

"Call me when you're ready to come home. Don't work all day, please!"

I got out of the car gladly, but with some difficulty and entered Old City Hall from the rear entrance facing only a couple of steps to maneuver. The elevator came down to that floor, thankfully.

Henry told me, as soon as I settled in, that Emily had brought Danny to a well respected child psychiatrist by the name of Zachary R. Rollins. The doctor had already met with Danny and the initial report was that all went well. Nothing I could do there but wait. But time was getting short--only about four weeks to September sixth and the long Labor Day weekend occurred just before the trial.

I asked Henry and Jordan to prepare for a meeting with me at one o'clock that very day to make sure I was brought up to date and that nothing had slipped between the cracks while I was away.

The mail was delivered about eleven that morning and there was a notice from the Suffolk Probate and Family Court to appear for a status conference with Judge Richard Talbot the following Wednesday. Talbot! What happened to Andretti? I wondered.

"Amy! Please have Henry and Jordan come in," I said to her in as measured a voice as I could manage.

As soon as they came in I didn't wait for them to sit down

"Did either of you know anything about Talbot sitting on our case instead of Andretti?"

They looked at one another and I knew instantly they had no clue.

"What do you mean?" Jordan asked, looking a little helpless.

"I just received a notice to appear before Talbot for a status conference day after tomorrow. Two days notice! What the hell is going on over there?"

They both looked at me and shrugged simultaneously as if they were on stage ready to perform a soft shoe dance.

Just as I was about to say something Amy buzzed me.

"Paul Jed on three." She said.

I thought to myself, now what?

"Ted, how are you feeling? I'm terribly sorry about your accident. I thought I'd be speaking to Henry this morning after I heard about all your injuries."

"I'm on the mend, Paul, What can I do for you?"

"I think your suggestion of a forensic psychiatrist is an excellent idea and the Governor will agree. But Ted, we have to start right away. Do you have anyone in mind?"

"As a matter of fact, I do. Dr. Justin Feingold. Have you ever used him?"

"No, but I've heard of him. Who hasn't? He's the leading psychiatrist over at McLean's and I'm sure he'll do fine. To save some time, I'll ask the Governor to schedule an immediate appointment. Feingold's a busy guy but this is a high profile case and I'm sure he'll agree. If Ms. Mitchell will also call for an appointment right away, I hope we can get started without any delay."

"That sounds fine Paul, but who's going to pay for all this?"

"Don't worry about that. I'll have the Governor pay for all the consultations it takes to get a final report."

"There's one condition to our agreeing to Feingold, Ted."

"Uh oh, Paul, here it comes."

"It's no big thing, Ted. It's just that those pictures you have of Emily could cause us some embarrassment. You've already received your restraining order and when the divorce is over you won't need one anymore. We've got a GAL, Dr. Monaghan and now, if we can agree, Dr. Feingold, so what's the sense of introducing those pictures at trial. If you agree to destroy those pictures, we'll agree to Feingold and let the chips fall as they may. What do you say?"

I had to think for a second--cause him some embarrassment, that's exactly what they're supposed to do.

"No deal, Paul. Feingold will diffuse the custody issue and reduce it to a question of what is truly in Danny's best interest. There will be no winner or loser, simply a clinical evaluation of the parenting skills of both parties."

"If you insist that those pictures be introduced we have a problem with Feingold. Let me get back to my client and I'll call you."

Not thirty minutes later Jed called back.

"OK, Ted. We'll agree to Feingold but the Governor is pissed. We'll just have to pull out all the stops and let the testimony about Emily and her habits carry the day."

"You'll do what you have to do, Paul. Thanks for calling."

When I hung up the phone I told Henry and Jordan that Jed agreed on Feingold. They both broke out in wide grins as though they just received a raise in pay.

"They agreed? What do you know! There is a God," Jordan exclaimed.

"What was all that about the pictures?" Henry asked.

"They wanted me to agree that we wouldn't introduce the pictures of Emily. I told them I would not agree. They caved, that's all.

One of you should call the courthouse and find out what happened to Andretti. And also, will one of you get me an update on Chuck Dawson's status? Call Emily and ask her to come in. Time is running out. Call Dr. Gerber and --"

All of a sudden the room started spinning and I felt dizzy. I had been sitting in my oversized chair behind my desk but the next thing I knew, Jordan and Henry were bending over me as I was lying in the floor.

"Leave him on the floor," Henry ordered Jordan as he knelt behind me and cupped my head in his hands, raising my shoulders somewhat.

"Just lie there Ted," Henry instructed.

"Don't move," Jordan added.

I started to get up but Henry had a firm grip on my upper body so I didn't fight him. My leg felt OK but my head hurt. The metal shelf on my abdomen apparently didn't move either what with all those bolts holding it in place.

"All right," I said, "Just let me lie here for a couple of minutes."

"Ted, I'm going to call Andrea and have her come and pick you up. You've done quite enough for your first day back," Henry told me.

I didn't fight them. I knew I could use a rest, but the adrenalin was still pumping from the events of the morning, when three people helped me get into the car for the ride back to Brookline.

The following day I felt a little better and, despite Andrea's remonstrations, I decided to go back to the office. I had to listen to all the reasons why I should stay home during the entire trip into the city, but I blocked all that out and by the time we reached the back entrance to Old City Hall, I couldn't wait to get out of the car.

As soon as I settled into my office, I called Clyde Lawler.

"Clyde, what's the story on the permitting for the new mall?"

"Ted, I was afraid to call you. I heard that you were in the hospital and I didn't want to add to your problems."

"Don't tell me that--"

"I'm afraid so. The last application the Appellate Board of Appeals was denied. All the other permits fell like dominoes. The whole project has failed."

"What about my money, my two hundred and fifty thousand dollars?"

"Your two-fifty just like my three hundred is gone. I wish to hell I never told you about this investment but I thought it was a good way for you to make some money in the short run. I'm sorry, that's all I can say."

I slammed down the phone and sunk into my chair. Two hundred and fifty thousand dollars! And that was just part of it. I only had about twenty thousand left on my credit line at the bank. Not enough to pay the expenses at the end of the month, and we had a month to go before the trial even starts.

"Jesus Christ!" I said aloud.

Henry and Jordan were ready for me Amy said when she buzzed me, but I told her to have them wait. I needed time to collect myself. After a while, thinking my options were limited or even non existent, I decided I'd try and borrow some money from my bank on an unsecured note-- if they'd do it. I had to force myself to put the problem out of my mind, I thought. I had to concentrate on this case. My salvation was to win the case for Emily--and get paid!

"Ask them to come in," I told Amy.

As soon as they came in the door, I could tell they were hesitant. It was obvious to me they were reluctant to burden me with the fast moving details of the case. Henry told me that Dr. Gerber's test results came back and Gerber was ninety-nine per cent sure that Danny was not the Governor's child. He couldn't stop there. Despite his concern for my health, he continued without skipping a beat.

"Mort Haller called after you left yesterday noon and said the Governor promptly made an appointment with Dr. Feingold. In fact, the appointment is today. I called Emily and told her about Feingold. He paused for the first time that morning."

"Ted, she was a bear. 'Not another psychiatrist' she bellowed at me. She became almost hysterical. I had to explain in detail that a forensic psychiatrist was your idea. I told her what a forensic psychiatrist was, what his job was going to be and why it would be helpful to our case. I didn't do as good a job as you but she finally calmed down. I told her that time was essential and she had to make an appointment right away; that Dr. Feingold was a very busy person and we were lucky if he takes the case on such short notice."

"There's more," he continued.

Judge Andretti recused herself from our case and Judge Talbot is rumored to take her place."

"Wow! That's fantastic," I exclaimed, summoning up enthusiasm I really didn't share. At least there's that, I thought to myself.

"That's three pieces of good news," I said.

Jordan piped in.

"I called Dawson Associates and spoke to Chuck. He said he could verify Lester's finding that the Governor manipulated two million dollars which should wind up in his personal account but there was more, much more. He asked if we could get the bank records of the Governor's campaign accounts. He thinks there's a link between those accounts and a mysterious source of income that's being transferred from one account to another. The mystery deepens when the funds that are transferred to his personal accounts are transferred on the same day of the week, every week, fifty-two weeks a year. Who the hell makes contributions like that?"

"That's a new twist of discovery for me. I've never faced that issue before. There's a status conference tomorrow. Why don't you spend the rest of the day researching whether it's a violation of privacy to obtain those records. Perhaps we could agree to redact the names of the contributors. Check the Federal Statutes too. There has to be a way to uncover a fraud even when the fraud involves campaign funds. I know the Congress conducts inquiries into misappropriations but I'm not sure what happens at the state level," I said to him.

"Perhaps the rightful person to make an inquiry is the State Attorney General," Henry, always thinking, added.

"Now, that's an intriguing thought," I replied. I was getting into it.

"The Attorney General, Anthony Mariani, just happens to be a friend of mine. More importantly, he's no friend of Brenden Mitchell." I paused, the wheels were turning.

"Get me the report of Chuck Dawson. Ask him if he'll sign his findings so far under the pains of perjury, you know like a full general audit. I'll take them up to Mariani and ask him what he makes of it all. Wouldn't it be cool if the Attorney General conducts the investigation for us?"

"You bet," Henry replied.

"And Jordan, don't lose sight of the business valuations Dawson Associates has to do for us. What about them?" I asked.

"I'll get right on it," Jordan replied.

After they left, I had mixed feelings of depression and excitement. Depression, when I considered all the work that lay ahead in only a month's time not knowing where the money was going to come from,   feeling the pain from my aching body and remembering my ugly appearance with little black hairs growing from the scar on my sliced cheek. It hurt to shave there. But, there was a sliver of excitement at the possibility of some help from the AG's office, Feingold and the prospects of a new judge on the case.

I called Emily and told her about the deal they offered about the pictures and that I refused. She expressed her gratitude. When I also told her about Dr. Gerber's results, there was no immediate response.

"Emily, are you all right?"

She still didn't answer. Then I heard her blow her nose and I could tell she was crying.

"After all these years-- What will I tell Danny?" she sniffed in a nasal voice.

"Don't tell him anything yet Emily. Let's wait and see how this information plays out. In the meantime we have a lot of work to do to prepare you for trial. Will you be up to it?"

"Don't worry about me, Mr. Eldridge. I'll be fine."

"OK then. Call Henry and make an appointment to come in for your initial preparation. I'll follow up with you when he's finished.

I have some good news for you. Judge Andretti recused herself. A new judge will be appointed to take her place."

"Oh my! That *is* good news. Thank God!"

I knew she wanted to talk some more but I kept the conversation short. I was exhausted. I was tempted to tell her about Charley Randell's discovery but thought better about it. Not yet, I said to myself.

I closed the door to my office when I got off the phone with Emily. I called Amy at her extension.

"Amy hold all calls for me will you please?"

I turned out the manor lamp on my desk which darkened the room even though some sun light entered through the blinds on the windows. I made my way to the leather couch, turned off the overhead lights, and stretched out, resting my head on the padded arm and fell fast asleep.

The Governor used his private phone. The phone in his office that no one, absolutely no one, not even Mort Haller could use. It was swept once a week by the State Police to make sure there were no bugs. It was six o'clock in the evening and the Governor had had a bad day. He was tired and strung out. Jed was on the phone almost constantly asking him for this piece of information or that, telling him about this problem or that, lamenting about all the work he was doing in order, the Governor was sure, to lay the ground work for his appointment to the Superior Court when this case was finished. He had to listen to Emily about how he was ignoring Danny's problem. He felt guilty about his lack of involvement with Danny's psychiatrist, Dr.Rollins. He hadn't even brought Danny to one appointment yet although he realized there had been only two meetings thus far.

Then there was the enigmatic Mort Haller. The Governor never delved very deeply into where the money was coming from that Mort managed; money deposited in accounts for his campaigns for Governor and money deposited in accounts for his fledgling campaign for the Senate. There was even money he knew that was deposited in his corporate and private accounts. Each time he tried to salve his conscience by asking some mundane question about finances, Mort would say, 'Not to worry. Leave all that to me'.

"Can I see you tonight?" he asked Rhea

"Oh God Brenden, no, not tonight."

"Please, I need to see you. The case is heating up and you're the only one I can really talk to," he hastily said to her.

"Brenden, the hearing is only a month away. I think we should cool it until the divorce is over. Besides, I'm scared to death about my involvement thus far. When I think of the possible consequences--"

"I know, I know but there's a light at the end of the tunnel-- although I guess you're right. We should wait until this hearing is finished," he paused but there was no response at the other end.

"There's not a day that goes by but that some wag talks about the divorce on the radio or some blurb appears in the paper. And the blogs--! So far most of the comments haven't hurt too much. They tell me the campaign for the Senate is still very much alive and viable," he continued sounding a little more up beat than he did when he started the conversation.

"I'm glad about that," she said to him, though still sounding nervous.

"OK then. I'll call you and keep you up to date. I love you."

"Bye, I love you too," she replied, thinking that she really didn't want to be brought up to date. In fact, she wanted to forget all about her participation in this divorce. Every time she thought about it she became nervous and upset, even at times ready to throw up. Keep me up to date, she thought. Puleeze!

On Wednesday, despite all the preparation it took to get me inside the courthouse, I was in Judge Richard Talbot's courtroom promptly at ten o'clock. Henry was with me but thankfully, Emily chose not to attend.

"It's only a status conference isn't it?" she asked.

"Yes," I replied, "but I want to give you the opportunity to be there. After all, you're paying for all of this." Yeah, right, I thought.

"I'm paying in more ways than one, Attorney Eldridge. I have to bring Danny to Dr. Rollins. I have to keep my appointment with Dr. Feingold. I have to see Dr. Hurley for my twice weekly session with him. Dr. Monaghan wants to visit us once more and that pest, Donald Long, is calling me all the time to try and schedule another visit.

And another thing; I'm having one difficult time making ends meet. Six thousand a month sounds like a lot of money but after the mortgage, food, clothing--I have to get Danny ready for school in a few weeks-- medical bills that are not covered by insurance--that's another thing, there is no provision for uninsured medical expenses in the Judge's temporary order. The psychiatrist's bills are enormous. Who's going to pay for this new guy, Dr. Feingold? And your bill, well that's astronomical. It's going up so fast, I'll never be able to pay it, no matter how much I get in this case .What then?"

She was on a roll but she had good reason to be upset. I could bring a motion to amend the Temporary Order but the trial itself was only a few weeks away. In truth, I should have been aware of that omission concerning uninsured medicals by Judge Andretti earlier. When the case was over, if we won, I thought, Emily would have enough money to pay for all the psychiatrists she would ever need and then some. She'd even have enough to pay my fee, I hoped.

I assured her that I had already spoken to Paul Jed and that the Governor agreed to pay for Feingold and his associate, the psychologist who would administer all the psychological tests. I told her how important Feingold's results could be.

"Do you understand Emily, that Feingold's diagnosis, his conclusions concerning your character and the Governor's character will probably carry the day as far as the question of custody is concerned. Feingold will also have the benefit of his psychologist's findings based on what the test results show."

"What about all the others? What have I gone through all this for if Feingold's recommendations will be so important? What about Dr. Monaghan? What about Long?"

"We couldn't control Long. That was an appointment by Judge Andretti to have Long function as her eyes and ears on the question of Danny's custody. But remember, we weren't too happy with Long back then so we both agreed on Dr. Monaghan. In fact, it was a victory for us to have the other side agree to the appointment of Monaghan. They only agreed because if they didn't they'd look like they were impeding the custody issue."

"Yeah, but I'm paying for half of Dr. Monaghan's fee," she said. She wasn't in the mood to cut me any slack, I thought.

"That's true, but just think, you only have to pay half," I said to her half kidding.

"I'm also paying half of Danny's doctor, Dr.Rollins. These halves add up, Attorney Eldridge."

Sometimes she's as sharp as a tack, I thought. She's come a long way since she first appeared in my office in early spring.

Paul Jed was also in the courtroom with only one of his bag carriers this time. We nodded in greeting as we took our seats at the opposite ends of the chairs strung out inside the bar for lawyers.

He looked tired, even distraught. His suit coat seemed to hang on him as if he'd lost some weight and his tie was knotted carelessly at least two inches away from the top of his collar. Sloppy, I thought.

Who was I to criticize? I looked like a refugee from the ER at Mass General Hospital with my leg still in a cast, a metal plate sticking out of my gut and a blazing scar on my face. I didn't look any better than my opponent, in fact, I looked a helluva lot worse, but at least my tie was pulled up tight--or was it? I checked. It was OK. Perhaps Jed thought that I was a little nervous and distraught when I fingered my tie. Well perhaps I was, just a little. It was a good thing. Trial lawyers never get too much of a bump on themselves because it's only a matter of time before they get knocked down. You can't win'em all, as the saying goes.

"All rise," the court officer bawled out as he came through the door leading to the Judge's chambers.

Right behind him was Richard Talbot, now in his fifteenth year as a Family Court Judge, who enjoyed the reputation as a knowledgeable, fair minded jurist; one who brooked no nonsense but one who had the patience to listen to the lawyers and witnesses even when they droned on and on. I knew all this from some experience with him.

I breathed a sigh of relief when I saw him. I had appeared before him several times and I knew he liked me. We'd met at bar association functions every now and then and even served on several continuing education panels together over the years. I knew I could expect a level playing field with him but he would, under no circumstances, give me any advantage.

He was heavy, with a full face marked here and there by brown blotches evidently caused by too much sun on his fair complexion. His chin was not distinguishable from his neck as the folds protruded above his shirt. His hair was a burnished walnut which fell, in a somewhat haphazard manner, over his ears. He had a ready smile until someone pushed him over the edge and then he became very quiet and spoke just barely above a whisper. This was very effective. The more he was pushed, the quieter he became until he had the attention of the lawyer who caused the uproar. At that point he would look at the offender and say something like, "If you continue to act like a seventh grader in my courtroom you will be made to suffer the consequences in open court in front of your client. The next outburst will cost you a five hundred dollar fine. Each additional outburst will cost an additional two hundred and fifty dollars. To be sure you understand counselor, that's seven hundred and fifty dollars for the second offense."

I was fascinated by the case that was called ahead of ours. It was a case involving Munchhausen by Proxy. The parent, a woman in this case, was a medical doctor who knew all the buzz words when she brought her eighteen month old baby to the emergency room. She'd tell the attending physicians that the child had certain symptoms which she rattled off like a trained pediatrician when, in fact, her license to practice medicine had been revoked in two states. The doctors would insert dyes in the baby's system, drains in his body, tubes in his nose and catheters in his veins when all the while the mother would be the center of attention as her child was undergoing tests. That, of course, was the reason for her bizarre conduct- putting the life of her child in jeopardy for the sake of attracting this kind of attention.

"What the hell is this?" Henry whispered to me.

"What a nut case she is."

Judge Talbot appointed a GAL, brought in the lawyer for the Department of Social Services to act on behalf of the child, suspended the mother's custody, and placed the baby in the protective custody of the Commonwealth. The father was nowhere to be found, at least at this stage.

Just another day in the Probate and Family Court, I thought.

It took quite a while for all involved in the Munchausen's case to gather their papers and exit and, engrossed as I was in the facts in that case, I didn't notice that the courtroom suddenly became packed with reporters.

Judge Talbot asked his clerk, Dolores Fairchild, to call the next case.

"Mitchell v. Mitchell," she intoned obediently.

I had to struggle to get up and reach the plaintiff's position at counsel table right next to the microphone, which stood between

Jed and me. I could feel all eyes on me as, at one point, one crutch slipped a little and I lost my balance before I reached my chair. Henry was right beside me though and lent a hand to straighten me up.

When Talbot looked up from whatever he was reading, he glanced over the whole courtroom, which had become hushed, save for a few feet that shuffled underneath their weight.

"The reason I asked counsel to attend today's session is to give me a status report on their trial preparation. I have some pretrial orders for them as well."

Jed approached the mike.

"Judge, are you aware that we already have pre-trial orders from Judge Andretti filed by her in June in compliance with which we submitted a list of witnesses several weeks ago together with our pre-trial memoranda?"

Oh brother, I thought. Here it comes.

"Attorney Jed, do you really think I am *tabula rasa*? I have read all the pleadings in order to prepare myself for today's hearing. I am quite aware of Judge Andretti's orders including the order that there will be no continuances. If it's all right with you, I thought I would up-date the orders since it will be me who will hear this case not Judge Andretti." His voice was dripping with sarcasm as he leveled a dagger-like look at Jed.

"Uh, well Judge of course--"

"Sit down, Attorney Jed."

He straightened himself upright in his high- backed leather chair before he continued.

"Allow me to set some guide-lines for this trial which will take place in only a few weeks time, on September sixth. First, there will be no cameras allowed. If it were up to me I'd also prevent the media from attending. In fact, if it were up to me, I'd conduct this trial in a closed courtroom. But we've come a long way since the Star Chamber and this is a public hearing, an open courtroom it will be and the public is indeed invited. But, I'm telling you all now," he paused and looked at those assembled behind the bar and those standing in the back of the room who somehow escaped the insistence by the court officers to be seated, "I will brook no outbursts or conduct not becoming the dignity of these proceedings.

Secondly, I want a new witness list from both sides a week before trial. I'm fully aware, as I said, that you submitted your lists a few weeks ago but let me prove something to you right now. It's true, isn't it, that since then you both have added at least one person to that list?"

Silence

"Well, is it true or not?"

"It's true Judge," I answered.

"Yes," said Jed.

"All right then," the Judge stated to us both and, at the same time, proved to all by that exchange that he was a jurist at the top of his game.

"Thirdly, I want an up-dated pre-trial memorandum from each of you at the same time you file your witness list.

Fourth, I don't want to be bogged down with what are called 'housekeeping motions' at the beginning of trial on the sixth. If you have those kinds of motions, including motions *in limine,* file them three days before trial and argue them that same day. I'll entertain motions to dispense with notice for your convenience.

Fifth, as I told you, I've read all the pleadings. Apparently you both intend to have this trial last until the end of the year sometime with all your witnesses. That's all well and good, but let me warn you. If there is repetition, if either of you drag out your questions on either direct or cross examination, I will call you into chambers and there I will warn you. If that conduct continues, I will impose fines in open court.

Lastly, let me tell you now. I will strictly enforce the rules of evidence, and be assured I know them just as I expect you to know them.

Any questions?"

Neither Paul Jed nor I said a word.

"Let me ask you then, what is the status of your preparation? You both must be ready for trial on the sixth."

I struggled to my feet.

"Your Honor, there are some events that are beyond the control of my opponent and me. For example, in order to assist the Court, we have recently agreed on a forensic psychiatrist who will endeavor to examine and test both spouses on their fitness to parent. He expects to be finished in time for trial but he is proceeding carefully and at great expense. In the event he needs more time, we hope Your Honor will accommodate us."

"Which one of the words, 'No continuances' don't you understand, Attorney Eldridge?"

"Thank you, Judge," was all I could say.

"All right, then. If there's nothing further, I'll expect your lists and memoranda in three weeks. Good day, gentlemen."

"All rise," said Jack, Talbot's court officer.

We cleared our papers from the counsel table and slowly made our way out into the corridor as I heard the clerk call the next case.

"Whew! That guy's something else," Henry said as soon as we got into the hall, which by now was crowded by reporters.

"Attorney Eldridge, Attorney Eldridge, what do you say about custody? Who will you have testify?" one asked.

"What's a forensic psychiatrist?" another demanded.

"Let's get the hell out of here," I said to Henry.

CHAPTER TWENTY

It's not such a strange coincidence that I know both the Lieutenant Governor and the Attorney General personally. They were both up and coming politicians when I was riding the circuit on the Superior Court and trying desperately to be appointed to the Appeals Court. I was in contact with both of them in those days; friends of mine also solicited them to speak to the Governor on my behalf, other friends contributed to their campaigns. Mary Hartigan, the Lieutenant Governor and I stayed in contact with each other after we graduated from the same college. Anthony Mariani, the AG, was actually related to Andrea through her grandmother's sister. Years ago, when her grandmother was alive, the whole clan would get together for summer outings, weddings and funerals and Tony and I, both budding trial lawyers, would go off by ourselves always somewhere near the keg that was tapped and talk endlessly about our cases, our careers and our family.

Tony was about two years older than I was which would make him about fifty. He was a tireless worker and scrupulously honest. After all, he was the Attorney General whose job it was to protect the people of the Commonwealth from fraud, corruption and unfair practices.

"Fraud and corruption," Henry said to me after we returned to the office after the hearing before Talbot. "That's exactly what we're trying to prove the Governor is guilty of. What better way to explore his illicit campaign funds than to alert the AG. We should also consider extortion, for cryin' out loud."

"Tony isn't going to go on a witch hunt and take on the Governor, a candidate for the U.S. Senate, unless he can be sure he's got him dead to right," I responded.

"If we get the affidavit of Chuck Dawson, pre-eminent CEO of Dawson Associates, stating he suspects that there is manipulation of bank accounts holding the Governor's campaign funds and the attribution of those funds to donors who make contributions on the same day of the week, fifty-two weeks a year, don't you think that would intrigue the person charged with the responsibility of seeing to it that political campaigns in this state are on the up and up?" Henry replied.

"Well, if you add what you just said with the fact that the AG has no love for the Governor and is politically ambitious in his own right, we might have a chance to convince him to start a covert investigation."

"Covert? What do you mean?"

"Well, I just don't think that the AG will go barging into the office of the Chairman of the Governor's Senatorial Campaign Committee. I happen to know that Tony has people on his staff that does investigative undercover work. If I can convince him to do just that; to have one of his staff confer with Chuck Dawson and conduct a separate investigation, it'll be a major victory for us."

"OK, I'll go over to Dawson's office today and see if I can't get his affidavit right away," Henry said.

The next day, Thursday, I called Tony and asked if I could see him.

"Sure, Ted, c'mon up," he said right away. "What's on your mind? Are you in the running for a spot on the Appeals Court again?"

"No, nothing like that, Tony, but I'd prefer to see you in person."

"Sounds ominous. Let me clear some things away and make room for you about eleven o'clock. How's that?"

"Sounds good. See you then."

I spent the rest of the morning doing what any one would do with half a brain: I researched the Office of the Attorney General in Massachusetts and, what was more important, what the jurisdiction and responsibilities of the office were.

The Massachusetts General Laws were pretty clear. They stated, among other things, that The Attorney General shall appear for the Commonwealth when the official acts of various state departments or commissions are called into question. I found out that Massachusetts has an independent state agency that administers campaign finance laws called The Office of Campaign and Political Finance which has jurisdiction over elections and, by definition the campaigns of those elections. Statewide candidates and committees are required to file monthly reports listing their receipts and expenditures with the OCPF and the frequency increases to twice monthly in the last six months of an election year.

It wasn't a giant step, therefore, to reach the conclusion that the Attorney General had the obligation to prosecute violators; those that ignored the requirements and those that defrauded the public by using fictitious names of donors.

I wrote down all the statutory citations and committed to memory the one or two that were right on point so I could not only convince Tony to act, but in truth, to show off a little. I also had Chuck Dawson's affidavit that Henry obtained yesterday.

The Attorney General's Office is at One Ashburton Place in the McCormack Building, just up the street from the Old Courthouse. It was usually only a three minute walk from Old City Hall but it took me almost a half hour as I hobbled up the hill carefully avoiding the stairs at City Plaza. Promptly at eleven o'clock, I was ushered into Tony's office.

He came from behind his desk with his hand outstretched and a big smile on his tanned, handsome face. He was just over six feet tall, hair the color of what my artist friends would call mars black mixed with sprinkles of grey and brown eyes that were dancing in time with his broad grin.

His grandmother came from some little town in Tuscany and unlike Andrea's side of the family, Tony and his family could speak Italian. He was sensitive to the profiling that hounded him throughout his campaigns and was fiercely defensive of his Italian heritage. Both his mother and father were Italian and he grew up in one of the apartment houses his father owned on Hull Street where each floor was occupied by some member of his father's extended family.

Tony went to the Elliot Elementary School on Charter Street and stayed in the North End all the way through BC High, Boston College and Boston College Law School. He was a "Triple Eagle" and damned proud of it.

We shook hands and clasped each other on the back before we sat down on his mahogany colored, leather couch.

"I heard about your 'accident' so called. Are you OK?" he said to me solicitously.

"That scar looks ominous."

"Honestly Tony, I'm having a hard time. I've been in therapy but I've got this case I have to pay attention to and I've got to be up and about. Moving around is painful."

"I know Ted. Everybody knows about the Governor's case, but you've got to take it easy. If you fall and injure yourself you won't be good for anybody, especially Andrea and the kids. How are the kids anyway?"

"That's another thing. Josh will enter BC in a few weeks and I won't be able to help him get ready because of this case. We're going to trial on September sixth. I won't even be able to help him move into his dorm. It's not that Andrea can't do whatever is necessary for him, it's just that I can't be there and I'll miss being part of his transition."

"And Mandy?"

"She'll be a senior at Brookline High. Hopefully I'll be finished with this case in time to take her around to visit colleges.

"And you? How're things with Joan and your kids?" I asked.

"They're all fine, thanks. What brings you up the hill from Old City Hall?"

"Tony, I need your help in a very sensitive, explosive situation that involves the Governor. Here, look at this," I said to him handing over Dawson's affidavit. I waited for a few seconds while he had a chance to look it over.

"We believe that the Governor is obtaining large sums of money from sources other than from his investments and his salary. Our only basis for that belief is that deposits are made in the Governor's personal accounts on a regular basis each week, all year. One possible source, we think, is the Governor's campaign funds. We've also uncovered about two million dollars that are unaccounted for--that doesn't appear on his financial statements. We think that also comes from the same source. The question is-- where does the money come from that's deposited into his campaign accounts? There's no way contributors donate the same amount of money every week, all year long. We think it's some kind of pay off; someone or some group is paying him every week. It looks to us that it must be from gambling, you know the bookies. He must provide some kind of protection for them in exchange for cash contributions. He then covers their contributions by labeling them as campaign funds and deposits them in several of his campaign fund accounts. There is evidence that he uses some of these funds personally and there is even some evidence that he deposits some of these funds into his personal accounts and into some of his business accounts."

"Well I'll be--"

"He must list phony names of contributors on his monthly reports to the OCPF," I said.

"Look at the frequency of the income he reports in his personal accounts," I continued, pointing to one of the Governor's personal bank account statements that I received from Paul Jed. "Almost the same amount every week, fifty-two weeks a year. That's simply not credible."

"No. It's fraudulent if those funds come from campaign accounts," Tony replied. "I can't believe it," he paused.

"Yet, I've known about the bookies in my neighborhood all my life. It was part of the scene growing up. Some of my friends were runners when they were just little kids. They'd take the betting slips to the bookies and bring them from one location to another. I haven't involved this office because I never had any actual proof. Besides, it was the Boston Police that looked the other way, or at least the few that had jurisdiction in the North End."

"The North End..." He shook his head.

"But now the violation is not bookmaking but fraud, perhaps extortion. Fraud upon the voters of this Commonwealth," I said.

"Fraud, each and every time he files his monthly report. What's even worse is that this Governor, this paragon of virtue, is participating in and protecting an illegal activity. Can you believe he's now getting ready to run for the Senate?"

Tony shook his head again.

"Do you have people on your staff that can look into these violations without letting them know that they're under investigation?" I asked.

"Of course we do. The question is Ted, whether it's the right thing to do. We'd blow the lid off this Governor's administration, destroy him publicly and prevent him from holding any public office, even dog catcher, for the rest of his life if we're wrong. But if we're right, he's sure to be indicted for criminal participation in promoting and abetting bookmaking activity and extortion and he'll be through politically," he stopped and became pensive. "All that is in addition to the sanctions imposed for violating the rules of OCPF," he continued.

"You know the old saying, if you're going to kill the king you'd better be sure he's dead," Tony said.

All those things, those things Tony mentioned that would happen to the Governor were exactly what I had in mind, I thought to myself.

"Tony, it's a matter of enforcing the laws of the Commonwealth. What the hell, that's what it's all about, isn't it?"

"OK, let me start someone on it and see what we uncover. We should begin in the North End. If we have the proof, and I mean proof beyond the shadow of a doubt, I'll get in touch with you. Who knows what the fallout will be but if we get the proof it'll be a blockbuster."

On the walk back to my office I was elated. I hardly noticed the pain in my leg and abdomen as I negotiated the downhill slope. I even tried to ignore the stares I got from passers by looking at my scar. To hell with them. If only Tony can complete his investigation in time for the trial, I thought. Wouldn't that be just the 'nuts?'

CHAPTER TWENTY-ONE

Governor Brenden W. Mitchell, with the help of his lawyer and his Chief of Staff, found out just who Dr. Justin Feingold was before ever agreeing to hire him. The Governor learned that Feingold had his office on Cambridge Street in the Bullfinch Building right in front of the Mass. General Hospital; that he was a world-renowned psychiatrist and even that would be an understatement; that he was mentioned for the past five years as a candidate for the Nobel Prize in medicine and was a tireless worker. He learned that although it would appear Feingold spends all his time writing books and articles and conducting research for cutting edge articles for publication in The New England Journal of Medicine, nothing could be further from the truth. He was told Feingold and his staff of psychiatrists and psychologists, including interns who are graduates of Harvard Medical School in training at Mass General and McLean, see patients every day.

The Governor, and he heard, just about every one else in Massachusetts, knew that McLean, a psychiatric hospital in Belmont, is affiliated with the Mass. General. Both hospitals are affiliated with Harvard and both enjoy a solid reputation in the psychiatric community. When the Governor was told that when Dr. Feingold sees patients at either hospital he has a trail of doctors, interns and third year students from Harvard following him on his rounds, asking questions, answering hypotheticals put to them by their teacher and listening to the patients' complaints, he was duly impressed.

There was more the Governor found out about this guy, this person who was to review the Governor's character, whether he was fit to parent, what kind of a person he was. No amount of investigation was too much, the Governor had thought. He knew there was a lot at stake here. He found out that a certain Dr. Samuel Freed was the psychologist in charge of Feingold's front line team. Freed's job was to administer the psychological tests and when they were completed, interpret them. The usual tests included the Minnesota Multiphasic Personality Inventory, otherwise known in the trade as MMPI-2 and the Million Clinical Multiaxial Inventory or MCMI-111. Additionally Freed liked to use the Sixteen Personality Factors Test, "16PF" to those who speak this language. Freed also used the well-known Rorschach Test to see what the person makes of the ink blots.

The Governor had met with Jed and Haller several times to consider whether it'd be wise to agree to Feingold, to have him become a major witness in the case to determine custody before ever hiring him.

"Why not?" Mort had said. "Don't forget we've got a woman who's a mental cripple. She's a goddamn drunk, takes drugs, can't control her kid, allows the kid to overdose on her watch and hasn't had the intelligence to earn one red cent in her entire life."

"I can't imagine Feingold reaching any conclusion other than it's in Danny's best interest that you be the sole custodial parent,"

Jed had said to the Governor. "Don't forget, we'll have the GAL on our side. Monaghan certainly will not conclude that Emily can have sole custody," he added.

The Governor had agreed to this procedure for several reasons. First, he didn't trust Dr. Monaghan. She was cool and clinical each time she visited Danny at Dudley Street. She maintained her distance despite the Governor's best efforts to turn his charm on her yet he couldn't get a read as to where she was coming from.

Second, now that Judge Talbot had replaced Judge Andretti, he wasn't sure what kind of impact Donald Long, the GAL, would have despite Jed's confidence.

Third, he was convinced that Emily was a dependent drunk, addicted to pain medication and not able to function as a full fledged custodial parent, just as Mort said. Her psycho-pharmacologist, for all his fancy title, was no more than her hired hand and his testimony, however much in Emily's favor, would not hold up to Feingold's analysis, the Governor thought. Even Danny's new shrink, Dr. Zachary Rollins, could only testify about Danny's mental health, not who the better parent was. Jed had reassured him of this. Danny, he was certain, was equally torn between his mother and his father and that was a "draw" as far as the Governor could tell.

If he was successful in obtaining custody he thought, he would be a single parent and that would certainly enhance his image for his run at the Senate. He could imagine pictures of Danny and him at the beach, at Danny's school, at Church; the loving father protecting his son from a debauched mother. Who could resist? Besides, Danny was getting to the age where he didn't need constant supervision. His sister Helen and the ever present housekeeper, Lilly, would be more than up to the job.

Perhaps maybe, just maybe he thought, Emily would fade at the last minute and this case would settle. At any rate, he was confident that Feingold would come down on his side so he agreed to submit himself to all the psycho-babble bullshit that he was told he had to endure.

Now, two days after the hearing before the new judge, the Governor was feeling depressed, insecure and worried about how his case was going, which was nowhere but to trial, he believed. He got up from his desk and went into his private bathroom. He locked the door, withdrew a brown vile from his trouser pocket and laid out two lines of powder on the sink countertop. He bent over and drew one line into his nostril with a loud sniff, touched his nose before sniffing some air and then he repeated the process with the other line in the other nostril.

After only a few minutes, although he felt invigorated, more confident, the goddamn divorce case was still on his mind. Why hasn't this fucking case settled he thought, getting angrier and angrier. Why should I wait for her to offer a settlement? What about all the promises Haller made about making sure the case would go away? Eldridge, despite his injuries, is forging ahead. Jed is chaotic, seemingly scattered. What will he be like at trial? And what, God forbid, if anybody finds out that I take a few drugs now and then to keep my spirits up. Jesus Christ but that would be the end. I can't let that happen. I must prevent this trial, he thought.

And what if I can't prevent the trial? What information will come out about me not being Danny's father even if there's no testimony about my taking any medication? How will that sound to the media? Why the hell didn't Jed try and get an agreement from them to make sure Emily keeps her mouth shut about that? How will Danny react when he hears what his crazy mother says about me? It's too bad those pictures weren't taken care of. I'll just have to show that she was out of control and I had to restrain her. His thoughts piled on top of one another. I just hope Feingold is the right guy.

What else? What am I paying these people for? Do I have to do all the thinking?

"Bess, get Haller in here right away!"

"Yes sir."

As soon as Mort opened the door the Governor started.

"Shut the goddamn door," the Governor barked.

"Now what?" Haller said trying to flash a patient smile.

"Look Mort, I've been thinking. We've already agreed on Feingold but let's make sure that we don't go to trial. Call Renzo, tell him that whatever he tried to do to Eldridge didn't work. Tell him to use his imagination; I don't give a shit what you tell him, just tell him this case must settle and he should make sure Eldridge is put out of commission.

"Why don't we make them an offer first," Mort replied. "Make sure we get Emily to agree that she won't testify about all that bull shit about you not being Danny's father as part of the deal. You've got plenty of money, assets. What the hell do you care if you give her half of what you've accumulated, half of what shows, anyway. That way there'll be no threat about any medication you're taking, the North End situation, Rhea or anything else. The only other issue is custody and that'll be resolved by all these shrinks, especially Feingold." Haller paused and leaned back in his chair.

"But that bitch hasn't contributed one dime to any of those assets."

"So what! You've been married to her for over fifteen years. She's entitled to half just on that basis alone," Mort replied.

"You know... I think you may be right," the Governor said after a long silence. "But if it doesn't work, if they don't take our offer within one week, I'm prepared to unleash Renzo and his crew to do whatever it takes.

Yeah, the more I think about it the better I like it. You know even better than I what to offer her. Put together a detailed package and tell Jed to contact Eldridge right away. At this stage, I guess I don't care so much about the assets as much as I do about what could come out in a trial that's open to the public. On the other hand, I don't want to give her any more than I have to. I'm going to run for the United States Senate, for crissakes, Mort. You'll be running the whole show and the benefits to us will be enormous, you'll see. Just get me out of this shit I'm in. The press and TV people will have a field day with Emily's testimony unless we settle.

Let's get right on it. Time is running short."

"Yes sir." Haller, like Bess learned long ago that that was the only answer the Governor wanted to hear.

CHAPTER TWENTY-TWO

Brian Woods pressed the buzzer outside the huge, dark, oak door instead of lifting the heavy, pitted brass knocker which hung just below the four square, leaded glass panels decorating the entrance of 10 Dudley Street. It was August, the middle of the week. It was hot, humid and sticky and Brian was bored stiff. He didn't play on the neighborhood Little League team, play hoops at the outdoor courts that doubled as driveways at every other house up and down Warren Street where he lived and he didn't go to the beach with his family like most other kids for the month of August. His mother had all she could do to keep the expensive house they lived in what with the paltry amount of alimony and child support she was receiving from her former husband.

His friend, Danny Mitchell was the only kid in the neighborhood he got along with, the only other kid who didn't like to play sports, the only kid who understood what it's like to have parents who're divorced and the only kid that didn't go to the beach in August.

"Hi Lilly, is Danny home?" he asked as the door opened.

"Sure Brian. He's upstairs in his room. Go right up. He'll be glad to see you," Lilly said sweetly.

"Who's that at the door, Lilly?" came a high-pitched shaky voice from somewhere out of the dark shadows of the warren-like interior of the cavernous house.

Shit! Thought Brian. I don't want to see that ol' bag as he hurried up the winding staircase to Danny's room as fast as he could.

"It's just Danny's little friend Brian, Ms. Prescott," Lilly answered.

Little friend my ass, thought Brian, even though he always liked Lilly.

Danny's door was closed as usual but Brian barged in, slammed the door against the wall and shouted, "Wassup bro?"

"Jesus Christ, Bri. Don't do that!" Danny was sitting on his bed with the pillows propped up behind his head playing with his Game Boy.

"So what happened to you? My mother told me they took you to the hospital over a week ago."

"She probably told you I swallowed some drugs, didn't she?"

"Well, yeah. So did you?"

"I guess, yeah, I did."

"What happened?"

'They pumped out my stomach."

"Did it hurt?"

"Naw, I wasn't in there long."

Danny leaned back on his bed and let out an audible sigh.

"Brian, how did you feel when your mother and father were going through their divorce?"

"I already told you. I wanted them to stay together."

"No, I mean how did you feel inside? Did your stomach hurt? Did you cry?"

"My father backed down. I guess he really didn't want my sister and me. That really bummed me out. We used to do a lot of things together, you know, go to baseball games at Fenway, Celtic games at the Fleet Center... things like that, but since he met this girl, Denise, he's been different."

Brian couldn't look Danny in the eye and he felt uncomfortable..

"No Brian, tell me. Were you crying? Because I'm crying all the time. I can't be the kind of kid my father wants and I can't -- I dunno, I'm just down, that's all, just down all the time. They're sending me to a shrink, for chrissake. My mother's seeing a shrink. Now they're talking about getting some fancy shrink for the both of them, I just found out."

Brian didn't say a word. Danny continued.

"When my father comes to pick me up he can't even come onto the driveway. He has to park the car in the street and toot the horn. They don't even speak to each other. And Aunt Helen is a pain in the ass; she doesn't even know I exist. My father dumps me off in this place and then goes about his business with one meeting after another."

"I try and keep busy by playing hoop in the driveway but my father never plays with me. We used to play "Horse" but not anymore. I always thought he was such a great guy, the Governor for cryin' out loud, I looked up to him and tried not to disappoint him but now I really don't give a shit. The only person I like around here is Lilly."

"What about your mother? How's she taking all this?" Brian asked.

"She's all right I guess. She's crying all the time, too. She's still taking her meds but she's not drinking as much," Danny told his friend.

"She totally pissed at my father and curses him whenever his name comes up but then she starts sobbing and feeling depressed.

217

I shouldn't be saying all this but my mother is barely able to cope with the divorce. When we were all living together, my father controlled every last detail. He paid the goddamn bills, balanced the checkbook, parceled out the money, decided on what to have for dinner and what I should do or shouldn't do. If we went on vacation, he'd tell us when and where we were going, what to eat and what to wear. Jesus, it was awful. It always bothered me to hear him put down my mother. God, he'd do an awful job on her. He'd tell her she couldn't do this right or that right. I'd often find her crying after my father went out for one of his nightly meetings after one of those fights.

Now, my mother tells me, the bills have piled up and she even has a hard time deciding what to make for dinner. She seems, I dunno, kind of scattered. I hear her crying, talking to herself when she doesn't think I'm listening saying things like she doesn't know if she can handle all this. She's in a daze sometimes. She leaves the dishes in the sink for days and the house is a mess."

Neither one said another word for a few minutes. Danny's eyes teared-up as he gazed out the window obviously trying to hide his face from Brian. Brian, aware of his friend's tears, was doing all he could to hide his own.

"What're you boys doing up there?" came the cry from Aunt Helen in her shrill, high-pitched voice from downstairs.

"Nothing," said Danny.

"Well you'd better come down here right now. Lilly has lunch prepared. And you can bring your little friend too, if you want."

The boys looked at each other and let out a howl of laughter.

"Come on my little friend," Danny said as they ran down the hallway to the stairs.

"Up yours," said Brian.

Time was slipping by. I was able to sign the twenty-five thousand dollar addition to my already over extended credit line at the bank but they refused to give me an unsecured loan of an additional fifty thousand. When I told them I needed the money right away, they at least made sure the loan closed in four days. I told them that the entire credit line would be paid off six months but they wouldn't give me a penny more.

The fact was, that I didn't have enough money to carry the office expenses, pay the experts in advance of their trial testimony, pay the new equity line, pay the existing first mortgage or pay the normal household expenses even with the additional twenty-five thousand. All I could do was juggle some payments and not pay others. What the hell else could I do?

Trial was only two weeks away when Paul Jed called me and, of all things, invited me to lunch at his office.

"Henry what do you think?" I asked my hard working associate. "Maybe he's throwing in the towel."

"In your dreams,"

"What the hell, I may as well hear what he has to say," I said.

When the time came for the meeting, I didn't prepare. I didn't know what the meeting was all about. I had my suspicions though. Opposing lawyers didn't make arrangements for lunch with each other unless there was something important to talk about, I thought.

I limped over to 100 Federal Street at 12:30 without my ever present brief case, no yellow pads, no nothing …just my pen in my shirt pocket sans the hokey plastic pocket protector. It was a good thing. I couldn't have managed any baggage with my crutches.

The lunch was a private, catered affair in the conference room at Jed's office. Nothing extravagant, just sandwiches and Cokes, just the two of us.

"Ted," Jed began as we unwrapped our chicken sandwiches and poured our Cokes.

"This coming week you've scheduled depositions of Dr. Lionel Gagne, Mark Conlin and Byron Hackett. I've prepared a short order of notice to allow me to take the depositions of Steve Lyons, Lester Begley and Charles Dawson. But honestly Ted, that's going to be a consummate waste of time for the both of us. There's also the question of whether the stenographer will have the transcript ready for trial which, as you know is just around the corner, without paying a small fortune for expedited copies."

"So here's the first proposal I want to make to you:

Let's both agree to forego the depositions and substitute written interrogatories. Each expert will state in writing, under oath, what he'd testify to at a deposition; what his valuations are and the method he used to obtain them. That way we'll have a written record of each person's testimony well in advance of trial so we can prepare our cross examination without worrying whether we'll get the transcript back in time." He looked at me expectantly.

Now I was well aware that depositions are, without a doubt, the most abused tool in the entire legal process, bar none. They are supposed to be a vehicle to obtain information in advance of trial in order to expedite the trial, to pare down the testimony in open court. If I was honest with myself, I'd have to agree that's generally what they do, but to get there, to get the final transcript which is also used to impeach the credibility of witnesses who are on the stand, the parties have to go through the often strident, discourteous, bellicose, confrontational, derisive, caustic and repetitious questions from the examiner. I knew Paul Jed was no exception to the rule.

Paul Jed, I was sure, would use every trick in the book at these depositions. Once he got beyond the nature of the question itself, I'd have to contend with how the question was asked. The stenographer wouldn't take down the decibel level or the dripping sarcasm that would accompany Jed's question. My experience with Jed in the past was that he's a master of that kind of conduct. Even his body language would be threatening. I learned that when, on many occasions, he'd lean across the table and ask his question eighteen inches from the face of the witness, he could bring tears to the most sanguine of them all.

The problems I had with Paul Jed in the past were no different from other problems I had with other lawyers. There's no supervision when the examiner, the deponent and the deponent's lawyer assemble in the privacy of the examiner's office. The stenographer's job is simply to administer the oath and record verbatim testimony and other statements. There is little if any restraint on the examiner. Oh, both sides stipulate that all objections are reserved until trial all right, with two or three exceptions, but although that agreement is assiduously made at the beginning of the deposition, it's violated constantly during the examination. What's worse is that, by pre-arrangement, the objections are used many times as a signal:

"I object," says the lawyer for the witness. "She doesn't understand the question."

"Do you understand the question?" the examiner asks.

"No" the witness says.

And so it goes.

It didn't take me long to come to the conclusion that I should agree with Paul Jed's suggestion. In fact, after only a few second's contemplation, I welcomed it. The money it would save would be enormous. Moreover, I wasn't in the mood to have to put up with him and his antics during three depositions. In the past I knew he sometimes made a habit of walking out of depositions in a fit of feigned anger. He even did that earlier in this case, I recalled. Besides all that, I was painfully aware that judges historically give only a slap on the wrist as punishment for such antics. Universally, judges abhor getting involved with discovery issues. I learned.

I took another bite of my sandwich, wiped the corner of my mouth with a paper napkin, took a sip of Coke and said to him,

"Paul, I think you've made a good suggestion. I'll agree."

He sat back in his chair and smiled in obvious satisfaction with himself. We were almost finished with lunch when he got up and excused himself.

"Ted, let me get the financial statements we both have filed to date. I'll be right back."

He left the conference room and returned shortly with a folder in his hand. He didn't sit down but went to the front of the rectangular shaped room and removed the cover on a screen which he pulled down from some apparatus suspended from the ceiling. On the conference table in front of the screen was a projector which was loaded with a disc apparently ready to go by the push of a button on the remote which I noticed for the first time beside the projector. It was really high tech stuff, I thought. My office simply had a blackboard.

Without a word Jed dimmed the lights and picked up the remote. He paused in the semi-darkness before he began.

I had to admit this performance was pretty effective. He had my attention.

"Ted, I've attempted to show all the assets of both parties as they appear on their financial statements filed thus far with the Court. I have here a copy of them for you to look at as we go along," he said as he handed me the Governor's statement and Emily's.

I watched him closely as he casually took something from his inside jacket pocket as though he carried it there all the time. At first I thought it was a pen, but then he extracted the point in a flourish and it turned out to be a pointer about three feet long when fully extended which he promptly used to rap the screen showing all the figures.

"Here you see three columns, each listing the assets that stand in the names of the parties," he said as he pushed the button or clicker or whatever it was on the remote.

"One column for those assets in Emily's name, one column for those assets in the Governor's name and one column for those assets in joint names."

He gave me a few minutes to compare the assets on the screen with the financial statements he gave me. I took my time going over each item to be sure he was correct.

"Ted, let's look at Emily's column first," he began as he again tapped the screen with his pointer.

"You can see she only has a small IRA in the amount of twenty-six thousand dollars in her name alone. I understand that was from her early employment before and shortly after the marriage."

I was getting aggravated by his pedantic delivery. He even assumed the air of a professor lecturing to his students. I just sat there and listened.

"Next, let's look at the Governor's column. Here you see a list of the assets standing in his name alone."

I don't know how much more I can take of this bull shit, I thought. All this information is on the financial statements. I said nothing.

"He has minority interests in three closely held corporations which he was involved in before the marriage. He is a limited partner in two real estate limited partnerships, which were formed before he even got into politics, well before his marriage to Emily. He has a 401K plan and a vested defined benefit retirement plan with the Commonwealth. He has a stock portfolio of about two million dollars most of which was accumulated without any contribution from Emily. You can also see he has a group of vested stock options in various flights from the same three corporations in which he owns a minority interest that I previously mentioned.

Let us turn now to the column headed Joint Property," he continued without skipping s beat.

Let us turn now---give me a break!

"In this column there is a savings account of six thousand, five hundred dollars, a checking account with a balance of two thousand dollars, more or less and of courses, the house. We have a value on the house of three million dollars," he said as he dropped his eyes from mine and rapped his thigh with the pointer as if it were a riding crop.

What was coming became perfectly obvious to me. It was not a new tactic. They'd try and saddle Emily with an over-valued house, the sale of which would have dire tax consequences, and they'd keep the liquidity and the corporate and partnership interests which would be valued so low as to be ridiculous. They'd rely on the Judge accepting their valuations base on three things: One, the Judge wouldn't understand the intricacies of the arcane valuation process. Two, their hired gun would carry the day over our hired gun. In other words, their experts would be better than our experts. Three, the Judge would agree that the assets that were the most valuable were accumulated before the marriage and thus were not subject to an equitable distribution to Emily. The Commonwealth Retirement Plan could be distributed to the parties in an unequal division based on the fact that they were accumulated before the marriage. Emily's share would be the subject of a "QDRO," a qualified domestic restraining order, which wouldn't be available to her until she's sixty years old. The other plans, the defined contribution plans could be distributed now but they'd be subject to a penalty for early withdrawal and they'd be taxable as ordinary income rates.

"Now Ted, if Emily took the house we could take those assets that're not worth much in exchange. The liquid assets could be divided but at least half would have to be set aside for Danny's school, college and graduate school. Emily would receive about five hundred thousand dollars in cash. That's a lot of money, Ted. Perhaps you'd want the money placed in a trust for Emily's benefit until she straightens herself out. The retirement plans shouldn't present any difficulty for us..."

"Don't go any further, Paul. Forget it. You're not right about the law. Your proposition is ridiculous. You're ridiculous," I said to him picking up the financial statements he'd delivered to me when we first sat down.

"There's no need to be personal, Ted. You're so goddamned high and mighty. Who do you think you are? You can't reject this offer, or don't you know even that. You have a duty to present it to your client."

"I'll present what you call an offer to her and you can count on it being rejected. There'll be no counter offer. See you in court, Attorney Jed," and I left without more. At least I got rid of those depositions, which would've been a disaster after this, I thought on my way out the door.

After Ted Eldridge left, Paul Jed leaned back in his chair at the conference table. Jed knew all along that this offer would be rejected out of hand. Goddamn Haller was so cheap, he thought. I told that son of a bitch that Eldridge wouldn't settle the case for that kind of money, Jed recalled. But no, he wouldn't listen to me. Well, we'll see what happens next.

CHAPTER TWENTY-THREE

When I got back to the office after my lunch with Jed I called Emily and asked her to come in. We made an appointment for the following morning. In the meantime I brought Henry and Jordan up to date.

"That's ridiculous," Henry said immediately after I was finished telling them about Jed's proposal.

"That's exactly what I told him," I said.

"To hell with him," Jordan chimed in.

"That's it for me today," I told them. "I'm going home early."

"Are you OK?" Henry asked

"Yeah, but Jed tires me out. Besides my leg starts to hurt later in the day and I need to get off it. My scar begins to throb sometimes as soon as I wake up. I'll see you in the morning. In the meantime, make sure we're in good shape with all our experts. They'll have to disclose their findings in sworn statements which we'll exchange for Jed's experts' statements. That has to be done this week. We've done this before so I know you know the drill. The exchange allows us to avoid depositions, thank God."

The next morning, before I met with Emily, before the mail was delivered, hell before I even had my second cup of coffee, a bike messenger came into the office and I saw that he delivered a stack of papers to Amy.

"Bring 'em on," I told her as I made my way back to my office, coffee in hand.

She brought the stack into my office with a sly grin on her face.

"Here's a bunch of love letters from your favorite lawyer," she said handing them directly to me. It was OK for her to joke about the envelopes she delivered; she didn't have to worry about their contents.

"What have we here?" I replied, knowing full well that it was nothing but trouble.

Sure enough, each of three envelopes contained a separate pleading. One was a motion for a continuance. Another was a motion for the Judge to appoint a mediator or an arbitrator to hear the case and the third was a motion *In Limine*, asking the Judge to prevent evidence from being introduced concerning the Governor's paternity.

"Shit!" I said.

"Is it that bad?" Amy said smiling at my frustration.

"It's worse," I said to her on her way out the door.

"Before you go, tell Henry and Jordan to come in and don't be so fresh," I said to her. I made sure she saw my smile.

After we were all assembled, I showed them the pleadings I had just received.

"I'll take care of these," I said pointing to the three envelopes and their contents, "But we have to start the homestretch before trial. We have two weeks before September sixth."

"We have even less than that," Jordan said. "There's Labor Day and that will cut into our schedule."

"No it won't. You'd both better plan on spending the next two weeks, including Saturdays and Sundays and Labor Day right here at the office.

Jordan, you have to contact Jed and mark our exhibits. You know the drill, all those exhibits we can agree to will be in three notebooks: one for the Judge, one for Jed and one for us. Those exhibits we can't agree to will be placed in three other notebooks. And Jordan, don't let Jed get away with placing any exhibits in the agreed notebook unless you are absolutely sure they are admissible OK?"

"Right."

"Henry, you have to prepare our pre-trial memorandum. Remember we have to submit it a week before trial. You'll also have to prepare our witness list. I'll work with you on that. Give me a draft in a few days."

"There's more. We have to prepare our witnesses and the cross examination of their people. I've already started on Emily's direct. I'm writing out every question and her answers. I'll also prepare her as best as I can for her cross. The Governor's cross too."

"Who will do the cross of Steve Lyons?"

"I'll take him," Jordan said

"Who'll do Gerber?"

No answer.

"Well?"

"Henry. You've drawn the short straw. It should be easy. He simply testifies to the results of his test."

"Not exactly," he replied

"He has to testify to the feasibility of the test, the procedure he used, the reliability of the hair follicle…"

"OK, you've got the idea," I replied with a satisfied grin.

"I don't look forward to it but I'll take the direct of Chuck Dawson and the cross of Lionel Gagne."

"Jordan, you'll keep track of the exhibits during trial. When I want exhibit number so and so, you'll take it out of the notebook and hand it to me. OK?"

"OK," Jordan said as he slouched down a little further in his chair as if the work load was a weight on his shoulders.

"Henry, the Judge will want suggested Findings and Rulings of Law right after the trial is finished."

"Well, he'll give us some time won't he?" Henry asked.

"He'll probably give us a week," I told him.

"I'll make sure we get the expedited stenographic record each day. It'll cost a small fortune but we'll need it. During the trial you'll make notes and prepare to write the Findings for the Judge."

"With all these witnesses you'll also have to make sure the next witness I call is ready. Have them on stand-by. You know, telephone alert."

"What about Charley Randell?" Henry asked.

"I'll take care of him," I replied.

"What about Dr. Feingold?" Jordan added.

"Look, I'll take care of Feingold, Monaghan, Hurley, Rollins and the GAL," I said. "Jesus Christ..."

"That's what you get the big bucks for," Henry quipped.

"Yeah, right."

"We always said this case was going to be a marathon. Maybe Paul Jed had his meeting with his associates just as we're doing and concluded that the case should be sent to a master or an arbitrator." I said.

"If it was sent out, we'd at least be sure of a hearing every day from nine to five in an atmosphere much more pleasant than a courthouse," Jordan mentioned.

"That kind of informal setting is just what Jed wants. He probably thinks the rules of evidence will be more relaxed and his lack of skills along those lines won't be as evident. I'm not going to let him get away with that if I can help it," was my reply.

"Anything else?"

"I hate to add to our problems," Henry interjected. "But what about the Attorney General?"

"I haven't heard a word from him. I'll call and ask him what the status of his investigation is. I doubt whether he'll tell me much until he's ready," was all I could say.

The next week before the hearing on Jed's motions I worked my tail off, gimp leg, metal plate holding my abdomen together and all. I clipped the hairs on my scar with a scissors but they still showed. Jordan and Henry were straight out as well and the tension around the office was palpable. Emily came in to review her testimony and she appeared resolute if not somewhat anxious. I read the affidavits of Jed's experts and used them to prepare my cross-examination.

My job was easy regarding the GAL. His report was expected a week before trial but I believed his work would be trumped by Feingold's testimony. Besides, his opinion was whatever it was going to be-- I couldn't change it even with an adroit cross-examination. I was prepared to compare his mediocre credentials with Feingold's more than impressive CV and thereby hope that the Judge would rely on Feingold. The only question I had was whether I was right about Feingold coming down against the Governor and supporting Emily.

The same was true regarding Monaghan. Her report was going to be almost unassailable. She has decent credentials, was agreed to by both sides and there was precious little I could do but hope her recommendation was in our favor.

I spoke on the phone with Danny's psychiatrist and concluded there was no problem there. That was about all I had time for before the hearing.

So here I was, three days after receiving Jed's packet of grief, sitting in the motion session waiting to be heard. As usual the courtroom was packed but this time there were no reporters, only litigants and their lawyers transfixed on their unique and very important motions, some engaged in actual argument, others like me just waiting.

While I was sitting there, I began thinking that there is a feeling among Family Law Practitioners that judges who sit in the Probate and Family Court should sit for only a term of years rather than be appointed for life as they presently are. These judges get jaded very quickly listening to all the travails of humankind day after day. I wondered what kind of mood Talbot was in today. I was sympathetic to the grind these judges went through. I went through the same thing when I was sitting. Actually, it's not the hardship that is so terrible. Rather, it's the deceit, the lies and the manipulations that are debilitating and pernicious. And, it's not just the litigants--it's the lawyers who're almost as bad. I was well aware that opposing lawyers insinuate themselves in their client's case, taking up their fight as if it was one of their own and the relationship with the opposition becomes contentious, even downright nasty. I remembered it well.

Still sitting there, waiting for the case to be called, I began to think of how Talbot was so patient in the past. I only hoped he'd be patient today. I guessed the truth is, he must lose it every once in a while. But if that happens today, I thought, I hoped he wouldn't embarrass the lawyers other than to order sanctions for their transgressions, mine included. I recalled I'd never heard him denigrate any individual litigant though, no matter how discourteous they were. He'd simply say, in his quiet voice, that he wouldn't tolerate one more such outburst or the person would be removed from the courtroom.

So, here I was in Talbot's courtroom sitting by myself inside the bar. Emily decided not to come. Henry and Jordan were too busy to come. Paul Jed was talking to Dolores Fairchild, Talbot's clerk, as though he was her best friend. Maybe she was, I thought. He received his inside information from someone. He was laughing with her as though he didn't have a care in the world, preening before the crowd, standing beside the clerk's bench as if he was center stage.

In each of the judge's chambers behind the closed doors of the courtroom, that mysterious place where lawyers are seldom allowed and litigants even less, the individual judges mark their exclusive territory with family pictures, personal books, toiletries in their private bathroom and desk paraphernalia. It's here in the private, serpentine passageways that judges meet one another and pass a collegial time of day as they go about their business.

That very morning, as Judge Talbot was on his way into the courtroom to begin the day's session led by his court officer, he was lost in the thoughts of what he'd just reviewed in preparation for the cases on his list that morning. In his reverie, he almost bumped into Judge Rhea Andretti.

"Well, Judge Andretti, excuse me. I was in another world. How are you?"

"I'm Ok, Judge," she replied, looking up and down the short hallway.

"Uh, Judge can I see you in your office for just a few minutes before you go in?" she asked.

"Certainly. Come with me right now. They can wait a little while longer. Jack you can go back in there," he said waiving Jack toward the courtroom.

Talbot opened his door and ushered Andretti in. They both sat side by side on the two chairs, in front of Talbot's government issued desk, not very far apart from one another.

It can't be, was Talbot's fleeting thought before a word was uttered. Has she been drinking? It's only nine-thirty in the morning!

"Judge," she began, "I've got thish problem..." she paused, looked out the window behind the desk and returned her gaze to Talbot. But it was apparent her eyes were glassy, vague and almost opaque.

"Rhea, have you been drinking already this morning?" Talbot asked in a soft voice.

She blew her nose on the handkerchief she'd been twirling in her hands, giving her a few seconds before she had to respond.

"I, I just don't know what to do. There is thish situatshun-" she whispered.

"Rhea, Rhea you can't go on today. You're drunk!"

"Yeah, well you're fat but I'll be sober in the mornin," she replied as she pointed an unsteady finger at him, laughing at her own joke. Instantly her laughter turned to sobs as she buried her head in her hands and cried uncontrollably.

Talbot was astounded. For an instant he didn't know what to do. Andretti was slumped over in her chair, her head not eight inches from her lap. Was she going to hurl? He thought.

He took his sport coat from his closet and put it around her shoulders.

"Stay here, Rhea. I'm getting Jack. He'll take you down the back stairs and drive you home."

Almost on cue, there was a rap on Talbot's door. Talbot jumped up and opened the door slightly to be sure it was Jack.

"Ah, Jack there you are. Judge Andretti is sick and can't go on. Will you take my car and drive her home? She lives nearby on Cedar Lane Way, I believe. Here are the keys."

He pulled the keys from his pocket and handed them over. At the same time, with his free hand, he assisted Andretti from her chair.

"Now Rhea, that's all right, go with Jack," he said.

"He'll take you home."

She got up and faced Jack on unsteady legs without saying a word.

Talbot gave Jack a look, which unmistakably conveyed the idea that this was a matter between them, as he looked back and forth a couple of times from Andretti to his court officer.

"Go ahead now. I'll go into the courtroom by myself."

Jack and the Judge walked arm and arm down the hall toward the door to the back stairs which served as the private entry way for the judges. The parking lot was at the foot of the stairs with the judges' parking spaces clearly marked, "Judge Only".

"Take care of her, Jack. Make sure she gets into her house before you leave her," Talbot instructed as Jack helped Andretti down the stairs.

CHAPTER TWENTY-FOUR

My thoughts were interrupted when Talbot entered the courtroom without his court officer. Dolores Fairchild, his clerk ever vigilant, cried out in a loud voice,

"All rise!"

Talbot looked a little disconcerted, not quite as sharp as I was used to seeing him as he somewhat tentatively and slower than usual, climbed the two steps leading to his high-backed maroon leather chair at the center of his bench.

"Call the first case," he said in a gruff voice.

"Mitchell v. Mitchell, case number 06 5638 D! Counsel take your seats at counsel table," Fairchild barked.

At least this time we were first on the list. Jed must've worked his magic with Fairchild earlier when they were laughing together

I thought. I wonder what he doles out to the staff at Christmas time in exchange for all the favors he gets.

Jed was the moving party so he was to begin.

"Judge, I have three motions before you this morning. I realize you said to mark these motions for hearing three days before trial but I understand that you assented to hear them today. How do you want to proceed?"

"Argue one at a time," was his curt reply.

Oh, Oh I thought. He's in one of those rare moods.

Jed took a deep breath and began with his motion for a continuance. This was a mistake, I thought.

"Judge I'm asking for a continuance in this marathon case. It's only been since early spring since this case first appeared on the docket and..."

"Attorney Jed! Which one of the words, 'No further continuances' don't you understand?"

"I know, Judge, but--"

"No 'buts'. Your motion is denied! Argue your next motion."

Oh brother, I thought. He's on the war path this morning.

Jed shuffled some papers he'd gathered together on the lectern before he was ready to begin, Judge Talbot glaring at him the entire time.

"My next motion, your Honor," Jed began in a most obsequious voice, "is a motion to refer this case to an arbitrator or a master.

He was instructed to proceed by only a cursory nod from the Judge.

"This case will take fifteen to eighteen days to try, Judge. Your entire docket during all that time will be exclusively Mitchell v. Mitchell; no other motions, no other hearings, no emergencies. It's simply not fair to the other people in this county who have a right to a hearing to have to wait.

Moreover--"

"What makes you think, Attorney Jed, that I won't be able to hear emergencies during this trial? It'll take you people a good half-hour to get set up each day. The stenographer alone takes five minutes getting her apparatus arranged to her satisfaction. By the time you both get your exhibits and other papers in order I can hear two or three motions."

"Judge, it's my experience that we'll be interrupted day after day with some kind of matter that needs to be heard expeditiously. I've even experienced whole days that are skipped for one thing or other leaving huge gaps in the trial. These gaps cause confusion and the rhythm of the case is destroyed."

There's trouble, I thought.

"Are you finished?" the Judge said almost inaudibly.

"Well, Judge--" Jed foolishly went on.

I slid down in my seat, having learned long ago that when the Judge apparently was on my side to shut my mouth.

"If the case is referred out, the litigants and witnesses will be in more comfortable surroundings and we'll be able to proceed day by day," Jed continued.

He has a death wish, I thought.

After a full minute the Judge was ready.

"Attorney," not even a last name, I thought. Here it comes.

"I have a duty to hear cases, not assign them to a substitute. Also, the courts of this Commonwealth are perfectly adequate for *all* the people, rich or poor. Additionally, Attorney, there's nothing in the Fourteenth Amendment to our Constitution that guarantees you a trial on a day to day basis. We do our best in this county. Sometimes people are inconvenienced. That's too bad. Your client may be inconvenienced. That's too bad."

"The reason for your motion hasn't escaped me, Mr. Jed," the Judge continued.

'Mr.' now is it, I thought. That's even worse than 'attorney'.

"If the case was referred to an arbitrator, the hearing would commence in the privacy of his or her plush office, without public scrutiny, without the media present and, more than likely, without regard to the rules of evidence. I've taken an oath to uphold the Constitution of this Commonwealth and these United States, Attorney Jed, and I'll not violate that oath under any circumstances."

"Your motion is denied."

Jed looked like he was going to faint, but he pressed on.

"My last motion, your Honor, is a motion *In Limine*.

"Proceed."

Jed looked all around the courtroom. Apparently satisfied, he began.

"Judge, there have been insidious rumblings that the Governor is not the father of Danny, the only child of the parties. The boy is fourteen years old. For fourteen years, he has believed that Brenden Mitchell was his father. Ms. Mitchell never said otherwise and they both lived their lives in a loving, caring way with Danny being the center of their attention.

Now, all of a sudden the defendant wants to introduce evidence that someone else, some stranger is the father of Danny. Is that in the best interest if the boy? What good will the introduction of that evidence do?

So, I ask you Judge, to prevent the introduction of any such evidence at this trial. It simply is not in Danny's best interest and that interest over-rides any other rights the defendant may have for its introduction."

"Attorney Eldridge?"

"First, these people have not lived their lives in a loving, caring way." I began. "They're getting a divorce for just that reason. There is no love or care or compassion shown by this Governor to his wife and there hasn't been for years.

This is a custody battle of the first water, Your Honor. There are a string of medical health care professionals ready to testify, solicited and paid for by both sides. For example, there is a forensic psychiatrist engaged by agreement of both the plaintiff and defendant who will testify based on therapy sessions and extensive psychological testing concerning the capacity of each of the parties to adequately parent this child. During the course of his investigation another physician, a urologist, uncovered from Ms. Mitchell the truth, according to her, that the Governor is not Danny's father. What's more important is the fact that I have scientific DNA proof that Brenden Mitchell is not Danny's father.

That lack of blood relationship may be an important element in the analysis of the character of the Governor to parent at all."

I was on thin ground, I knew, but I let it fly.

"Anything else, Attorney Eldridge?"

"No sir."

"I'll enter an order. You both will hear from me."

"Thank you."

"Call the next case, Ms. Fairchild"

CHAPTER TWENTY-FIVE

"There's something strange going on there for sure," Tommy Bresnahan, an assistant AG, was telling his boss.

"One of our stalwart investigators has been working over the records at Mitchell's campaign headquarters and her findings thus far indicate some substantial manipulation of the books," he continued.

"Like what?" the AG inquired.

"Well, up until about two months ago there was a weekly deposit of twenty-five hundred dollars into various bank accounts listed as "Campaign Funds, Brenden Mitchell for U.S.Senate". Oh, there was a slight variation each week, but the difference was only miniscule. That's over ten thousand a month, every month, month after month, if you catch my drift. Then, all of a sudden two months ago, the deposits were reduced to almost exactly two thousand a week or about eighty-six hundred a month. They've been at that level ever since. There are spikes here and there but the deposits are startlingly consistent.

There's more. The only records we were shown were the bank records. There were no records of the source of the money. Where did the cash come from?"

The AG wrinkled his brow as he listened to his assistant.

"It's a violation of the OCPF not to have the records available at the campaign office," the AG said finally.

"I'm going to tell you something in confidence, Tommy. Ted Eldridge, the lawyer for the Governor's wife in the divorce case everyone's talking about, tells me he thinks the Governor is getting a rake-off from the bookies, perhaps the ones in the North End. He tells me he thinks the Governor has the local cops in his pocket. He also tells me that the Governor is using those funds for personal expenses. Now that I think of it, he's probably funding his divorce case with campaign funds. God knows it must be costing him a small fortune."

"I'll be goddamned," Tommy exclaimed..

"That's major criminal activity. He could be indicted on the strength of what you just told me alone. The indictment would be enough to destroy any of his political ambitions and even put the rest of his term in jeopardy at the State House."

"If it's true. Remember the allegation comes from the Governor's adversary in a divorce case."

"Well, what do you want me to do, boss?"

"Who has been conducting the investigation so far?"

"Her name is Deidre Hennessey. She young but she's bright."

"We have to have a plan before we select the person who will carry it out. The key, obviously, is to get the records which show the names of the contributors. The answer to that question lies with the Governor's Chief of Staff, Mort Haller. I think we need more of a heavy-weight from this office than a young Deidre Hennessey to confront Haller. That means you, Tommy."

"No problem. I'll get right on it."

"It doesn't end there though, does it?" the AG said.

"We have to find out where the money comes from if it doesn't come from contributors and it sure as hell doesn't come from them."

"We've got the makings of a major crime that could shake up this state like never before. The question is," he continued, "what are we going to do about it? We can't bring in the FBI. We certainly can't bring in the Boston Police when there are allegations of corruption in the force itself. That leaves the State Police."

"And so?"

"And so I'll make sure they conduct a covert investigation. It shouldn't take too long. The bookies we're initially interested in are in the North End. We'll start there. God knows I can point them in the right direction. I've always looked the other way thinking that bookmaking there was solely within the jurisdiction of the Boston Police. I only hope none of my relatives are involved."

Tommy turned to go.

"One more thing, Tommy. Ted Eldridge is a friend of mine. In fact he's part of my extended family in a way. His wife is a cousin of mine. I'd like to help him out, if I can, by getting this information to him in time for him to possibly use it in his divorce case. We only have less than two weeks."

"I understand. As I said, I'll get right on it, boss."

As soon as Tommy left, the AG called the Commander of the Massachusetts State Police, Peter Britt, and told him the whole story.

"Jesus Christ," Britt exclaimed. "Are you kidding me? The Governor?"

"Yeah well, that's what we want to find out," the AG replied.

"I've got just the guy in mind. I'll get him in here right away."

"Thanks, Peter. I certainly appreciate it."

Two days later, on Wednesday, a short, swarthy, bald- headed man about forty-five years old entered a small store -front on Salem

Street in the North End. The store only sold lottery tickets, nothing else. The glass case in front of the clerk was filled with all the different variety of tickets. Behind the cash register were rows of tickets ranging in cost from one dollar to five, each denomination featuring a different game, the numbers of which had to be scratched out. The quick-picks were on a separate roll. There was a small shelf just before the glass case where those players who had to circle numbers could fill out slips.

The tiny room was dense with stale cigarette smoke even though no one was there except the old man behind the counter. He was dressed in jeans and an old, grey undershirt, the kind with straps around the shoulders and a scooped neck.

"Red Sox-Yankees this Saturday, eh pops?"

"Big game," the old man replied.

"What's the bet?"

"It's all even."

"Here's a hundred on the Red Sox."

The old clerk looked into the eyes of the bald man.

"I don't know you. I only sell lottery tickets," he told him.

"Look pops. I was told I could place a bet with you so don't give me that shit," the bald man said grabbing the old man by his undershirt. As he did so he made sure the clerk noticed a Glock .38 stuffed in the waist of his pants on the left side, just above the pocket.

"OK mister, fill out this slip and I'll place your bet."

"I'm not filling out any slip. *You're* the one who'll fill out a slip. Jot down a receipt for the "C" note and write after it the words 'even -Red Sox Wednesday August 21st'."

"Not on your life," the old man replied. "I'll take your bet but I ain't writin'down nothin'."

"All right. I ain't writin' down nothin' either," the bald man said.

"Here's my hundred. We have a bet, right?"

"Right," came the reply.

The bald man left and got into a black Ford Taurus parked further down Salem Street out of sight of the old man's store.

The driver leaned over the passenger seat and opened the door.

"Did he notice the wire?" the driver asked.

"Not a chance. Let's go."

The next day the old man was visited by another plain-clothed, deep tanned, well dressed officer from the State Police by the name of DellaPenna. He showed him his badge as soon as the last customer left and they were alone. He knew he didn't have much time, so he got right to the point. He placed the recorder on the counter and pressed the button marked 'play'.

When the recording was finished he said, "Tell me who receives the money and covers the bets you make, and tell me quickly before we're interrupted. If you tell me right now, this instant, my office will look the other way about your involvement."

He could tell the old man was frightened. He didn't have to wait long.

"The clearing house is Renzo's Restaurant, OK? The guy there is Guiliano Rigali. He controls the whole thing."

"Thanks," he said, picking up the recorder just as another customer walked in. He couldn't wait to get out of that stinking place.

"Well, now we're getting somewhere," the AG said to Tommy as he was informed of the progress on Salem Street the very next day. Tommy had received a phone call from DellaPenna that very morning bringing him up to date.

"What happened with Mort Haller?" the AG asked.

"After doing a dance, he finally brought me the books showing the names of the alleged donors. After a fight and some threats, he allowed me to copy the ledgers. We ran a random sample check and found out that more than half of the names were phony. When I asked him about that later, he shrugged and blamed the discrepancy on the poor quality of the volunteers at the headquarters. I could tell he was pretty shaken up though."

"What about the Governor's personal bank accounts?"

"We were lucky there," Tommy replied.

"All the bank accounts were subpoenaed by Ted Eldridge and they were copied for him. Haller referred us to Attorney Paul Jed. Haller said something like 'they've been looked at by everybody else, why not you?' We simply asked Jed for another set. They show an enormous amount of money being spent on the divorce case and other household and personal items, trips, vacations, clothes, alimony, child support, you know, the whole thing. But they don't show where the deposits come from. Eldridge could trace income from the Governor's salary, dividends, income from his real estate holdings and the like, but Eldridge didn't have access to the campaign accounts.

Thousands of dollars in the Governor's personal accounts must come from those campaign accounts. There are also large withdrawals of cash with no accountability. We also think there are assets of the Governor that he acquired from these campaign accounts."

"How much money are we talking about?" the AG asked.

"We figure almost five hundred thousand dollars were siphoned off just this year so far," Tommy replied.

"And that doesn't include the assets. God only knows how many assets came from those funds. There's over two million un-accounted for I understand," the A.G. said.

"It looks to me like Haller is responsible for collecting the 'donations' and the Governor is responsible for spending the cash."

"Yeah, I agree. What's next?" Tommy said.

"I'm going to coordinate with Britt, the Commander of the State Police. He's approaching the problem from another perspective. He'll hopefully be in a position to tell us where the money is coming from that feeds the Governor's appetite for spending so much money."

Della Penna was dressed in a dark blue suit, white shirt and blue and red tie as he made his way into Renzo's at three-thirty

Saturday afternoon. The lunch crowd had thinned out and the early birds hadn't yet arrived.

He sat at a table in the corner away from the windows, away from the small, cozy bar but against a wall, which provided him with a view of the whole room. He couldn't have been more conspicuous despite his efforts. A waiter eventually approached him dressed in black trousers, white shirt, black bow tie and a red cummerbund.

"Can I help you, sir?"

"I'll have a Campari and soda," DellaPenna said.

"Here's a menu and I'll be right back with your drink."

As the waiter turned to go, the customer asked, "Are you Gulie?"

"No sir. Gulie's out of the hospital now over a week. He's in re-hab. He's got a knee replacement but he should come hobbling in here any time now. This is his first day back to visit Renzo. He's in the kitchen. Do you want me to tell him that you're here?"

"Yes, please. Tell him there's a friend who'd like to speak with him."

Ten minutes later, Gulie came out of the swinging doors leading from the kitchen by pushing his shoulder into the door and stopping it from closing with his crutch. He maneuvered the other crutch through the opening and let the door swing close. Della Penna watched.

"Do I know you?" Guiliano asked.

"Not yet," came the reply. "Please sit down for just a few minutes. There's something I have to tell you that you'll be interested in," the bald man said enticingly.

Gulie hesitated and then sat down with difficulty, propping his crutches against the wall.

When the Della Penna opened his suit coat, Gulie shifted in his seat and watched carefully as Della Penna took out only a wallet.

Then Della Penna flipped open his wallet and showed his State Police identification to Guiliano Rigali.

"Allow me to get right to the point. We know you're operating a book out of this restaurant and have been for quite a while. We also believe the owner, Renzo Andretti is involved. He'd have to be blind and stupid not to know what's going on here."

Guiliano said nothing.

"Look, why don't you save us some time. Go and get your boss and tell him to come out here and sit down with us."

With nothing more than a shrug Gulie got up carefully and hobbled into the kitchen.

"We've got some trouble, padrone," he said to Renzo as Renzo was pounding some veal with a wooden mallet on the large, butcher block table in the middle of the kitchen.

Renzo said nothing.

At that instant, Gulie recalled a conversation he had with Renzo when Renzo came to the hospital to visit him.

"What d' you want me to do Gulie," Renzo had said.

"I recognized the son of a bitch," Gulie told him. "It was that detective that does all the work for Eldridge's office, Charley Randell."

"This was a pay back, you know, my friend."

"I know boss, but as far as I'm concerned, that bastard Randell and the goddamn lawyer can swim with the fishes."

"I feel the same way but let's get something out of it for our trouble."

"What d' you mean?"

"If we do something like that we should do it on behalf of the Governor, not ourselves. That way we get a benefit."

"What do you have in mind?"

"I talked to Haller yesterday", Renzo had told his chef. "They said they were attempting to settle the case with a generous offer. The first offer wasn't accepted by Eldridge so they're not sure what they'll do. They haven't been able to get together yet to decide. But if the case doesn't settle they're going to want us to get involved. At that point, we'll be doing a trick for the Governor and, at the same time, a little pay back for you. Capisce?"

Renzo finally looked up from the now flattened veal.

"There's a guy out there from the State Police. He says they know about our operation and he wants to speak with you and me. He sent me in to get you. He's sitting at table 24," Gulie said.

Renzo untied his apron strings and lifted the apron over his head. He rolled the apron up in a ball and threw it in a corner, near the refrigerator.

"Why don't they go after criminals, murderers, robbers, pimps and the rest for chrissakes? Everybody bets. What the hell--"

They both walked slowly up to the table where Della Penna was sitting sipping his drink, Gulie lagging behind, struggling with his crutches.

"Please sit down."

Gulie and Renzo complied. Renzo sat down and Gulie leaned his crutches against the wall as before, then slid into a chair, keeping his leg extended outside the legs of the table.

The Della Penna had his wallet out as Renzo pulled his chair up closer to the table while Gulie tried to give himself more room.

"I'm a State Trooper," Della Penna said, showing his badge to Renzo.

"I told your assistant that we know you're running a book here. We know some of the locations that are in operation in the North End but, you know what? We really don't give a shit. What we're interested in is who gets the rake other than you."

He paused and looked into the eyes of the two sitting opposite him.

Della Penna continued. "I don't even want you to tell me the names of the cops who've been blinking and are obviously being paid off. Those guys will be taken care of by the Boston Police Department if at all. We're not investigating them.

Here's my proposition. If you tell me the name or names of those who're participating other than you, we'll shut down the book but you won't be prosecuted. We'll shut down the satellites but we won't prosecute them either. Booking has been going on in the North End since Paul Revere and even after we shut you down we're sure it'll start up again, so you figure it out."

"On the one hand you stand to be prosecuted with all the publicity that goes with it. I understand Judge Andretti is your daughter, sir. How would she like it to see her father's name all over the Globe and the Herald?"

"And you sir," the trooper said looking at Guiliano, "You have a son at B.U. we found out. How would he like seeing his father's name linked to an indictable crime?"

He folded his hands in plain sight on the table, sat back in the chair and after a few moments, took another sip of his drink.

"On the other hand," he continued, "all you have to do to avoid all that is give me the name or names I want. Right here. Right now."

CHAPTER TWENTY-SIX

"Stop badgering me for chrissake," Brenden Mitchell was complaining to his lawyer Sunday morning.

Paul Jed was putting the Governor through his paces by simulating Ted Eldridge's cross examination.

"I'm only trying to get you used to the kind of questions you'll be asked on cross. It's not going to be pretty. You simply must not get aggravated and learn to take your time before you answer. We have to prepare. This case might not settle."

Jed could see that the Governor was wound tighter than a major league baseball. He fidgeted in his chair, barked his answers at Jed, and was easily distracted.

"Let's get this over with," he told his lawyer. "I've got other problems."

"OK. We've finished with your direct. I think you'll be fine with that. It's the cross I'm worried about. Let's go through it again."

"Look Paul, let's cut the bull shit. Go back to that son of a bitch with an offer he can't refuse. You say Eldridge got back to you after he talked to Emily and said, 'no dice' to the offer we made, right?"

"That's right. He made no counter offer—a flat out rejection."

"The one thing that prevents an agreement is custody, wouldn't you say?" said the Governor.

"I could back off on that and agree to shared legal custody. They tell me that because we live in close proximity to one another, shared custody would work. Is that right?"

"Governor, you talk like you've never heard of that possibility before. I told you that shared custody was an option the first day you came in here."

"Well, maybe you did, but at that time I was so pissed off when Emily said I wasn't Danny's father that I wanted an all-out fight for custody."

"Custody wasn't the only thing that prevented an agreement, Governor. The property settlement we offered was also rejected. Mort told me to low-ball them the first time around. Eldridge didn't even let me present what we offered as alimony and child support. We'd have to sweeten the pot considerably before we could possibly hope to settle this case. And Governor, trial is only a week away."

"What about all those investigations that've been going on? Have we heard from whatshername? Dr. Sheila somebody--"

"I'm expecting her report tomorrow morning. She said she was going to messenger it to Eldridge and me by ten o'clock."

'The other guy?"

"I don't think his report will hurt us at all."

"Feingold?"

"We'll see."

"OK then. Let's prepare a new offer, one last time before we have to take more drastic steps. Give the bitch seventy-five per cent of all the assets on my financial statement. Shared custody, that should do the trick. Gagne's associates, Graham and a guy by the name of Foley did a tax analysis for me and a valuation of all my assets. Use that. You'll see it when Gagne comes in to prepare with you tomorrow.

Offer her six thousand a month alimony and two thousand a month child support. The alimony will be tax deductible so that kind of break-down is beneficial to me. I figure Emily will get about five million in assets. Just make sure the house goes to her. I'm more interested in the other assets, even at only twenty-five per cent. The rest of the details I expect you to take care of."

After Jed wrote down all that the Governor had told him, they continued with the simulated cross examination, but the spark was gone. Their hearts weren't in it, Mitchell could tell. After only a half-hour more, the Governor picked up his notes and headed for the door.

"Call me or Mort as soon as you hear from whatshername tomorrow," he said on the way out the door.

As soon as he left, he called Ted Eldridge.

"Ted, I've finally talked to my client and I think I have a proposition that you'll like. Can I see you tomorrow at eleven o'clock? I'll go over to Old City Hall.

"That's OK by me. I'll be here."

"Thanks. See you then."

When I received Jed's call, I was in the middle of preparing Chuck Dawson, my intrepid business expert, for his direct examination. Trial was only a week away but I wasn't worried about Dawson. It was a sheer joy to listen to him expound on valuations. I only had to present an outline to him and he took it from there. I didn't have to worry about his cross examination. He knew more about methods of valuation than Paul Jed could ever assimilate in a lifetime.

253

After he left, I called Jordan and Henry in to tell them the news of Jed's call.

"What the hell, he's bidding against himself," Jordan exclaimed.

"Boy, they really don't want to go to trial, do they?" Henry chimed in.

"Yeah, well, we can't assume a thing. Let's get back to work."

Without any more, they left and the underlying intensity in the whole office resumed. The office was more than intense; it was a mad house. Henry, Jordan and I each waited impatiently for the secretaries to get caught up with the tapes they left in the trays. The system was agreed to years ago. Lawyers would dictate onto tapes and the finished tapes would be placed in the trays for typing. First come, first served, senior partner or not. The secretaries were strung-out and crabby. Usually on a Friday the office would pay for a catered lunch and the staff would spend a half-hour in the morning laughing and joking about what they were going to order and who was going to share with whom. Not this Friday, when the trial was going to start in four days with the holiday intervening. The overtime pay really wasn't worth giving up a whole Labor Day weekend for, they made clear. The only way to even come close to compensating them was to give them time off after the trial—a number of days off greater than they would have had if they didn't work straight through the weekend and the holiday.

Precisely at ten o'clock the following morning, Amy brought a large envelope from Dr, Sheila Monaghan. I opened the fifteen-page report and skipped to the bottom line for her recommendation. "Shared legal and physical custody" was her opinion.

That's bullshit, I thought. It's simply a 'cop-out'. This puts us in a bind. That ass Donald Long isn't going to be good to us and that means our only chance for full custody rests with Feingold— and I haven't heard from him and probably will not until the trial begins. I wondered what Jed would say. I wondered whether the Judge would allow Gerber to testify. I wondered how Emily's testimony would come down. Charley Randell's testimony should be dynamite or won't it---?

"He's here," Amy said.

I went out to the reception area to greet my *good friend* Paul Jed and escorted him into the large conference room rather than the conference room that's cozier, more intimate. I wasn't looking for intimacy.

"Coffee, Paul?" I asked as we sat down across from one another. The conference table had yellow pads, pencils and pens available for our guests. We even had napkins with the firm's name imprinted on them, real coffee cups, not cardboard, a carafe, spoons, sugar and a small pitcher of cream, not milk. A little over the top perhaps, but this was downtown Boston.

"Why thank you, Ted. Yes, I'll have some coffee," he replied.

I poured and, just so he wouldn't feel uncomfortable, I poured myself a cup also. He put his own cream and sugar in so I didn't have to do that at least.

He placed the cup to his lips and although I knew the coffee was hot, I somehow wasn't surprised when I heard him slurp his first sip and dribble some coffee down his chin. He grabbed one of our napkins and, without a word, placed his cup back on the saucer, wiped his chin, settled back in his chair and reached for his briefcase.

"Ted, I've been preparing for trial just as I know you have, but I thought it would be worth one more try to see if we can reach an agreement."

"I'm happy to hear any proposal that's better than the one we were talking about in your office the other day," I told him.

"Before I begin, I want you to know that what I'm about to offer you is all I got. There is no more. This is our best shot."

"So what you're telling me Paul, is that this is a "take it or leave it' proposition, right?"

"No, no. I didn't mean it like that. I only meant that I've worked up the Governor to get as much as I can from him.

Let me lay it out for you," he began.

"Will you need the blackboard?" I asked him with a straight face.

He didn't get it

"No thanks," he said sincerely.

"First, Emily will receive seven million dollars in assets including the house. The difference between the value of the house and seven million is four million dollars, which she will receive in cash. We've figured this to be a 75-25 split. Of course, the value of the Governor's interest in the corporations and the limited partnerships is included in the five million.

Second, the rest of the assets, such as the defined benefit plan and any 401k plans will be divided 75-25. We'll get a court approved order transferring the ownership in the defined benefit plan along these lines.

Third, the Governor will pay Emily six thousand dollars a month alimony and two thousand as child support. He'll pay all of Danny's reasonable medical and dental expenses. College expenses will be decided later. For example, if Brenden Mitchell is elected to the Senate, he'll pay the entire expenses of Danny's college. If not, we'll just have to wait and see.

Fourth, we'll accept Dr. Monaghan's recommendation, shared physical and legal custody of Danny.

Keep in mind that the Governor will still pay two thousand a month as child support even though he has shared custody.

There you have it," Jed said, shifting his position in the chair and crossing his legs.

I didn't say anything for a moment. Finally, I said,

"It's apparent that you've given this some thought Paul, and I will do the same. We don't have much time so I'll, try and get Emily in here this very day."

"That'd be great Ted. Thanks for the coffee."

He got up to go, then paused.

"You know Ted, I want you to know that I've gotten over my disappointment over not being appointed to the Superior Court seven or eight years ago. At first, I held you responsible, mainly because you were the one who was appointed. But now, in this case, you've handled yourself like a perfect gentleman."

Whew, I thought. Is he blowin' smoke? Trying to soften me up? Is he that devious?

"Well thanks, Paul. No sense we don't treat each other with civility. I'll get back to you as soon as I can."

When he left, I asked Amy to get Emily on the phone for me while I composed my notes from the meeting I just finished.

Several minutes later the morning mail was delivered and it contained the report from Donald Long. That meant I received Monaghan's report and Long's report in the mail, both on the same day, an incredible coincidence. Just as I suspected, Long's recommendation was that the Governor have sole physical and legal custody of Danny. He provided what amounted to an equal division of time between both parents, but the bottom line went to the Governor. By such a recommendation, he covered his ass. He did what the Governor wanted on the one hand and at least approached what was right on the other.

Another letter I received was from the bank. They told me I was in arrears on my credit line and one month behind on my mortgage payment; that if I didn't pay the arreages within thirty days, they'd start foreclosure. There was no way this trial would end and a judgment enter in thirty days, I thought. Foreclosure would buy me some time, but how much? What if Talbot enters a judgment that's not in Emily's favor? Where will I get the money I owe? Shit!

There was always the hope the case would settle, I thought before I picked up the phone to talk to my client. Perhaps I should sell it to her. If Emily agreed, I'd have my money within weeks. She had a lot to lose if she insisted on going to trial. She certainly wouldn't get from Talbot what Jed offered. No, I thought. Let her make up her own mind. I'll give her my opinion, my recommendation, but she'll decide.

"Emily, how does it feel to be a millionaire several times over?" I said to her when she got on the line.

"What?" she said. I knew I'd spoken too fast.

"You'd better come in here so we can talk about the offer I just received from Paul Jed," I said to her more slowly.

An hour later, I was still explaining the package to her: the plusses and minuses, the risk of trial, the benefit of settling. All seemed to go well until I got to the part about custody.

"Emily, we received both reports from the investigators. Donald long recommended physical custody to the Governor--"

I heard her gasp. She produced her handkerchief from out of nowhere and covered her trembling mouth with it. I pressed on.

"Dr. Monaghan recommended shared legal and physical custody. Part of this settlement offer from your husband is that he will agree to Dr. Monaghan's report. He'll agree to a shared custody arrangement. In other words, your time with Danny will be fifty-fifty."

Her eyes became slits, her mouth pursed and her fists clenched as she shot me a direct look.

"Tell me," she began, "How the hell can shared custody work when Brenden and I can't even communicate. We really don't even like each other. There's no way we can talk things out in a shared custody arrangement. Think of all the details that have to be agreed upon to make something like this work. Who drives Danny to school? Who picks him up? Who takes him to the doctor? Who spends time with him when his father is out campaigning all day? Every weekend? Do you honestly think we can agree to substitute visitation days when something comes up that prevents one of us from exercising our regular visit?

No! I won't agree! It's not a matter of how long Danny will be with me. He'll be with me for the same amount of time no matter what those so-called experts call the custodial arrangement. All Brenden wants is the victory. He won't parent, drive, cook, clean, buy clothes, take Danny to church, check his school work or anything else that requires time spent with Danny. He just wants the title. He wants to control the major decisions involving Danny's life. I wouldn't be surprised if he intends to somehow use the fact that he's the custodial parent in his campaign for the

Senate. I won't stand for it. To hell with the money, it's Danny that I have to protect."

"You realize Emily, that our only hope for sole custody lies with the recommendation of Dr. Feingold. Your testimony will help, but it'll be Feingold who will carry the day."

"Well, let's go with it then. I'm ready," she said.

I was disappointed. Jed's offer was within a heartbeat of being accepted. My money problems would've been over. This case would end—finally. But...nothing I could do.

I called Paul Jed and told him I'd see him in court, no deal.

Haller was waiting for the call. Everything was on the line with this settlement offer he knew. He could hardly wait to hear from Jed. When he did, when Jed told him the case didn't settle, he was dumbfounded.

"Mort, all he said was 'I'll see you in court'. You know what that means. We have to get ready for the Governor's testimony now, I mean right now."

"Oh Jesus Christ! That means big trouble. I'll get back to you."

"Wait a minute, Mort! We have things to talk about. You owe me almost two hundred thousand dollars. It'll be a helluva lot more if we go to trial. What're you people going to do about it?"

"Not now, Paul. Not now. Please! I'll get back to you."

Mort went into the Governor's Office.

"We have to talk."

"Shoot"

"No, not here."

"Where?"

"Meet me in an hour at the Algonquin Club. We'll talk there."

In the Algonquin club's library on the second floor, Mort settled in one of the Empire chairs. The governor sat opposite him in a red leather couch.

"They didn't accept our offer," he began.

"I'll be a son of a bitch!"

"So we'll have to get ready--"

"My ass, we have to get ready. I'm ready. Call Renzo! Let's put plan 'B' into operation. They'll get more than they bargained for. If this trial goes on I'll be ruined. Ruined!"

"Look, Brenden, the trial is now," Mort said using his boss's first name for emphasis. I'll call Renzo but we still have some ammunition to use against Eldridge. Don't forget, Emily is no prize. She'll look like a drunk when these shrinks get finished with her. Her testimony about drugs is completely unsupported. What else is there? Sure, they've got some pictures but the press, the public, will never see them, they're impounded. The question of custody is open. You've got a better chance than Emily has. Talbot will never give her seventy-five percent of the assets"

"Back and forth, back and forth, for chrissakes. What a fucking nightmare!"

They stayed at the Algonquin club another half-hour before Mort had a chance to call Renzo from the club's phone, after the Governor left.

"They didn't accept the final deal. There's nothing left to offer them," Mort said.

"What do you want me to do?"

"Take him down."

CHAPTER TWENTY-SEVEN

September sixth was a Wednesday. At six A. M. when my alarm went off, it was cloudy, unseasonably cold and downright bleak. By the time I reached my car it was raining and the clouds became even blacker. By the time I reached Old City Hall the wind picked up and the rain came down in large pellets against my windshield, stripping a lot of leaves off the trees and causing some to stick like glue to the roadways and sidewalks.

I was nervous. I still get nervous on the day a trial begins. The thought that the trial will be governed by strict rules of conduct is the one thing that settles me down. No grandstanding as in a deposition. No interruptions as in a motion session. Well, OK, hardly any I thought.

The four days before the weekend and the holiday itself were nightmares of nothing but work. People were all away from their offices downtown, away from their telephones, even their cell phones were shut off so every effort to reach somebody ended in frustration. After Labor Day, we crammed a whole week's work into one day, Tuesday, to try to catch up with those we couldn't reach earlier.

We had one piece of good news that came in with the morning mail, Tuesday morning. Judge Talbot denied Jed's motion *In Limine*. His order, however, alerted both sides that evidence about paternity might be limited. I honestly didn't know what the Judge meant by that but I was prepared and so was Dr. Gerber.

The Suffolk County Probate and Family Court is located on the fourth floor of the newly constructed Edward W. Brooke Courthouse. The dedication ceremonies took place only four years ago in October 2002 and, as I've said to many people, the newness hasn't yet worn off. The courtrooms are all commodious, the acoustics are exceptional, the floors are shining and the chairs inside the bar as well as the benches outside the bar gleam with polish. Compared with Worcester or Cambridge, Suffolk is a palace. In Cambridge for example, in order to get to Courtroom #5, called "The Dugout", clients, lawyers and witnesses have to walk past a locker room filled with green, government issue, metal lockers stretching along the corridor for about fifty feet. Once past that, there are busy restrooms for men and women, which open directly onto the corridor leading to the courtroom. Up a few steps beyond the disinfectant odor from the toilets, across a rather narrow hall sits "The Dugout".

Henry, Jordan and I looked like a small military cadre on our way to the courthouse early Wednesday morning. Henry and Jordan each pushed or pulled a two-wheeled cart on which were piled red, expandable, document folders loaded with the pleadings files, the correspondence files, the miscellaneous files and a file for each witness, theirs and ours. I limped along with my crutches, metal screws in my pelvis, a titanium rod in my left leg and an ugly red scar across my face. For some stupid reason I wanted to be with them. No cab for me, I had to hit every rut in the road.

We prepared our exhibits in large, black, three ring binders. There were six of these: one set for the Judge, one for Jed and one for us. In addition, we had a large leather, zippered bag, similar to a garment bag, which contained our charts and graphs. Finally, there was my tan, leather, trial bag with my initials just below the handle, which I considered to be my good luck charm, given to me by Andrea when I opened my office at Old City Hall. I had all I could do to keep up with Henry and Jordan as I hobbled along, but the effort gave me something to think about as I put one foot in front of the other, using my crutches as another pair of legs. At least I didn't have to carry anything.

None of us said a word as we made our way over Washington Street, down State Street and over Congress Street; about a twenty minute walk with the carts and the crutches to the courthouse. The rain hadn't let up; the wind was coming from the northeast directly in our faces and the sidewalk was slippery from the accumulation of fallen, wet leaves. Maybe I should've taken a cab after all, I thought.

Parked illegally on the street by the side of the courthouse were two TV trucks with a small staff of people milling around outside the cabs. In front of one of the trucks, an attractive young woman was holding a microphone in her hand and was speaking before a camera. Another TV truck had jumped the curb and was parked on the stone pavement directly in front of the entrance. A long line of people snaked out the front door, each person having to be stripped of any metal, their pocket books emptied, their bodies explored by a wand, which covered them from head to foot before gaining entrance through the magnetic arch, into the vestibule and access to the elevator banks. The exceptions to the queue were lawyers who simply had to show their bar cards indicating that they were in good standing before the Board of Bar Overseers of the Supreme Judicial Court. Depending on the mood of the court officer, sometimes even lawyers had to empty their pockets of metal, keys and pen-knives.

Once inside the courthouse we showed our bar cards to the court officer who was tending the security apparatus. I held my breath hoping we wouldn't have to take all the files off the carts for inspection. We looked like we had prepared for some kind of an invasion with all our trial material. Fortunately, probably because he saw I was a cripple, he waived us through after we unloaded our personal items into the trays and passed them through the x-ray machine.

As I stepped through the arch however, every alarm in the system must have gone off. The reason was obvious of course. The court officer looked knowingly at my cast and waived me through with a sympathetic look. What he didn't know was that the metal plate holding my pelvis together would have shorted the whole system out even if the cast was removed.

There was a throng in front of the elevators and not just a few people were heard to say, "There's her lawyers." One reporter stuck a microphone in front of me and asked, "Any comment before the trial, counselor?"

"No comment," was all I said.

Emily was to be my first witness and she was waiting for us, sitting on the bench outside the courtroom. I told her to be sure and dress conservatively; no diamonds, no pearls, no Rolex watch, no short skirt, and no cleavage. I was almost sure I didn't have to give her that lecture but I've been burned before. I could see the moment I saw her that she was dressed like a lady. Nothing fancy. She wore a conservative navy blue suit, a white blouse and a simple gold necklace. Her brown hair was cut so that it fell just over her ears and tapered to the base of her neck. Her blush and eye shadow looked to have been expertly applied and her lip-gloss was a muted pink.

"Emily, you look lovely," I said to her. It not only was the truth but I wanted to give her some confidence, some security.

"Thank you," was her only reply. I could tell she was nervous.

"Sit there while I go inside and make some arrangements," I directed. "I'll be right back."

I had arrangements to make all right. The question that had to be answered right away was who was going to go first. I knew I had filed my complaint before Jed. I also knew we had checked the docket and made sure we had filed first but I didn't trust Jed or his connections in the courthouse. He had filed his own complaint for divorce and I was not going to be taken by surprise when the case was called and Jed stood up to make his opening argument.

Inside, the courtroom was jammed. There wasn't a seat to be had. Even the chairs inside the bar were filled with lawyers who had come to watch the proceeding.

I had to wait my turn in front of Dolores Fairchild's desk, leaning on my crutches, as there were lawyers who evidently had tried to mark some motion for hearing today hoping to get a front row seat. She would have none of it.

"There's only one matter on for today," she said over and over as the line quickly thinned out.

"Dolores, there's no doubt that the record shows I filed first, right?"

"Actually there was some doubt this morning when I came in, Mr. Eldridge. Someone had listed Brenden Mitchell as the plaintiff and the procedure memo given to the Judge had Paul Jed going first. Someone must have been confused because Brenden Mitchell is the plaintiff all right. He filed a cross complaint for divorce but you filed first. I changed Judge Talbot's memo accordingly, not to worry."

"Thanks Dolores."

Yeah, sure, someone must have been confused, I thought.

Jordan and Henry were busy stacking our files against the wall and around the counsel table. The exhibit books were distributed to Jed's table and to Dolores for the benefit of the Judge. Jordan had to leave after the files were taken out of their expandable document folders. I knew he wanted to stay but there simply was no room for four of us at counsel table. Besides that was the game plan all along.

Emily was sandwiched between Henry and me at counsel table, which was stacked with files and notebooks. Amid the cacophony of the courtroom, a hush suddenly came over the crowd as the Governor of the Commonwealth of Massachusetts made his entry.

He acted as though he had just entered a political gathering for his benefit as he waived to bystanders, smiling, nodding and looking resplendent in a grey double-breasted suit, stark white shirt and a red power tie. He immediately took his seat next to Paul Jed at defendant's counsel table, shot his cuffs displaying huge, gold cuff links, a Patek Philippe watch and calmly folded his hands in front of him, looking like a conquering hero.

The courtroom din started up again as soon as he was seated and there was nothing left for me to do but wait for the trial to begin.

I didn't have to wait long.

Jack sing-songed the ancient "cry" in a stentorian voice and told everyone to be seated after Judge Talbot sat down. There was a shuffling of feet followed by a surprising silence.

"Call the first case," the Judge ordered.

Obediently, Dolores called out, "Mitchell v. Mitchell, Suffolk Divorce 065638 D.

Those who will testify please stand." Emily and the Governor stood up.

"Do you severally solemnly swear that the evidence you are about to give in the matter now in hearing shall be the truth, the whole truth and nothing but the truth, so help you God?"

"I do," they both intoned.

There wasn't a whisper in the courtroom.

"Proceed," the Judge ordered.

With some considerable effort, I stood up to the microphone, which stood between the counsel tables and placed my notes on the lectern.

"May it please the Court," I began.

I outlined what I expected to prove for about thirty-five minutes. Too long! There's nothing that can't be said in fifteen minutes, but I thought I had no choice. I labored over the expected testimony of Donald Long and Dr. Sheila Monaghan—boring. I droned on about the testimony of my real estate expert, Steve Lyons, equally boring.

After twenty minutes, just as I thought I was losing the Judge, I began to outline the sexy stuff. When I got to the part about what I expected my detective, Charley Randell, to testify to at least in general, there was an audible gasp from the gallery. When I outlined what Dr. Gerber was going to say about DNA testing there was such a commotion that the Judge had to insist on quiet.

Even so, the noise escalated when I described the existence of our forensic psychiatrist and that we expected his results any day now. When I got to the part about the unexplained cash, which our expert Chuck Dawson would testify to, there arose such a commotion that the Judge declared a five-minute recess and warned that if, upon his return, there were any more such disturbances, he'd clear the courtroom.

I still had not heard from The Attorney General's office so I didn't have a chance to drop that bomb before the recess was called. I simply had to wait before I could call Bobby Della Penna from the State Police and Tommy Bresnahan from the AG's office, if I could use them at all.

When I made my way back to the counsel table both Emily and Henry told me I'd done a good job. From the look on the Governor's face, I guessed that maybe I had.

While the Judge took his five-minute recess we didn't have much time, so we all stayed where we were. I looked at Emily to be sure she was all right and I thought she looked OK.

After Judge Talbot settled in his chair upon his return, he nodded to me as a signal to begin.

"My opening is concluded, Your Honor," I said.

"Attorney Jed?"

"I'll waive my opening now Judge, and open at the conclusion of the plaintiff's case."

"Call your first witness, Attorney Eldridge."

"Emily Mitchell," I replied, as I struggled to my feet.

Emily rose from her chair at counsel table and took the stand, which consisted of a lectern attached to a platform. On the platform, one-step up from the floor, was a chair for the comfort of the witness. A microphone was affixed to the lectern. The stenographer was in her place in front of the witness so as not to miss one word.

"You've already been sworn," the Judge said to her. "Be seated if you'll feel more comfortable," he continued.

Emily sat down and as soon as I saw she was settled, I began.

I took her through her years of education, the early years of her marriage, her employment history, the birth of Danny, the fact that she had the primary responsibility of his care, the role she played in the Governor's political life, her contribution as a homemaker, her health and finally the Governor's conduct towards her during the marriage. I introduced the photographs into evidence and with a flourish, I showed them to Jed by placing them demonstrably in front of him at the defendant's table.

"No objection," he stated.

I showed the pictures to Emily and bore in on the bruises, the hematoma, the swelling, the indignity, the hurt until I got what I wanted. Emily began to sob uncontrollably.

"Lunch recess," the Judge said as he rose from his chair.

"Two o'clock."

At lunch, I really had to get away, to be alone with my thoughts. I was never hungry anyway at noon and I didn't want to get bogged down with any details that I thought Henry could handle. I took a walk around Faneuil Hall even with my crutches, stopped for a bagel and coffee and watched all the tourists go by while sitting with my leg straight out wrapped in its cast.

In the afternoon, I began again with Emily. Not too long after Talbot resumed the bench, I went into her finances in detail, her paltry assets standing in her name alone and finally had her explain the strained relationship she shared and still shares with her husband. She testified to his ego and his insistence on complete control of all matters affecting the family; how he told her, on so many occasions that she was good for nothing and how that hurt her. But, I saved a kicker.

"Ms Mitchell, is Brenden Mitchell the father of Danny?" I asked.

The pervasive undercurrent of noise in the courtroom became hushed.

"Objection!"

"I already ruled on your motion, Mr. Jed. He may have it."

"No, he is not."

"What were the circumstances of your marriage approximately nine months before Danny was born?"

"Objection."

"Overruled."

"Brenden and I had a horrible argument one night after dinner. He slapped me hard across the face and I fell to the floor. Blood squirted from my nose and my lip was bleeding. I decided I would not take any more of this abuse so I told Brenden to get out or I'd call the police."

So far so good, I thought. Keep going.

"He packed his things and left. We were separated for about five or six weeks when I was asked out to dinner by an old acquaintance of mine. One thing led to another and yes, we were intimate that one night. A few weeks later I found out, I was pregnant. I was beside myself with remorse and guilt. Brenden was renting a small apartment on Beacon Hill at the time. I don't know why he hadn't move in with his sister; probably because her husband, Arthur Prescott was still living. Anyway, I went to his apartment one night shortly after I found out."

At this point, the courtroom was like a tomb. Not a sound. Not even a cough. No shuffling feet.

"Go on," I said.

"Well, I knew what I had to do. I was dressed in a skirt, a blouse--well, you know, I knew his preferences. I told him I missed him. We had some wine and before long, we were in bed. The very next day he moved back in with me. Within a month, I told him *we* were pregnant. He was very happy about it. We'd been trying for years you see. I knew he wasn't the father of Danny but what was more important at the time was he didn't."

She paused and looked down at her hands folded on top of the lectern. She had a smile that was inscrutable, certainly not embarrassed, in fact, a little self-satisfied, I thought.

"Now at some point did your husband recently move in with his sister?" I asked after giving her a chance to catch her breath.

"Yes."

"What did he take with him?" We had rehearsed this area to a "fair thee well" so I knew what she was going to say.

"He took clothes and some of his toilet articles; some other items with him."

"What did he leave?"

"He left some clothes and other paraphernalia, items in the bathroom."

"What items did he leave in the bathroom?"

"Among other things he left his comb and his brush."

Atta girl Emily, I thought.

"What did you do with his comb and brush?"

"I scraped the brush with his comb to get his hair on the comb. I then put the hair in an envelope and brought it to Dr. Hans Gerber. I gave the envelope directly to him."

That was a long way around but I had to establish the chain of control.

At that point we were finished. It was three o'clock when I finally said, "Thank you, Ms. Mitchell, that's all I have."

"Your Honor, I move that her testimony, starting from when she began with an 'argument with the defendant', be stricken from the record," Jed blurted out.

"Denied."

Jed sat back down and began to gather some papers in front of him in an effort to look unperturbed by the Judge's ruling, I thought. I could tell he didn't want to start his cross at that point. He didn't want to start one day and have a gap in the testimony until the next day; he'd lose the impact, destroy the rhythm. I didn't blame him but I wasn't going to agree to adjourn until tomorrow. This is a dogfight.

As I sat down at counsel table, I leaned my crutches against the bar behind me and looked directly at Brenden W. Mitchell. The look on his face left no doubt in my mind that the Governor would not soon appoint me to the Appeals Court. He shook his head, a scowl on his lips, but I knew he was shaken. His face was blotchy with pink and white patches and his eyes were almost closed in concentration as he stared at me. I smiled at him, that's all I did, as I took my seat.

No sooner had I sat down when Jed got up. "Your Honor, it's late. May I request we adjourn until nine o'clock tomorrow morning?"

I bolted from my seat and kicked over my crutches in the process.

"Judge," I said. "We have an eighteen-day trial in front of us.

Every hour is precious. We'll be here forever if we begin to cut the trial day short."

"Proceed now, Attorney Jed," the Judge instructed.

Jed strolled to a point directly in front of the witness stand and stopped about fifteen feet away. He assembled his notes on the corner of the defendant's counsel table and held what appeared to be an outline in his hands.

"Madam, you're on drugs aren't you?"

"Objection," I said.

"Overruled."

"I take medication, yes."

"Tell us what medication you're on."

"I take Lithium."

"You started out taking Valium, didn't you?"

"Yes."

"And then you progressed to Zoloft, right?"

"I object to the word 'progressed'." I said, rising.

"Attorney Eldridge you are simply to object. Nothing more. Do you understand?" Talbot said to me without even looking at me.

"Yes sir," I replied.

"Overruled."

"Answer the question, Ms Mitchell," Jed continued.

"Yes."

Atta girl Emily, keep it short and sweet. Don't volunteer, I thought.

"Are you aware, Ms Mitchell, that Zoloft is a mood elevator whereas Lithium is prescribed for bi-polar symptoms?"

"Objection!"

"Sustained."

"What were your symptoms at the time your doctor--let's see-- oh yes, a psychiatrist, Dr. James Hurley, prescribed Lithium?"

I had to hand it to Jed. That was a good recovery, I thought.

"Some days I'd feel sad, other days I'd feel OK."

"Dr. Hurley is a psychopharmacologist, isn't he?"

"Yes."

"Tell us, just what is a psycho pharmacologist?"

"He prescribes medication."

"Does his prescription include three and four glasses of wine every night while you're taking Lithium?"

Another gasp from the gallery.

"I object!"

"Overruled."

"Well, does it?"

"I don't drink three or four glasses of wine every night."

"How many do you drink?"

"I'll have a glass of wine at dinner. That's all."

"What would you say if I told you that your husband says you drink three and four glasses of wine every night, and then pass out on the couch while Danny fends for himself and later goes to bed?"

"That's a lie! I haven't had any wine since he left."

Oh, Emily! That's not the right answer, I thought.

"Isn't it true that you lose control of yourself when you're in your manic phase?"

"Objection!"

"Sustained."

"Isn't it true that when you're depressed you go to bed and can't function?"

"Objection!"

"Overruled."

"When I get depressed sometimes, I take my medication."

"You are aware that Danny attempted suicide when he was under your control, aren't you?"

"Yes," she said in a barely audible voice.

Hang in there Emily. I thought she was beginning to lose it.

"Where were you at the time?"

"I-- I'm not sure."

"Were you curled up in a ball lying in bed during one of your mood swings?"

"Objection!"

"Sustained. Re-phrase."

"Were you completely in control of yourself at the time your son attempted suicide?"

"Yes."

"How can you be sure, you don't even know where you were?"

"I-- I don't know."

"Now Ms. Mitchell…"

"Tomorrow morning, nine o'clock," Talbot said, rising from his chair.

"All rise," Jack instructed.

There followed a clamor as reporters rushed out the door to beat the crowd. Everyone left in the courtroom was talking to his or her neighbors in groups of three and four apparently all talking at the same time, not listening to anyone.

I made my way to the witness stand, gimp leg and all, took Emily by her arm, and guided her down the single step from the platform. "I didn't do so well, did I Mr.Eldridge?" she said speaking close to my ear.

"You were fine, don't worry," I assured her.

"Holy shit," Henry said as soon we reached counsel table. "What a tight ship Talbot runs. He doesn't fool around, does he?"

"That's the way it ought to be," I said to him. "Ask the clerk Dolores, if we can store some of these files in the courtroom overnight, Henry. We'll only need the files of our witnesses to take with us," I said as I grabbed Emily's arm and led her through the throng of onlookers still in the courtroom.

Outside, in the hall, reporters were ready for us, some with their cell phones still in their ear.

"Who's the father?" one shouted in my face.

"When does Randell go on the stand?" another demanded.

"How much money is unexplained?" someone asked.

"When does Dr, Gerber go on?" asked another.

I answered with "No comment" each time and decided that Emily and I would take the stairs rather than risk being cooped up with some reporter, or worse the Governor and his entourage, in the confines of the elevator. I had second thoughts about half way down as I struggled from stair to stair with the crutches and my cast even with Emily's assistance.

Back at the office I prepared Emily for the questions I thought would be asked the next day. I hadn't told her the details about what Charley Randell had uncovered for fear that she would either be so angry she'd lose it or tell one of her friends which would almost certainly get back to the Governor. Now was the right time I thought. I planned to call Charley at some time; at a point when I thought he'd make the greatest impact. When I related the whole story to her, she was angry all right, but after she calmed down, she also was empowered, somewhat galvanized and more confident about her forthcoming testimony, I believed.

After she left I forced myself to think of something pleasant, something other than this trial if only for a few moments. It didn't work. I lamented the fact that I had missed bringing Josh to his first day at Boston College. He'd left last week during our hectic preparation and I didn't have the time to go with him. Andrea filled me in on some details but I had to say my goodbyes the morning he left. I had mixed emotions. I was happy for him of course, but I knew that, just like when he was issued his driving license, the event was another right of passage. Soon he would be gone.

CHAPTER TWENTY-EIGHT

When Renzo finished his conversation with Mort Haller, he spoke to Gulie.

"They want us to terminate the lawyer," he said.

"That's OK with me."

"Think about it, Gulie. What's in it for us other than to punish them for what they did to you? After all, we were pretty rough on their guy. Wiping him out? Is it worth it? Do you think that doing away with a prominent lawyer who's representing the wife of the Governor won't cause all hell to break loose, not only here in the North End but all over the state? Our friends in Springfield won't be too happy."

"Your call, padrone," Gulie said.

"Let's see if we can stall for a few days, you know, let them know we're involved but something less ...ah less ..."

"Like what, boss?"

"Find out if this lawyer, what's his name?"

"Eldridge."

"Yeah, whatever. See if he's got any family who's old enough for us to place a call, let them know he's in trouble. Maybe that'd shake him up, take his mind off this case, y'know what I mean?"

"Y'mean tell someone in his family that we're gonna do him in?"

"Yes, Gulie, that's exactly what I mean."

"Let's take a pass for a few days and see what happens, OK.?"

"OK."

The three of us, Emily, Henry and I, arrived at the courthouse the next morning and if there were crowds before, there were even more now. Jordan remained at the office preparing memoranda for my direct testimony of Randell. Last night the evening news, on all the local channels, was filled with the day's events complete with pictures of the Governor entering the courthouse and Emily and me leaving. The morning Globe had the proceedings on the front page of the City & Region Section above the fold. They printed almost *verbatim* the remarks I made in my opening, which probably accounted for the throng of people gathered outside the front door expecting to see a blood bath. I frankly hoped they wouldn't be disappointed.

Nothing had changed inside the courtroom. It was jammed. Jack was busy telling people they would not be allowed to stand; they'd have to find a seat or leave. Emily seemed relatively calm but I knew she wanted to get her cross-examination over with— who wouldn't.

When she resumed the stand Jed started right in.

"Now Ms. Mitchell, suppose you tell us the name of the person you allegedly slept with, the person you claim is the father of Danny."

Well, that didn't take long, I thought.

"I object," I said to the Judge, not only rising from my chair but walking toward the bench with the first crutch I was able to grab.

"I'll hear you, Mr. Eldridge," the Judge said, looking up from his notes.

"The name of the person is completely irrelevant," I began. "The only issue is whether the defendant is the father of Danny, not the name of the person who really is his father. Whoever he is, he's leading his own life; perhaps with a wife and children of his own. It would be an invasion of his privacy to compel the disclosure of his name some fifteen years later. We're not seeking any child support from this person nor are we looking to absolve the defendant of his obligation to support Danny. We simply want the record to disclose that the Governor is not the father of the child for purposes of custody."

"How will the revelation of the fact that the defendant is not the father of the child affect the issue of custody?" the Judge asked me.

That wasn't an easy question to answer. I did the best I could.

"My answer has to be that blood is thicker than water, Your Honor. In a custody hearing even the most insignificant fact may tip the scales one way or the other."

The Judge paused. He was thinking. That was one of the things I liked about the guy. I liked his answer even better.

"Sustained."

Apparently unperturbed, Jed forged ahead.

"So you admit to committing adultery, Ms. Mitchell. Is that right?"

"That was fifteen years ago," Emily replied with a tone in her voice.

Oh oh, Emily, don't develop an attitude, I thought.

After beating the subject to death for a few more minutes without making any headway, Jed abruptly changed the subject and asked her some questions about her financial statement, trying to prove her expenses were padded. He wasn't getting anywhere with that either. I prepped her until she was confident about dollars and cents and her answers were forthcoming. What was equally important, we made sure the figures added up. She had substantial needs she said and she showed a large shortfall on her financial statement. She didn't have enough to meet her every day expenses and neither did she have enough to meet Danny's she made clear.

Jed knew when to quit.

"That's all I have. Thank you Ms. Mitchell," he said to her.

"I have nothing further, Judge," I said, and with that, Emily's testimony was finished.

I disturbed the background noise, which escalated as Emily took her seat and brought about a hush from the crowd when I called, "Dr. Hans Gerber."

He was easy to examine. He'd testified many times before and was perfectly comfortable and relaxed on the stand as he gave his oath to the clerk. I established his credentials even though Jed stipulated that he was a qualified expert as soon as he took his seat in the witness box. That was an old trick, that kind of stipulation. But, I took fifteen minutes making sure his lengthy *curriculum vitae* was testified to and made part of the record.

His testimony was rather simple. He examined the hair follicles on the comb, which Emily had delivered to him and tested them for a DNA match- up with the swab he had taken from Danny's mouth. There was no connection. The test results were ninety-nine percent accurate. In Dr. Gerber's opinion, Brenden W. Mitchell was not the father of Danny Mitchell. That's all I needed. I was content to let Jed try to shake the testimony of this celebrated doctor.

"That's all I have, Your Honor," I said taking my seat.

More background noise, foot shuffling, stage whispers clearly audible.

Jed strolled to a spot on the floor in front of the witness stand and unbuttoned the front of his suit coat. He placed his notes on the corner of the clerk's bench this time and looked directly at the witness.

"You had to make an important assumption in conducting your experiment, didn't you doctor?"

"The DNA test is pretty much *pro forma*," Gerber replied.

"That may be true but you had to assume that the hair follicles were really the hair follicles of Brenden Mitchell, isn't that right?" Jed said boring in.

"I was told they were."

"You didn't know for a certainty that they were from the head of the defendant, did you?" Jed asked.

I was tempted to object. Asked and answered I thought but I kept my seat.

"No."

"In fact the only person who told you that they were Brenden Mitchell's hair follicles was the plaintiff in this case, Emily Mitchell, right?"

"That's right."

"Your Honor, I move that Dr. Gerber's entire testimony be stricken," Jed said.

Talbot appeared to look at his notes. He rubbed his jaw, looked at Jed and me and then down at the bench again.

"I won't rule now," he said. "I'll reserve judgment and take his testimony *de bene*."

"I have no further questions," Jed said, turning away from the witness as though the witness had some communicable disease.

"I have no questions. Thank you Dr. Gerber," I stated. Jed did a good job creating a doubt to a test that was virtually a lock I thought, but there was nothing I could do.

It was getting along towards the noon recess and I was anxious to get rid of all the testimony about custody except for the testimony of Dr. Justin Feingold. I hadn't heard from him but I expected to receive a call from his office any day now. In fact, I thought he was rather late in getting back to Jed and me. Nothing to do but wait, I thought. I was placing all my custody eggs in one basket but I had no other choice if I wanted Emily to carry the day.

I decided to submit the report of the Guardian *Ad Litem*, Donald Long, rather than put him on the stand. His conclusions were a matter of opinion and, since the Court appointed him, I couldn't impeach his credibility to any great degree. Let Jed put him on if he chose.

I struggled with whether to put Dr. Sheila Monaghan on the stand, however. Her report was not the official report of a Court appointed G.A.L. but I thought I could win the argument to submit her report instead of having her testify based on the fact that she was appointed as a result of an agreement of both sides.

Jed and I approached the bench at my request in order for me to submit Monaghan's report *in lieu* of her testimony and, to my surprise, Jed agreed with me. We cut off two days of trial time with that agreement alone.

After the noon break my next witnesses were, of necessity, boring. Steve Lyons testified to the values of the real estate in the real estate trusts. His testimony went in smoothly. We had worked together for years and I was able to get to the bottom line of his opinion of value very quickly. On cross Jed tried to impeach his credibility by questioning the comparables he used but he wasn't successful in the least.

Lester Begley testified that he examined three boxes of the defendant's business and bank records and found that the Governor reported income substantially less on his Federal and State income tax returns than the deposits in his bank accounts indicated. He also testified that he found two million three hundred fifty thousand dollars in assets of some kind that were not disclosed on the Governor's financial statement which he submitted to the Court under the pains and penalties of perjury.

On cross-examination, Jed tried to establish that the Governor's unreported income was not his personal income, therefore not reportable. He tried to show that the two and a half million Begley found was, in reality, money in the name of a trust and therefore not in the name of Brenden Mitchell. I wasn't sure what kind of impact this had on the Judge.

By four o'clock, it was obvious that Jed was finished with Begley and the Court adjourned until nine o'clock the next morning.

That evening the six o'clock news was awash with the Governor's tax omissions and undisclosed assets. The radio talk shows were unforgiving. The bloggers had a field day. The Globe the following morning had letters to the editor criticizing the Governor, his administration, and just about everyone connected with him. Additionally, there were eight op-ed pieces written by both the paper's liberal and conservative columnists castigating him. Dr. Hans Gerber was quoted in a major article in the Health Science Section but the article never mentioned that Ms. Mitchell herself delivered the Governor's hair follicles used in the DNA test to the good doctor.

On Friday, the third day of trial, I called Chuck Dawson to the stand. After his credentials were testified to, I began.

"What bank accounts and other private accounts of the defendant did you review in preparation for your testimony here today?" I asked him.

"I looked at all the documents that Attorney Jed provided in the Governor's answer to the plaintiff's document request."

"Where did you find those documents?"

"I received them directly from Attorney Paul Jed."

"In addition to the private financial accounts of the Governor what other accounts did you review?" I asked.

"I was able to review the Governor's campaign accounts," he replied evenly.

"What accounts were they?"

"Both his gubernatorial campaign accounts and his newly opened campaign accounts for his possible run for the Senate."

"How did you obtain those accounts?"

283

"I copied them from the records at the Attorney General's Office."

"What did the records consist of?"

"They were in two parts. One part showed the bank accounts and the other, a separate part, showed a book of the list of donors, you know, contributors to the Governor's campaigns."

"What did you find?"

"I found that there were deposits in these accounts on a very regular basis. By that I mean there were deposits of almost the same amount every week, fifty-two weeks a year on the same day."

"How much are we talking about?"

"There were deposits each week totaling twenty-five hundred dollars until recently, then they were reduced to two thousand dollars and they remained constant thereafter."

"Did you find out where these funds came from?"

"Yes, in the separate book, there was a list of names of donors to the Governor's campaign next to each amount contributed as the source of these deposits. But, there was no address next to the names or any other information, for that matter. Moreover, the amounts donated didn't add up to the amounts deposited. We also checked the names that were listed and found that many of the names simply did not exist."

"What else did you find?"

"In the past twelve months alone I found over a million dollars that wasn't accounted for."

"What happened to that money?"

"I was able to trace some of that money into the Governor's private bank accounts, about half of it, but I believe the rest was withdrawn as cash."

Now there arose in the courtroom such a din that the Judge had to stand up to get the attention of Jack who was striding down from his perch toward the crowd in an attempt to quiet them. In all my years as a trial attorney, I never saw a judge use a gavel or say anything like, "Quiet in the courtroom!" from the bench. I, as a judge, certainly never did. Talbot didn't either. His chubby face was red with exasperation as he simply turned and walked out of the courtroom without a word leaving the whole scene to Jack to restore order.

Brenden Mitchell appeared to be livid. His arms were waiving animatedly as he looked to be scolding his lawyer about something, no doubt about the fact that his campaign accounts were ever released in the first place.

After order was restored, Jack left the courtroom to bring the Judge back in. When he was settled, Dawson resumed the stand.

"What did you do with the information you uncovered, Mr. Dawson?" I continued.

"At your request I brought the information to the Attorney General of the Commonwealth of Massachusetts. The AG's office told me that they had begun an investigation as they too had compared the information from the campaign accounts with the Governor's private accounts and..."

"Objection," Jed bellowed over the rising noise of the crowd, standing up from the defendant's table.

"Sustained."

"Move to strike what the Attorney General's Office told him," Jed continued.

"Motion granted. What was told to the witness by the Attorney General's office shall be stricken." Talbot answered, almost shouting over the din that ensued.

The noise had turned into an uproar as if a bomb had gone off. In many respects, a bomb did go off. For a second the Governor appeared apoplectic. Jed looked speechless. After only a few seconds more, apparently, the rest of the assembly processed the information they'd just heard and, as if understanding the ramifications for the first time, the noise level was cacophonous.

For the second time the Judge left the bench without a word. He couldn't have been heard over the noise level anyway. Even Jack didn't attempt to quiet the crowd for a few minutes. Some reporters rushed out the door to make phone calls to their editors. Some people left to escape to the hall in order to avoid the clamor in the courtroom. The rest, those who stayed, were talking animatedly with one another until Jack quite forcefully, ordered them to be quiet or else leave the courtroom immediately.

Dolores Fairchild left the courtroom for a few minutes and on her return, we were advised that the Judge had declared the noon recess; that we'd resume at two o'clock.

I had to get away, to be by myself again. I grabbed my crutches and hobbled down the back stairs and out to the fresh air. This time, instead of going to Faneuil Hall, I walked up to Cambridge Street and had a bagel and coffee at Finagle a Bagel. I started reading an abandoned Herald which I found on the chair next to me but it seemed that every page had some mention of the trial so I stared out the window instead, lost in my thoughts, which were too complicated to even try and sort out.

At two o'clock, Chuck Dawson resumed his place in the witness box and we waited for the Judge to come out. I remained seated and, I must admit, I had a feeling of satisfaction watching the Governor's look of disbelief, of utter consternation, remembering all those years when this Governor, this bastard, refused to give me the time of day. The case wasn't over though. There was a long way to go. Don't get cocky, I thought to myself.

When the Judge returned to a quieted courtroom, he stood behind his high-backed leather chair and waited for the crowd to become even quieter.

"If this kind of conduct continues I shall be forced to clear the courtroom and conduct the rest of this case before video cameras, rest assured, I will have no hesitancy."

He sat down and again nodded for me to continue.

"Mr. Dawson what else did you do with that information?"

"I conferred with your accountant, Lester Begley and together we put together a chart showing the added assets we uncovered in the Governor's column. We also added the cash that was withdrawn from his campaign funds to his personal accounts."

At that point, Henry got up and placed the chart on a tri-pod in the center of the courtroom for all to see. Jed wasn't the only one with a pointer and I began going through the Governor's assets one by one, point by point, so to speak.

"As you can see, in the first eight months of this year there has been deposited in the Governor's personal accounts five hundred eighty- three thousand dollars over and above what the Governor received from his salary and the income he reported from his other investments," he said as he directed my attention to the first column with a nod of his head. I dutifully pointed to it with the tip of my pointer.

"Moreover, last year there were similar deposits but not quite as high, only three hundred twenty-two thousand dollars," he continued as I pointed at another column showing the figure.

"Did you compare his deposits to his Federal Income Tax return?"

Jed was halfway up, ready for an objection but he sat back down.

"Yes, I did."

"What did you find?"

"There was no mention of three hundred twenty-two thousand anywhere on last year's return."

"How many years did you account for in your analysis?"

"We went back five years," Dawson said, looking straight at the Judge.

"Did you reach any conclusion about the amount of funds from these campaign accounts that have been accumulated by the Governor over the years that are not accounted for in his list of assets on his financial statement?"

"Objection."

"Overruled."

"Absolutely," Dawson said as I pointed to another column.

"How much was that?"

"Two million three hundred-fifty thousand dollars."

Now despite the Judge's admonition, another clamor arose although this time not quite as raucous as the last. I thought, for a split second, that the reason was the crowd wasn't able to comprehend the gravity of what Dawson had just testified to but, on second thought I guessed they were afraid they'd all be expelled from the courtroom if they let themselves go.

Talbot saved face I thought, by ignoring the outburst. He simply stood up and announced,

"Monday morning. Nine o'clock!"

"All rise," Jack instructed and opened the door leading to the Judge's chambers for the Judge's exit.

At that point, whatever emotions were suppressed by the crowd before, were let loose with abandon and the courtroom was bedlam. I looked across the table at the Governor who was slumped down in his chair as if attempting to lose himself from the crowd --but to no avail. A group of five or six people gathered all around him and at last, he arose from his slump and was escorted out by two State Policemen on either side of him. I hadn't noticed the two officers before but they certainly made their presence known as the Governor looked as though he could hardly walk on his own without their help.

I had prepared one more question for Chuck Dawson, about the amount of cash that was withdrawn directly from the campaign accounts by the Governor, about a half a million dollars, but I didn't get the chance.

I made my way out with Henry's assistance and Emily closely followed. I nodded in the direction of the ladies room for Emily's benefit and Henry and I escaped to the men's room for refuge from the madding crowd.

Once inside, we looked at the bottom of the doors of each stall to make sure they were not in use and waited for the three guys standing at the urinals to finish their business and take their leave.

"Jesus Christ," Henry said exhaling and shaking his head.

"I've never seen or heard anything like it. Ted, you were great."

"All you have to do is prepare," I replied.

"Jed will have all weekend to prepare his cross-examination," I continued, somewhat resignedly.

"So what!" Henry exclaimed. "There's nowhere for him to go. What can he possibly do?"

"Well, we'll just have to see won't we," I replied.

After a few more minutes, the crowd had thinned out considerably. We met Emily and risked going down in the elevator rather than attempting to negotiate the stairs again. Nevertheless, when we reached the ground floor, a bevy of reporters rushed up to us, their microphones in their hands, shouting their questions at us.

"What's the AG going to do, Mr. Eldridge?"

"How did Dawson get the records from the AG, Mr. Eldridge?"

"When's the forensic guy going on?"

"Aren't you just trying to smear the Governor?" one reporter asked with a sneer on his face.

I gave them the obligatory answer, "No comment," and attempted to carefully limp through the throng. Emily, Henry and I made our way back to Old City Hall without saying a word to one another as we were surrounded by media and others almost all the way. I must've made a pathetic looking figure struggling with my crutches. Why didn't I just call a cab for chrissakes, I thought. On the way, I glanced at Emily and could tell by the expression on her face that she was happy. I was pleased to observe that although questions were directed specifically at her by a couple of die-hard reporters, she didn't say a word in response.

CHAPTER TWENTY-NINE

The Governor ducked his head as he entered the back seat of the state police cruiser. His two escorts sat on either side of him.

"Where to Governor?" asked the State Police driver, "The State House?"

"No take me home, Mike," the Governor replied in a shaky voice. He used his cell phone and contacted Mort Haller.

"Mort, meet me at my house. I'm headed there now."

Fifteen minutes later the Governor almost ran through the throng of reporters gathered outside the front entrance of 10 Dudley Street accompanied by his two police guards. When they reached the front door one officer said, before turning away,

"Will you be all right, Governor?"

"Yes, yes, not to worry," he replied.

"OK then. We'll be right outside if you need us. Our instructions are to remain here until we're relieved."

Five minutes later Mort Haller rang the bell and was let in by Lilly.

"Oh Mr. Haller, I'm so glad you're here. The Governor just came home and he looks terrible," she said guiding him towards the elaborate staircase, a wrinkled brow creasing her forehead.

"Don't open the door for anyone else, Lilly," Haller said to her as he mounted the stairs.

As he opened the door to the Governor's room, Haller found the Governor lying on his bed, fully clothed, leaning against two pillows he'd propped up, his arms behind his head his legs fully extended in front of him. Haller also noticed some residue of white powder on the glass end table by the bed.

"Did you know, Mort, that this is Danny's room when he stays with me," the Governor said in a low, almost inaudible voice.

"And this was my room when I was a little boy," the Governor continued wistfully, a tear brimming each of his eyes.

Mort said nothing in reply but pulled up a chair and sat down by the side of the bed.

"Governor, we'll get out of this. Those bank accounts are subject to human error. They have no proof of where those funds came from. They have a list of names that don't jive. So what? Mistakes can be made."

The Governor raised a limp hand from behind his head and waived it at Mort as if dismissing him and what he had said out of hand. His eyes were half-closed as if he was in a trance, unfocused.

"You know, before Monday you should see your doctor, get some help. It'll make you feel better, help you to sleep."

"Mort, be a good fellow and bring me a bottle of scotch that's in the liquor cabinet in the dining room, will you?"

"Are you sure that's what you want?"

"Hell yes. Monday is a long way off."

"Don't forget, Brenden, Jed has yet to cross examine Dawson and you haven't even taken the stand in your own defense," Haller said to his boss, using his first name in a rare show of familiarity.

"When you do, when Jed puts your case in, there'll be a different story, you'll see."

"Mort, are you serious? Didn't you hear what they've collected against us? They have millions of dollars of unexplained funds in my personal accounts that came from campaign contributions and you and I know that that money is *not* from campaign contributors," the Governor said wearily.

"It's only a matter of time before they link it up to our North End activities," he continued.

"Look, Governor, you'll win the custody battle. You have Donald Long in your corner. You even have Dr. Sheila Monaghan recommending joint custody. I'm sure Feingold's testimony will be in our favor. So what if we've misallocated some funds? It happens all the time. The public will soon forget when we step up to the plate and acknowledge our mistake and correct the accounts."

"Mort, we should settle now before it's too late," the Governor said to his chief of staff.

"I'm afraid we've already offered the maximum to them and they've rejected us. The issue is custody as far as they're concerned and, as I've told you, we're going to win that issue," Mort replied.

"How about that bottle of scotch, Mort? I'm getting tired of all this right now."

"Look Brenden, just promise me you'll see Arnold Bennett in the morning and get something to boost your outlook on this case. To be honest with you I called him on my cell phone on the way over here and, although he's the busiest doctor in North America, he said he'd see you tomorrow right here in your own home at nine o'clock. We need you at your best when you take the stand so don't sleep through the appointment. OK?"

"Sleep through? I haven't had a good night's sleep in weeks. Now I'm going to get that scotch myself--"

"No, I'll have Lilly bring it up on my way out. Just relax tonight and I'll call you after you see Bennett in the morning. Take care of yourself, Governor," Mort said to his boss on his way out the door.

When Lilly brought the scotch for the Governor, complete with a bucket of ice and a small carafe of water next to a short glass inscripted with the initials BWM, she announced he had a call from Paul Jed.

"Yes, what is it Paul?"

"I'm just calling to tell you that I don't want you to worry. All cases have their ups and downs and we'll be OK when our case goes in. I'll see you tomorrow in my office and we'll go over your testimony again, OK?"

"Yeah, sure. I'll be there at eleven o'clock Paul. G'bye."

After Jed hung up the phone Brenden Mitchell dialed Rhea's number.

"Hello?"

"Hi. I needed to call you."

"How's it going?"

"So far it couldn't be much worse."

"Yeah, that's what I've heard through the courthouse grapevine. How are *you* doing?" she asked.

"To tell you the truth I'm barely making it."

"What's wrong?"

"I can't sleep. I'm worried that the misplaced funds of a few million dollars will be traced to sources that could destroy me."

"Well--"

"There's more. Did you ever think what would happen to us, to you, if they ever found out about our relationship?"

"Brenden, I think about it all the time. Our relationship is one thing but to have that relationship going on while your case was being heard before me is what's causing me to come close to a nervous breakdown."

"Well, I think we're all right there. At least I hope so," the Governor replied. "Can I come over and see you tonight?" he whispered to her, his lips close to the phone.

"Are you out of your mind? Of course you can't," she exclaimed.

"But I need to see you," he said.

"Brenden, get a grip on yourself for chrissake. I can't see you tonight or ever again if I'm going to keep this judgeship."

"But Rhea, we've taken so many precautions. No one will find out."

"Brenden, I've spoken to my father. I told him about us and he was livid. He said something about speaking to you or to Mort Haller and that I shouldn't worry about how you would react if I explained I couldn't see you any more."

"Well I'll be goddamned. That son of a bitch is the cause of me getting into possible trouble with the Attorney General's Office."

"W--What?"

"Rhea, your father, Mort Haller and I have had a deal going for years where we've shared the profits from the bookies in the North End. It's possible that the whole thing will be found out by the Attorney General's Office and we'll all go down the drain, you included."

"Oh my God!" Her hands started to shake. She tried to get control. "It's no surprise that my father is involved with the bookies, but you!"

"Rhea, your father was very ambitious for you as you were for yourself. We needed the money for my campaigns. I was elected, you were appointed. It was a win -win situation all around."

"I--I," she stammered. There was a long pause.

"OK, I see what's happening here," he said to her after waiting for her response.

"Goodbye, Rhea," he said to her softly as he carefully hung up the phone.

The Governor grabbed a fist full of ice and dropped the cubes into his crystal glass, filled the glass to the brim with scotch and gulped down half of it. It was going to be a long night.

Promptly at nine o'clock the next morning Dr. Arnold Bennett saw Brenden Mitchell. The doctor told the Governor that he was prescribing Paxil to get him out of the doldrums and enough Ambian to last well beyond the end of the trial to help him sleep at night.

Later that morning Mitchell met with his lawyer and the session actually cheered him up a little. The thought crossed his mind halfway into the meeting that he didn't know whether it was what he was hearing from Jed or the Paxil at work that elevated his mood.

Jed explained to him that there was no connection between the two million three hundred-fifty thousand dollars that Lester Begley found and the assets the Governor disclosed on his financial statement. Jed spoke about an *inter vivos* trust that held title to the funds, over two million dollars. The fund was actually in the name of the trustee, the Mayflower Bank and Trust Company.

"What about the half million they found in my bank accounts?" the Governor asked.

"Brenden, that was just a temporary loan. After all you are going through a contentious divorce. Your wife is a drunk and it's clear you will be awarded custody or at least shared custody. Your expenses are more than you ever dreamed and you needed that money for just a short period of time."

"The expenses are certainly more than I ever dreamed, that's for sure," the Governor replied, somewhat relieved. They worked through the noon hour and when they were finished, Mitchell climbed into the state police cruiser that had been stationed outside Jed's office all morning and directed the driver to take him home.

Once home, he avoided the TV but the Globe and the Herald were on the hall table where Lilly usually deposited them. The headlines screamed at him as he passed by and he couldn't avoid picking both papers up and carrying them off to his office/den where he began reading every word. When he finished, his melancholia returned, worse than the night before. By mid afternoon, he still had not eaten any breakfast or lunch but he just wasn't hungry.

He took his medication and went up to Danny's room to lie down for a nap, hoping to escape the reality of the events that seemed to engulf his very being and bring down a pall that was suffocating him. He forgot all the things his lawyer had told him earlier and despite the turmoil that his mind was embracing, he was able to drift off into a tortured half-sleep.

By seven-thirty that evening, the late afternoon sun found its way through the heavy curtains covering the westward facing windows and suffused the room with a mellow, ambient light that, for the first few moments when the Governor opened his eyes, gave him a feeling of tranquility. It wasn't long, however, before he remembered the events of Friday's court session and the allegations of Charles Dawson and the problems he faced in light of Eldridge's opening statements.

Mort Haller had called and left a message for the Governor to call him back but he just wasn't up to it. He found Lilly in the kitchen and she made him a sandwich which he ate right there at the kitchen table without saying a word to her. She escaped to her room leaving him alone. His sister was nowhere in sight. The house felt like a tomb.

After he finished his sandwich he retreated to Danny's room with a bottle of scotch, some ice in a glass and a magazine he hoped would divert his attention from the turmoil in his mind. Usually after a few scotches his eyes would close and he'd be asleep on the couch or in his favorite chair only to wake up, go to bed and sleep through the night. This night, however, he could not sleep, the magazine was not a diversion, the scotch kept him awake and he was increasingly nervous and disconsolate.

He took a couple of Ambian tablets and, just to make sure he could get to sleep, he took two Paxil capsules.

CHAPTER THIRTY

I couldn't help but read the papers. I tried to avoid the TV but it was impossible. I certainly avoided the blogs on the internet. Over the weekend, the media were full of themselves, cocky with all the information they had to devour and then spew out, like ambergris to the ravenous public. Friday evening news programs speculated that the Governor would be indicted. Anchors from all three local networks as well as other locals had an excitement in their voices that indicated a major story--one that wasn't finished yet and one that would have a major impact on the Commonwealth, they all said. Stay tuned they implored. ABC, NBC, CBS and CNN picked up the story line on their national news programs later in the evening.

Saturday morning the Globe had front page stories from three different reporters each with a slightly different slant but all three predicting doom for the Governor. The Herald didn't hold back. They came right out and called the Governor "A Crook-- Governor steals five hundred eighty three thousand from his campaign funds," the article screamed. Another lead article called upon the Attorney General to act, to indict the Governor on grounds of fraud and abuse of campaign funds. Evidently, they didn't bother to look up the statute to get the correct name of the violations or the General Law that governs them.

Sunday showed no respite. The papers didn't let up. The TV stations were relentless. The gossip on the streets was about nothing else. But, there was no new information. There was only speculation about how the case would turn out and what was in store for the Governor. Some people predicted jail. Others were less sanguine; perhaps more jaded, and predicted that he'd beat the allegations "like all politicians do".

My phone didn't stop ringing all weekend. I tried to escape the house on Sunday by trying to visit Josh at his dorm on the BC campus. I finally tracked him down in a coffee shop where he was sitting with four of his friends but I could tell he wasn't too thrilled to see me as soon as we made eye contact. After all, it had only been a couple of weeks since he left home. I knew he wanted to establish his independence even though we lived only ten minutes away but I honestly thought that he'd be rather proud of how my trial was progressing since it was all over every newspaper and TV station in the state. At least that's what I thought before I spoke with him.

"Hi," he said as he left the table where his friends were sitting and walked up to where I was standing.

No "Dad". No hug. No warmth. His eyes were not even focused on me but were darting around the room as if he was greeting someone with the plague, as if he was afraid of something.

"Hi," I responded but caught his body language so I kept my distance.

"I just wanted to stop by and say 'hello' since I wasn't able to help you move in. How are you doing?"

"OK," he replied. "I'm making a lot of friends. My roommate is a great guy. My courses are going to be tough but they seem to be interesting—How's the trial going?"

"Well, the trial seems to be going OK. Have you read about it?"

"Uh, no, not really. I've been busy with school, books; you know all the stuff that happens in the first few weeks of freshman year."

I was surprised at his nervousness. I hadn't seen him in a while but --

"What's the matter, Josh. You seem afraid of something, even me."

"I'm not afraid of you dad, I'm afraid *for* you."

"What do you mean?"

"Let's go outside," he said.

We sat on one of the cement benches which formed the perimeter of a small patch of grass outside the building.

"I got a call from some guy who told me that if you didn't settle the case, you'd be dead in a week," he told me. "The guy hung up right away. I never heard his voice before. I called mom right away and she told me not to worry; that this kind of threat happened before; that I shouldn't say anything to you about it because you've got too much else to worry about. But, honestly Dad, now that you're here, I can't help myself."

He put his arm around my shoulder and hugged me. I could feel him shaking; felt the tears.

"Josh, don't worry. Those kinds of calls happen to a lot of people, actors, actresses, sports figures, politicians and yes, even lawyers. Your mother was right. All you have to do is study hard and don't worry about me."

After another ten minutes, I left. He was in better spirits and I was pissed. Those bastards, I thought. I'm not quitting. I'm going to win this goddamn case –and get paid!

I was worried about the money I owed and how the amount was adding up. I worried about Andrea and how she kept Josh's call a secret from me; what it was doing to her. The details of the case crowded my thoughts, pushing everything else to the back of my mind. I worried about everything!

I stopped by Old City Hall to look at the mail and there, finally, was the report of Dr. Justin Feingold, all twenty-three pages of it including test results, diagnosis and recommendations. It wasn't mailed but rather was slipped under the front door of my office. Right then and there, I decided to forgo the one question that remained for me to ask Dawson. Instead, I was going to put Feingold on the stand first thing Monday morning. I called his office and, of course, he was not in on a Sunday, but the answering service asked if my call was an emergency.

"It certainly is," I replied. I didn't have to pretend I was desperate, I was! Dr. Feingold called me back ten minutes later and that sweet, kind, brilliant gentleman agreed to testify first thing Monday morning, or at least right after Jed's cross examination of Chuck Dawson.

On Sunday morning, Brenden Mitchell felt a little better after sleeping on and off during the night, thanks to the Ambian he'd taken. He was groggy and a little unsteady but, overall, not as bad as he felt yesterday. He forced himself to remember the positive things his lawyer had told him on Saturday and to make sure he didn't slip back into one of those states where he almost teared up. He took another couple of Paxil tablets.

The Sunday Globe however brought him back to reality and the problems he had to face this coming week at trial. Was it possible he could prevail over Emily, over Eldridge, over Dawson? What could he do but go press forward and rely on Paul Jed to make good on his promises.

Mort Haller stopped by and attempted to cheer him up but, frankly, he couldn't wait for him to leave. He was getting tired of his saccharin bullshit and his blind faith that everything would turn out all right. He stayed in the house all day, didn't answer any phone calls and tried to lose himself in reading the newest New Yorker Magazine.

By Monday morning, I was ready. I couldn't wait to get started. When we arrived at the courthouse, it was again jammed with media people, lawyers and courthouse aficionados who were assembled outside the building waiting for the cast of characters to arrive. We waded through the throng, were waived through the security arch and didn't say a word in answer to all the questions shouted at us on the way in. We, that is Emily, Henry and I continued our way up to the fifth floor courtroom and again avoided the gathering of reporters who were intent on getting a read on what was going to happen during the course of the day.

"Who's your next witness?"

"Who's the father, Ms. Mitchell?"

"When does the Governor go on, Mr. Eldridge?"

Nothing. I said nothing.

I was surprised when I entered the courtroom and saw Brenden W. Mitchell already seated with his lawyer at counsel table. He looked like a derelict who had slept during the night on a pile of cardboard stretched across a park bench in Boston Common. He was haggard looking, pale, with dark circles under his eyes, and a vacant stare from his pupils, which appeared to be almost opaque.

I wondered whether Paul Jed had received Feingold's report yesterday, Sunday, as I did. I was so excited after reading the report and arranging for Feingold to be on telephone notice this morning, that I forgot to ask him.

The courtroom was as crowded as before but was strangely subdued due in large measure, to the admonitions of Judge Talbot no doubt. We barely had time to sit down when Talbot emerged from the doorway following Jack, who stood at attention as the Judge passed him on his way up the two stairs to his bench, crying, "All rise. All those having anything to do before the Honorable, the Justices of the Probate and Family Court, now sitting in Boston, in and for the county of Suffolk, draw near, give your attention and ye shall be heard. God save the Commonwealth of Massachusetts."

I didn't know whether Jack was instructed by Talbot to open the court session with the traditional "cry" or whether he was overcome with the pageantry of the proceedings thus far, but it was unusual to hear him to say the least.

It took only a few seconds for the assembly to take their seats and quiet down.

"Attorney Eldridge?" Talbot inquired inviting me to proceed.

"No further questions, Your Honor," I said. I could hardly wait to have Jed finish his cross-examination of Dawson.

"Attorney Jed?" the Judge said in the form of a question asking, in that manner, whether Jed was ready for his cross.

Jed got up slowly, almost dramatically and approached a spot directly in front of the witness.

"Mr. Dawson, you are a paid expert, are you not?"

"Yes. I am paid."

"You are paid by whom?"

"Attorney Eldridge, who bills his client."

"How much?"

"Six hundred dollars an hour."

A gasp from the crowd.

"How much was your retainer?"

"Fifteen thousand dollars."

"How much have you been paid to date?"

"Forty-five thousand"

"That doesn't include your testimony on Friday or today, does it?"

"No."

"Now as a paid expert you found over two million dollars that you said was unaccounted for by the Governor. Is that right?"

"Yes."

"Are you aware of the Governor's estate plan, Mr. Dawson?"

"No."

"You mean to tell this court that you state unequivocally that there is two million dollars unaccounted for without looking at the Governor's estate plan?"

"Well, yes that's correct."

"Mr. Dawson, I hand you this document marked exhibit twenty-three for identification and ask you whether you can identify it?"

"It says it's a trust."

"Whose trust is it?"

"It says Brenden W. Mitchell."

Jed took a copy of the trust, walked over to where I was sitting, and plopped the trust on the table in front of me with an utter look of contempt.

"Your Honor, I offer it," Jed said handing the original to Dolores, the clerk, with a self-confident smirk on his face.

"I object."

"Overruled."

"May I be heard, Judge?"

"No. Proceed, Attorney Jed."

"Do you know how this trust is funded, Mr. Expert?"

"Objection," I bellowed.

"Sustained. There is no room for sarcasm. Mr. Jed. Proceed."

"Look at the schedule attached to the trust. It shows that the trust is funded with two million dollars, doesn't it?"

"Apparently."

"Do you know who has title to that two million dollars, Mr. Dawson?"

"I suppose the trustee does."

"And who is the trustee?"

"The Mayflower Bank and Trust Company."

"It's not the Governor of this Commonwealth, is it?"

"No."

Jed walked over to his counsel table and picked up another yellow pad with some handwritten notes in it before he began again.

"Now, the second point you made was that some five hundred thousand dollars was deposited into the Governor's personal accounts from his campaign accounts, is that right?"

"Yes, approximately."

"Because of fees like yours, you are aware of the cost of this litigation are you not?"

"Yes, somewhat."

"Are you also aware that candidates for office sometimes lend their campaigns money from their personal accounts?"

"Yes, I'm aware of that."

"Are you aware that candidates sometimes also borrow from their campaign accounts when they are faced with extraordinary expenses such as a divorce of this magnitude?"

"Well, I guess so. I'm not sure."

Jed turned his back against the witness, walked toward his counsel table, turned to face the Judge and said with a tone of utter contempt,

"No further questions."

While Jed was examining Dawson, I feverishly thumbed through Mitchell's trust and finally, on the second to the last page I found it.

With the trust in my hand I approached the witness.

"Look on page forty-two of the Governor's trust, Mr. Dawson and tell us what you find?"

He turned each page slowly until he came to the page I directed him to. He looked up at me.

"What does it say there about what the Governor can do to this trust?"

"It says he can revoke it any time he wants."

"If he revokes the trust what happens to the two million dollars?"

"It reverts to the Governor."

"No further questions," I said to the Judge.

The background noise swelled as Chuck Dawson stepped from the witness box but not enough for Talbot to take any threatened measures. I couldn't wait to call my next witness but I had to call him on his cell phone to tell him I was ready.

"Judge, may we have a fifteen minute recess?" I pleaded.

"Fifteen minutes," The Judge replied.

I looked at Jed and the Governor to see if I could detect whether they had received Feingold's report but they showed no indication of any distress. In fact, Jed appeared very smug and satisfied with his treatment of Dawson. Even the Governor looked a tad relieved although he still looked like a refugee from some street shelter.

I called Feingold on my cell phone, being careful not to let anyone hear me, and sat with Henry and Emily and waited.

Not ten minutes later, as the crowd was milling about chatting with one another about the events that had transpired and, no doubt, anticipating what was to come, Dr.Justin Feingold entered the courtroom. Although I'm sure he wasn't recognized by but a hand full of people, he had such a presence, such a carriage, that he instantly became the focus of everyone's attention as he nodded to the Governor, to his counsel and then to Emily and me. He looked like the professor from Harvard that he actually was, not some slick snake oil salesman from the big city. He stood exactly in the middle of the two counsel tables and looked perfectly comfortable and at ease. I didn't dare approach him as I wanted him to maintain his impartiality.

"All rise."

The courtroom quieted down instantly.

"Attorney Eldridge?" the Judge inquired.

"I call Dr. Justin Feingold," I said in a loud voice.

"What!" came a cry from Paul Jed, standing up from counsel table and moving toward the Judge.

"Judge, I saw Dr. Feingold come in just now but I thought he was delivering his report personally. To this moment, I still haven't seen it; I never received the report from Dr. Feingold. How can he be put on the stand?"

"I never…"

"Side bar," Judge Talbot barked, cutting Jed off without another word.

We both assembled at the side of the Judge's bench, out of the hearing of all but the stenographer, who was busy setting up her machine to record every word.

"What's this all about?" the Judge asked.

"Judge Dr. Feingold is the forensic psychiatrist we both agreed to. He and his associates conducted their investigation but I haven't received his report," Jed exclaimed, his eyes darting back and forth between me to the Judge.

He turned to me and asked, "Do you have his report?"

"Yes. I found it slipped under my office door yesterday, Sunday about noon."

"Well I'll be damned. I never received it," Jed said more to the Judge than to me.

The Judge leaned away from us in the direction of the witness who had taken his seat in the witness box and asked Dr. Feingold, "Did you deliver your report to both counsel yesterday?"

"I gave two copies of the report to a messenger service with instructions to deliver one to each lawyer's office yesterday about eleven in the morning," Feingold answered.

Apparently satisfied, Talbot declared a fifteen-minute recess.

"Call your office Attorney Jed and see if the report is there," he instructed and rose from his chair.

"All rise," Jack said in his usual way.

Fifteen minutes later I saw Jed enter the courtroom with his client. They both looked like they'd been on drugs. They both had a vacant stare and moved slowly and deliberately toward their counsel table as if in a trance, without saying a word to one another or to Jed's associate for that matter, who'd been sitting there waiting for their return.

Jack saw them enter and exited the courtroom to fetch the Judge.

"Side bar," the Judge said as soon as he sat down. He nodded at Jed inviting him to report as we gathered at the Judge's bench.

"Judge, the report was delivered yesterday all right but not to my office," Jed explained.

"It was delivered to the office next door by mistake and wasn't brought over until this morning after I had left for court. I've only had a chance to skim it. I can't be expected to cross examine Dr. Feingold having just received the report, Your Honor."

"No. You're quite right, Attorney Jed. We'll resume at two o'clock. That should give you enough time. After all Dr. Feingold is your witness as much as he's Attorney Eldridge's." The Judge got up and turned to exit the courtroom.

"All rise," said Jack.

It was about eleven A.M. when court was adjourned so Jed would have about three hours to comb through Feingold's report. He wouldn't like what he read, I thought, but that's the way it is. There's not much he could do. He certainly couldn't attack Feingold's credentials. The doctor's conclusions were the result of his investigation, his very thorough investigation, and there was not much Jed could do to impeach his findings. What Jed had in his favor was the report of Donald Long and the report of Dr. Monaghan. Because those reports were in evidence and marked as exhibits, he could read every word into the record when he put his own case in--- with no cross examination from me.

When the Judge resumed the bench at two o'clock, I lost no time in calling Dr. Feingold. I noticed him and how he was dressed for the first time that day.

He looked as if central casting selected his wardrobe for a 1950's movie: charcoal grey slacks, tan button-down shirt, dark brown knit tie and a brown corduroy sport coat. When he sat down I saw he had on dark argyle socks and penny loafers. I looked to see whether the sleeves of his sport coat had patches on the elbows and, sure enough, there they were.

He was sworn in by Dolores and settled himself confidently in the witness chair.

I started in by asking him about his credentials in order to qualify him as an expert, which was necessary to allow him to give his opinion about his findings, when Jed piped up:

"I stipulate that Dr. Feingold is an expert," he said. Same ol', same ol', I thought.

It took me ten minutes to put on the record all the information that appeared on his C.V. If this case was ever appealed, I wanted the Appeals Court to be able to read from the record what kind of a witness this person was.

I was always able to recognize that in a long, protracted case such as this one was turning out to be--no surprise-- that everyone gets tired of it after a while. Moreover, surprisingly, it doesn't take that long for the attention deficit span to kick in. The judge loses his patience, the plaintiff's lawyer cuts corners to keep the judge's interest, the defendant's lawyer feels rushed as the judge has known what the case is all about hours, if not days ago and even the court officer begins to nod off.

With that in mind, I started right in.

"What did you do to prepare for your testimony today?"

"I conducted several interviews with both the husband and the wife. I spoke with the child on two occasions, I spoke with the mother's psychiatrist, Dr. James Hurley, I spoke with the assistant headmaster at Danny's school and I referred the testing elements of my investigation to Dr. Samuel Freed who administered the psychological tests to both parents."

"What was the purpose of your investigation?"

"To determine as scientifically as possible, the psychological traits of both the mother and the father."

"What did you find?"

"Can you be a little more specific?"

"What characteristics of the Governor did you find relative to his ability to parent Danny?"

"I found that the husband has a tendency to present himself in a favorable light, to deny problems or personal shortcomings and even to aggrandize or overvalue himself."

Atta boy, I thought. Let's have the rest of it.

"What else did you find?"

"I found that he, the husband, exhibits sensitivity to criticism, coexisting with a tendency to externalize blame."

You could hear the proverbial pin drop in the courtroom.

"How did he externalize blame?"

"During the marriage he blamed his wife for his shortcomings."

"Did you reach any conclusion regarding any other interpersonal relationships between the husband and wife?"

"Yes. There wasn't any."

"What do you mean by that?"

"The husband constantly undermined the wife's parental authority when, on a few occasions she tried to discipline Danny and he denigrated just about everything else she did. She seldom had any response to him other than to disagree with him. He was a rigorous disciplinarian, she was more of a loving, forgiving parent."

"Is that all?"

"No. The parties are unable to agree on even the simplest of common matters."

"How does that affect parenting?"

"Because their parenting methods are so divergent, a joint custodial arrangement, whether legal or physical, is out of the question."

Oh baby. I'd better stop when I'm ahead, I thought.

"Thank you, Doctor. That's all I have."

"Judge, I offer a copy of Dr. Feingold's report as exhibit number 275," I said, handing the report to Dolores.

"No objection," Jed replied in a voice barely audible.

Jed again got up slowly, still apparently in the trance I thought he was in when he first came back into the courtroom. His shoulders were slouched and his chin was in his chest as he began, almost reluctantly it seemed, his cross examination of Feingold.

"There are two people here, aren't there, Dr. Feingold?" he began.

"What do you mean?"

"Well, you only testified about the Governor's shortcomings. What about Ms. Mitchell's?"

"I wasn't asked about them."

"I'm asking you now!" Jed shouted at the witness, coming out of his lethargy.

"I object," I said.

"Keep your voice down, Attorney Jed," the Judge intoned.

"Overruled," he continued.

"Didn't you find that Emily Mitchell is suffering from mild to moderate symptoms of a major depressive illness?"

"Yes."

"That she remains symptomatic with unexpected stresses, sleep disturbance, difficulty concentrating, difficulty getting herself to places on time?"

"Yes."

"And that she suffered from a depressive illness from which she continued to be symptomatic?"

"Yes, I told you."

"You found out that Danny took an overdose of drugs and had to be rushed to the hospital when he was under the care of his mother, Didn't you?"

"Yes."

'Tell me Dr. Feingold, are you familiar with the report of the GAL?"

"No."

"You didn't bother reading it?"

"No."

"Why not?"

Oh, oh I thought. That's your first mistake Attorney Paul Jed.

"I was conducting my own investigation. A very thorough investigation, I might add and I didn't want to be influenced by anyone else's. A lawyer's investigation is not quite up to our standards," he continued.

"You spoke with Ms. Mitchell's psychiatrist didn't you?" Jed asked gaining his rhythm, picking up his momentum.

"Certainly."

"And it says right here in your report that he told you she suffered from major recurring depression, isn't that right?" he asked the witness pointing to the page in the report where the quote was typed.

"Yes."

"And you'll admit, Doctor, that if Ms. Mitchell was experiencing a major depression episode she would not be a fit parent at that time, would she?"

"No, she wouldn't."

"Didn't you find that Ms. Mitchell was quite nihilistic, had low energy, was negativistic; that she was overwhelmed by daily guilt, fear and anxiety and she didn't wish to be alive when she was not functioning?" Jed asked, reading from the report.

"At times."

"Didn't you find that Ms. Mitchell was passively suicidal?"

"Yes, at times."

"And aren't you aware that in the evenings she'd consume two and sometimes three glasses of wine in addition to the medication she was taking?"

"She doesn't drink any more."

"Really? Since when?"

"For several weeks now."

Jed continued to read from Dr. Feingold's report but I could see he was trying the Judge's patience repeating over and over the same findings.

Finally, Jed said, "I have no further questions."

"I only have one or two, Dr. Feingold," I said.

"Other than the difficulty Ms. Mitchell has sleeping or concentrating or being late, does she have any other symptoms?"

"Ms. Mitchell suffers from a mild to moderate depression as a result of which she experiences those symptoms."

"Does she take medication for these symptoms?"

"Yes and her psycho pharmacologist has prescribed a certain drug for her."

"Does the drug work?"

"It certainly does."

"Is she now able to avoid periods of depression where she contemplated suicide in the past?"

"Most certainly. The medication helps her avoid almost all the symptoms she had complained of other than trouble sleeping and concentrating. As for being late, I think we all suffer from that malady periodically."

"Thank you. That's all I have," I said.

"No questions," Jed exclaimed.

"Tomorrow, nine o'clock," Talbot said and left the bench.

"All rise," said Jack.

CHAPTER THIRTY-ONE

The Governor made his way out of the courthouse, through the crowds of reporters and on-lookers, flanked by the two State Police officers that previously accompanied him and left Jed to make his way on his own. The cruiser sped away towards Storrow Drive following the Governor's order and, as before, Brenden Mitchell entered 10 Dudley Street leaving the two troopers on guard on each side of the entrance. It looked more like 10 Downing Street, London than the Prescott mansion in Brookline, Massachusetts.

The Governor's sister, Helen Prescott, was standing in the entrance vestibule when Brenden came in.

"Brenden, you look just awful. Come into the kitchen and I'll make you a cup of tea the way mother used to do. It will make you relax and we can talk. We haven't really talked since this nightmare started and I want you to bring me up to date. What is that trollop of a wife of yours up to now?"

She gently guided her brother toward the kitchen and he followed her without any protest. She could have guided him into hell and, the way he felt, he'd offer no resistance.

He sat at the old kitchen table where Lilly usually took her meals and watched with vacant eyes while Helen retrieved an actual tea kettle from the cupboard and began boiling water.

He was overwhelmed by a feeling of sadness mixed with a sudden bout of melancholia sitting at the kitchen table of his childhood with his sister making tea as his mother did when he was a little boy. He was in the same kitchen, with the same faucets and cupboards, the same wallpaper and wainscoting, the same wooden floor--nothing had changed but himself. Oh, how he'd changed, he thought gloomily.

"Now Brenden, tell me what's happening that's making you look so sad," Helen said placing the cup of tea and saucer, of course, in front of her brother.

Brenden Mitchell didn't answer at first. He simply sat there looking at his sister, his eyes brimming before he wiped them with his handkerchief.

"Helen," he said finally. "Do you think I overvalue myself?"

"Brenden! What are you talking about? Of course not. You're the Governor of this Commonwealth and you deserve to be. Is that what that wife of yours said?"

"Do you think I externalize blame?" he continued as if he hadn't heard a word she said.

"Brenden W. Mitchell, you stop that kind of talk right this very minute," she scolded.

"You are my brother and I love you. I will not hear of any such nonsense," she exclaimed altogether forgetting about her tea.

The doorbell rang but they ignored it until Lilly came in and announced that Mort Haller was at the front door.

"The policemen asked me if I would get your permission for Mr. Haller to come in," she said.

"Yes. Have him come in Lilly, thank you," the Governor said to her.

"I'm sorry Helen. I have to speak with Mort," Mitchell said as he got up from the table, leaving his sister sitting alone.

When Mort arrived, Brenden Mitchell and his chief of staff went into the den where Lilly asked if she could get Mr.Haller some tea and refill the Governor's cup.

"No thanks," they both said in unison and sat across from one another in matching, comfortable chairs.

"Mort, I'm finished," Mitchell said with a long sigh.

"I can see the headlines in the Globe and Herald. 'Governor Mitchell diagnosed as one who denies problems and personal shortcomings' they'll scream. Governor Mitchell is said to 'overvalue himself' the editors will cry. Governor said to 'externalize blame', they'll say. No, Mort. I'm done. There'll be no run for the Senate. I'll be lucky to finish out my term as Governor."

"You've got to get hold of yourself," Mort said. "You look like hell. Remember who you are. You're the guy who was once robust, full of vigor and confidence. You can't appear in court looking like this.

I am your friend and I'll always be your friend Brenden. Yes, this is a difficult time for you, for us, but we'll come out of it. So you don't run for the Senate now. Who's to say that six years from now you won't be a formidable candidate?"

"That's kind of you, Mort. You know I don't even want to go to court tomorrow. I want to let Paul Jed handle the rest of the case. I don't think I can face everybody."

"Well you can't do that, I'm afraid. You have to testify when your case goes in. Besides, have you ever thought that you're going through what just about everybody has to go through in a divorce case when there's a contested issue of custody?"

"Yeah, well everybody isn't the Governor," Mitchell said. "What's more, everybody doesn't have their career come to an end during a trial either," the Governor continued.

"I'll be O.K., Mort just give me some time. I need to rest."

"I'll leave you then. Call me if there's anything..."

"Yes, Yes. I'll see you in the morning."

After Haller left, Mitchell went back into the kitchen where Lilly made him a sandwich, which he really didn't want but took the plate she offered up to his room, Danny's room, and stretched out on the bed.

Here I am, he thought, lying in the semi-darkness of the fading September sun light, the Governor of this Commonwealth about to have my career, my reputation, my marriage even my relationship with my son ruined by this goddamned divorce case. In this very room I dreamed of achieving such noble goals, he remembered. Where did I go wrong? He sat up on the edge of the bed. What's the matter with me? Of course I know where I went wrong. I took money illegally, I looked the other way while crimes were being committed, I've taken drugs, I'm guilty of adultery! What could I expect?

He lay back down and thought about his mother and father; what would they say, what would they think about his ignoble collapse. They wouldn't be able to bear watching television or reading the papers as the media was merciless in their condemnation of him, he thought. Helen, at least was spared the embarrassment. She seldom watched television or read the papers.

He got up and went into the bathroom where he attempted to pour out two Ambian tablets from the bottle but half the tablets spilled out into the palm of his hand. He stared at the handful of sleep producing pills and saw another equal amount left in the container. He hesitated, tears were brimming in his eyes, his throat was constricted and his stomach was churning. He looked at his reflection in the mirror and was startled at what he saw: a defeated old man, without honor, without a future, without a wife and disgraced before his son.

He emptied the rest of the Ambian tablets into his hand and turned the faucet on in the sink. He picked up the glass and fingered the initial 'M' on it with his thumb for a split second before filling it with water. He hesitated-- he stopped-- sighed and poured the tablets back into the bottle. No, not now, he thought to himself. He swallowed two tablets and went back to bed.

He was right about the media. The television stations were relentless, unforgiving and every one of them trumpeted the character traits testified to by Dr, Justin Feingold. The talk show hosts discussed with their callers whether the Governor should resign. The vast majority stated unequivocally that he should.

CHAPTER THIRTY-TWO

Tuesday morning was another gloomy, cloudy, rainy day, mirroring, I supposed, the feelings of the readers of the headlines of the Globe and Herald. It was their Governor after all; their state that was held up to ridicule by the national press, by the syndicated columnists and the news anchors from coast to coast. There was sadness, a universal feeling of betrayal of the residents of the great Commonwealth of Massachusetts by their elected Governor. Even the most vitriolic news commentators sort of shook their collective heads in shame as they related the facts in excruciating detail of what had befallen their leader.

Even I, as bad as I wanted to retaliate against this pompous ass of a Governor, was tired of this case, tired of jousting with Jed, tired of Emily, tired of the money problems that were haunting me and the threats to my life. I couldn't wait to get the whole thing over with. That didn't stop me from calling my next witness though, even as I knew his testimony would blow the lid off this courtroom.

"I call Charles Randell," I said loudly, as soon as I got the nod from Talbot to proceed. For a second I glanced over at Jed who looked pale and wan sitting there with his hands clasped on the table in front of him. His client sat stiffly in the chair beside him gazing blankly, straight ahead.

After he was sworn and gave his name and address to the Court I started right in.

"What is your occupation?"

"I am a private detective."

"Are you licensed as such in this Commonwealth?"

"Yes I am."

'Were you hired to perform any service in connection with this case?"

"Yes, I was hired to conduct a surveillance on Brenden Mitchell."

"Was that all you were hired to do?"

"No. I-- at least my firm, was also hired to conduct surveillance on the comings and goings of Judge Rhea Andretti."

A huge clamor erupted in the courtroom. Some people even got up from their seats and rushed out the door evidently to call their editors or their TV stations with the latest shocker to be revealed in this case.

Jack raised his arm and approached the throng behind the bar.

"Quiet please. Quiet please," he instructed in a loud voice.

I looked at Talbot to see whether he was going to stay or leave the bench. I was surprised to see a startled expression on his otherwise enigmatic face.

Apparently, the crowd remembered Talbot's threat to close the courtroom in the event of any future disturbances for they quieted down rather quickly.

"Who hired you?"

"You did."

"What was the reason you were watching Judge Andretti?"

"I got a tip that she was into her own nocturnal affairs and, since she was the Judge assigned to your case, I thought..."

"Objection!" Jed bellowed rising from the defendant's table.

"Sustained," the Judge answered.

"Did you personally conduct the surveillance on the Judge?"

"No. My associate, Jake Bauer did."

"Did something happen to Mr. Bauer as he was doing his job?"

"Objection!"

"Overruled."

"Well, tell us what happened to him," I continued.

"He was mugged twice while watching her townhouse on Cedar Lane Way."

"By whom?"

"I really don't know."

"What did Mr. Bauer find out?"

"Objection!"

"Sustained."

"What did you learn, if anything, about the surveillance your firm conducted on the Judge's activity?"

"Nothing, really. She went to Bar Association meetings and the like but she otherwise stayed home. It wasn't until later we found out what was going on."

"Objection. Move to strike all after 'she otherwise stayed home'," Jed exclaimed.

"Sustained, all after 'she otherwise stayed home' shall be stricken."

"What was the purpose of the surveillance conducted on Brenden Mitchell?"

"We, uh... you wanted to monitor his comings and goings."

"For what purpose?"

"Objection."

"Overruled."

"To obtain facts enough to show that he was committing adultery."

"What did you do?"

"I watched where he went at night."

"What did you find out?"

"Well for the most part he went to meetings. He, of course went home to his sister's house when he had custody of his son but he never took him anywhere that I could see. On three or four occasions though, I followed him, in the evenings, to a townhouse at 18 West Cedar Street. I went to the tax collector's office and the public records there showed that the house was owned by Dr. and Ms. Barry Styles. I asked a few of the neighbors and found out that the Styles' were in Florida while their house was being renovated."

Jed got up to object but sat right back down after a look from Talbot.

"What did you observe?"

"The first two or three times the Governor parked his car on West Cedar Street and went in to the Styles' house even though it was dark inside."

"What did you see then?"

"Actually, nothing. No one went in and the place remained dark during the entire time the Governor was there."

"How long did he stay in there?"

"About two or three hours, each time."

"What happened next?"

"The last time I saw him enter 18 West Cedar Street I went around the corner to Pinckney Street and saw him exit the back entrance of number 18, cross Cedar Lane Way and enter the doorway of Judge Andretti's house. He stayed there for two hours and twenty-five minutes. I saw him leave the Judge's house about eleven-thirty P.M and enter the back door of 18 West Cedar Street. The lights were still out at the Styles' residence when he went in. After only one or two minutes I saw the governor leave number 18, get into his car and drive away."

"What was the date you last saw the Governor leave Cedar Lane Way?"

"The evening of August 19th."

"At that time was Judge Andretti still assigned to this case?"

A collective gasp arose from the crowd.

"I really don't know the answer to that question...but you do," Charley answered with a slight smile.

"That's all I have. Thank you, Mr.Randell."

Paul Jed stood up. His face was ashen but he spoke with a commanding voice.

"Your Honor, I move that this whole line of questioning be stricken."

"I'll hear you, Attorney Jed."

"There is absolutely no proof, other than the detective's word, that the person who entered Cedar Lane Way or 18 West Cedar Street was the Governor but even assuming the Court believes this paid witness, what is wrong with a person visiting another at eight forty-five in the evening? There is nothing on the record to show that there was any romantic involvement between the Governor and Judge Andretti. This whole line of testimony is inflammatory and calculated to disparage the good name of Brenden Mitchell. The consequences to the defendant are so grave, so devastating as to outweigh any consideration this Court might give to allowing the testimony to stand."

Jed's forehead was wet with perspiration, the rest of his face was red, he tried not to show his hands but I could see they were shaking, as he took his seat next to his client. The Governor, who previously sat bolt upright, looking straight ahead with a blank stare, now sat with his head bowed and his hands clasped on the table in front of him. Pathetic!

"First, there is no reason to disallow this testimony on the ground that the witness was paid," I began.

"The conduct of the defendant is certainly an issue in this case. There does not have to be an eye witness to adultery. There seldom is. All one has to do is prove 'opportunity and inclination' which we certainly have here. The Governor and the Judge didn't meet four times at night at her house just to play cribbage," I said repeating what Henry had told me.

"Besides Judge, the meetings themselves, irrespective of whether there was sex involved, were an abomination. How in the world can this Court countenance any private meetings between the Defendant and the very Judge who's sitting on his case?"

I struck a cord I could tell. The Judge had a disgusted look on his face as the crowd murmured what I believed to be their disapproval of the conduct I'd just related.

"Motion denied," the Judge said immediately as I sat down.

Another outburst came from the crowd and Jack again had to quiet them down.

"I'll take the noon recess," Talbot said in a voice that was barely able to be heard.

"All rise," Jack, the very busy court officer said in a loud voice.

I hadn't noticed Emily all morning but when I did, on my way back to the table, she was beaming.

"Oh, Ted-- Attorney Eldridge, you were just great," she said to me, kissing the scar on my cheek. I smiled at her and nodded to Henry, who knew from experience that I wanted to get away to be by myself. Nevertheless, I simply could not escape the throng of reporters who were waiting for me in the hallway outside the courtroom.

"Do you have any other witnesses about adultery?" one asked.

"Where's the kid during trial?" asked another.

"How much longer," said one.

"What do you think the Judge will do, Attorney Eldridge?" shouted another.

"No comment," was all I said.

I didn't dare take the elevator. I didn't want to be stuck in close quarters with a slew of reporters all badgering me with questions. Yet I still had to hobble along, unsteady on my feet, as I opted for the stairs in hopes that only a few would follow me. No such luck.

All the way down they kept up a stream of questions to which I never responded. Once outside, I headed for Quincy Market but the questions never abated. Finally, I turned on the group that was following me and said to them:

"Please give me a break. I need some time. I will not answer any questions, so please back off," I told them.

They left me alone and I proceeded laboriously, to the coffee shop at the entrance to the South Market Building. There, I was left in peace as I sat on one of the benches outside and watched all the tourists go by without apparently a care in the world. I wondered what Jed would do, what questions he would ask on his cross examination of Charley Randell. But the damage was done, or almost done to this Governor. I wasn't finished. I still had the problem of connecting the Governor to the rake off from the bookies in the North End. How could I get that into evidence? I had planned to answer that very question when Court was adjourned later today. DellaPenna? Bresnahan? Could I get their testimony in? Their conversations with the bookies and with Renzo would be excluded as hearsay, wouldn't they? Well, first things first.

CHAPTER THIRTY-THREE

When I returned to the courthouse I made my way through the crowd again, still refusing to answer any questions, took the elevator up to the fourth floor this time and actually pushed my way through the group of reporters gathered in the hall and those waiting inside the courtroom, sat down heavily at counsel table next to Henry and let out an audible sigh.

"Jesus, but I'll be glad to see this case finished," I said to him.

"I know what you mean," he replied just before Emily returned to her seat next to us.

Henry told me that the Governor with his two State Troopers flanking him left in the two-toned blue state cruiser at the noon recess for parts unknown, sans Paul Jed. Unashamedly, we joked that he had to go somewhere to take some medication to help him get through the day.

"What do you think will happen to the Judge?" Henry whispered to me out of Emily's hearing.

"Henry, she's going to get disbarred," I replied, whispering back to him.

"I'm not so sure," he said to me, shaking his head.

After the Judge resumed his seat and the usual courthouse shuffle and undercurrent died down, Jed got wearily to his feet. I wouldn't have traded places with him for all the money in the world. He looked like a beaten man and his client-- his client looked worse.

I worried that I didn't have much of a chance to prepare Charley for his cross examination but he was a big boy, he could handle Paul Jed on his worse day. Besides, all he had to do was stick to his basic story which we had rehearse to a fair-thee-well.

"Mr. Randell, you are a private detective are you not?"

"Yes."

"You perform your duties for hire, right?"

"Right."

"How long did you have Judge Andretti under surveillance?"

"For several weeks."

"And for all that time you never saw her participate in any gathering, any meeting other than a legitimate Bar Association meeting, isn't that so?"

"Yes, that's so."

"And you never saw her in a bar or, for that matter in anyone's house other than her own, that's true also isn't it?"

"Yes."

"And of course you are intimately familiar with the Judges social friends, right?"

"No, I'm not."

"So you don't know whether the Governor and Judge Andretti are good friends or not, do you?"

"No."

"Now, Mr. private detective for hire, where were you standing when you first observed a person enter Cedar Lane Way on the night of August 19th?"

"Objection."

"Overruled."

"I was about fifty yards away from the entrance to both houses, one on Cedar Lane Way and the other on West Cedar Street."

"You must have been standing on Pinckney Street, right?"

"Right."

"And it was dark, right?"

"Yes."

'Those fifty yards are about half the distance of a football field, to put it in perspective, that's also true isn't it?"

"Yes."

"And yet, as dark as it was and as far away as it was, you think it was the Governor of this Commonwealth who entered West Cedar Street and Cedar Lane Way that night. Is that right?"

"That's my testimony."

"And you don't know for a certainty that no one was home at 18 West Cedar Street, do you?"

"Well, the lights were out."

"Are you telling this Court that you could see every light in that house at once from where you were standing?"

"Well no, but I could see one whole side of the house."

"You'll admit that there are at least four sides to a house, won't you?"

"Uh"

"You have to answer, Mr. Detective."

"I guess."

"And the only reason you concluded that Dr. and Ms. Edmonds were not at their residence on August 19th is because someone told you they were in Florida, right?"

"Well no. The house was dark."

"Do you conclude that every house that's dark has no one home?"

"I also relied on what I was told."

331

"Do you rely on everything you're told?"

"Well--"

"You don't know of your own knowledge whether anyone was home at 18 West Cedar Street on the 19th of August, do you."

"No, I guess not."

Suddenly the doors to the courtroom burst open and Jordan Levy from my office, exploded into the courtroom, followed by a group of reporters and even cameramen none of whom gave any evidence that they were interrupting the trial or, for that matter, whether they cared.

"Here, what's going on?" Talbot exclaimed, peering down at the melee before him.

"Judge, may we have a short recess?" I hurriedly asked.

"Fifteen minutes," Talbot barked and promptly left the bench.

Jordan rushed up to the counsel table out of breath and breathing hard with the breath he had left and dropped an official looking document in front of me.

"Ted, look at this. The Governor has just been indicted!" he sputtered.

I couldn't believe what I was looking at. The indictment was against Brenden W. Mitchell, handed up by the Suffolk County Grand Jury dated September seventh, for matters concerning corruption, extortion, participation in illegal betting and violations of the regulations of the Committee of Campaign and Political Finance.

"The investigation of the Attorney General's Office in conjunction with the State Police finished their investigation and presented their evidence to the Grand Jury which had already been convened and they didn't waste any time handing up the indictment," Jordan told me between gasps for breath.

"They also indicted Mort Haller, the Governor's Chief of Staff," he continued.

"I called the Attorney General's Office and they told me they intend to present the indictments to a specially named prosecutor

who will present his findings to a Special Grand Jury that's going
to be appointed by the Crime Commission," Jordan continued.

"Ted, of course you can read the charges in the indictment
into the record as it's a public document," Henry added, his voice
rising over the hubbub.

"I know, Henry. I just have to digest what's just happened. I
don't know what Paul Jed and his client will do now. Let's see if
we can get an adjournment until tomorrow."

I looked over at the Defendant's table and saw Paul Jed and
one of his associates surrounding the Governor who held his head
in his hands, looking as though he was about to expire. Jed put his
arm around the Governor's shoulders and I could see he was trying
to hold him together as his body was shaking as if he was in the
throes of having been heavily medicated-- on his way out.

The noise prevented me from concentrating on what had just
happened. Emily looked confused although I was certain she knew
the news was devastating for her husband. People were running
around the courtroom actually shouting at one another as Jack
stood helplessly by.

I noticed that Dolores Fairchild left the courtroom madhouse
that was getting worse by the minute and escaped to the privacy
of the area behind the closed doors to the rear.

After a few minutes she re-entered the courtroom preceded
by Jack, evidently for protection, and announced that court was
adjourned until nine o'clock tomorrow morning. That was all right
by me.

Jordan, Henry, Emily and I made our way through the throng
and, curiously, not one reporter asked me any questions. Emily, her
head bent as if she was a full back plowing through the line, also
escaped any inquiries. We waited in front of the elevators for one to
open, standing on the threshold of the entrance preventing anyone
from getting in line ahead of us. As soon as the door opened, we
all piled in. Henry pressed the 'close' button before anyone else
could join us and we were deposited into the lobby of the building
without a word being said by anyone. We all made our way out of

the building without being jostled or even delayed. The media had too much on their minds to even give us a second look.

The Governor must have had a head start as I saw him get into the cruiser with his two body guards as we walked across the wide stone pavers in front of the Edward Brooke Courthouse, on our way to Old City Hall.

The window of the cruiser was open and Paul Jed was bending down to talk to his client who was seated inside between the two troopers.

"Governor are you all right? You're welcome to come to my office and decompress, have a little Scotch and we'll review your direct testimony," Jed said to his client.

The Governor thought to himself, what a blockhead. That's the last thing I need right now. Get me away from here, from him, from the whole goddamn bunch.

"No thanks, Paul," he replied. "I'll see you first thing in the morning. I'll meet you in your office at eight o'clock. That should give us enough time to brush up, eh? Thanks for everything," the Governor said ominously.

"Take me home," he said to his driver.

CHAPTER THIRTY-FOUR

We, Jordan, Henry and I, arrived at Old City Hall, having bid Emily goodbye and, as we walked in the front door of the office, we were greeted by cheers. The office staff had gathered around us abuzz with the knowledge of the indictment. They were full of questions, had the office TV on and were as excited as I've ever seen them. They worked hard getting us to this point so I didn't care that it was evident by the cups and saucers strewn about that they had gathered around the conference table like a bunch of kids, drinking soda and coffee while watching the news casts.

The three of us sat down with them and extolled them with trial vignettes that made them alternately laugh and become sad. The Governor's plight was sad. *Sic transit* gloria *mundi,* I remembered saying a long time ago, although I had an empty feeling this time around.

I couldn't bear to do any work for the rest of the day so I went home. Andrea was happy for me but she knew enough not to ask too many questions. I never told her about my conversation with Josh. She knew from past experience that I didn't want to relive the traumas of the day by relating the details to her. I spent some time in the afternoon paying attention to Mandy whom I had neglected for several weeks. She was preparing for her SAT's and Andrea was taking her to colleges in and around Massachusetts. Mandy and I were always in synch with each other so it was no big deal to become reacquainted. She knew about the trial of course, but she too didn't ask many questions. Besides, all she had to do was turn on the TV or the radio to get a blow by blow description of what was going on. As a senior, she knew enough to keep her own counsel in the halls of Brookline High and not give away any family secrets.

Before dinner I sat in my usual chair and watched the news on ABC. I purposely avoided the local news but even Charles Gibson covered the trial in detail, especially the part about the Governor and his Chief of Staff being indicted.

The soothing sound of the ice cubes in my scotch tinkling against the glass as I stirred them with my index finger didn't help me drive out the demons in my mind. I kept thinking of the events of the day with mixed feeling of relief and sadness.

Henry was right, I thought. I didn't have to worry about the hearsay problems that would arise if I put the guy from the State Police on the stand. What was his name? DellaPenna. I had a similar problem with the Assistant A.G., Tommy Bresnahan, if I put him on. Neither of them could testify to the conversation DellaPenna had with Guiliano Rigali. I didn't want to call either Rigali or his boss, Renzo, based on the promise the AG made in exchange for their cooperation in naming Mort Haller and the Governor. Now, with this indictment being a public record, all I had to do was read the charges into the record.

But wait a minute, I thought. The charges are just that, only charges. The indictment is only the government's allegations against the defendant. He won't be found guilty, if at all, until after a criminal trial. But so what, I continued with my musing, sipping my scotch slowly. The indictment alone is enough to bring down this Governor. But is it enough to have Emily win sole custody and a seventy- five percent share of all the assets? That's what I was looking for—and to get paid!

The Governor thanked his driver and again was escorted from the car to the front door of 10 Dudley Street by the two State Troopers. They resumed their vigil as Brenden Mitchell entered the house he grew up in, full of memories of a kinder, gentler time. Lilly inquired if there was anything she could get for him as she met him in the vestibule but he waived her off and went into the living room in search of Helen.

The whole downstairs was dark. No lights were on and even the filtered light coming through the curtained windows on the west side of the house was dim casting early Fall diminishing shadows over the large oriental rug highlighting, to some extent anyway, the rose, ivory and blue colors that made up its traditional pattern.

Helen was not in her usual chair under her reading lamp. Mitchell went into the kitchen, certain he'd find her there but he only found Lilly cleaning up after a late lunch.

"Can I fix a sandwich for you?" she asked again.

"No thanks," he replied wearily and continued to look for his sister in the den.

He found her there sitting on the couch in front of a television set. She looked transfixed as she stared straight ahead looking at the news and was apparently so engrossed in what she was watching she didn't hear her brother come in.

"So now you know the whole story, eh Helen?"

"Oh Brenden, I didn't hear you come in," she said to him as she looked up at him.

"Brenden, I'm so sorry," she continued after a few moments.

He sat down next to her and switched off the television set with the remote.

"I--I just don't know what to do. I don't know which way to turn. The divorce, the trial is-- it's just too much for me," he said to her in a voice barely audible.

She didn't respond right away. She wanted to try to let him get it all out of his system.

"I don't have a prayer to beat this indictment, Helen. They can trace money right from the bookies to my campaign accounts. Mort set the whole thing up of course, but I'm the beneficiary so I can't escape blame. I could say I merely borrowed the money to fund this divorce, but that doesn't answer the question of where the money came from in the first place," he said holding his head in his hands.

"The characterization of me by Dr. Feingold was devastating," he lamented, tears now forming in the corners of his eyes.

"The testimony about me not being Danny's father--Helen I--I can't face any more of this," he continued in a muffled voice, trying to stifle a sob in front of his sister despite the fact that she always mothered him in times like this when he was little.

"Brenden, of course you're Danny's father. Don't you dare think otherwise," she exclaimed putting her arm around his shoulder.

"Where is Danny, by the way? Why hasn't he been around here for the past week or more?" she asked.

"He's at Emily's mother's house in Osterville, I guess," he answered.

"You *guess*? She said, accusingly.

"Don't start, Helen," he said to his sister blowing his nose.

"Well, it's just that I miss him," she responded. "So does Lilly," she said.

"Oh, I know that I can get on his nerves but honestly Brenden, he brightens up this whole place when he's here. He'll be here after the divorce is over won't he? I mean, you'll still be able to have contact with him, won't you?"

You mean after I get out of jail, Brenden Mitchell thought.

While sitting there Brenden thought of his father, Harold Daniels Mitchell, friend and companion to people in power all over the United States, people of status. What would he think of me? And mother? What would she say? The daughter of Thomas and Mary Plummer, high society of the Back Bay for years, what would they think?

Oh God!

He got up from the couch, kissed Helen on the cheek and went up to his room, Danny's room, and pulled the shades. He sat on the edge of the bed for a few minutes and finally got up, went downstairs and told his sister he was going out for a few minutes.

"I'll be right back," Lilly, he said to her on the way out to the garage.

As he passed the two troopers he told them he was going to the store...that he needed to be by himself for a little while and they shouldn't worry.

"I'm sorry Governor but we've got our orders. One of us will have to go with you but don't worry, you can act as though we were invisible."

"Ok, I guess," he said to them.

"But, if you must know, I'm only going to the package store."

"OK, Pete here will go with you," one of them said.

Pete got into the passenger side of the Governor's car and they drove off. Five minutes later the Governor parked in front of his favorite package store and asked Pete to stay in the car while he went in to make a simple purchase.

"OK, Governor. I can watch you from here so I guess it'll be all right," Pete replied.

As soon as Brenden Mitchell opened the door to Dillon's Package Store he was greeted by three clerks and even a few customers like a long lost friend.

"Hang in there Governor," one said. "We're your friends here, Brenden," another declared.

"Good luck, Governor," another said.

Brenden Mitchell offered his thanks and made his way to the cooler in the rear of the store. He paused by the case which displayed the champagnes and, not seeing what he wanted, searched for Maurice Depping, the owner.

"Maurice, I'm looking for a special bottle of champagne. Do you have any Cristal?"

"Well, you must be expecting a victory, Governor. That's the top of the line. I have two bottles right here out of sight," he said reaching down to a separate cooler under the counter shelf.

"I just need one," the Governor replied. He paid for the champagne with his debit card and left the store.

He didn't say a word to Pete on the way back to the house but simply dropped him off at the entrance to the front door to join his buddy before parking the car in the garage. He paused for a second in the vestibule wondering whether he should get a champagne flute from the sideboard cabinet in the dining room --but then he thought better of it. Just the bathroom glass is good enough, he thought. He did go into the den however and retrieved a pen and some paper from his desk before proceeding up then stairs to "his room".

After the hearing Emily went directly home. Her phone didn't stop ringing all afternoon but she didn't answer it. The first thing she did was call her mother and ask to speak with Danny. After being assured that he was alright, even though he answered her questions in monosyllables, she spoke to her mother.

"He's doing fine, dear. Don't worry. The tennis courts are still open at Wianno and he's found a friend who goes to school down here to play with. Don't worry about him missing a few days of school, Emily. He'll make it up after this nightmare is over for him."

"What else is he doing other than playing tennis," Emily inquired.

"Oh, he and his friend are sailing 'J's' at the yacht club. At least I think they're 'J's'. Whatever, they seem to be having a good time."

"Well-- OK and thank you mother. This trial will be over quicker than I originally thought."

"How is it going dear?"

"It's had its ups and downs but lately it's going quite well. Haven't you been watching TV or listening to the news mother?"

"Oh, as soon as that stuff comes on, dear, I turn it off and I certainly don't read about it in the papers. I also try and keep Danny away from the news and the TV but I can't say I've been too successful."

"Well, I'm glad he's there. Thank you again," Emily exclaimed to her mother.

"Not at all dear. Call tomorrow, OK?"

"OK."

Emily went into the kitchen and opened the refrigerator door. There on the side door was a cold bottle of SIMI chardonnay. She poured herself a half glass and sat down on her favorite chair in the den and kicked off her shoes. She felt elated at the progress Ted Eldridge was making in the case. She turned on the TV with her remote and clicked on a local talk show which featured one of the Boston Globe columnists as a host for the program..

"He's finished," the columnist was saying.

"Can you imagine?" his co-host replied, "Indicted, for crying out loud. The Governor of the Commonwealth and his Chief of Staff. I just can't believe it. Taking a payoff from the bookies in the North End... For what? For a few thousand bucks?"

"And what about the use of that tainted money to fund his campaign for the Senate?" the columnist replied. "What about the campaign laws he's broken by using campaign money to pay for his divorce? Can he be any dumber?"

"I can't believe what's been happening to him in this divorce case. Did you see how the shrink painted his character? He just about said outright that he had a serious mental problem and needed some substantial behavioral modification," the co-host replied.

"Well, he might as well resign right now. The longer he stays in the public eye the worse it'll be for him," the host stated.

Emily finished her drink, thought about pouring herself another drink and resumed her place in front of the TV. She clicked to a different channel and surfed the guide in frustration before finally turning the set off. The house was silent and lonely. She was lonely. There was no noise. She had no responsibility to prepare dinner. No husband to prepare dinner for. No Danny pestering her asking when dinner would be ready. She went into the bathroom and took the bottle of lithium tablets from her medicine cabinet and tried to remember whether she had taken the prescribed dose this morning.

I feel so depressed all of a sudden, she thought. Why? Things are going all right. What have I got to worry about? she said to herself. I'm old. That's it. I'm old, she thought. What the hell will I do for the rest of my life? Who will bother with an old lady like me? Danny will be gone in three or four years; off to college, God willing. And then what? Who cares about money? What will I do with myself?

She sighed as she looked at her image in the bathroom mirror. She had circles under her eyes, her roots were showing, her cheeks were depressed against her high cheekbones and she was pale and drawn. She didn't dare look at the rest of her body in the full length mirror in the bedroom.

She attempted to pour two tablets out of the bottle but a whole hand full came out in her hand. She looked at the pills, looked at herself in the mirror-- and carefully poured the pills back into the bottle.

"Danny, sweetheart, what did your mother say on the phone?" his grandmother asked after she'd hung up from talking to her daughter.

"Nothin."

"Well, what did you say to her?"

"Nothin."

"Now Danny, that's not nice. Talk to me. Tell me what she said."

"We just talked for a couple of minutes. She wanted to know if I was all right."

"Are you?"

"Am I what?"

"Are you all right Danny?"

"Yes, I'm OK."

"You've seen the news on the TV haven't you?"

"Yeah, I guess."

"How do you feel about what's happening to your father?"

"I dunno."

"Do you care what happens to him?"

"Yeah, sure, I guess."

"Your mother and I think that you will be able to go back to your own house and live with her. How do you feel about that?"

"OK, I guess."

"You'll be able to see your father on some weekends and go out to dinner with him once or twice during the week. Will you like that?"

"Yeah."

"Danny, what's the matter with you? Can't we talk? Heavens, I've been trying to see how you're feeling so I can help you. Don't you understand?"

"He never bothered with me before why do you think he'll bother with me now," Danny blurted as he stood not three feet from her. He turned and ran out the front door crying.

Oh God. How will this kid ever make it? she wondered.

The Honorable Brenden W. Mitchell opened the door to "his" room and carefully placed the bottle of champagne on the nightstand next to his bed. In his other hand he held the pen and paper he had retrieved from the den both of which he deposited on the small table in front of the curtained windows. He went into the bathroom and rinsed out the bathroom glass he used every morning, picked up his two bottles of pills and brought the glass and the pills to the nightstand. He opened the bottle of Cristal and poured the pale liquid into his glass, filling it half-way. He carried the chair, usually placed in front of the closet, over to the table, picked up his glass of champagne and sat down.

He paused, looked out the same window he so often looked out at when he was growing up and began to write:

Dear Danny,

You will be surprised to receive this letter from your father. I thought it might be too late for me to tell you things--things I haven't had the time to tell you in the past; things I should have told you long ago. Things like, I love you. But I have failed you in so, so many ways. I thought I could, at the very least, attempt to let you know how I truly feel.

I think of all the Little League games you participated in that I didn't bother to attend, all the conversations at dinner I missed because I was too busy, all of your school work I ignored and never bothered to see whether you needed any help. I am overwhelmed with regret.

Becoming a State Senator and then the Governor of this state, even a candidate for the Senate of the United States should never have stood in the way of me showing you how much I love you. I would trade my entire career for a second chance to be the father you deserve.

But there will be no second chance. You will hear terrible things about your father in the coming months. Some things will be the truthful, others will be exaggerations of the truth, but one way or the other, I never intended to hurt you.

In this letter I ask your forgiveness. I beg you to rise above the calamity I have caused and show the world who you really are, and yes, the family you came from. You have a proud heritage given to you by your grandparents, sullied by my stupidity yes, but a part of you nevertheless.

And so, my son, I bid you goodbye. I love you.

Your father

The Governor put down the pen, drank the rest of his champagne and walked back to the nightstand. He refilled his glass, emptied the two bottles of pills into his hand and washed them down with the rest of his Cristal. He stretched out on his bed and closed his eyes.

CHAPTER THIRTY-FIVE

Wednesday morning, the sixth day of trial, was one of those late summer days that could have dawned just as easily in early August. I was up and ready to go before the sun shot its rays between the slats on the Venetian blinds in our bedroom.

I left the house before anyone was up, listened to my iPod in the car and reached Old City Hall just as the custodian, Drew, was sweeping the front plaza. Drew was one of those guys who never said much. He could convey his feelings, however, with a smile or a frown, sometimes with nothing more than a grunt.

This morning I couldn't tell what kind of mood he was in. He had a slight smile on his face that appeared at the corners of his mouth which accented deep wrinkles in his cheeks. But at the same time, I noticed his eyes were half closed as he pushed the large broom across the large stone pavers, seemingly lost in thought. I got the impression that something happened to him that he could not quite figure out.

"Mornin'," he said.

"Morning, Drew. Everything O.K.?"

"I guess."

He looked away from me and stared down at his broom, not moving. I got the impression that I did something wrong to him the way he ignored me. I mean, he never said much but I always could tell he was glad to see me.

I limped up the stairs to the elevator bank. I had enough to worry about. When I opened the door to the office, no one was there either. I made the coffee and brought my second cup of the day with me into the large conference room, using only one crutch. I sat at the table and spread the file of Charley Randell before me.

Let's see, I thought. Jed was in the middle of his cross-examination of Charley when Jordan interrupted the hearing with the news of the indictment. Do I have any re-direct? What shall I do about the indictment? I could call DellaPenna or Tommy Bresnahan to the stand but I'd have that hearsay problem when I asked them to relate their conversation with either Renzo or Giuliano Rigali. Henry was right of course. I could read the indictment into the record but the indictment alone is not a guilty finding, so what good is it? Besides, it may not be allowed in. What if Jed objects on the ground of relevancy? How is a criminal indictment relevant in a divorce case? The criminal acts were not committed against Emily.

I was in the middle of this thought process when Jordan opened the front door and, without stopping, came rushing into the conference room.

"I can't believe it," he said breathlessly.

"Can't believe what?" I replied

"What!! You haven't heard the news? The Governor is dead. They found his body this morning in his bedroom. The cause of death hasn't officially been announced but the news media all say he committed suicide. Suicide! Can you imagine?"

All I could do was stare at Jordan. After a few seconds I realized my mouth was open yet I couldn't speak. My hands started to shake and I grabbed the edge of the table to steady myself.

There were so many thoughts running through my head that I couldn't think straight. What about Emily? What about Danny? What should I do? Did I contribute to this catastrophe? Of course I did! Drew? Did he know when I came in? Was I too confrontational trying this case? That's the way it goes, isn't it? Could I have been more collegial? More accommodating? Did I have to be so goddamn aggressive?

"What're you going to do?" Jordan asked, falling heavily into one of the conference chairs .

All I could do at that point was shake my head. Not only were my thoughts mixed but so were my emotions. I felt sad, resigned, remorseful, even to some extent relieved, but I couldn't separate any or them. I couldn't make sense of them.

I got up and made my way into my office. I couldn't stand Jordan looking at me expecting answers and I had to get away and be by myself. The phone started ringing but I didn't pick it up. I wasn't ready to talk with anybody. I wasn't sure I was ready for anything at that point.

In my half daze, the time went by and soon the office was filled with the entire staff. Jordan must have alerted them to my fractious mood as not a soul came knocking at my closed door, not even Henry.

A few minutes later, I hadn't made much progress in sorting out my thoughts or my mood so I decided to face the tempest and by that, hoped to be able to come into focus.

The entire group was congregated in the conference room talking in hushed tones when I entered. They stopped their chatter and looked at me expectantly, as if I had the answers to all their questions.

"Well, what do you think of that?" I said.

They all started to answer at once. I couldn't hear one over the other. I forced myself to smile at them, turned around and limped out the door. I had no idea where I was going but I had to get away.

As I left the elevator, I imagined everyone was looking at me accusingly. Were you the lawyer who caused the Governor to kill himself? Stop it, I told myself. You'll drive yourself crazy. It wasn't your fault. You tried a difficult case, that's all.

I went out the back way, crossed Washington Street, State Street, Congress Street and into Faneuil Hall again in search of a peaceful interlude on one of the outside benches, in the hope that by watching the people go by I'd be distracted from my guilty feelings.

Emily had a fitful night's sleep. She woke up almost on the hour from one AM to six before falling back to sleep. At seven she awoke feeling as though she hadn't gone to bed at all. She went into the bathroom and observed, with a sigh, that her countenance hadn't changed from the night before.

She brewed some coffee and turned on the television set on the kitchen counter.

"-- and so ladies and gentlemen, thus ends the political life of our Governor. An ignominious term in office if there ever was one. An autopsy is expected but there is a question of who will authorize the procedure since the Governor's spouse is suing him for divorce.

In other news…"

"Wha…What?" Emily said aloud. "Did I hear right? An autopsy? Jesus Christ! What happened?"

She switched to another channel in time to hear the commentator say: "The Governor, Brenden W. Mitchell, is dead apparently from an overdose of drugs. As soon as we learn more we'll be back to you. In the meantime, that's all we have for now."

Emily was dumbstruck! She couldn't believe what she'd just heard. At that moment, the phone rang. She went to the table on which the phone rested with an unsteady gait, her hands trembling.

"Hel...Hello."

"Emily dear--"

"Who is this?"

"Emily, this is your mother. Are you all right?"

"I just now heard the news. I can't focus. I can't talk to you now, mother. I'm sorry," she said as she hung up the phone.

Oh my God, she thought, as a flood of memories overpowered her. Brenden dead? How could this be? She pictured him as he was twenty years ago, strong, vigorous, and confident; rich yes, not only in money but in family tradition which always meant so much to him. How she loved him then. What happened to us, she thought as she started to get dressed.

What shall I do? What about Danny? Oh my God! Danny what will he think?

She went back to the telephone and dialed her mother's number.

"Hello." It was her mother.

"Mother, please put Danny on the line."

" Hello." Danny's voice was barely audible.

"Danny, sweetheart, are you OK?"

"Yeah."

"I'm coming right down to Osterville to be with you." Despite her best effort she began to cry.

"Danny, we'll be all right. Please don't worry," she said between sobs.

She heard nothing on the other end.

"Danny, honey, say something! Are you sure you're OK?"

"Yeah, I'm OK."

"Well, please put Grandma on the line and I'll be there as soon as I can. Remember, I love you, all right?"

"All right."

"Yes dear," her mother said calmly.

"Mother, is he OK?"

"He'll be fine. What are you going to do?"

"I'm coming right down. Danny and I need to be together. I'm supposed to be in court this morning but under the circumstances I really don't give a damn. I'll see you soon."

Emily Mitchell finished getting dressed all the while thinking about what would come next. She continued to cry silently, her tears falling on her freshly pressed blouse as she tried to steel herself against what she knew would be an onslaught of media attention. What would I say to them? What happens to the divorce? How do I feel? Oh God, I'm not even sure of how I feel.

As she prepared to open the door leading to the attached garage, she looked out of the front windows of the livingroom.

"Oh no!" she said aloud.

She saw at least ten reporters or cameramen or whatever they were standing on the sidewalk in front of the house.

Thankfully I don't have to go by them, she thought as she entered the garage, opened the automatic door and backed the car out. She turned the car around and headed down the driveway with her windows close tight. As she passed the throng she was almost blinded by the flashes that went off from the cameras.

"Do you have a comment, Ms. Mitchell?" she heard one say.

One actually was courteous enough to offer condolences: "I'm sorry for your trouble, Ms Mitchell," one said loud enough to be heard over everyone else.

Emily nodded in the direction of them all and drove away toward Route 128 and Cape Cod.

Danny hung up the phone after talking with his mother and went outside so his grandmother couldn't see he was crying. My father, dead? My father? Is he really? Of course he is, he thought while walking among the fruit trees planted next to the patio in the rear of the house. His grandfather planted them before he died over eight years ago and Danny always loved them. I'm at fault , he thought. They'd be still together if it wasn't for me. Now what? The small orchard brought him no peace. How will I get along with just my mother? I wish I could stay right here with Grandma. But school? What about that? I do like it at Brookline

High. And Brian, my best, no, my only friend? I really miss him even when I'm here.

His thoughts were running together now. It won't be so bad to go back to Brookline as long as Brian is there, he thought. I wonder how my mother will survive all this. Will she go back to drinking when this case is over? What about her medication? He couldn't stop crying and he was afraid, overwhelmed with guilt.

His grandmother came out with a Coke in her hand.

"Here dear, drink something cold," she said to him as she joined him by the apple trees, their branches now bending and ladened with ripe fruit.

"You know things will begin to look up when this case is over and you're back in school. Your mother will be fine, don't worry about that," she said to him as she put her arm around him and continued walking.

"If you want, we can arrange for you to go to a first class prep school, even board there. Would you like that?"

"Do you think if I didn't cause their break-up there'd be no divorce and my father would still be alive?" Danny said through his tears.

"Danny! Don't you dare think that. You had nothing to do with the divorce between your mother and father. They just couldn't get along after a while. It happens to adults all the time. Your father made some political mistakes which got him into trouble, mistakes that other politicians have made for years. It's just that your father was a proud man and couldn't face the consequences."

"Well, I guess--"

"Listen to me. There is a lesson your father would want you to learn from all of this. That lesson is that when people make mistakes, they have to face up to them; not run away and hide. Just like you, young man, have to face up to these troubles and not run away and hide. Understand?"

"Yeah, I guess so," Danny mumbled.

They continued their stroll and Danny's Grandmother noticed he'd stopped crying. This kid will be all right, she thought. Prep school! That's not a bad thought. He'd be away from the glare of the

media, away from the ups and downs of his mother's rehabilitation-
- not a bad thing to consider at all.

Paul Jed, an early riser, turned on the news first thing in the
morning. He was flabbergasted! His first thought was 'There goes
my judgeship'. His second thought was 'There goes the trial'. No
defendant, no case, no divorce, no judgment, no fees. How in hell
will I be paid now, he lamented.

When he arrived at his office his secretary told him that there
was a partners meeting in the conference room scheduled for nine
o'clock. Promptly at nine, all the partners had gathered which was
strange in itself as the meeting was called without any notice. They
all had tight schedules but they must have made adjustments to
attend the meeting this morning.

Before the meeting, Jed called the Court to request that he be
allowed to start at ten o'clock instead of nine. He was informed that
the Judge had arranged to begin at eleven o'clock and that the clerk,
Barbara Hancock, was in the process of notifying all parties.

His four partners took their accustomed seats around the
conference table and the meeting began as soon as they were all
settled. The senior partner, Donald Cooper called the meeting to
order.

"Paul, we're here because we're concerned about the two
hundred forty-three thousand dollars that's on the books in this
Mitchell case," he began.

"Now that the Governor is dead, the case will end and there
won't be an order for counsel fees. In fact, as you know, all the
property will belong to Ms. Mitchell and to the trust the Governor
had set up. Whether the two million will stay in trust or not is of
no consequence to this firm. It won't be available for our counsel
fees in any event.

So Paul, we were wondering what you intend to do about
collecting the outstanding fee?" Cooper asked.

Paul was speechless. His mind was racing, searching for the
right response.

"What am I going to do? What does anybody in this firm do when the fees go "south". We have to eat them, that's what we do," he replied.

"Do you think Ted Eldridge will ask his client to contribute to our fees?" Jim Flahive, his other partner asked.

"After all, she'll walk away with the whole estate," he continued.

Paul couldn't believe what he was hearing. Not one word about the calamity, the tragedy that befell the Governor of the Commonwealth. Not a word about all the months of work he put in, now all shot to hell. They were concerned with the outstanding fee, that's all.

"I don't know. Frankly, I'll be too embarrassed to ask," Paul finally said to them.

"Too embarrassed! Too embarrassed!" Donald Cooper shouted.

"This is our bread and butter, Paul. A quarter of a million dollars is not something we can just write off. The firm carried you, paid all your expenses, while all the while you continued to take your normal draw. Hell, we all continued to take our normal draw. Now what? We just walk away from over two hundred thousand dollars? I don't think so," Cooper stammered.

"Look Paul. Be reasonable. At least go before the Judge and see if you can solicit his help in convincing Eldridge or his client that, in all fairness, we should get paid. What do you say?" Flahive pleaded.

"I'll do my best," Jed managed to say as the meeting came to a close.

Back in his office Jed sat down and rested his head in the palm of his propped up right hand, elbow on the desk.

I'm just as bad as those guys, he thought. I was litigating this case without regard to the money it was costing everyone involved. What the hell, I was litigating this case so I could get a judgeship. Who's worse, those guys or me, he asked himself.

He packed his briefcase with yellow pads and two files he brought with him from court and left for the eleven o'clock session ordered by Judge Talbot. He wondered whether this would be the last time he would appear in this case. The thought followed him all the way to the Brooke Courthouse.

CHAPTER THIRTY-SIX

Judge Rhea Andretti arrived at the Courthouse early on Wednesday, the thirteenth of September. For the past month and a half she had been beside herself, depressed and frightened. She never was so careful as she was on the bench lately. She was patient while dealing with not only the lawyers but the litigants, even the *pro se* people. She felt that someone was always looking over her shoulder and she didn't dare display any of the temper she knew she was reputed to have.

This morning, she was in pitiful shape. The recent developments splayed all over the television and radio about the Governor's indictment just about sent her over the edge. In court, just yesterday, she caught herself thinking of the last conversation she had with Brenden Mitchell and was thankful that the affair was over. Her mind continually wondered when she should have been paying attention to the proceedings in front of her. What was she thinking? she said to herself about a million times.

As she sat down at her desk in her chambers, recently painted light blue and pink at her insistence to lighten her moods, she noticed a large white envelope someone had placed in the middle of the desk addressed to her, "The Honorable Rhea Andretti".

She gasped as she read the return address in the upper left hand corner: Massachusetts Judicial Conduct Commission. Her hands were shaking as she carefully slit open the flap and unfolded the single page.

"You are hereby notified that the Judicial Conduct Commission will hold a hearing on Monday, September eighteenth, at nine o'clock A.M. at the offices of the Commission. 11 Beacon Street, Boston, Massachusetts in connection with allegations of judicial impropriety made against you, a copy of which is enclosed herewith. You are hereby advised to engage counsel."

Eleanor Lappin, Chairperson

Her first thought was of Renzo. What will my father say? His heart will be broken if I'm censored. Worse, she thought, I could be disbarred. Oh God! She started to cry.

At eleven o'clock the courtroom was being vacated by the lawyers and their witnesses who had just completed their hearing before Judge Talbot. I had received a call from Emily telling me that she wouldn't be at the hearing, that she was on her way to the Cape to be with Danny. That was all right by me. I wasn't up to holding hands with a widow who would send mixed signals about her emotional condition.

The benches behind the bar were occupied by only a handful of spectators, some of whom may have been media people. I couldn't tell. It was strange. No clients, no noise, only Jed and me, the clerk, Dolores Fairchild, Jack and Judge Talbot.

"Call the case, Ms. Fairchild," then Judge instructed.

"Mitchell v. Mitchell," the clerk announced obediently without the formality of reciting the case numbers.

I arose, still in some pain, still with crutches and stood by the microphone between the counsel tables.

"Your Honor no doubt knows what has happened since our session yesterday. I am saddened to have to report, on the record, that the Defendant is dead. That means the case is over and there is nothing further that can be done. Therefore, I move that the case of Mitchell v. Mitchell be dismissed."

Talbot just sat there for a full minute before responding.

"As a matter of law, Attorney Eldridge, I know no such thing," he said quietly.

"The only thing that will prove to me that the Governor is dead is the filing of the death certificate. Your motion is denied."

Of course, I said to myself. What a bonehead!

"You're quite right, as usual Your Honor. I shall file the death certificate along with a motion to dismiss as soon as the certificate is ready.

"And I certainly shall assent to the motion, Your Honor," Jed said.

"In that case we are adjourned," the Judge said.

On the way out, Paul Jed approached me in the corridor outside the courtroom.

"That was one helluva case, Ted. I'm glad it's over. I can't believe what happened to the Governor and Mort Haller. And then to have the Governor take his own life, a strong man like that. It's a shame!"

"Yeah well, I'm sorry it turned out the way it did," I replied, hoping to end the conversation. No such luck.

"Uh, Ted. We've got almost a quarter of a million dollars on the books at my firm. Now that the case is over I don't think Talbot can order Emily to pay our counsel fees. Do you think that now that she's going to acquire the whole estate either outright or through the trust, could you see if we could get paid?"

I stood still in my tracks. Did I hear right? Emily to pay Jed's counsel fees? Is he kidding? If he didn't have the brains to demand that his fees be paid by the Governor as we went along that's his fault, although I certainly understood where he was coming from. I could've been in the same boat. Maybe he expected payment in some other fashion, a judgeship maybe?

I decided on the spot to let him down easy.

"I doubt it, Paul but I'll ask Emily. If she agrees, I'll be back to you." But don't hold your breath, I thought.

Now that all the assets would belong to Emily, I breathed easier. I'd be paid and I wouldn't even have to wait. Paul Jed wouldn't get anywhere with Emily, I was certain.

CHAPTER THIRTY-SEVEN

EIGHTEEN MONTHS LATER

Number four, wearing the blue and crimson of Taft School, took the pass from his shooting guard under Taft's hoop after a Deerfield score which tied the game. It was Winter Parents Weekend and this was the last game of the season.

He slowly dribbled the ball to the center line with his right hand and deftly switched to his left and cut to his left as the Deerfield guard stretched out both hands in front of him. He looked to the center, at the low post, but the big guy was covered. He quickly switched hands again and moved to the top of the key, dribbled back with his left hand, turned, brought the ball to his right hand, jumped and pushed the ball toward the hoop, finishing the shot with his fingers loosely splayed out in front of him. Nothing but net!

The buzzer sounded, the game was over. Taft: 42. Deerfield: 40

"Danny baby!"

"How to go!"

"What a shot!"

"Nice game, Danny!"

"What a game!"

The rest of the team exploded from the bench and engulfed the starting five on the floor. They were soon joined by the Taft cheerleaders and the entire student body who had occupied the bleachers, swarming around the team and shouting for joy.

Danny's shirt was soaking wet with sweat. His face was red resulting as much from the compliments he heard as the strain of the game. He looked over the heads of the crowd attempting to find his mother as he was jostled to and fro by the student throng.

He smelled her distinctive perfume before he spotted her. She looked beautiful, better than ever. Better than at any time in the past year or so, as she got on with her life and visited him often at school. She came down to Watertown almost every weekend and, beginning almost immediately in that first September of his sophomore year at Taft, he could see a change in her.

The change really escalated when she announced her engagement to Dr. James Hurley, her psycho pharmacologist. Danny could see that he was a good guy, not only to his mother, but to Danny also. Last summer for example, right after the wedding, the three of them spent a month in Italy in a little town called Forte Dei Marmi, right on the beach on the Versilia Riviera. Jim and Danny, when the three of them weren't at the beach, played hoop at least three times a week. Jim, it turned out, played basketball for Harvard and still had a great jump shot.

In the evenings, when Jim and his mother didn't dine together alone, which was not all that frequent, the three of them would enjoy the different delights the town had to offer.

Danny could see the change in himself too. His mother was joyful and at peace. Jim was more than friendly and was kind and thoughtful. He missed his father at times, but all in all, he was pretty happy with the way things were going.

There were kids at Taft who'd been there since freshman year or before and, at the beginning, he worried about whether the bonds forged among them would prevent any new kid from breaking in. He needn't have worried. His classmates, in fact the entire student body was friendly, courteous, and accepting. He fit right in almost from the first day.

"Danny, sweetheart. I'm so proud of you," Emily said as soon as she was in ear shot. She was joined by Jim who was also beaming with pride.

"That Italian jump shot couldn't have been prettier," Jim said, smiling.

Danny was content. His world was together, his grades were A's and B's and-- he had a girl friend.

"All rise!"

We entered from the left of the court room, single file, all three of us. The courtroom was more than splendid with large portraits encased in heavy, gilt frames on the walls between large, floor to ceiling, curtained windows.

There was a hush about the place, almost like a sanctuary, with wall to wall carpeting inside the bar upon which the lawyers tread silently, speaking only in modulated tones to one another.

This was only my first week on the job. Governor Mary Hartigan, God bless her soul, had just sworn me in as an Associate Justice of the Massachusetts Appeals Court the week before. She had become the Governor on the very day, in fact within the hour that Brenden Mitchell's death was announced.

The swearing-in ceremony was not elaborate. After all, I'd been there before. It took place in the Governor's Office at the State House where my Amherst classmate, now Governor of the Commonwealth, produced her own personal Bible upon which I took the several oaths to preserve, protect and defend the Constitutions of the United States and the Commonwealth of Massachusetts.

Andrea, Josh and Mandy were the only family members in attendance. We drank champagne in paper cups, and for just a few minutes, we all reflected on how we arrived at this place and time.

The Governor informed me that Mort Haller had engaged a lawyer and was gearing up for a battle that he was likely to lose. After all the time spent in discovery and motion after motion, a trial date had finally been set. She predicted six months in jail, five years probation and hundreds of hours of public service.

Judge Rhea Andretti was disbarred, the Governor had told me. She didn't fight the proceedings, didn't engage a lawyer and was contrite and obviously humiliated throughout the hearing process. For that reason, more than likely, the Commission recommended that her suspension be subject to re-instatement after two years.

The bookies in the North End were not prosecuted she said. After the whole story was related, no charges were ever filed against Renzo Andretti, Guiliano Rigali or, for that matter, against Charlie Randell.

So, here I am, an Associate Justice of the Massachusetts Appeals Court, endowed with my very own parking space and several court officers to do my bidding; I'm approaching fifty years of age, my judicial future looks promising and at home, I still have to take the garbage out.

Printed in the United States
93742LV00006B/49-96/A

9 781434 330918